1,000,000 Books

are available to read at

www.ForgottenBooks.com

Read online
Download PDF
Purchase in print

ISBN 978-0-243-11900-4
PIBN 10786706

This book is a reproduction of an important historical work. Forgotten Books uses state-of-the-art technology to digitally reconstruct the work, preserving the original format whilst repairing imperfections present in the aged copy. In rare cases, an imperfection in the original, such as a blemish or missing page, may be replicated in our edition. We do, however, repair the vast majority of imperfections successfully; any imperfections that remain are intentionally left to preserve the state of such historical works.

Forgotten Books is a registered trademark of FB &c Ltd.
Copyright © 2018 FB &c Ltd.
FB &c Ltd, Dalton House, 60 Windsor Avenue, London, SW19 2RR.
Company number 08720141. Registered in England and Wales.

For support please visit www.forgottenbooks.com

1 MONTH OF FREE READING

at

www.ForgottenBooks.com

By purchasing this book you are eligible for one month membership to ForgottenBooks.com, giving you unlimited access to our entire collection of over 1,000,000 titles via our web site and mobile apps.

To claim your free month visit:
www.forgottenbooks.com/free786706

* Offer is valid for 45 days from date of purchase. Terms and conditions apply.

English
Français
Deutsche
Italiano
Español
Português

www.forgottenbooks.com

Mythology Photography **Fiction**
Fishing Christianity **Art** Cooking
Essays Buddhism Freemasonry
Medicine **Biology** Music **Ancient Egypt** Evolution Carpentry Physics
Dance Geology **Mathematics** Fitness
Shakespeare **Folklore** Yoga Marketing
Confidence Immortality Biographies
Poetry **Psychology** Witchcraft
Electronics Chemistry History **Law**
Accounting **Philosophy** Anthropology
Alchemy Drama Quantum Mechanics
Atheism Sexual Health **Ancient History**
Entrepreneurship Languages Sport
Paleontology Needlework Islam
Metaphysics Investment Archaeology
Parenting Statistics Criminology
Motivational

The TWENTY-FIFTH MAN

The Strange Story of Ed. Morrell, the Hero of Jack London's "Star Rover"

BY

ED. MORRELL

Lone Survivor of the Famous Band of California Feud Outlaws

AUTHOR OF
"THE NEW ERA PENOLOGY," "THE DEMON,"
"IN THE SHADOW OF THE JAIL DOOR,"
"JIMMY AND THE JOURNEY'S END,"
"PRISON BORN" and other short stories

NEW ERA PUBLISHING CO.
MONTCLAIR, N. J.

COPYRIGHT 1924
BY ED. MORRELL
All rights reserved, including that of translation into foreign languages, including the Scandinavian.

+ B
M829t

771923

THE GLOBE PRESS INC.
MONTCLAIR, N. J.
1924

*Dedicated
to
The Submerged Tenth
of the World with Deepest
Sympathy and Understanding.*

FOREWORD

A human document is always interesting, especially when the individual concerned has learned some great moral lesson as a result of his experiences; but, when a man has been tortured well nigh unto death, and punished for things of which he was not guilty, and then has been able to rise above the baser human passions and forgive his enemies, he has achieved a victory that the ordinary man finds it difficult to understand. The autobiography of such a man is doubly interesting.

One cannot read the "Twenty-Fifth Man," the life history of Ed. Morrell, without pondering over the sublimity of the soul of man. Ed. Morrell was never a criminal in the ordinary sordid acceptance of the meaning of the word. It is not difficult, for those who have been pioneers in the West, to understand and appreciate the motives which actuated him and his associates in levying war against corporations which were plundering the country and robbing the settlers of their homes and property. Those of us who have lived in the West for a generation and are thoroughly familiar with its development, know that for many years the railroad corporations dominated the politics and economic life of the people in the various states. The crimes perpetrated by the hirelings of the corporations were many and unrevenged. Thousands of men have suffered from the iron heel of persecution by great railroad corporations. Ed. Morrell's story is the story of one of them.

Towering over and outweighing in importance the economic struggle, which was the underlying cause of his troubles, is the victory of the man himself. His victory over a barbarous prison system is tremendous. The contribution of Ed. Morrell to society in calling attention to the cruel, inhuman and utterly indefensible prison system, is a service that only men like him are competent of rendering. Prisons and felons are misnomers in the light of modern medical knowledge and psychology. The tragic consequences and the price society must pay as a result of the unintelligent method of dealing with crimes and those guilty of violating the laws of society is appalling. The stark cruelty, the unrestrained hatred and passion, the unreasoning desire for revenge and punishment and the unsympathetic attitude toward problems affecting the reformation of the criminally inclined, makes progress in this line necessarily slow and it is the work of such men as Ed. Morrell and the document he has prepared of his experiences, which will help most toward bringing about a day of better understanding.

GEO. W. P. HUNT
Governor of Arizona

Executive Office
  State House
    Phoenix, Arizona,
      July 12, 1923.

INTRODUCTION

In 1923 I was privileged to be that one fortunate human being chosen by Ed. Morrell to aid him in launching "The American Crusaders" for the advancement of "The New Era Penology," with executive headquarters at Montclair, New Jersey.

When I say fortunate human being I do not mean that this should be stressed lightly, for of all coveted boons within the privileges of the life of man there is none greater than that of being allowed to share in the creation of a structure which has for its purpose the humanizing and forwarding of conditions that will aid humanity in striving for higher and better things, physical, moral, spiritual.

Officially I am Secretary-Treasurer of "The American Crusaders," but I am more than that. I am the devout follower and pupil of that master who is giving to the world a new dispensation which can be likened only to the Sermon on the Mount. Jesus Christ suffered prison. More He faced the supreme sacrifice on Calvary. Ed. Morrell suffered a martyrdom in prison so appalling that any human being not having conquered all sense of pain, physical, mental moral and spiritual, would have welcomed the crucifixion of Christ as an avenue of escape from such horrible tortures.

Through my close association with Ed. Morrell I have pored over the manuscript of the "The Twenty-Fifth Man" so that I am very familiar with its facts, its power and its purpose. I have gone into the public record of Ed. Morrell covering the past fifteen years and examined files of authoritative facts, letters from eminent men and women in every walk of life; statesmen, Governors, jurists and leading authorities, not to mention the highest literary celebrities, renowned men of letters, scientists, leading psychologists, doctors of medicine and alienists. In fact leaders in every activity of life have contributed their portion in glowing terms of praise and appreciation in recognition not only of the dynamic personality of the man, but for the message he has been ordained to give to the world.

I have examined carefully the files of newspapers covering a period since 1908, shortly after Ed. Morrell's pardon from life imprisonment at San Quentin, California. They are irrevocable documentary evidence to prove that Ed. Morrell is the father of "The Honor System."

He it was who gave to the world the first glimpse of the new vision. He it was who put it into force by actual field work, moulding public opinion in the far Western States between the dates of 1908 and 1915.

I confess that at times I have been exercised over the fact that Ed. Morrell would allow the credit of advancing this new concept to be appropriated by irresponsibles parading in the guise of "prison reformers." It seems inconceivable that people who have followed closely the awakening of the public conscience to this new vision could be led astray regarding the true author and inspiration of all this marvelous work.

During the early years when the "Honor System" was announced in the Far West, Ed. Morrell carried on a series of mass meetings all along the Pacific Coast States, arousing public opinion to the highest pitch. At such a time one would think that these so-called "prison reformers" would have lent a helping hand to further the work.

Not so these paraders of self-righteousness. Rather they took the stand as carping critics. Their slogan was that Ed. Morrell was trying to "commercialize prison reform." And now after nearly fifteen years of personal sacrifice and physical hardships unbelieveable, when the "New Era Penology" is given to the world, these same "reformers" stand baffled because they can perceive no vulnerable spots for the avaricious fingers of the plagiarist to dig in and appropriate to his own credit the birth-right and heritage of Ed. Morrell.

Their latest "war-cry" is this: "Ed. Morrell is not offering anything to the world that we don't already know." "His claim to the authorship of a new system of penology is not based on facts,'' or ''it is common knowledge that many of the salient features of the new system have been tried and discarded as impractical, visionary.''

Ed. Morrell is known and loved by thousands who have heard his voice in behalf of Society's misfits. He is an actual living demonstration in the art of self-mastery. This marvelous man while alone, a grim life convict, dead and forgotten in a dungeon, discovered his real self. The great inner power unfolded in the darkness of his living tomb.

It has made him stand out alone among the immortal convict characters of history, ''Jean Valjean,'' ''The Count of Monte Cristo,'' ''The Prisoner of Chillon.'' But these are only fiction characters, while Ed. Morrell is real, the one living man who has had experiences equal to if not greater than any of these three or the famed author of ''The Pilgrim's Progress,'' who found himself in a dungeon.

It was the discovery of this great power and the understanding of it that rescued him from his appalling prison life and eventually brought him back to the world with a determination to conquer, to make it see that the Social Code of Ethics cannot be beaten into a man.

It is impossible to attempt to outline the bigness of this man. The all important fact is that he seemed destined to undergo these strange experiences. They were unusual, almost fantastic, but they preceded the dawn of that new consciousness.

In the terrors of a dungeon the real Morrell was born. The truth of his own being was revealed to him, and with it came such powers that he conquered even his enemies, the very dungeon itself, and finally the prison with its bolts and bars.

Many celebrities owe their inspiration and success to the life and personality of Ed. Morrell. Jack London often said that through contact and close association with Ed. Morrell he was enabled to grasp many deeper glimpses of the subconscious self. He credited this man with moulding his later and more mature mind. Jack London's masterpiece ''The Star Rover'' is the proof of it.

In giving to the world the story, "The Twenty-Fifth Man," Ed. Morrell, its author, has contributed a human document of gripping interest. It is not only replete with stunning human interest episodes. It is more. "The Twenty-Fifth Man" will prove to be a great addition to American literature, surpassing anything of its nature ever attempted.

Eminent literary critics who have passed judgment on the manuscript predict that the story will establish its right to be classed as the true American Prison Epic.

DR. RAYMOND S. WARD

Montclair, New Jersey
February 1st, 1924.

AUTHOR'S PREFACE

This volume has been presented as a story. Hence it is not overburdened with quotations regarding sources of authority. However it may be pertinent to say that a clear periodical record may be found in the Congressional Library at Washington, verifying the historical events given in the story.

The problems presented in the dungeon awakening and the wanderings in "the little death" may be interpreted in many ways. However, they will be perfectly clear to those qualified to understand them. For the benefit of others who might doubt that there are human beings alive today who are privileged to leave their bodies and visit distant lands and other ages I quote remarks by an eminent scientist which have just been published as if in verification of the material contained in this book.

"The possibility of traveling forward into the future and backward into the past is an idea that has always had a singular fascination for the human mind. Romancers without number have toyed with it. The amazing wonders of visiting the streets of ancient Babylon or of imperial Rome, or of coming into the world five, or fifty million years hence, indeed surpass almost any other conceivable miracle."

"We are somewhat accustomed to guesses at the bizarre experiences in fables of the mysterious East or in the fantastic tales of fictioneers such as Jules Verne or H. G. Wells, but seldom has a scientist of established reputation dared to risk his prestige by voicing the opinion that this is humanly possible."

"Consequently no one was quite prepared for the shock which Capt. A. G. Pape, who is the honorary secretary to the Edinburgh and Cothians Branch of the Royal Anthropological Institute, suddenly put forward his amazing thesis, which he declares has been developed and proved in experiment by a new school of scientists and philosophers in Edinburgh.''

"These investigators, he maintains, have developed 'aeroplane' or 'time-machine' minds, capable at will of flying into any past age, of actually witnessing any event in the history of the earth, from the time when it was a blazing mass of incandescent gas and fluid metal down to the present day. Every one of us, he declared, has within him undeveloped faculties which, if properly cultivated, will enable him to accomplish the same feat — to leave his present body behind to travel through Egypt at the time of the Great Rameses, and actually to witness the slaughters of Marathon, Gettysburg, Waterloo or the Marne.''

"Captain Pape's pronouncements naturally created the nearest approach to a 'scene' that the British Association dignity permits. A storm of questions, criticism and denunciation has been playing about the daring young scientist's head ever since. But he sticks to his theory and claims that time and the future discoveries and experiences of man will justify his assertions. He predicts the development of a new race type, a coming race of supermen, all of whom will have the fully developed 'time-machine' faculty.''

" 'These inherited faculties may be obtained by any one, but only by means of an utter renunciation of self. He must learn to forget himself and all his petty desires. Having achieved the proper state of mind, a task by no means easy, and which implies a vast amount of concentration and renunciation, one who wishes to try this great experiment will have to sit alone in a quiet room and will himself back to any definite place and period. His physical body meanwhile remains at rest but his mentality is transported by impulse to some other place and other time'.''

" 'It is necessary to realize that there is around us a vast world unseen by most of us, but not necessarily invisible. That is, it can be perceived and lived in by men who have developed certain little known faculties of their minds by the mental process briefly mentioned. It is possible for them to explore and study the unseen world of the past precisely as ordinary men have explored and studied the world that is within the present reach of all of us'."

" 'There are actually men now living who have these mysterious faculties in complete working order and are able to use them to obtain a vast amount of vital information about the nature and history of man, and about the world which most of us are unable to see. It is no picture or mere vision which passes before the eyes of these investigators, no unreal panorama which unveils itself on a stage. It is an actual living in the so-called past'."

" 'We Anthropologists can easily recognize the features of this new race type, features which will become more accentuated in the coming centuries. We call this coming race the Austral-American. It is already known and recognizable. It is a fact and not merely a belief'."

" 'We as a school of thought and science most certainly detect a new race, clean cut, which is now forming. This new race will be the great race of the future'."

In 1912 I gave the immortal Jack London much of my dungeon experiences, particularly those vivid wanderings in "the little death," while undergoing torture in the strait-jacket in the dungeon of San Quentin. This material was later incorporated in a story called "The Star Rover." Darrell Standing, the composite character, was used by London to carry over these weird and fantastic experiences.

At the time of the publication of London's masterpiece critics all over the world railed at the impossible situations, and denounced it in the strongest language. Since then students are beginning to view the daring attempt of London in a very different light. Those who are versed in the occult, and psychologists see in these mind projecting pilgrimages much food for thought. And now, in the twenty-fourth year of the twentieth century thousands of serious minded men and women are at last beginning to realize that the age of miracles has just begun. Mind projection is not merely a speculative theory. Many know it to be a concrete fact of physical life.

For the benefit of the reader of this story, "The Twenty-Fifth Man," I desire to state emphatically that the experiences of mind projection in "the little death" were very real to me, because I not only projected my mind through the power of self-hypnosis out of the dungeon and into the big living, moving world of today, influencing the lives of some who were destined to play a great part in my future life, but also I explored time through the ages reliving lives that I had lived just as surely as I live the present life. More, I was privileged in the dungeon to understand many strange complexities of my checkered career and the purpose for which I had been marked for suffering.

The rest of the story, particularly that pertaining to our atrocious penal system needs no comment other than to express the hope that it may prove a powerful agency toward awakening the conscience of a lethargic world to the horrors and brutalities of our jails, to the end that a new era will dawn for humanity.

ED. MORRELL

March 1st, 1924

CONTENTS

Chapter		Page
I	SAN QUENTIN PRISON, THE SING SING OF THE WEST. A FOLSOM TRANSFER	1
II	PRISON MUTINY	12
III	MUTINY AND COUNTER MUTINY	23
IV	SIR HARRY'S PRISON DRAMA UNFOLDS	38
V	THE KNUCKLE VOICE	48
VI	A STORY IN KNUCKLE TALK	56
VII	A MYSTERIOUS MEETING	72
VIII	DETECTIVE SMITH ELUDES A TRAP, THEN LAYS ONE	86
IX	THE BATTLE OF STONE CORRAL, TURNING POINT IN THE LONG YEARS OF OUTLAWRY	93
X	A FAKE MESSAGE. A JAIL HOLDUP	109
XI	A WILD RACE TO THE KINGS RIVER BRIDGE	120
XII	A BLOODLESS BATTLE AMONG THE CLOUDS	129
XIII	THE LOVE OF LIFE. LOST IN A MOUNTAIN STORM	141
XIV	CAMP MANZANITA, STRONGHOLD OF THE OUTLAWS	154
XV	A BANDIT IN THE ROLE OF A COLLEGE STUDENT	169
XVI	THE FIGHT AT SLICK ROCK	179
XVII	A MINER'S CABIN AT SULPHUR SPRINGS	192
XVIII	A QUICK RETREAT TO CAMP	210
XIX	THE FALL OF CAMP MANZANITA	220
XX	AT THE END OF THE TRAIL	231
XXI	"JUDGE LYNCH," THE AMERICAN MOB	241

CONTENTS (Continued)

Chapter		Page
XXII.	RAILROADED TO PRISON	251
XXIII	FOLSOM, THE JAIL OF THE "OCTOPUS"	260
XXIV	LIFE IN A MAN-KILLING JAIL	269
XXV	TORTURE, A FINE ART AT FOLSOM	284
XXVI	A PRISON TRANSFER	297
XXVII	THE BLACK TERROR OF SAN QUENTIN. THE REVELATION	308
XXVIII	A DOUBLE JACKETING, A PROPHECY	327
XXIX	RELEASE FROM THE DUNGEON, THE PROPHECY UNFOLDING	343
XXX	THE PROPHECY FULFILLED, A PARDON	358
XXXI	YEARS IN RETROSPECT	365
	AMERICAN CRUSADERS BULLETIN	375

THE TWENTY-FIFTH MAN
*The Strange Story of Ed. Morrell,
the Hero of Jack London's "Star Rover"*

CHAPTER I

SAN QUENTIN PRISON, THE SING SING OF THE WEST.
A FOLSOM TRANSFER.

BULKED upon a rocky point, jutting out into the North arm of San Francisco Bay, stands a medieval structure. From the top of Mt. Tamalpais it resembles a feudal castle on the Rhine, massive, turreted, with square donjon and frowning loop-holed towers, and a trail for horsemen leading up to the rampart on whose battlements pace human beings, reminding one of the wielders of tar-pot and lead-ladle.

The inclosure is rectangular, its door iron studded, swinging on ponderous hinges. It occupies a strategical position, impenetrable from all angles, grim, forbidding, an overwhelming sight even when softened to a shadow by the white mists of the bay.

Approaching, the trail becomes a road, with battlements, walls manned by guards armed with modern weapons, and towers, the vantage points of defense. What resembled the Donjon of the Lord, or Baron, is but the Administration Building, the iron studded door a man-gate, and so on until the Feudal Castle, increasing in its severity, is San Quentin, one of the largest prisons on the North American Continent.

At the man-gate the feudal likeness ends. Once within, San Quentin, as its name implies, is Spanish. The four cell houses are long, low and squatty, grouped in parallel lines four deep, opposite the Captain of the Yard's Quarters. There is a patio too, with fountains and a great variety of shrubs.

San Quentin at the time of which I write, after nearly half a century's existence, had made history as a notorious man-killing jail — inhuman, terrible, the very flagstones standing as mute accusers against the shocking brutalities committed there in the name of the law, on defenceless victims.

The visitor, being permitted to go no further than the balcony of the Administration Building, where he might enjoy the garden, flower scented air, and a silence, which to him was not oppressive, usually believed he had glimpsed an idyllic Utopian scene. How could he penetrate what lay beyond; how know the true San Quentin, a sinister place black as Hell, a volcano, a smouldering cauldron vomiting forth blighting vapors, poisonous and all consuming?

He was not allowed inside, and how could he observe that even the windows of the Female Department facing the garden were heavily coated with drab paint and nailed down, lest the soul starved inmates might see its flowers or breathe their fragrance.

He never visited the "Bull Pen," a corral no larger than a small city block, where nineteen hundred convicts were herded together like cattle in the stock yards of Chicago, during hours not devoted to man-killing toil in the Jute Mill.

There was no way for him to discover that every type, race, creed, and color; good men, bad men, strong men, weak men; defiled and defilers, moral and immoral, healthy and sick; bright eyed vigorous boys just emerging from adolescence, and men, pitted and pocked from every imaginable disease; all rubbed cheek by jowl so near that cheerful garden upon which the proscribed might never gaze.

The visitor was naturally unaware of the "Bull Pen's" fetid mist of stifling, sickening odors. He never could have guessed that, surrounded by water on the outside, there would be an absence of it within. If he did, he must surely have believed that in later years, the Warden with a penchant for novelties who had constructed a swimming tank of approximately ten by twenty feet, had solved the problem. He heard the whispers about this luxury having cost the taxpayers around twenty-five thousand dollars and there his knowledge ended. He never could have learned that its popularity waned immediately after the grand opening; that the confined of San Quentin found it to be a pool of innoculation instead of a health giving agency, and were forced back to the time honored "bucket brigade,"— those who washed doing so within their cells,— while the "Bull Pen" odors continued as stifling as ever.

Thus, having looked upon the flower garden from the balcony, the visitor departed, believing he had seen a great prison, satisfied that conditions within were ideal. Most institutions are investigated that way, with perhaps a good dinner thrown in at the Warden's house for the professional "whitewasher."

To a student of penology, San Quentin must have represented a strange admixture of insanity and coddling paternalism under the cheap pretense of a system, with brute force and ignorance answering for rules and regulations. He alone might realize that nineteen hundred men were crowded in a place foul and stench ridden, hardly large enough to house comfortably five hundred, that everything about it was unsanitary, that clubbings and beatings by inhuman guards were the order of the day, that prisoners were pitted against one another to the utter destruction of the good by the bad, and that the enforced silence was oppressive and unnatural, producing an abnormal condition of mind.

Like most prisons, San Quentin was ruled under a system of blind stupidity, and thus I found it. I was standing alone, thinking over this very situation when someone approached me.

"You're a Folsom Transfer. I have it straight from headquarters that word has been sent down the line to crush you. Hell is going to pop in this prison. We want to pull off a big rumpus in the Jute Mill but, if the mob ever gets started and we lose control, there'll be killing and every one of us will be hung. What do you think about it?" asked Happy Jack, a prisoner who knew me.

We were in the "Bull Pen." It was my first Sunday in San Quentin and my Folsom ring around stripes were too noticeable. In order not to attract attention, he moved away immediately after I explained my desire to try first to make good here, not having been given a chance in Folsom. I was a lifer, and there were friends with money who could aid me if I kept a clean record. I told Happy that I would answer later on, as to what part I should play in the strike.

The trouble hinged around the mess hall, that storm center of all American prisons. The food beggared description. The common diet, — beans in all stages of decay, unseasoned, unpalatable — was served twenty-one times a week. The odors from the meat, purchased by the Commissary Department through a system of collusion with favored political contract bidders, would turn the stomach of even a healthy dog, when its scattered portions reached the stew pots of the general mess. The few scanty vegetables served were frequently rotten, and the flour, merely the scrapings from the mills, was full of weevils, soggy, black and unpalatable, spelling dysentery and death to those who made it their sole reliance; while the State paid the very highest prices for food which never reached the convicts of San Quentin.

Graft had been an accepted chronic condition even at Folsom, but it had never developed to such an abandon that the vilest food was served, tho we were constantly hungry there through short rations. While I was still at Folsom rumors were rife that the cap would soon blow off of the inferno on Frisco Bay with a mutiny worse than any that had ever occurred in the history of the country. Only the spark of some overt act was needed to precipitate it.

Folsom had only grumbled, but San Quentin moaned and groaned in terrible silent ferment. The hospital and the old tubercular ward were filled to capacity, and dungeon and punishment cells were jammed full of convicts who had already dared protest. San Quentin was rife with an unspeakable atmosphere of suppressed murder, and only awaited the responsibility of leadership. Something was holding them in check. Perhaps news that had seeped in of an impending transfer from Folsom of twenty-five desperate convicts, the worst ever confined during the history of that institution. Among them might be a leader.

It had just turned dark as the man-gate opened to admit our zebra striped line of sullen and dark visaged creatures, leg shackled, hand shackled and manacled, with a heavy bull chain which bound us twenty-five proscribed men rattling ominously at every step.

The convicts incarcerated in the front tiers of the cell building facing the offices stared in mute amazement at the gruesome sight, then as tho by magic, joyously passed the word on to the rest of the prison confined. When they heard we had arrived, San Quentin became a beehive of buzzing sounds.

We had been tanned and blackened by the blistering suns of the Folsom Rock Quarries until we looked like Mexicans. We had eaten nothing since our morning meal of "bootleg coffee," dry bread and a scanty pan of beans, and it had taken all day to ride from that prison in the Northeastern section of the State, to San Quentin, locked and bolted like cattle in a Southern Pacific car. We were famished and weak, while those poor convicts who were not physically robust were hardly able to stand.

The manhandling Folsom escort guard stepped among us, the heavy clanging bull chain fell to the stone flags of the prison yard, and in pairs we were marched to the general mess. God, what a meal! San Quentin food was even worse than we had anticipated. It had lain served on the table for hours awaiting our arrival, cold, clammy bull stew in tin pans, dry, soggy bread and "bootleg" in tin cups, that unpalatable mixture of burnt bread crusts, oats and other ingredients crudely compounded, the curse of every American prison. There were salt and pepper on the table. There were half gallon jugs of deadly acid, a substitute for vinegar.

We twenty-five famished transfers from Folsom choked over the "bull stew." Some of the more weakly became sick, while one daring convict who had attempted to gulp what was on his heavy tin plate aroused us all with a sudden motion, in which he exhibited the large molar tusk of a mule. We learned later that a mule which had broken its leg near the prison inclosure mysteriously disappeared. It had come to light in the stew pots of the general mess for prisoners on the day of our arrival at San Quentin.

None of us spoke a word, but the low, grumbling jail sound could be heard. The silent system prevailed at that time in the general mess, and the rough, brutal guards pounded their heavy clubs upon the flagstones as a sinister warning that order must be maintained. We dared not protest then, smothering our feelings like the other nineteen hundred in San Quentin for the big day when all should burst forth in terrible mutiny.

Hunger maddened convicts, hunger maddened masses outside of prison walls,— they are all alike. We had been half starved at Folsom, had been train riding all day, and tho famished it was impossible even to bolt down the slop placed before us that night in San Quentin, and even then we had more to learn of what was done with the food before it arrived at the old rough wood tables.

The fifteen minutes allowed for eating had soon passed, and it was a welcome relief to be herded out. The regular prison staff were plainly disgruntled, gruff brutal orders showing their attitude. This would mean extra work and their general feeling was mirrored in the actions of the Captain of the Yard, "Take them to Hell below," he grumbled under his breath, stepping from his private office to confront us lined up before him. "Why the Hell should I be bothered with them tonight? Clean out one side of the dungeon and lock 'em up there."

We listened dejectedly to the strange order. Its true meaning did not dawn upon us until lodged in six of those dungeon cells. The punishment dungeon after that long day of hard travel,— and we wondered what next! There was no thought of segregation. They thrust us in by "the first come first served" method. The lanterns vanished,— doors clanged shut. We were in darkness, without even so much as a blanket and had not been allowed to bathe or wash our hands and faces after the ordeal of transfer through a scorching hot valley. In misery we twenty-five sank exhausted to the cold stone floor of San Quentin's dungeons.

Even that first Sunday after our transfer, without Happy Jack's timely warning I could see that trouble was brewing. On that same Sunday there was a strained feeling of unrest in the "Bull Pen," where nineteen hundred men were crowded together. Contrary to the customary din and noise, sinister silence prevailed. It was the only place where no attempt was made to control the actions of the convicts, but on this day freemen with clubs moved about among us. Rifle guards on the wall above held us under relentless scrutiny, every little while exchanging signals with their fellow freemen in the yard.

We Folsom Transfers were hideously conspicuous, still wearing the grimy convict stripes of that prison as a badge of incorrigibility, and the guards watched for the least excuse to place us under arrest. I was marked as a leader, having been pointed out to every freeman as a notorious desperate character, a life convict, an ex-bandit, a bad man who would surely start something at the first opportunity. But even with all this against me, I still determined to make good, and until I could be convinced of the general intention toward me at San Quentin which was not so much a private lockup of the railroad company as Folsom, I had urged my friend Happy Jack to wait for his answer.

I was put to work in that Hell of San Quentin, the Jute Mill. More than a thousand others were there also, making grain sacks amid the deafening clatter, in air filled with jute dust so thick at times that it was hard to distinguish more than vaguely a faint outline of the blue coated guards who stood over us with loaded clubs to see that we turned out our one hundred yards of cloth each day.

It was indeed an inferno, where men with faces painfully drawn to a tensity strove miserably amid the jarring roar to perform the required weekly task. The alternative was to spend Saturday and Sunday in the dungeon on a bread and water diet if they failed or even so much as incensed a guard. Then they must return, pale and haggard, on Monday to accomplish an amount of perfect work hard for a well man to produce, and in fetid air, amid pandemonium likened only to the tortures for lost souls which Dante depicts,—surrounded by the murmur of the jail, ever enduring in the form of bitter imprecations and vile oaths hurled upon the white slave task masters of the State's proscribed and damned.

In San Quentin the same discontent was evident in the Jute Mill as that which I had noticed in the "Bull Pen" the Sunday following our arrival, but it all centered around the food, not the unthinkable conditions of labor. Even this employment was better than idleness, though faithful service merited nothing where the iron heel prevailed as a system. A prisoner without friends, money, or political pull had no rights that even the lowest and most brutal guards deigned to respect. It was not the Jute Mill, the long grinding hours of toil with every human emotion suppressed, the nights in prison dens, stench ridden and degrading, but the impure food which was furnished by the Commissary Department when the State paid for the very best. They might trample on all other rights of the unfortunate convict, but the condition of food is at the bottom of every prison riot, without exception.

I was bent upon making good even in this hopeless situation, intolerable at any time, but impossible to a life convict. At the end of about a week in the Jute Mill I was summoned to the Captain's office. He had received my punishment record from Folsom. I stood rigidly at attention listening while he read it aloud. It sounded more like a death warrant, and when he had finished I tried to speak.

"I'm doin' the talking," he cut in. "You just listen and listen damned close. I am putting a special watch on you, and the first time you bat an eye, by God yer' going to hit the hole!"

Again I made a feeble effort to speak, but this brutal manhandling Captain called for silence, repeating the trite, sinister warning, "The first time you bat an eye, I say, you'll think Folsom was paradise in comparison to this place. Go back to your work! 'Cons' don't do no talkin' here, understand?"

Without another word I dejectedly returned to my work and I knew then I had many obstacles to overcome. Happy Jack was correct. Still, I wanted to make good, to demonstrate by every act my honest intention of doing right. I was young, healthy and strong. My outdoor life had made me so, and I did hope that some time I might gain liberty through the front gate. Most prisoners feel the same before the machine begins its grinding process to leave them crushed and broken.

In a few more days I began to taste of real bitterness. A guard accused me of crowding and brutally jerked me out of line. I tried to defend myself, but a convict's word never stands against that of a freeman at any time, much less if he is to be broken.

"He's a bad actor and I've had my eyes on him for several days. He's trying to stir up trouble, Captain," the guard explained.

"Dungeon! Twenty Days!" The sentence was pronounced before I could scarcely draw a breath. Two burly guards held me firmly by the wrists, each trying to twist my arms out of place as they pushed me away from that autocrat who ruled the City of the Living Dead.

In the dungeon I was chained to the wall, on a bread and water diet, only to be brought back to the office by the same guard shortly after my release. "This stiff is trying to stir up trouble all the time," the brute guard whined. "He keeps dog-eyeing me, Captain. Worst man in my section."

I was asked to give a reason for my actions but remained silent. They knew that I was raging and desired nothing more than to hear me break loose on a tirade that would furnish grounds for more punishment.

"An officer's addressing you," prodded my inquisitor, the Captain, "and when an officer speaks, answer, damn you! Do you understand?" He lifted his loaded cane as if to strike me.

I remained erect and motionless before him, knowing the game too well to be decoyed into breaking my silence.

"Put him in the hole for thirty days, and see that he don't get too much bread and water." There was anger behind the command. He had failed to make me cringe. My spirit was not yielding fast enough.

After that I saw much of the punishment dungeon, grew accustomed to being chained by one foot, to a shivering body and a cold stone floor, to chilling air, to darkness and dampness. I had not even so much as a blanket.

Until he was moved, the same guard was always responsible for my torture. He openly boasted of taking this means to avenge the death of a relative, a gunman and bloodmoney hunter who had been killed by the California Outlaws during a chase.

Evil and vicious indeed is our American Prison System. It permits of all sorts of abuses. Instead of being constructive and curative, it becomes but a destructive agency. It is retributive and criminally vicious in every sense of the word, vomiting forth a spawn stigmatized as ex-convicts to go out and poison the social stream, having been trained to commit worse criminal acts than those for which they were first apprehended. Thus Society's Juggernaut, the criminal punitive machine, that incubator of crime, becomes at last an even greater menace to the helpless and defenceless citizen than the unapprehended criminal.

When my tormentor who started the persecution had left, there were others to take his place to try to instill in me a fear of their guns and clubs,— to make me docile and meek. Innumerable were the excuses found for punishment. Times without number I was sent to the "hole" until, as in Folsom, my prison life became a case of just in and out of the dungeon, even tho I bent every effort to obedience.

This gained me nothing for, as Happy Jack had warned that first Sunday after my entry into San Quentin, "word had been sent down the line to crush me." I could see that I was doomed, a hopeless lifer, and an undying hatred sprang up within me toward everything that smacked of restraint. My decision was quick. I would undertake the dangerous task of leadership. The food was unthinkable, and nineteen hundred convicts were protesting.

CHAPTER II

PRISON MUTINY.

It was morning. The great Jute Mill was in full operation. The clatter and bang of loom shuttles with a nerve racking din, told the story of daily grind. Everything appeared as usual on the surface. All were in their places, even the guards. Only the air was different. It seemed surcharged with something terrifying. Those same guards must have sensed it. Silent, restless, uneasy they looked about, their customary brutal bravado gone, a menacing atmosphere of tension prevailing.

I was working on a loom under the tutelage of a convict weaver. That morning my trips to the cobs house for new supplies were frequent. I grasped every opportunity to pass a word here and there to trusted men, on the last one gliding unseen with my new supply of cobs to another part of the Mill where Happy Jack stood, alert and anxious.

"What's the word, Ed?" Happy whispered nervously.

"Pass the signal in ten minutes. That will be ten o'clock sharp. Give me a chance to return to my station so that everything will look right. Remember, each man must stand firm, above all else guarding against the first bad break. Are you sure of everyone? If we lose control we'll pay the penalty with a rope."

On a Sunday about three weeks before this great day, Happy Jack and I with twenty-three others had held a meeting. It may be hard to understand how so many convicts could gather together in San Quentin prison openly and without interference.

There were big dormitories on the ground floor of the front cell house facing the offices. Room tenders were in complete charge there and, during the hours on Sunday when the other prisoners were forced to remain in the

"Bull Pen," they rented them out to groups of moneyed convicts. The money circulation within the prison walls was from three to fifteen thousand dollars and while the poor and friendless alternately sweltered in the sun or became drenched with rain, suffering all manner of inhuman torture for the slightest infraction of rules or for nothing in instances where they had been singled out for crushing, a favored few were wined and dined in these rooms at five dollars a plate. Until complaint at the imposition made it dangerous, for such occasions food was taken from the guards' and officers' mess or even the larder and storehouse of the Warden. When the freemen grumbled a decided shrinkage in the meager rations of the unfortunates who must subsist solely upon prison fare was evident. It was an underground system of graft almost as baneful as that practiced by the Commissary Department in the letting of contracts, a collusion between confined and confiner for which the major portion of nineteen hundred men must suffer in silence.

The convicts were helpless, tho well aware of the situation. They knew that in those big rooms food was set up as daintily as in some of the leading hotels in the country, that gambling went on there without interference from the minions of the law,— faro, poker, stud and draw, three card monte, chuck luck, honest John, and even the negro game of "rolling bones," and that heavy tolls in the form of a head price of graft were exacted from each of the moneyed owners of some particular game. They were also conscious of the staging of opium parties often to bring about the first downward step toward the complete demoralization of some callow youth, these debaucheries scarcely causing passing comment, much less a reprimand from the hardest task masters of the institution. Pampered prison pets could break rules with impunity and the convicts all knew that those who could afford the price in cold cash did anything and everything according to the whim of the passing moment, while dumb, stoical and submissive the remainder of nineteen hundred men suffered in silence.

But the time of reckoning was near. Taking advantage of the very system we were seeking to destroy, it had been possible to charter room number five in the front cell house building for a handsome sum of money. At the appointed hour of room lockup on Sunday morning when the other convicts were forced into the "Bull Pen," by two's and three's we filed inside, apparently to banquet. No questions were asked because we had paid the price in cash. The door was locked behind us and absolute privacy was secured, not even the room tender being admitted.

Happy Jack was appointed chairman. He called the meeting to order and two plans of mutiny were considered, another's and my own. The first was an attractive program. It required one hundred picked men placed in strategical positions in offices, kitchens and dining rooms, even in the homes of officials outside the prison walls. Some had already been employed in the Commissary Department, in the Administration Building, in the stables and in roustabout gangs of "Bull Pen," hospital, cell blocks and general mess.

At ten o'clock on a working day, each unit of the one hundred would perform its part independently of all others. Captain of the Guards' offices and guards' quarters were to be taken first. The convicts would then don freemen's uniforms, and decoying rifle guards from their posts of duty on the walls by telephone calls to report at the office, would take their places. Freemen about the prison must then be put in the common punishment dungeon while general lockup should be declared for all convicts who were not leaders, so that the mutineers might work unhampered.

Some ruse would bring the Warden and all those connected with his residence to the prison and then the rest of the freemen, women and children on Point San Quentin were to be brought over and crowded into cells while escape was being effected.

This man's mutiny plan also called for the mining of the institution so that complete destruction would result, the walls to be shattered, and gatling gun posts wrecked, and the Jute Mill with its millions of dollars worth of machinery to be utterly demolished. The greatest wreck of a penal institution since the days of the Bastille should take place according to the program.

There was no interruption during his reading, and even I could not refrain from admiring the mind capable of conceiving a plot that portrayed such a remarkable power of organization. This man was a dominant character. Of course he functioned toward evil, but it was a clear case of misdirected energy, only more forcibly emphasizing the hellishness of a penal system which allows such qualities to go to waste. What a terrific power for good he could have been in a different environment.

My project was indeed mild in comparison to his. It involved the capture of the Jute Mill, officers and guards there to be held as hostages until the Administration, through the Warden, compromised. I had read the demands to be presented by a committee from the Jute Mill who should parley under a flag of truce, and then took up a discussion of the other plan, dissecting it for bad points. The worst feature was that there could be no assurance of protection for freemen or women and children when the nineteen hundred convicts should leave the prison beyond control of the committee, to roam the foothills after years of incarceration under a brutal system of suppression. Lives would undoubtedly be sacrificed, profound horror created throughout the country, and the one hundred responsible for carrying out the plans of mutiny, who could not possibly escape far, would be executed by the speediest method to avenge deeds of the others.

Mine was accepted by a majority of twenty-three votes, the author of the first program and his crony no doubt withholding the two. It had been agreed after a careful weighing of every phase of the situation that my connection with the plot should never be known except to the other twenty-four conspirators, that they should stand between me as chief instigator and the hundred trusted prisoners who were to take active part: If the officials had even become suspicious of me as the directing mind I would have been placed under arrest; or perhaps, in keeping with their intense desire to crush me, framed on a murder charge by some "stool pigeon" for which I should be hanged. Such acts as killings during prison riots are usually performed by "stool pigeons" or even guards. Thus marked leaders, in the absence of evidence, may be sentenced to die. More subtle intriguery goes on at those times in prison than in a court of Fifteenth Century France, and I was depending upon the resourcefulness of Happy Jack who knew and understood our men and my position.

Three weeks had now passed since that meeting of twenty-five. After speaking to Happy Jack I had returned to my station. The guard was eyeing me strangely when something happened! It came with the suddenness of an explosion, only this one was reversed. Instead of silence broken by a loud rending crash, the jarring noises of the Jute Mill stopped on the instant of ten and the calm became oppressive. Machinery, millions of dollars worth, that had been working at top speed ceased to operate and not a sound of any kind could be heard, not even a voice or a stir among the thousand or more men who had been busily employed but a moment before.

The silence was more overpowering than the noise. Minutes lengthened into seeming hours of anxiety. In reality it was only a short time before sounds of talking broke the hushed stillness. It was the jail whisper rising into loud speech, strange and foreign to all of us convicts so accustomed to suppression. Then came the screeching hyena-like gibbering of a strike mob staccatoed by sharp words and hurried commands from those brave dependable men whom

THE TWENTY-FIFTH MAN

Happy Jack had declared we could trust implicitly with the duties of assistants. In groups of five and six they moved about methodically from position to position, each of them brandishing a keen edged dagger. I overheard the orders they gave to the guard at my station.

"Say, good little man," said one, "stay right where you are and see that all of your men remain in their places. Just keep your nose clean today. Arrest the first man who disobeys or tries to damage one scrap of machinery and we will attend to his case instantly."

Satisfied I hurried away as there was a great deal to do. I knew that Happy Jack had successfully executed my order to have each guard supported by a group of trusted men. These were sworn to protect him with their lives and also to help him watch the machinery. We did not propose to allow wanton destruction which would mean grave loss to the State.

I had two big burly convicts sent to guard the door of the Superintendent of the Mill. He stood in his office, pale and worried. Everything else had been done so that in less than half an hour we were in complete control. More than a thousand prisoners stood rigidly at attention while ever vigilant our assistants moved about ready to cope with the slightest evidence of a breakdown in the plan or any attempt at counter mutiny by some of the professional "stool pigeons," the most dangerous characters in prison, perverted creatures who prey upon fellow convicts to their own personal advantage, immunity from punishment or a furthering of chances for parole or pardon.

I was again with Happy Jack in the rear of the Mill. Instinctively glancing toward the position of the guard who was responsible for my downward dungeon career, I found him missing. Happy Jack told me that he had escaped with two others notorious for their cruelty, fleeing through the engine room and gaining the top of the wall by a rope which the rifle guards lowered. I was pleased to learn this, as their absence insured a more orderly mutiny. Had they remained the temptation for revenge might have been too strong in the hearts of some of the oppressed. I felt no apprehension for the rest of the seventy-five freemen now under rigid captive control, because it was customary to assign the more level headed guards to Jute Mill duty, where they were less protected than in the yard. Already they were sighing with relief as the time passed without an overt act being committed, and in some sections they were standing about with groups of their former charges laughing and joking over the new turn of affairs.

The committee to go before the Warden and the Captain of the Yard had been selected. To avert suspicion Happy Jack appointed me one of them. With the Captain of the Jute Mill Guard in the lead we stepped out through the big doorway where he raised his hand as a signal that we might pass safely through the gate and into the protecting inclosure of the prison proper. Guards who completely manned the encircling wall dared not fire into the Mill lest the lives of the freemen might be endangered. For the same reason we were safe.

I was keenly alert to sounds, and felt pleased that all was still quiet back in the Jute Mill. How I dread to think of what might have happened had we been foolhardy enough to drive the guards out instead of holding them prisoners. Not a freeman would have respected the State's machinery sufficiently to protect it and in order to make the affair really spectacular for the outside world, gatling-guns would have been turned loose, and at that very moment the work of destruction and bloodshed would have been well advanced.

The Warden was a senile man, trembling and palsied. I don't believe he had ever been inside of the prison any further than the offices. He did not come to meet us in front of the Captain's headquarters. The only other man present besides the Captain of the Yard was the Turnkey, an old experienced officer, cool headed, courageous, the one man at San Quentin who could boast of the love of convicts and freemen alike.

"Are you boys the committee from the Mill?" asked the Captain of the Yard, glaring at us with loaded cane in hand.

Not uttering a word, we nodded our heads in unison.

"Who is spokesman?"

Feigning forgetfulness he glowered impatiently at me when none replied on the instant. "You are one of the Folsom Transfers, eh?" His head moved slowly up and down.

"Yes sir," I replied.

"And what may be your name and number?" He knew me only too well.

"I am convict 16,766, by name, Morrell," I said.

"Ah, you're Morrell? It seems to me I've heard of you before. Of course you are the leader, uh?"

Divining the Captain's purpose of trying to single me out as a fitting target on whom to cast the blame for all the trouble and anything that might occur during the whole riot, what Happy Jack had hoped to avoid by making it appear that the leadership had been scattered among a hundred or more with no particular head, I determined to evade the trap.

"Leader? No, Captain," I replied. "The trouble resulting in this strike was an old story long before my transfer from Folsom. They chose me as one of the committee, doubtless to have a mixed representation. The duty was thrust upon me without the alternative of accepting or rejecting. But, now that we are here we had better get down to business."

He did not interrupt me and I continued, "Time is a precious factor in the whole proceeding. We five have been sent by the convicts of San Quentin to lay their grievances before the officers. If we are not back in the Jute Mill in one hour the lives of five guards will be sacrificed in reprisal."

"What is the complaint?" stammered the Warden, stepping to the door, his palsied trembling increased by the fear that an attempt might be made against his life.

As an answer to his query, one of the committee handed me a paper on which were written the conditions for compromise with which I was only too familiar. I read them aloud,—the first a demand that the Commissary Department be cleared of prison pets and the Commissary General be removed at once; the second, a demand that the Warden make an investigation of the food supplies and that those connected with their purchase through bids be prosecuted for graft, the old food being destroyed and emergency orders made immediately, pending new bids.

The discharge of the Steward of the general mess and the removal of the convict chief cook from the kitchen, the new chef to be appointed by popular voice of the prison were, the third and fourth requirements. The fifth called for the removal of the head baker who was to be punished by a forfeiture of all good credits and brought before the Board of Prison Directors on the score of grafting, making bread from maggoty flour and encouraging his convict assistants to commit unmentionable acts while performing their duties. All "stool pigeons" and prison pets holding positions as waiters in the general mess were to be assigned to the Jute Mill; clean, reliable, efficient men being appointed in their places. Not the least important demand was the sixth calling for a new Captain of the "Bull Pen" and cell houses, — the removal of the Chaplain as a "parasitical, snivelling hypocrite, a grafter and traducer of hopes of unfortunate convicts for future reformation," and the substitution of some good public spirited woman for the terrible brutal Matron of the Female Department.

The seventh was a provision that no prisoner should be confined on bread and water any longer than ten days and that a mattress and two blankets must be supplied anyone sentenced to the punishment dungeon. The last called for the return of all personal property stolen from the convicts under the pretense of carrying out prison rules.

The conclusion contained a promise that honest effort by the Administration to comply with the demands would be met by a spirit of hearty co-operation on the part of the prisoners who would make every effort to obey all rules, maintaining order and discipline throughout the institution to the end that San Quentin should be a model prison that would gain the sympathy of the people of the State and world at large. In addition was the demand that the Warden or Captain return to the Mill with the committee, in person giving a solemn promise to carry out all of the provisions faithfully.

When I had finished reading, the officials retired to the Captain's private office. We heard their voices distinctly. The Captain of the Yard was talking excitedly to 'the Warden interrupted only by the arrival of the Commisary General and the Captain of the Guards, a swaggering braggart who delighted in giving orders to fire upon the convicts,— a man thoroughly hated and despised.

Again and again the recriminating words of the Captain rang out,— "By God, I won't do it! If I go down there and give the convicts my word it must be kept. I will not be the goat. This is all your fault anyhow," he shrieked, denouncing the weakness of the Warden. "I have warned of a day of reckoning and the marvel is that it did not come long ago."

There was some interruption, then he continued, "You damned grafters would like to make me the goat, but my hands are clean and I don't propose to be placed in the door that way. Why don't you go down to the Mill, Warden, and you," he sneered to the Captain of the

Guards," "or you, Commissary General?" the voice rasped on.

"No, you know damned well that you don't dare put your noses inside! Afraid you might be torn to pieces and rightly so! You are a bunch of cowards! There are only two men who would dare confront those convicts, myself and the Turnkey. If I go, I must know where I stand beforehand. Are these demands to be granted and carried out?" Tho hard, the Captain of the Yard was a man of his word, and he did not propose to be made a catspaw.

"Yes, yes! Everything will be fulfilled. Make your promises and I will back you up, but for God's sake, Captain, go down and end it all," the Warden groaned feebly. "I will stand by you and everything will be all right."

We could hear the roar of the mob in the Mill. They were calling loudly. The hour was up, and springing into the Turnkey's office, I grabbed the 'phone. Happy Jack answered. "What's the trouble?" I asked.

"We are losing control! This mob is going crazy!"

"For God's sake, hold everything in check," I shouted, "the committee are all safe and we will return to the Mill in a few minutes!"

Again Happy Jack urged, "Belts are being cut, and if something doesn't happen quick, Hell will jar this Mill to its foundations. Don't lose any more time, Morrell!"

The Captain with the customary catlike tread had entered the office. His face was pale and grim. "Let me have that 'phone," he shouted, snatching the receiver from my hand and shoving me aside. "This is the Captain of the Yard," he shrieked into the mouthpiece. "Your committee is safe. They are returning to the Mill with me, and if there is one dollar's worth of machinery destroyed down there, by the Eternal God, I'll hang everyone of the leaders of this mutiny." He banged up the receiver and stalked out into the yard, commanding us sharply to fall in line and lead the way.

CHAPTER III

MUTINY AND COUNTER MUTINY.

At the Jute Mill door we were met by an ear splitting demoniacal roar, scarcely a human sound, inarticulate, menacing. Brave as he was the Captain turned white and instinctively stepped back. He seemed to be living his whole life over again in the brief space of a few seconds. The Turnkey, a Godfearing man, never blanched nor batted an eye. His cool demeanor amazed even us. He must have had a clear conscience.

All semblance of order that was maintained in the beginning had gone. The leaders had lost control. Breaking away, hundreds of striped creatures, howling and angry, surged toward us in the front of the Mill. Vainly the men who had taken charge brandished knives and shouted. They were lost in this mob of furious convicts. Sensing the danger I mechanically shoved the Captain of the Yard over to a table used for inspecting sacks. It was about five feet high and offered a good vantage point, commanding the entire human mass so densely packed in that section of the Mill.

Springing onto the table I grasped the Captain's hand and swung him up beside me, then turning, faced the mob and shouted for order. Instantly the twenty-four other leaders took up my command that they listen to the Captain who had come to talk.

"To Hell with the Captain!" The voice was a signal sound of that destructive element to be found in every mob. It stirred them on to recklessness, and I shuddered for the Captain's safety. There were some who hungered for his life. This would mean the rope for me and perhaps many other innocent men. I had taken the desperate chance of leading this mutiny solely in the belief that there would be no bloodshed. Something must be done.

Mechanically I clapped my hands, shouting for order.

Happy Jack and his brave supporters began moving among the rioters, striking blows and cracking heads to be dressed later in the hospital. They were "stool pigeons" ever the disturbing element, who were loathe to allow such a splendid opportunity for personal gain to pass. They might injure and even kill and then tell stories that would please the ears of the officials. This time they had failed, hopelessly outnumbered. The noise died down.

I spoke calmly and without interruption as one of the committee of five who had gone to lay our grievances before the officials and told them that the Captain had returned with us to give assurance that our demands would be granted. I asked them to accord him the same friendly treatment that he had given their committee when at his mercy, and then advised the Captain to speak.

As if addressing a sympathetic audience he went over the whole situation, explaining how he had tried in vain to have things remedied, which were entirely out of his jurisdiction, but that he now stood before them as the directing authority to give his word that these conditions would end at once, except a few which were entirely in the hands of the governing body,— The Board of Prison Directors,— namely the removal of high officers holding departmental positions, and the arranging of requisitions for new food supplies. He again gave assurance that the spirit of this protest would bear good fruit and concluded by commanding that the convicts return to their work, maintaining order in the prison so that harm would come to no one.

One of the leaders jumped to the top of a loom. "Let's give three cheers for the Captain," he shouted.

A hearty resounding roar indicated the good will of the convicts. It was the first cheer, loud and long. This was followed by a second which, to the great chagrin of all who desired order was lost in a series of catcalls and jeers.

Again came that miserable bellow. "To Hell with the Captain! He's nothing but a dirty watchdog, and the truth is not in him. He'll lie his contemptible soul into Hell and ring the change on himself in the next instant. Take my advice, burn the Mill down! That's the way to bring our condition before the people."

The voice ceased as abruptly as it had started. Someone had taken this man in hand. Perhaps a club had fallen upon his head, but the damage was done and again the destructive element was gaining control. It looked like trouble, even bloodshed. There was not a minute to lose and jumping into the breech again my voice rang out commanding silence.

This time I made sure of painting a picture that even the most hardened might glimpse his danger, should the day's work end in bloodshed.

Once more came a challenge from the midst of the tightly packed mass. "Who the Hell are you that we must listen? How do we know but you're a 'stool pigeon' transferred from Folsom? Get down out of there and let some of the men we know speak for us."

Happy Jack's voice rose high above the buzz, hurling a string of imprecations at my unknown accuser. There was a moment of silence, and acting quickly, I continued my speech.

"Our friend wonders who I am?" I shouted. "He lies when he says he doesn't know me. He is a barking dog without a bite, anyhow. Now if that tough bully will only come forward and show his face, when this excitement is over I will make him eat his words like the dirty yellow dog that he is."

By a happy thought the mob had been turned into a merry laughing body, almost childlike in its simplicity. They were won heart and soul, and three cheers loud and long followed.

Again I cut in. "All in favor of accepting the Captain's promise, raise your hands like men." It looked as if every hand in the Mill was held up high. The battle for law and order had been won. Millions of dollars worth of the State's machinery remained intact. Every man returned to his station. The Jute Mill was again in motion and San Quentin became once more as orderly as before. It was all over so far as we were concerned.

The siren blew announcing our midday meal. We were counted one by one as we filed out through the man-gate to the general mess. The meal was just a little worse than usual, but all were happy in the thought that this day would mark a new epoch for the future. There was a noticeable air of self-assertiveness on every face. It usually accompanies a victory.

Those sitting at the first tables were finished almost before the end of the line had come in. They began to march out, amazed to learn that they were to go straight down the mess hall to the upper yard. This was customary only in the evening for general lockup. A word would have set the dining room aflame, but before that could occur the head end of the line already emerged into the open and mutually obeying, as human beings are so prone to do at times of crisis, they responded to the lockup bell, automatically going through the routine without a murmur.

A blinding madness gripped the mutineers. There was only one answer to this sudden performance. They should have returned to the Jute Mill for work. Since they did not, each in his heart believed he had been tricked. It looked like a well laid piece of treachery and many were convinced that the Captain of the Yard had betrayed the confidence reposed in him.

By means of the jail murmur message after message passed around from those occupying cells in the building facing the offices, one to the effect that there was a terrific commotion in the Captain's headquarters. He was exonerated. The other officials had double crossed him, and the report was circulated that the Captain of the Yard had left through Liberty Gate in a terrible rage.

The mutiny had been concluded and San Quentin was quiet again. It was over so far as we convicts were concerned. However, to all appearances, a real mutiny was now being staged, an official one.

The walls were heavily manned by rifle guards. Extras with clubs were detailed inside of the prison. Convict trusties in spick and span uniforms were carrying messages around the institution. It became, as if by magic, a beehive of activity while we sullen prisoners looked on in silence, waiting for the outcome of the new turn in affairs.

"Kids' Alley," one hundred twenty cells on the ground floor, was cleared of its occupants. Convict roust-about gangs moved the furniture from them, carrying it to the front of the cell houses facing the offices, and by about four o'clock all was ready for the great weeding out upheaval.

My cell was located in "Murderers' Row," where lived all of the dangerous "lifetimers." I was one of the first to be divested of my clothes and dragged forth naked to a narrow cell in "Kids' Alley," about four and a half feet wide, eight feet long, and seven high, made of solid stone. I had been marked as a leader, and one by one seven others were thrust in with me. Cramped and miserable, it seemed impossible that we could live.

All afternoon the weeding out continued while officers, blue coated and heavily armed, flitted around through the buildings placing notes into the hands of "stool pigeons" who in turn passed them on to the despicable element known as prison rats and pets. In certain cells immunity from torture was offered those who would join in the sinister plot to make the official mutiny a success, and by nine o'clock that evening, at a signal from headquarters the order was given "to raise Hell and keep it up."

Instantly pandemonium broke loose, a weird bedlam, a mutiny staged for the outside world to hear about. What a strange contrast to our orderly protest in the morning! For the moment we eight crowded together in the tiny cell, forgot our misery, pain and slow suffocation,— did not even see the unrolling of the large prison fire hose, so absorbed were we in the frenzied shrieking and clatter of the hired mob. It was drawn into "Kids' Alley" and the huge nozzle held against our door, while still we were unaware of our fate.

"Damn them, give them water, plenty of it," snarled a voice, and a great stream of icy water burst into the cell striking the back wall with terrific force and spraying down upon our naked bodies so heavily that we were almost hurled to the floor! We dodged, crowded, and finally stooped low to avoid being struck directly by the full force of the stream. It was strong enough to kill. Like a cloudburst it poured in. Our teeth chattered, cries went up to Heaven. Some would have fallen and drowned in the water which was now waist deep if the strong had not acted as a support.

Were they going to drown us like rats within the narrow confines of the tanklike cell? The water was creeping up higher and higher, and now we had to stand erect to hold our chins above it. At last they withdrew the nozzle and took it to the next cell and we stood there in the dead of night, straining every muscle to the utmost to keep from collapsing.

If I live a hundred years I shall never forget the horrors of that night with the water trickling out but slowly under the bottom of the door, packed together like sardines, holding up the fainting and collapsed, listening to the groans and cries of agony that issued from every cell in "Kids' Alley," and waiting hour after hour for the cold water to seep out. From shoulder high it gradually receded until we were standing waist deep, then knee deep, and by ten o'clock the following morning ankle deep. We had stood all night, and half crazed, half frozen, we crouched in miserable heaps upon the floor.

The howling din of the paid rioters had never subsided during the entire night. Word was passed around that reporters from the metropolitan press were arriving hourly to hear the noise from the only mutiny the world at large should know about, and to make the seriousness of the situation more impressive, several of the Board of Prison Directors had arrived and were holding an almost continuous session in the office of the Warden.

Repeatedly the reporters asked the Warden for an explanation of the trouble, for the causes behind the great uprising, and as often he would point his finger and ejaculate in pained alarm,— for this Warden was a good actor, — "Do you hear them now? Listen to that! What can you do with such brutes, who openly defy every law of God and man?"

The official mutiny sounds continued as if to give his words more force, and ringing his hands in an agony of grief he protested pitifully, "I don't know what it's all about. I have been too lenient, and I suppose this is the price I must pay for conducting an institution along humanitarian lines. I know I shall be blamed for it all. Oh, those Folsom Transfers!"

"I didn't want those convicts brought here,— desperate characters every one of them, and from the day they entered San Quentin we have slowly but surely lost control. They have demoralized this prison." The Warden paused, noting with pleasure the effect of his dissertation. If he could only win the press, he knew that his Administration would be strengthened. The infamy to which such a man will stoop is appalling. His knew no bounds, and with a final exclamation he cried, "I will not be accused. My case must be taken to the people. I can prove that I fought against the transfer of those evil brutes, and I know that the Governor will support my claim."

Such acting, and he was really putting it over. Why not? The convicts were not allowed to be heard, and the infamous play was carried along splendidly through the coöperation of the Warden's convict pets and prison rats in the big San Quentin cell houses.

The battery of reporters still surrounded the Warden in one corner of his large palatial private office. Some were suspicious, and insistent about finding a cause for such a tremendous prison upheaval. The Warden sensed his position and became more determined in his efforts to enforce the advantage already gained. He parried many thrusts and queries leveled at him by the older and more astute news gatherers. At such times he would frantically grasp at one of the many long poised telephone connections leading out from his central station to various ramifications of the big penal institution. His rasping, whining commands were given in jerky disconnected sentences, denoting to a keen student of human nature, the coward and tyrant at bay driven to desperation.

At last he reached the Governor by long distance 'phone, just what he wanted more than all else. Hardened news campaigners sensed a "scoop" and being permitted the freedom of the offices they listened in rapt attention to the whining voice.

"Governor," he called, "San Quentin is in open mutiny. I need at least a regiment of soldiers to protect the prison. I won't be responsible for the consequences if you fail me now. The place has gone entirely mad. Those Folsom Transfers are at the bottom of the trouble, and they are already tearing the buildings down."

What the Governor had to say in reply, of course, the reporters could not determine other than to perceive that the Warden became still more agitated. Slowly he hung up the receiver and resting his head upon his arm posed in the woeful attitude that one would expect to see in a man whose great hopes had been rudely crashed to the ground. If he succeeded the world would hear only of the mutiny, the official one. The people of the great State of California would never know of the peaceful protest against graft in the Commissary Department. The real cause of the prison mutiny was to be cloaked and the convicts were to be depicted as inhuman monsters without the pale of the law, just common prison brutes.

When a riot ends it always begins in prison. Whatever the convict starts is invariably concluded by the officials in a destructive manner. The helpless convict protests against prison wrongs hoping that word may seep through the thick walls of the jail to an unsuspecting public. Where the convict leaves off servants of the State take it in hand, committing acts of violence and destruction so that the innocent may be condemned and the public mind poisoned against them. I have studied such manifestations for a quarter of a century. Investigation shows not one instance where the convict is criminally responsible for the damage done. Our public servants are most frequently the real offenders, their slogan usually being that the world must never know the true cause of prison troubles.

During the few hours of the convicts' mutiny of San Quentin, there was neither bloodshed nor destruction of public property. The Jute Mill with its millions of dollars worth of machinery was under their control and neither a vicious act was committed nor a freeman injured. When the convicts surrendered upon assurance that their demands would be reasonably adjusted, the officials violated every tenet of equity and justice by starting the real mutiny. They committed the most appalling damage to public property that has ever occurred in the history of American Prison Riots, and this vandalism was engineered by the Warden and some of his subordinate officers duly sworn to obey the law and discharge a sacred duty to the wards of the State. His tools were the prison pets and "stool pigeons" who lent proper coloring to the picture for the outside world.

The first night of the riot had passed at San Quentin. The effect produced upon the representatives of the press had been good. Delegations of citizens who had hurriedly come to San Quentin to learn at first hand the nature of the trouble, stood a safe distance from the seething danger within the walls. Many of them were grouped around the Warden with blanched faces, horrified at the earsplitting pandemonium.

Still the Warden was not satisfied. He wanted more to participate in the disturbance. The horrible opium traffic flourished throughout the prison at this time, and on the second night, prison rats and trusties passed to and fro through the cell tiers supplying irresponsibles with the drug and all other convicts who could be tempted to partake.

The noise and clamor grew steadily worse. Sheriffs' posses from adjacent counties were hurriedly summoned and camped on the hillsides to guard the prison against a break. Sounds could be heard for miles around, and the unthinking public made excursions by boat to Point San Quentin to listen in amazement to this exhibition of open rebellion in the State's largest penal institution. Outraged Society stood aghast, wondering what would be done next by those terrible convicts, pitying and sympathizing with the State's political servants.

On the third day many of the convicts were dope maddened, and goaded to action by the blue coated assistants of the Warden, to their insane pandemonium they added destruction. Averagely decent men became gibbering savages shouting for vengeance, blindly striking out at inanimate objects, attempting to throttle unfortunate cell mates and throwing down all barriers of decency.

The battery of special writers still surrounded the Warden, prodding him with leading questions. They were not permitted to interview any of the convicts of the prison proper but "stool pigeons," who had been primed with official stories to strengthen the Warden's plaint.

The Warden was still acting. Every little while he nervously jerked himself from the swivel chair, pacing up and down before his imperturbable inquisitors. Now and then he rushed to a window, throwing the sash up and theatrically sweeping his hand in the direction of the great cell buildings, from which issued the most insane racket ever heard in the history of any penal institution. "There," he shouted repeatedly, "listen to that! Tell me, you men who think you know so much about this stuff and nonsense called brotherly love and kindness,— tell me how you are going to practice such methods on brutes like these. Why, my God, men, don't you understand? They'd tear you to pieces like a pack of mad wolves."

"Here's an answer to your damned prison reformers," the Warden went on, with a great show of indignation. "Here's an answer to your maudlin, sentimental, busybody women, who have been preaching about coddling criminals, evil brutes, lawbreakers. I have tried to please them, and now things have reached such a pass that even the lives of us servants of the State are not worth a plugged nickel. Here we have the results of their demoralizing public agitation. If they had not opposed me in my rod of iron policy for such beasts, this disgraceful exhibition could never have happened."

The old political, con-wise Warden was putting home his final words that should be given the public, and the noise issuing from the cell houses only too forcibly clinched them. "Why men, last week these unruly criminal ruffians had the effrontery to make a demand upon me for feather pillows to replace those of straw prescribed by law for every penal institution in the land." The Warden sneered, and then he laughed.

The San Quentin Mutiny lasted fourteen days. The hired rioters had burnt themselves out, and were in a stupor. Quiet prevailed. "Kids' Alley" had been filled and the overflow placed in the dungeons. For thirteen long days and nights, we had waited to know the outcome, struggling against sickness, hunger, cold, and even death. On the fourteenth day, still naked, I was dragged from the horror chamber, given an old pair of trousers and a shirt, and barefooted and bareheaded, marched before the Warden and a quorum of the State Board of Prison Commissioners.

"He is the ring-leader," shouted the Warden. "I have all the facts in my possession. He is the twenty-fifth man of the Folsom Transfer. Gentlemen of this Board, behold the brains of the riot. He started this trouble."

What did my protestations of innocence amount to against the word of a tyrant, a man utterly devoid of the first principles of common justice or decency, a man who would not hesitate to swear away the life of an innocent victim in order that he might vindicate his rottenly notorious mal-administration of the second largest prison on the North American Continent?

Tho weak from loss of sleep and hunger, my poor shrivelled body hardly able to stand erect, I feebly tried to defend myself against the cowardly accusations of the Warden, pleading that if given a chance, I could prove that my conduct throughout the whole affair was exemplary,— further, that I was directly instrumental in saving several million dollars worth of the State's machinery, not to mention my efforts toward helping to keep the peace. Then they silenced me. I was not permitted to plead in my own behalf, or even to produce witnesses.

"Solitary confinement, all privileges forfeited!" The words struck me like a cannon ball. Had I not been a lifer, no doubt many years would have been added to my original sentence, as in the case of Happy Jack and the others who had so bravely sacrificed themselves to an orderly mutiny and the protection of the State's machinery.

After my release from solitary I became a target for any "stool pigeon" who wished to curry favor with the officials. They were always ready to listen to stories about the twenty-fifth man of the Folsom Transfer,— the man who hád led the San Quentin Riot. Henceforth, my life was to be one long siege of torture. Then, the notorious Sir Harry came to prison. I was a marked man, and through the fatality of the tangled threads of my prison life, made to order for him.

Sir Harry was a forger and bigamist, internationally known, a man who had served many terms, a "stool pigeon" and an informer on his unsuspecting prison pals. My first impression was that of distinct aversion for him. In time this was partly overcome by his smooth demeanor and apparent interest in me. I knew little of his previous history then, and his gaunt appearance combined with an air of having been done a grave injustice tendéd to soften my antipathy. In addition he made it known that he was a man who would do anything to escape from prison before his term expired, and craving for freedom myself, I conceived a plan.

In less than two months, through his slick ways and small "stool pigeon" work, he had been appointed assistant to the Captain as private clerk.

"The rest will be easy now," I suggested. "This old Administration closes soon. There will be a new Warden and for a time, confusion. There is a fellow here who forges as well as you can, and, for safety, he will do part of the work. Also there are two friends besides him whom I would like to get out. You can gain possession of our commitments. He will make counterfeits, changing the term of imprisonment and dates so that we will all be released in the regular way within a few months after the new officials come in."

Sir Harry was to fix up the books in the office, and thus it was arranged so that there appeared to be no chance of a double-cross. He soon brought me our four commitments, commenting that the fifth was his own, and that he preferred to change it himself. Two days later, the other forger had the commitments ready. They were complete even to the seals, and looking them over Sir Harry averred with great feeling, "Those are fine. Almost as good as I could have done, but you ought to have seen mine. It's perfect. Only one year instead of four, and I'll be going out in five months. I am changing the books now, but those which the Captain may see will have to be left to the last, after the new crowd gets in."

The original commitments were burned in a cell that night. We four convicts began to feel good. As short timers we now made every effort to keep out of trouble pending our release. Only a man serving life can understand the strange metamorphosis that goes on within a human being when he realizes liberty is near at hand, to be gained without injury to anyone.

Then Sir Harry came to me one day with the news that he intended to leave the office. "The Captain thinks a great deal of me already, so I'll just throw a fit in his presence and when I come out of it, I will ask to be assigned to a night job in the dining room of the 'red front'," he said.

"How about the rest of the books?" I asked.

"Why," he laughed, "you're slow. This move only strengthens the game. I'm after a night job that permits me to go anywhere in the prison and I can slip over to the office to do the remaining work at the proper time. Then too, in case by any chance they should spring those commitments or we should fail in getting the County records outside destroyed and a backfire should occur, someone else would be in the job and that clears me and all of us."

I was relieved at this explanation, never having asked to see Sir Harry's forged commitment, and believing that it had been changed like the others, forestalling a double-cross. I did not dream that he had left it intact and was at that very moment working out an entirely new scheme.

All my life I have been governed by intuitive promptings. Invariably they have never failed to guard me in hours of danger. This time I unwisely ignored my first impressions of the man, Sir Harry, his suavity no doubt blinding me to his true character. As a result this fatal blunder brought down upon me the most appalling condemnation that was ever inflicted upon a human being in the red record of prison history.

CHAPTER IV

SIR HARRY'S PRISON DRAMA UNFOLDS.

The cell door banged open and two guards pounced upon me. Ordinarily the least sound awakens me, but on that Sunday night I heard nothing until the intruders were inside and clutching at my throat.

"They've come to kill me this time," I thought, resisting as they tried to pull me from my bunk. Then I was struck on the head and grew weak and dizzy. In a short while I realized that my mattress was being torn to pieces. They were searching for something.

"Where are they, damn you, where are they?" demanded a gruff voice.

I made no effort to ask questions, fearing further assault at the hands of my brutal warders. The search went on until the place was wrecked completely. At length, when they were satisfied that their quest could not be solved, I was dragged out into the tier and stood up against the wall while one of my brutal tormentors menacingly faced me, blackjack in upraised hand, poised to strike if I made the least show of resistance.

"Let us take him below," the other remarked as he stepped clear of the cell. "The Captain will raise Hell if we lose any more time. Better get a wet towel and wipe the blood off that fellow's face," he cursed, "or else we are liable to get in bad with the main 'screw'."

In another instant, I was pushed and shuffled along the tier to the prison yard below. I had no clothes on, and in the middle of that frosty night those guards marched me, almost naked, across the yard to the punishment dungeon where the Captain and the Warden stood waiting.

"Well, did you get a gun on this one?" a voice asked, cursing roundly as they shoved me in.

"Not the sign of a gun," replied a guard.

The Captain snorted angrily as he helped to drag me into one of the cells. He locked the door quickly as if fearing I might escape, and left me without an explanation in the cold dark tunnel-like dungeon.

I was not alone for long. Soon, a commotion started, doors began to clang, there were sounds of men being dragged in bodily, and moans and groans of pain. At last above the din, I recognized the voice of one who was in on the commitment deal. I called out to him and he replied that we were all double-crossed, that the whole thing had been tipped off and we were up against it hard.

Thinking he referred to the commitments I suggested that all we would have to do was to keep quiet, adding, "But I don't understand this talk about guns."

"Don't say any more," he advised. "There may be 'stool pigeons' locked up down here."

I became silent, but my mind was active in an effort to solve a deeper mystery than the changing of commitment papers. It would not account for the present situation, and in my terrible plight I forgot all about my bruised head and bodily sufferings.

In the morning the other prisoners quickly ascertained by counting up that there were no "stool pigeons" among them, and a babel of tongues so filled the place I could scarcely distinguish more than that a jail-break had been planned among some of the lifetimers.

"What was that talk about guns?" one asked another.

"Damned if I know," came the ready response from each of them.

"I was standing at my cell door waiting to be let out when the watch dogs sneaked up quick and nailed me," said one.

"We all had our clothes on," another added, "and that makes it look bad. It will be hard to explain why we were dressed at such an hour of the night. Whoever gave it away was on the inside, because the prison 'screws' knew just which cells to open.''

But the ever recurring question was, "Does anybody know anything about guns?" No one could solve that mystery and they all decided to tell the truth when put on the carpet.

The talking ceased. Men were entering the dungeon armed with pick handles and soon the confined were being prodded and bruised to force someone to tell where guns were hidden. But all to no purpose. These poor unfortunates knew nothing, and the screaming and cursing accompanied by pleadings for mercy made me shudder.

There were nineteen lifers locked in the dungeon. They had hoped to escape, but now everything was lost and as the torture increased with each denial that there were any guns, the air became surcharged with agony and cries to God to let them die.

It was a hideous nightmare to me, but mild in comparison to what followed. One by one, men were taken out and put through a painful gruelling third degree, each admitting frankly that he knew nothing about any guns, which only further tended to convince the officers that it was a conspiracy of silence, one convict shielding another. They were dragged back to the dungeon, most often unconscious, to be pitched upon the stone floor, awakening in feverish delirium, broken, raving and moaning, sobbing and babbling.

I was the last to be manhandled, and my very consciousness of the sufferings of those who had gone before caused me more real pain than if it had all been inflicted upon me. They dragged me out, and for the second time in my life I experienced the sensation of having chairs shattered from the impact of my bruised body, of fainting and being restored again, not to be questioned about the California Outlaws this time, however, but to be commanded to surrender some guns of which I knew nothing.

If guns really did exist there would have been no reason why I should have endured such awful torment. To divulge the secret could affect no one else, since the officers insisted that I alone had planted firearms in the prison. However, to them, my denial was stubbornness and so the ordeal went on until overcome, my body being unable to stand any more torture, I was dragged back into the dungeon cell, there to recuperate for the next siege of manhandling.

When I came to, they were still prodding my companions, taking some out again for added tortures, while a few were removed from the dungeon as insane. Whenever the officials entered, they stopped at my cell to ask if I was ready to tell about the guns.

Thirty-six days passed and the nineteen confined in the dungeon had dwindled down to one, myself. It was agreed that I alone knew where the "plant" was, and they decided to make me tell. There was no use trying to reason. Even when I explained that the fact I was in bed asleep when they opened my door proved I had not been included in the contemplated jailbreak, the answer was a sneering suggestion that I was "just slicker than the rest and did not propose to run the risk of being caught dressed."

More than a month of questioning, torture, and dungeon darkness I had endured, and then came my trial before a Board of Prison Commissioners, an arbitrary court from whose decision there was no appeal. The strong cigar smoke in the courtroom made me dizzy and sick, and several times during the long trial I nearly collapsed as they bullied and cajoled me for information regarding those guns, which did not exist so far as I knew.

The chief inquisitor of the Court badgered me insisting that I had the firearms buried within the prison walls, but all to no purpose. I stoutly defended my innocence against the almost insurmountable opposition. True, this Court sincerely believed in my guilt and could not be censured for the hostile stand they had taken since, if guns were planted within the prison walls, all of the lives of the freemen in the institution were in danger.

At last, goaded to desperation and like a wild animal fighting with its back against the wall, I demanded as an act of common justice that I be confronted by my accuser. Silence ensued. The members of the Court whispered in undertones one with the other, then the President mildly rejoined that the Warden of San Quentin Prison had preferred the charges against me.

Like a shaft of light piercing a dark cloud it dawned upon my dazed brain that someone had framed me and the Warden of the Prison was to shield the real informer. Jail intriguery was at work, plot and counter plot, and I was marked for the sacrifice. Then the Court made an offer of mercy.

"Convict, 16,766, if you will surrender the firearms you will only receive a mild punishment. Refuse this extended offer of leniency made to you by the Court and your last chance is lost."

I remained stoically silent, not knowing what else to do. I could not surrender firearms and I could not induce a revelation of my innocence to this unfeeling tribunal. My last hope had vanished.

Slowly the presiding Judge uttered the dread sentence, "Solitary Confinement for the Balance of Your Life."

A hushed silence pervaded the Courtroom and old hardened newspaper men stared blankly at each other. Not a word was spoken. I had no guns to surrender. They were non-existent. I was framed, and like the impact of a bullet the awful sentence of life, in a solitary dungeon of San Quentin, fell upon me.

My original sentence was life imprisonment,— now life in a solitary dungeon made two life sentences,—thus life on top of life. What little hope I held as a lifer was lost. Henceforth my days until death should end the misery, must be dragged out in the drab silence of a dungeon cell.

Innocent, but doomed to death! In fact I did not know all of the details why I had been sentenced to life in darkness until sometime later. Sir Harry was dragged into solitary and locked in a cell near mine. It was only for a short time, but long enough that I could learn the full extent of the plot.

He had received the coveted job in the "Red Front." He had never changed his own commitment, but while pretending to work with me on the commitment plan had persuaded all of the other lifers that he would go the limit to help them escape. His first advances were repulsed by these convicts old and prison wise.

In order to demonstrate his good intentions he suggested that he would not only get a night job in the "Red Front," but that he would also steal some drugs and dope a guard to prove how easily it could be done on the night of the proposed break. Sir Harry had lost interest in my commitment plan the moment he secured his coveted position, but he shrewdly kept me in ignorance of this fact and also of his scheme with the other lifers for a night break.

On the other hand Sir Harry had informed the Captain of the Yard that some lifetimers were planning an escape, that they had confided in him, and that he would lead them to believe he was helping while obtaining information.

The intriguery — the double-crossing! His whole plan was so hellishly ridiculous in its conception that under any other condition than serving a life sentence in solitary I should have laughed outright, for tho terrible, it was humorous to believe that this sickly slimy creature, a bigamist and forger, could play so many parts with such consummate effrontery and still escape detection.

Of course the Captain knew this was a wonderful opportunity. "With the Administration so nearly at an end, if we can expose a big prison plot for a night break I might hang on for another term," the Captain thought. "Let her ride," he finally exclaimed to Sir Harry after some deliberation.

True to his promise to the lifers a guard fell asleep at his post of duty, heavily drugged. He was discharged and strange to say, here again the diabolical Sir Harry had worked a wheel within a wheel for he heartily disliked this particular guard and had thus brought about his downfall. He knew that the Captain was strict on account of the expected break.

Henceforth Sir Harry began to act the role of a martyr in the service of the Warden and Captain. His elastic step was gone. He dragged himself into the office frequently with face drawn as if undergoing a heavy strain, only to report slow progress each time.

"It is too much on me, Captain," he often said. "I can't stand this any longer."

In reply, Sir Harry was only patted on the back and requested to be game and see it through. He was rapidly gaining in their good will for his efforts in behalf of the Administration.

To convince the Captain that there was to be a real break and to impress him with the seriousness of the plot he finally informed him that the lifers had proffered a guard five thousand dollars to smuggle in some guns. "They will be given to me tonight," he ventured, "and you don't have to take my word for it either. The cook in the 'Red Front' is one of your 'stool pigeons.' You can have him watch and report whether or not it is true."

For some time Sir Harry had made it a point to speak mysteriously and in whispers to the night guards in the cook's presence. At last this "stool pigeon" became suspicious that strange things were going on. He cut a hole in the screen between the kitchen and the dining room so that nothing might escape him.

Sir Harry named the night on which firearms were to be smuggled into the prison. It happened to be the night that a good natured unthinking guard had agreed to bring in a large package of prime cigarette tobacco. This was a common occurrence, but Sir Harry had arranged it to look unusual.

At midnight the "stool pigeon" cook saw the innocent guard slip a box into Sir Harry's hands. This had the desired effect. The cook informed the Captain in the morning.

A little later Sir Harry went over to the Captain's office announcing pleasantly with his hands shoved deeply into his trouser pockets, "Well, Cap, I got the guns all right." He had by now assumed an air of familiarity with this autocrat of the prison, so strangely in contrast to his former whining obsequiousness which all well trained "stool pigeons" practiced in the presence of the Captain of the Yard.

"They came in last night," he went on, "and have been planted in the lower yard. The break will occur next Sunday night. Your 'stool pigeon' saw the package handed over to me," and then and there Sir Harry's imagination ran wild.

Breathlessly the Captain demanded that he be led immediately to the hiding place of the guns.

But Sir Harry had another card to play, which would explain the non-existence of the weapons tho it might cost a life that was absolutely innocent of even the slightest connection with the plans for his prison break.

"Morrell and I just planted the guns," he added, his eyes narrowing.

"What!" shrieked the Captain in despair. "Planted the guns with Morrell! By God, man, are you crazy? Planting guns with Morrell, and I gave you credit for having brains! Heavens, man, you should have brought them to me. If I fail to get possession of those firearms at once, by the Eternal, I will have you shot if it costs me my life as a sacrifice! Get out before me, quick, and lead the way as fast as you can."

Affecting an alarmed expression, Sir Harry apologized. "God, Captain, can't you understand? These men knew the guns were coming in last night, and if I had not produced them, they would have been suspicious and the whole plot would then have been spoiled."

"Don't lose any more time," angrily shrieked the Captain. "The damage can be undone if you hurry. Dig up that plant, I say. Take me to it now! What in Hell did you mean anyway, by planting the guns in the lower yard?"

Sir Harry appeared overcome with grief as he staggered from the office dramatically making his way slowly toward the lower yard followed closely by the Captain.

"My God," he gasped examining the ground, "they're gone! Don't punish me! I didn't mean any harm!"

What a fiendish imagination! There were no guns, and still he persisted, trembling and ashen colored, weaving the tangled thread of an impossible story that was to swear away my life.

The Captain was in a rage, and began to abuse Sir Harry, who then made his past master play. "Don't be foolish, Captain," he urged. "Morrell has lifted the plant all right, but those guns will be distributed among the men in preparation for the break, and we'll get them Sunday night. They won't attempt to use guns before that time, so everything is safe."

But the Captain was still furious, and driven to desperation Sir Harry changed his tactics, assuming an air of offended dignity. "I am through with the whole business," he exclaimed. "After all I've done for you people,— after all I've risked,— these men would kill me like a dog if they knew,— you now treat me only with rank ingratitude. If you and the Warden would leave me alone, I'd get the bunch, guns and all, but now you can go ahead and finish it yourselves."

It was the Captain's turn to change front. He grew very gentle as he realized they could do nothing without this man who held in his mind the solution of the whole plotted escape to its minutest detail, including the names of all of the guilty prisoners. He tried to quiet Sir Harry.

"I'll go ahead on only one condition," Harry finally replied after divining that the desired effect had been produced, "that is that I shall receive a pardon as soon as all is over, because my life in this prison wouldn't be worth a cent. Sooner or later some of the bunch will murder me, besides, what I'm doing for you means a lot."

When the Captain took it up he said the Warden agreed this was the best move to make and promised to see that Sir Harry should be granted a pardon for his great service in behalf of the State.

"All right, then," Sir Harry chortled, "I'll go on with it, but don't bother me any more. Even now someone might have seen me down in the lower yard, and if so that will surely queer the whole thing."

One of the men in the plot had spent weeks making skeleton keys for the cells and he was to be released first in order to open the other doors. On the fatal Sunday night he stood dressed and in readiness while the guards who were supposed to have been doped dragged me to the dungeon, under the impression that I, Morrell, was the arch criminal of the prison plot.

The man who had made the keys was caught redhanded. The other lifers followed, but none of them possessed any guns, and thus it had finally dwindled down to just me. They were sure I had lifted Sir Harry's plant, taking the weapons somewhere else for future use, and until I produced those imaginary firearms, I was doomed to darkness and silence.

CHAPTER V

THE KNUCKLE VOICE.

It was mercifully called solitary confinement where I, the doomed victim of a prison plot, was to spend the remainder of my life. My dungeon cell was four and a half feet wide by eight feet long. It allowed me but three short steps and a turn on the fourth as exercise. I had an old straw tick on the floor and two blankets. A scanty meal and water were shoved in through the bottom of the grated door once every twenty-four hours, and by that it was possible to keep some track of the passing time. Silence and darkness completed the tragedy. I was alone, a grim life convict dead and forgotten in a living tomb.

I was alone except for Jake Oppenheimer, "the Tiger of the Prison Cage," the only other man in the history of San Quentin who had received such a sentence. I might as well have been alone in the dungeon since my only companion lived thirteen "tombs" away — too far to speak to even if we had been permitted. Silence, loneliness, darkness was our lot. We two in the dungeon had to lie there day in and day out with no occupation, no opportunity for mental improvement, without common physical necessities.

Not a scrap of reading matter of any description was permitted in solitary, not even the commonly accepted New Testament of the Bible. If it had been, I could not have seen the print, for during the brightest part of the day only a faint streak of dull, murky light penetrated into the dismal room where the solitary cells were located. This came through a painted window from the corridor and thence to my cell.

I was hardly able to see my hand before my face, but added to the darkness was silence, indescribable — stifling. It was broken only by the catlike tread of the guards. In that room their deathlike watch over the solitary cells even palled upon them, and they had the freedom of a large space, could talk to each other and smoke or mayhap read if they were intelligent enough, and could leave the prison inclosure going far from solitary after a certain number of hours each day. They had the relief of human companionship, they mingled at will with the outside world and yet they have been known to become affected by the atmosphere, some even going insane.

The terrible mental battles which I fought are impossible of conception by one who has never known imprisonment, not to mention existence for any length of time in solitary silence. If I could only have talked to the "Tiger" it would have been more endurable, but sealed in this prison tomb it seemed humanly impossible to communicate with another so far away.

The loss of mind even before death could intervene appeared inevitable for me. Most of the hours of each day, like a lion in a cage I paced to and fro in that crypt of horror — three steps and a turn on the fourth — thinking, thinking, thinking, for there was nothing to do but that or sleep and I was a notoriously light sleeper.

As the months dragged their weary length out into years my thoughts ran wild, and in the mental battle which ensued I developed an amazing power of vizualization. I began to invent, creating devices mentally, drawing plans upon the walls of my brain, completing each and then starting in on something new, at last experimenting in self-induced hypnosis, daring even to project my mind out and beyond the confines of San Quentin to distant lands and loved ones.

From that I delved into a system of irrigation, conjuring up from the seeming depths of nowhere various methods attempted since primitive man's first struggles with the soil. Through this amazing research work, I developed a system of overhead irrigation which conforms as nearly as possible to a natural rainfall. It is used successfully today in arid sections of Far Western States.

A mental fog bank swept over my mind at intervals. Then, everything would go blank.

Now, in desperation, I took up a new line of stimulus, and soon discovered that I received great relief in playing checkers, vizualizing both sides of the game with as much enjoyment and competition as if at grips with an opponent.

One time a few flies strayed in from the outside. During the brightest part of the day, when the sun was high, a vagrant ray of light would straggle in from the corridor through the painted window of the great solitary room and thence, in its transit, along the wall of my cell. It was a bright spot and after making the acquaintance of my flies I found a new pastime to lighten the burden of long hours.

I began to study our much despised housefly, discovering many traits which appeared amazing to me. He was almost human, sensitive to pleasure and pain.

My hearing was abnormally keen making it possible to detect sounds almost inaudible. The buzzings registered different degrees of emotion. The revelation was marvelous. To my crude mind it was uncanny.

I established the sun spot as a danger line, snatching at the flies and trying to catch them if they rested upon it. They soon learned that I would not harm them if they remained out of this zone. The fact that I could never catch them on the sun spot proved that they understood perfectly. From any other part of the wall I could gingerly pick off the fly in my fingers.

In my first attempts to hold them captive they would emit strange vibrating sounds which would change instantly to a soothing buzz when released. At last, satisfied that I did not intend harm they seemed anxious that I hold them in my hand. After this they never showed any signs of fear and forgot all thought of our strange association lost in the ecstacy and joy of play.

One little trick that amused me particularly, was a desire of the flies to rest upon the extreme tip of my nose. This was a coveted spot, and great rivalry existed among my little friends for its vantage point. The lucky one who first secured the place would fight his companions off fiercely, buzzing loudly as if teasing them at every attempt to crowd him from the spot. Occasionally I lifted the little demon up bodily. At this he would plainly sulk, showing evidence of anger at me for daring to interfere, while one of others would dash for his place emitting a cackle of derision at the discomfiture of his opponent, who, as the convicts would say, for the remainder of the day "showed a grouch against the world."

Oh I knew all my flies! Each was distinctly an individual. The multitude of differences between them was surprising. I knew the happy-go-lucky fellow, always willing to give way to the others for the sake of peace,— the nervous one, the phlegmatic one, the demon of the bunch expressing in every act and sound the selfish swinish nature. The Beau Brummel of the crowd was there too, a real dandy always preening himself, his strut denoting that he thought the very universe revolved around his ego.

In my little colony of friends I soon realized to my own satisfaction that I was closely studying a miniature world of humanity, every emotion being expressed there, love, anger, envy, and hate. Believe me, when I say I am serious, that our despised insects and houseflies possess all the traits of civilized man even to his callousness. But I was able bodied, and a healthy human cannot always content himself with such amusements. I must find something new with which to occupy the twenty-four hours of each day for the balance of my life. Was it possible my jailers wanted to produce a madman?

Again I was back on my hobby of self-hypnosis. Prone on the floor, I would stare fixedly at my shining sun spot, until my eyes dilated as large in proportion as the very sun itself. At last unconsciousness! My powers grew marvelously, until I even experienced the sensation of wandering, of being someone else, another self than the dull, hopeless life convict in a dungeon cell. Still there was little definite in these glimpses. They started concretely enough by my leaving the cell and journeying out beyond the walls of San Quentin, but only to end in chaos.

The time came when I felt that my reason was surely going, and even grew fearful of thinking, inventing, playing games, lest insanity should be the ultimate outcome. Again I commenced wondering about the man thirteen cells away. If I could but communicate with him! It would save me and perhaps him also if he had not already become mentally unbalanced.

The "Tiger," that only other human who had ever received such a sentence as mine, had entered the life of silence before me. Perhaps he had by now succumbed to the inevitable. A plan flashed into my mind. We might talk by sound, a tapping on the wall, but it should be a secret code that no one else could unravel. The guards, the warders must not know.

An old escaped convict from the Island of Saghalien had long ago imparted to me the secret of the Siberian Square, created by a famous doctor, a Russian Nihilist of the inner circle, during his imprisonment in the fortress of St. Peter and Paul. I decided that my Sphinxlike code should be a system based upon the square and worked it out completely. But how was I to get the code initials to the "Tiger?" This problem taxed my ingenuity to the utmost. We were too far separated to speak, and had nothing with which to write notes, even if the distance between thirteen cells could have been spanned.

I devoted hour after hour each day to rapping out slowly the first five key initials of the square upon my dungeon wall. Occasionally a tapping response would come from him, indicating clearly that he heard, but only further establishing the fact that my efforts were futile, since he

THE TWENTY-FIFTH MAN

could not grasp the code. Then I gave him the twenty-six letters of the alphabet in consecutive order. He followed, repeating each one of the sounds after me, denoting that he understood the meaning. I then gave them to him according to the system, placed in parallel lines within an imaginary square made up of twenty-five smaller squares with an extra one for the letter (Z).

	1	2	3	4	5	6
1	A	B	C	D	E	
2	F	G	H	I	J	
3	K	L	M	N	O	
4	P	Q	R	S	T	
5	U	V	W	X	Y	Z

THE SIBERIAN SQUARE
The knuckle voice of the dungeon, a sound language now used in nearly all jails of the world.

There were five spaces each way. (A) was thus: one, space, one; or two short taps; (B) one, space, two; or one short tap followed by two short taps, and so on for the other three letters of the first line of five, each of which started with one short rap, being the first group. (F) commenced the second line and was two, space, one; or two short taps followed by one. (J) was two, space, five; or two short taps followed by five. (Y) was the fifth letter in the fifth line being five, space, five and (Z) being the letter in the odd square became five, space, six.

I went over it in code repeatedly, but to no avail. Each day as I grew tired of tapping I would throw myself down upon the old straw tick trying to make my meaning clear to the "Tiger," through the power of mental pictures. If he would only see it as I had it in my mind, the problem would become a simple one.

For nine months I had tried to teach the "Tiger" my knuckle talk. In desperation I had exhausted every imaginable resource to convey to him what to my mind appeared to be a very simple problem in the A, B, C's of the English Language, but all to no purpose. I was baffled. Still I could readily understand how the poor "Tiger" failed utterly to grasp the meaning of my incessant tapping. He had already sunk into the abysmal swamp of despair through the most unmentionable tortures ever inflicted upon a human being in the history of jails. He was a State made demon, a two legged, man-killing jungle beast with all the finer sensibilities blurred by inhumanity.

I wanted to converse. The companionship of a common language tho we might never see one another would help him and save me from a like condition. Toward the last of those nine months I had given up hope of his understanding my sound taps, resorting to the uncanny measure of trying to transmit the Sphnix mystery of the knuckle voice to him mentally.

For a long time no sound came from the "Tiger." Was he dead, or had he perhaps left the dungeon? Then, like a dying man grasping at a straw I made the final effort, a superhuman one, throwing all the force of my will into it. I listened intently. An unmistakable sound! I was frantic with joy. The "Tiger" had rapped the alphabet in code! Now he was slowly spelling out words. In a few days we were talking, tho feebly at first.

He said that he had tried for months to figure me out, finally giving up,— that the weird ticking sound was like the empty diversion of an insane mind. The "Tiger" had thought me mad,— believed that the tragedy of my sufferings had blotted out everything and that the fancies of the bereft had made me think I could thus communicate with him.

"Did it never occur to you," I asked, "that in my continued tappings of the twenty-six letters, I had some code through which we could communicate with understanding?"

"No," he replied, "I could gain nothing intelligible until now. It came just like a flash,— a vision,— the picture of a square seemed photographed upon the wall, made up of twenty-five small squares in lines of five each containing the letters of the alphabet and an extra one for (Z), the twenty-sixth. If it hadn't been for that flash, I believe we never would have talked."

I was immeasurably pleased, not only because we could talk, but his picture of the Knuckle Code proved that my first real experiment in mental telepathy with the "Tiger" had been successful, and I knew that once our minds were in accord we would achieve marvelous results. Still for the present I should be satisfied with knuckle talking. This system of transmitting the unspoken word was to solve one of the hardest situations in my life, and to help pass the time in that period before I learned the greater things concealed within a human mind.

CHAPTER VI

A STORY IN KNUCKLE TALK.

"What in Hell are you tapping on that wall for?" demanded the head warder peering into my cell.

This man was exceptionally brutal and had never even so much as exchanged a word during all the time since I had been confined in solitary. Prior to his advent as head warder in charge of the tomb of the living dead, he was known as one of the most brutal manhandling guards of the line in San Quentin. He had been a gattling-gun post man and also handled a club as a convict herder. He was a notorious boaster and openly aired his hatred for all convicts, being in return despised by them.

In order to dispel his suspicions and to create the impression that I was going insane, I mechanically went on tapping with my knuckle, moving to different positions along the wall of the cell until I finally stood facing the door, still maintaining my tap, tap, tap. Curiously puzzled he moved away.

The "Tiger" loudly called with stacatto raps, not knowing the cause of my sudden interruption, and cat-like our shrewd manstalker jumped from my cell to his. Again I heard the gruff voice, "What the Hell are you tapping on that wall for?"

The "Tiger's" answer evidently riled the warder for I could hear sinister threats of manhandling as a reprisal for his spirit of insubordination.

Henceforth, our knuckle talking was destined to meet with grave and unexpected opposition on the part of our erstwhile jailers. At last came the day when they not only understood that our tappings had a real purpose, but that we had established a communication whereby we could converse freely.

Our warders held a council of war to devise some means of depriving us of even this much coveted boon of mercy. They resorted to measures of punishment such as denying us the scanty meal served once every twenty-four hours, for periods of as long as five and ten days at a time, and often cut off our ration of water for two and three days until we were almost dying from thirst, but all to no avail. They might succeed in preventing it for short periods tho never permanently, for, when the night watch came on, often bringing a sleepy guard we could knuckle talk a streak until morning without interruption.

It mattered not to the "Tiger" and me, buried in a living tomb, where daylight and darkness were as one, for we could rest and sleep any time while knuckle talking had now become a luxury. It was about this period that I had consented to tell the story of my life to the "Tiger," and he had answered, "I want it all, Ed., every word of it, and from the beginning."

"I have seen so little of the world and life," he pleaded, "that your story will be a great treat. Please begin now."

"Before I launch into the real story," I remarked, "you must understand something of the early troubles that led to the feud between the settlers of the San Joaquin Valley and the Railroad Company."

"The land agent of the company had sent circulars inviting settlers from all over to come into the great San Joaquin Valley, particularly to Fresno and Tulare Counties and make their homes upon the sections that had been given them by the Government as a bonus for the construction of the road," I rapped. "In the circular the prospective rancher was assured that once the patents were granted the company would sell to those who had the best right to buy, at the rate of unimproved land in that vicinity. This was approximately five dollars per acre. Better offers that outsiders might make were not to be considered. These settlers were to be accorded 'first privilege of purchase and were to be protected in their expenditures'."

"Peaceful homeloving people from all over the country answered the call of the railroad land agent," I went on, "going through the struggles of the early pioneer, enlarging their rough shacks into spacious ranch houses, constructing miles upon miles of wire fence, and building great irrigation ditches, converting a thirsty desert waste into fields of wheat and fruitful garden spots."

"The thrifty settlers were so busy they had no time to worry over the long delay in receiving titles to their homes. Not the least of their troubles was the debt from excessive freight and tariff rates for hauling grain to tide-water, there being no competition. It became so bad, at last, that freight such as farm implements and needed supplies coming from the far East, tho it might be sidetracked for hours at their own station, could not be delivered until first taken to San Francisco at forty cents, from there to be reshipped to them at fifty cents or more a ton."

"The short haul tariff tyranny was spelling ruin to the farmers and no redress or relief could be gotten through pleadings to the courts. It really seemed as if the railroad must own the State from the Governor down to the most petty officer. The railroad commission was openly accused of bias while it was common gossip that the company maintained a million dollar lobby at the State Capitol during each session of the Legislature."

"But, to cut a long story short," I continued, "after seemingly endless trouble things reached a climax. The ranchers had two bad years and the following was to be a banner one. They had spent thousands of dollars in improvement, never doubting the integrity of the promise of the land agent. And now when they were just on the verge of being able to get out of debt, the storm broke."

"These people had braved a wilderness to create homes only to be informed suddenly that their lands were for sale by the railroad, to anyone who would pay the price asked, not at the unimproved cost of about five dollars per acre, but for staggering amounts ranging from twenty-seven to as high as sixty dollars. Besides this, they had lost their last fight in the courts for a reduction of grain rates throughout the State, which would forestall their making any money during the fruitful year.''

''To add fuel to the fire the land agent had the effrontery to offer them an opportunity to lease their own lands, which they hotly refused to accept, realizing it would be an open acknowledgement that they did not own them. Test cases were fought in the lower courts but lost. Then they referred them to the United States Circuit Court in San Francisco.''

''In the meantime the railroad company had already listed their land for sale in nearby real estate offices, beginning to deed it over to strangers who were doubtless dummy buyers. Ejectment proceedings started immediately.''

''Feeling satisfied regarding the coming decision from the higher Court the ranchers banded together to protect themselves, and tho they had sworn not to fire the first shot, battle became inevitable. The United States Marshal with deputies and railroad men armed and apparently ready for trouble came to continue the work of eviction. While the leaders of the banded ranchmen were conferring with them, it started. A shot was fired by someone. Instantly as if by magic, guns were brought into action and the roar of battle aroused the entire countryside. Irregular shooting followed and then silence.''

''The death toll was great that day. Wives and mothers were left helpless and alone, while remnants of the bands of doughty ranchers were scattered all over the San Joaquin. It was called 'the Mussel Sleugh Massacre,' terrible in its consequence; but still the people waited, hopeful regarding the outcome of those test cases. They were not left long in doubt. Brief and cold was the final decision of the highest Tribunal, which stated that titles to the land in question were in the plaintiff, the railroad company, and that the defendants had no title and their possession was wrongful. 'There must be findings and judgment for the plaintiff, and it is so ordered,' concluded the Court."

"Immediately the railroad announced that they had withdrawn from any further fighting and that the trouble must be settled in Washington. The ranchers knew now that the company was making an extreme stroke as Congress does not allow the use of troops for civil purposes. This move made it a case between Government and settlers so that the whole United States Army could be sent in if necessary to drive those people from the land they had improved a hundredfold through promises that were never intended to be kept."

"Further resistance was futile, and as each notice of ejectment was served the poor ranchers packed the few personal effects that could be carried, leaving their homes and sadly trecking back into the mountain districts, there taking up small claims on hog and cattle land."

"Needless to say they were disgruntled, even bitter, feeling such hatred toward the railroad which had deprived them of their homes, that they believed no act of vengeance could be considered criminal provided it harmed none save the dread 'Octopus'."

"From their midst," I rapped the "Tiger," "sprang the California Outlaws of whom even to this day none are known but the leaders. The families of most of them were not aware of their connection with the attacks against the railroad. Railroad money from the express cars was their sole interest, passengers never being molested and the United States Mail being held inviolate, always."

"Of course, the men who were recognized leaders have paid dearly for their depredations of outlawry. They called me 'the twenty-fifth man,' the youngest member of the bandit gang. When, upon my capture, I failed to reveal its history or even the other names, I was marked for the sacrifice and my doom was sealed."

The "Tiger" remained silent as he so often did when reflecting. Finally he urged me to continue, asking for some of the wild escapades which he knew no one could tell but me. Luckily it was night with a sleepy guard on watch, and through the medium of the knuckle voice, I started the story, rapping it to him thirteen cells away, spelling each word out upon the wall of my dungeon, the only time I have ever told it to anyone.

We of the living dead were cursed, reviled and punished for even this slight diversion to occupy the mind, so during the day when alert ears caught our little ticking sounds, the thread of my story was often broken. But on this night I continued without interruption, tapping him the story of a strange robbery, the first of its kind in the history of this country.

The noted night flier Southbound from San Francisco was brought to a dead stop in the San Joaquin Valley, I had told the "Tiger." The long train had been moving swiftly over the lonely stretches of country North of the Mojave Desert when, through the drizzling rain came sharp gun reports and the crash of high explosives.

Heedless of warnings some of the more daring passengers snapped up their windows and in alarm discovered that engine and express cars were gone. They felt sure that all means of escape had been cut off so that robbers could take their time in the cars, but none came and after an hour of anxiety they heard the puffing engine, felt a welcome jolt, and were soon on their way again.

The conductor said that the engineer had been off his time schedule and was bending every effort to make it up. He turned at the command, "Stop and be quick about it," gazing into the barrels of a shotgun.

"Don't make any fuss, but obey orders," the same voice admonished.

There were two masked men fully armed. One had jumped from the roof of the express car onto the tender of the engine. It was going at full speed. He even asked for the emergency brake. The other climbed down the rear of the express car. One hand on the coupling pin, with the other he returned the fire of the brakeman.

The two bandits forced the engineer to run the express car up the track. In a few minutes they had shattered the safes with dynamite and had rifled them of their treasure in railroad money. The crew were ordered to carry the sacks a short distance. A bomb was set off on the eccentric of the huge overland engine, and soon the bandits were lost in darkness.

It was the first time dynamite had ever been used to open an express car, and the only time on record that robbery was ever committed on a train where passengers were not made the victims. Also the United States Mail was untouched, clearly proving that the robbers only intended to injure the railroad company. The passengers remarked at the time that the Mussel Sleugh Tragedy and others of its kind were being avenged.

The locomotive and express car were badly injured and with great effort the heavy train was dragged into Fresno.

The railroad officials made a hurried survey of the wreck, minimizing the startling phases of the robbery and appearing alarmed only at the loss of schedule by this noted flier. They did not even stop to remove the shattered express car. A heavy Mallett compound engine was coupled on, and soon the long train was sweeping through the wide stretches of the hazy San Joaquin.

The man-hunt for the train robbers was inevitable and keen interest centered upon Visalia, the County seat of Tulare County. From early days this frontier town had maintained a hard reputation. Everyone said that more questionable characters lived there than in any place of equal size in the world. It was the storm center and magnet point for opposition against the "Octopus," the railroad company, and all eyes turned toward it in hope of locating this new outlaw band.

Within the confines of Visalia could be found in those days, the true Western two-gun man-killer. Its Spanish-town was the center of a redlight district made famous by the notorious "Hole in the Wall," a saloon and dance hall where the Spanish Fandango was still a part of the program. Also it had been the headquarters of the band of "forty thieves," and of the noted bandit Joaquin Murietta and others.

Now the railroad company, in its frenzied effort to run to earth the perpetrators of this strange and daring crime against the safety of its lines, had turned Visalia into a seething mass of blood-money hunters, gunmen with notched weapons and bad reputations hungering for the head-price that had been placed upon the bandits.

Visalia had, of course, long since shed its frontier appearance, substituting real buildings for the old fashioned lean-tos and shacks, but its main street was still unpaved, dusty and bedraggled with stray dogs and other domestic animals idling about unmolested. Occasionally a band of horsemen might swish up or down it, leaving a blinding cloud of dust in their wake. This was all that broke the sleepy inactivity — while the blistering midday sun baked everything to a brown,— except a continual rattle of glasses in the dives and low groggeries where the pungent odor of stale beer indicated that the habitues were trying to keep cool.

At evening, when the trade winds blew across the Valley of the San Joaquin, Visalia, as of old awoke with a bang, ready for another night's lurid history. Screeching fiddles, twanging mandolins, and the loud thud of bass drums with the shouting of dancers and quick bark of six shooters, told the tale of the town's usual mode of relaxation.

This hectic life among a people who openly boasted of an abhorrence for honest employment in the majority of cases, naturally attracted the attention of blood-money hunters seeking the rendezvous of this latest band of robbers. There was no other logical place to turn, because they had disappeared with the bags of gold as if the very ground had opened and swallowed them.

After months of tense excitement over the attractive rewards for the bandits dead or alive, and just when interest was beginning to wane a repetition of the great Pixley Train Robbery occurred. This time the Big Limited Southbound was held up at Goshen. Again the same two mysterious strangers, cool and daring, performing their work without a hitch, smashed the express car, blew open the safes and rifled them of their contents, then slunk into the darkness. No one was injured.

Excitement once more reached a fever heat. Suspicion pointed directly against Visalia. This time a box of watches from the express car was found upon the veranda of the home of an unpopular preacher, a man who had busied himself in the feud between the ranchers and the "Octopus." The box of watches contained this message, "A present from the train robbers to a flunky of 'the Beast,' who enjoys an annual pass over its lines."

Hundreds of gunmen representing the lowest, most murderous element from the border of the British Northwest to the Mexican line flocked in, many of them making their headquarters around Visalia's Spanishtown. The good citizens of the entire Valley, knowing the railroad feud, breathlessly awaited the outcome, many hoping that the bandits would not be caught, instinctively feeling that they would prove to be friends or even neighbors of good standing.

The "Octopus" and the State of California doubled the rewards for the capture dead or alive of the bandits, and the wrangling of gunmen increased as they anticipated winning the big stake. The nearby mountains teemed with strangers, carrying guns and looking wildeyed while they breathlessly sought to kill for the alluring head-price, each hoping that he would be the first to fire the death shot and drag the victim down to the Sheriff's office. But again the outlaws disappeared, leaving not even the vestige of a clue, and it was believed they had fled from the country. The bandit news was relegated to the second and third pages of the big dailies and finally ceased to appear.

On the night of August 3rd, 1892, occurred the last of the great series of train robberies in the San Joaquin Valley. Suspicion fell upon a quiet little home in the outskirts of Visalia.

Pinkerton agents insisted that they had tracked a stranger there, a man who proved very talkative and boastful, and altho he might not have participated in the many crimes, he never-the-less seemed to be well acquainted with details and inside information of the robberies and they thought he should be brought in and compelled to give information to the proper authorities.

The Sheriff laughed heartily. "Gentlemen, you are dead wrong about that place. It's the home of one of Tulare County's most respected citizens. He is the father of a large family. His name is Chris Evans and he is now the foreman of our Grand Jury. I insist, gentlemen, you are mistaken," he exclaimed. "Regarding his boarder, John Sontag, every one of us knows him. He has been there for many years and is upright and honest."

"We are not after them," the Pinkerton men insisted, "but the stranger claims to be a half brother of John Sontag and has gone to that house."

Big Bill Smith, the head of the railroad detective department, came in at that moment, urging action at once. Still laughing, the Sheriff commissioned one of his deputies to accompany Smith. In a short while they returned to the Sheriff's office with the stranger. After a grilling he was thrown into a cell. He must have given incriminating evidence because Big Bill and the Deputy Sheriff hurriedly left the County Jail again, making direct for Chris Evans' home.

Approaching the place, the deputy remarked, "There goes John Sontag now. See, he is just entering the back door."

Evans' oldest daughter, a pretty girl of about sixteen, responded to their knock at the front of the house. To the query of Big Bill Smith she replied that Mr. Sontag was still downtown. She did not know that he had returned and was resting in his room at that moment.

Big Bill, sure that he had seen him and not the girl's father, cursed, "You're a damned liar!"

It was a dreadful mistake, which nearly cost Big Bill his life for the father heard the loud slurring remark. Notorious for his quick temper he sprang into the room with a six shooter.

There was an exchange of fire. It awakened John Sontag who stepped in with shotgun poised. The officers were retreating. Big Bill Smith did not look for the gate, plunging head-foremost through the fence palings. The Deputy Sheriff fell badly wounded. Now, the irate Evans stood over his still form, lowering the gun slowly as he recognized a former friend. He did not shoot, but turned his attention to the fleeing railroad man-catcher, by this time lost in a cloud of dust, his pace quickened to a mad flight by the sound of banging guns.

When the noise died down, Evans and Sontag stared blankly at each other. They realized a terrible tragedy had occurred in their lives. No time could be lost now. Quickly gathering up some ammunition, the two men bounded into the officer's buckboard and fled toward the foothills of the great Sierra Nevada Mountains.

Contrary to its early morning lethargy, Visalia was awake. Whistles and firebells loudly sounded the alarm. Gunmen ran to and fro in confusion while others dashed through the streets on horseback, until clouds of dust enveloped every road leading to the foothills. The man-hunt was on. Visalia was in the limelight again, commanding front page attraction, not now as the abiding place of the old famous band of forty thieves or of the Mexican brigand, Joaquin Murietta, but of a new and unique gang of outlaws. Once more the pulse of her underworld throbbed with excitement. Its population of notorious badmen hourly increased with the influx of new blood-money hunters, men of grave questionable repute arriving like hungry hounds on the scent of the chase.

The bandits did not go far. They stopped in a secluded spot until their trail had been hopelessly lost, retracing their course homeward again after dark. Their arrival was reported by spotters who lay in hiding near the Evans' homestead.

Two old railroad detectives, wise in the game of man-hunt, hurriedly recruited a posse from the hordes around the "Hole in the Wall," low characters always ready to pick up a little easy money regardless of how dirty or cowardly the job might be. No guilt had been established against the two good citizens of Visalia other than the gunplay in self protection. They had avenged an insult offered a little girl, the daughter of one of them, and now both were to be hunted as outlaws.

Among the desperadoes who joined the posse was one Oscar Beaver, a badman about town. He demanded an opportunity to fight the outlaws single handed, boasting of his deadly aim and the certainty that he would bring them back. The two men organizing the death legion, shrewdly accepted Oscar for front rank honors. They went at once to the home of Evans, the former good citizen, veteran of the Civil War, noted Indian Scout under Custer and many other famous generals of the frontier, a man game to the core and a recognized dead shot.

"They're in the barn," Oscar hissed. "I'll creep up close and nail them as they come out,— kill them on sight. I'm going to get that big reward."

The rest of the posse remained at a safe distance. Oscar, the badman, glided along the ground on his stomach, crouching in the weeds about thirty feet away, silent and like a serpent ready to strike. The barn door slid open. A large heavy topped buggy was backed out, and the father and mother of seven little children, who were at that moment asleep in the house, stood near in silent farewell embrace. Sontag held the horses.

The flash of a gun stunned them for an instant. Mechanically Evans shoved his wife back into the protection of the barn then grasped his shotgun and fired, coolly remarking, "Evidently the fool killer is abroad tonight."

His aim was unerring. It had made him a great soldier. A stir in the darkness, a thud and groan, marked the closing of Oscar's career. The badman who had come there to murder, crumpled up and lay silent, while the two outlaws sprang into their buggy and fled toward the mountains amid a shower of bullets fired by the other man-hunters.

The next day news was given out that a Deputy Sheriff aiding in the search for train robbers had been brutally murdered by them. But to most of the valley and mountain people who knew him, the death of Oscar Beaver was heralded by rejoicing. "He was one of the worst characters of that section," they explained, "having taken part in the Mussell Sleugh Tragedies, aiding in driving the unfortunate ranchers from their homes on railroad lands."

Chris Evans was now called the Leader of the California Outlaws, and John Sontag, his lifelong friend, was known as an able Lieutenant. There was no evidence to connect these men directly with any of the depredations committed against the "Octopus," but a sinister shadow had fallen across the threshold of the little home. A boastful stranger changed the current of their whole lives. Sontag's half-brother came like the shadow of doom.

Weeks passed, all very much alike except for occasional skirmishes between the outlaws and posses. The railroad loudly clamored for action, charging openly that the peace officers of Tulare County were in collusion with the bandits. This was unjust and shameful. Those men were brave and sincere in the performance of their duty tho naturally hampered by the vast number of friends the fugitives possessed throughout the entire valley and mountain regions. But the company's purpose was soon evident. They sought justification for their next move, which was to virtually usurp the duties of the County authorities. This was done at once by commissioning into their service every badman and gunfighter that money could buy. Posses were formed which started a campaign of terror throughout the peaceful mountain settlements, where the innocent, even women and children were no longer safe from the railroad's hired thugs.

Henceforth a strange contradiction was manifest. Mountain people stood aghast before the wanton acts of brigandage committed by these men parading as peace officers. Timid women on mountain trails were openly insulted, and the supposed outlaw band of hunted men often found it necessary to come to their rescue against those sworn to uphold the law.

One of their men who was brought into the mountains, known locally as Sam Black, claimed to be a Deputy United States Marshal from the Mexican Border. He was a hungry looking ruffian with notched gun indicating that he had not only killed his man but many men. The side partner with whom he swaggered about had just completed a long term in prison for a heinous offence and both were shunned, dreaded and despised. The climax came one evening after dark on the outskirts of Camp Badger, a lonely mountain settlement.

Black and his cowardly partner had been watching the cabin of a young married couple. When they discovered that the woman was alone, her husband being away in the logging camps, they forced the door and brutally attacked her. Her screams made them fearful of danger. Both of them quickly slunk away into the heavy manzanita brush before help could arrive.

In desperation, the mountain people sent word of the tragedy to the outlaw band. Picked men were ordered into the district to stalk the perpetrators of this new outrage. They lay in wait for Sam and his partner to return to camp, greeting them with heavy fire. The noted gunman fell crumpled up on the trail, while his pal dashed into the underbrush.

Wounded, the Deputy Marshal crawled into the cabin and under the floor concealed himself out of range of the bullets. Early next morning he was taken to the valley, wounded badly, one leg being amputated as a toll, a reprisal for his cowardly act. But this not deter him from committing more atrocities, his final and crowning crime being the wanton murder of his employer in San Diego. He was sentenced to life imprisonment, doubtlessly saved from hanging by the influence of the railroad in whose service he had pursued the train robbers.

Here the "Tiger" interrupted to ask if he was still in San Quentin.

After a series of quick taps, which in the knuckle voice denoted a laugh I replied, "No! He died on the day I entered San Quentin as a transfer from Folsom. Died from an attack of heart failure. He had been ostracized by all the convicts of San Quentin and it was said his fear that the dagger might be thrust into my hand to avenge the honor of the California Outlaws, brought about his sudden ending. His partner, the infamous Tom Burns, met a belated death at the hands of a cowboy in Arizona. I heard that a group of them danced a jig upon the pine box which contained his body."

"That, Jake, will prepare you for the big story," I told the "Tiger" thru means of the knuckle voice. "It gives the proper setting for the drama."

"It starts out good," he exclaimed. "Please don't bother about explanations. I am anxious to see where you come into the picture."

We had revelled in knuckle talk on night shifts for nearly a week. Our guards had thrown all caution to the winds, being drunk during the greater portion of that time; and though exhausted from the continual tapping, I did want to go on with the story, but something very unusual happened. The Captain of the Yard made a complete change of guards in solitary from the chief down. This could only spell trouble for the "Tiger" and me. Our knuckle talk must stop. We must study our warders, their habits, their inclinations, their good points and their bad ones. If some were sleepy, we would do most of our talking while they were on duty, but woe betide us if they discovered our faint low tapping.

Days went by, and the "Tiger" was growing impatient. The silence palled upon us both, and I decided to go on, but we had to be cautious.

"I am going to tell you an interesting part of the story now," I finally rapped the "Tiger." "It will be the tale of a great detective and gunman, the turning point in my life," and once again the knuckle sounds were bridging the space thirteen cells away.

CHAPTER VII

A MYSTERIOUS MEETING.

Big Bill Smith, railroad detective, had made his headquarters in Fresno, the County seat of the County in which most of the big train robberies had occurred. He lived at the Grand Central Hotel. I stopped there with the intention of meeting him.

The big dailies had played Smith up in lurid type as the "Sherlock Holmes of the Wild West," until the people of this bustling town believed that a great hero was in their midst, often forming in groups to stare and whisper as he passed by. Either through fear of losing their esteem upon closer association or for the more deep-seated reason that Fresno was the hotbed of friends of the outlaws who thrust notes under his door and sent letters of warning by mail, he never spoke to anyone or lounged in the lobby of the Hotel, and I gave up hope of a chance meeting.

Detective Bill Smith was always grave and mysterious, hating the men who had committed outlawry against his company as if the injury had been personal. He was a pitiless watchman, capable of denouncing, even crucifying his own brother if he should unfortunately run counter to the law. Stern, silent, reticent, he was a man who had never been known to smile. There were some who called him "yellow at heart," because of his inglorious retreats before a withering fire from the outlaws, but he never resented such accusations, preferring to allow his next whirlwind performance to demonstrate that he was far from being gun-shy, doggedly following every clue, silent and devoid of emotion.

I had studied him carefully, and at last decided upon a plan of action, sending a bellboy to his room one day with my card, requesting an interview. It was granted only after Big Bill felt satisfied from the boy's description that I did not appear to be at all dangerous.

To my timid knock, a gruff voice answered, "Come in!"

This man-catcher was standing erect, to one side of the room as I entered, hands thrust deeply in the side pockets of his coat. He looked at me furtively, his sharp menacing eyes almost hidden beneath a narrow protuding forehead and a pair of shaggy eyebrows. His black flowing mustache concealed the mouth so that I could not determine whether it was cruel or weak. The man's whole appearance was far from prepossessing, and I felt a distinct shock of aversion. I was fearful of the outcome of this first meeting.

"Your business! Well, what is your business with me?" he demanded impatiently.

Without another moment's hesitation, I plunged into the purpose of my mission, concluding by telling him that I was familiar with his work and had come to offer a plan which would bring about the capture of the outlaws, provided however that he would do the square thing by me.

"Oh, I get those kind of steers every day and if I listened to all of them I wouldn't have time for anything else," said Big Bill concealing his interest, tho disconcerted. "But to come down to business," he added shrewdly, "what information have you that would be of the least interest to me, young man? What do you know about the outlaws? Do you know the leaders, or any of their friends?"

Then followed a series of questions through which I remained silent, finally explaining, "Here's what I wanted to say. I have a friend serving twenty years in San Quentin, who was a former member of the outlaws and a close personal friend of the leader. If you help me get this man out I can join the band through him. After that, you know, the rest is a mere matter of detail."

"Who is this friend of yours?" asked Detective Smith, with an awakening curiosity. "How long has he been in prison, what did he do to get there and what do you want me to do if I can use your services?"

The outlaws did have a friend in prison so my answers were satisfactory and I made the demand that he appoint me an operative on his staff with the usual salary and expenses, adding that in the event the bandits were captured through my efforts I wanted equal credit and a full share in the standing rewards. "But in order to make all this possible, you must have my friend pardoned at once," I concluded.

"Sit down," directed Big Bill, interested at last. "Tell me something about yourself."

I did, and his many searching questions were almost in the nature of a third degree, until at last evidently satisfied the great detective ended our interview with an appointment for the following evening.

This time he came to the point more quickly than I had anticipated. "Look here Morrell, I have considered your offer carefully and am ready to take a chance with you. I admit your plan appeals to me, tho frankly I don't believe you can deliver the goods." Here his shrewd face hardened. "If you do, I'll show you I'm a man of my word," he remarked. "You will be given every ounce of credit due you, likewise your full share in the reward and so far as getting your friend out of prison is concerned, why that's easy. Show me you're on the level and I'll have him out in jig time. Meet me in San Francisco the early part of next week," he concluded. "I'll make arrangements for your work to begin at once."

My third meeting with Detective Bill Smith took place in San Francisco in the following week. With an apparent studied ease of expression he plied me with further questions regarding myself, questions which on their surface would indicate that they were prompted more by afterthought than any real intention to entrap me. Nevertheless they were keenly subtle and showed he had been industriously checking up all my statements to him.

Smith eyed me strangely as if to determine the extent to which he dared trust me. He was searching the very depths of my being to detect flaws, perhaps even a weak spot. Could it be possible that the keen detective had measured me correctly and was now about to uncover my dual role? But his next speech put me at rest completely regarding my fear of exposure.

"Morrell," he ventured, "I have full authority and am responsible to no one for the staff in my charge. I employ and dismiss when I please. Your salary will be five dollars a day and expenses. You must submit a daily report in writing to me, checking up everything that you do, including your expense account."

"Here are your credentials," he continued, handing me a paper, "in the event that you need to show your hand at any time, but I warn you, young man, to be careful of that document. If your connection with me becomes known, it will surely spell 'curtains' for you." Our interview ended by Smith inviting me to have lunch with him before returning to Fresno to take up my work.

Over the meal that night many phases of the plan for my activities were discussed. Smith was ambitious to pull off some big spectacular windup to the reign of outlawry. He was daring even to the point of madness, and I could see that those working under his orders were but mere pawns in his bloody game. "There isn't a doubt in the world that this ruthless man-stalker would not hesitate to sacrifice my life to gain his selfish ends," I thought as I listened to the coldblooded details of the scheme he had in view.

At this time Smith had been thoroughly repudiated by his cowardly retreat from the Battle at Jim Young's Cabin. The press had unmercifully lambasted him and his man-killing gunmen. He was still smarting under the merited condemnation and would go to any extreme to redeem his lost prestige. Try how I would it was impossible to get him to talk upon the details of the fight on Pine Ridge. It was such a one sided affair that I could see he keenly felt the disgrace, desiring to have it considered a closed chapter.

Here Jake interrupted my tapping. "I say, Ed, you haven't told me anything about that fight."

"No, Jake, I was just coming to it, when I had finished with Smith and my introduction to you as a full-fledged detective."

"Yes, the Battle of Jim Young's Cabin as it was called marked the undoing of the great Detective Bill Smith. He never recovered his standing after that."

"Prior to the Battle of Jim Young's Cabin, the bloodmoney hunters had blustered about through the mountain settlements openly hurling defiance at the outlaws and branding them as 'a bunch of cowardly thieves, who would not dare meet their adversaries in open encounter'."

A month passed after the outlaws made their sensational escape from Visalia, I had told the "Tiger," and the chase cooled down to a mere situation of watchful waiting. The Stage Station at Mill Creek in Fresno County was the gathering place of the hordes of man-killers. The barroom was never empty and liquor was consumed in quantities by these thirsty "fire eaters." From this central station the spies of the posses went out in all directions in search of information regarding the movements of the outlaws. On the night preceeding the Battle of Pine Ridge suspicion fell upon a ranch house near the Barton trail.

After dark Big Bill Smith and thirteen others of his gunmen including Burke, the half-breed, who was in charge of two Apache Indian Scouts from the San Carlos Reservation in New Mexico, filed out of Big Bill Traywick's Saloon at the Stage Station on Mill Creek. Slowly the long line of gunmen trailed toward the Barton Ranch and took up their positions, closely encircling the place and waiting patiently for the first streaks of dawn, to open battle with their trapped quarry.

THE TWENTY-FIFTH MAN 77

Smith's information was accurate. His spies had told him that the outlaws were at the Barton Ranch and would remain there all night. A battle was surely imminent.

The ranch folks were moving about. The posse was restless and at last one of the more daring of the gunmen ventured from his crouching position and walked boldly toward the barn where the housewife was busy milking. This fellow, Vic Wilson, stood out head and shoulders over the balance of the posse, and why not? He was reckoned a dead shot having a Border reputation as a man-killer. He had twenty-four notches cut on the barrel of his long pearl handled seven shooter, and only the evening before at Bill Traywick's saloon in the presence of an admiring group of his cronies he had filed the preliminary cut of another one on his gun, vowing "this will be for the Leader of the California Outlaws."

"Good morning Mam, have you seen anything of *Christ* Evans?" he asked in sarcasm.

Angered the woman stood up and faced her intruder. "No, I have not seen Mr. Evans," was her quick rejoinder, "but when you see him you'll see Hell."

She went on about her work ignoring the man entirely. Nonplussed he returned to his companions remarking, "Wrong again!"

The posse were grouped together in a dry wash near the Barton Ranch. They were holding a council of war. Some of them were disgruntled, and openly accused Smith of leading them on "a wild goose chase." They were cold and hungry from the long night's vigil and in no friendly mood to consider further plans of their leader for that day at least.

Just then a mountain spotter broke through the underbrush on the other side of the dry wash, calling out to Smith who walked briskly toward him. They conversed in low tones for a few minutes. Once more Big Bill was all action. His eyes fairly blazed as he shouted exultantly to his sulking gunfighters, "Come on men. This time I will show you the real fireworks. The outlaws are resting at Jim Coffey's Cabin down on Sampson Flats. We will hit the Barton Trail for Pine Ridge. We can stop there at Jim Young's Cabin and have breakfast, to be fit for the fight. I figure it will be all over by twelve today."

Burke and his Apache Indians led the way and soon the long trudging line of gunmen were winding their slow course up the steep trail to Pine Ridge. They passed the farm belt and dragged into the tall timber, refreshed by the cool air and spurred on by thoughts of the reward for capture "dead or alive" of the outlaws. Only small shafts of light could penetrate through the trees during the long march, and when they emerged suddenly out into a clearing on Pine Ridge they were blinded by the strong early sun, for a moment not seeing Jim Young's Cabin directly before them.

Again, Big Bill Smith was wrong. His secret spies had given him the double-cross, leading him directly into a murderous man-trap. All night one of them had been watching the movements of the posse around the Barton Ranch, and knowing that the outlaws were to leave Sampson Flat before daylight, this man who broke through the underbrush to speak to Smith, had intentionally given the information, hoping to lead him and his posse into that difficult region while the outlaws were detouring away and around the base of Pine Ridge South to safety in the Tulare Mountains. He, like so many of the mountaineers who were staunch friends of the outlaws and sworn enemies of the "Octopus," was playing with Smith as a cat with a mouse, while enjoying the reward of a spy.

By a strange trick of fate the bandits, instead of carrying out their prearranged program, had retraced their steps making directly for Jim Young's Cabin. They, too, wanted a refreshing breakfast.

Chris, the older of the two outlaws, was seated under the window facing the open garden directly in front of Jim

Young's Cabin. The younger man, his partner, was busily engaged preparing the early morning meal. Every little while the vigilant outlaw would drop the paper he was reading and glance outside taking in the surrounding clearing and lowering his gaze each time, apparently satisfied of no lurking danger. Suddenly, an unusual sound attracted his attention. His sharp hearing had caught the neighing of a horse.

Instantly the bandit leader became, once more, the alert scout of old. Hardly changing a muscle of his set features he coolly surveyed the panorama of gunfighters trooping in at the gate. When satisfied with his inspection he turned as if making a casual remark to his partner. "I say, John, don't move from that spot. Stand bolt upright where you are. If you step across in line of the door you will be seen. We are trapped like a couple of rats in a blind hole."

"There are thirteen of them including Burke the halfbreed and the two Apache Indians, and Big Bill Smith is leading," he continued. "We'll surely have to fight our way out this time. As a signal I'll open fire from the window, and when I do you charge from the door."

The one window and door, which the posse was approaching, were the only means of exit, and as the foremost manhunters came to within about twenty feet of the cabin, a screen of shotgun fire burst forth and two fell. The outlaws, acting as on one impulse, stepped through the open door repeating the shotgun fire, this time rolling up the posse in confusion at the gate.

The Apache Indians, true to their native instinct took in the situation at a glance, and hopping like jackrabbits, concealed themselves behind the large bowlder which formed a part of the fence, starting to employ Indian tactics from this secure vantage point. The rest of the posse, the pale face gunfighters, scurried for shelter shouting loudly for mercy. Not one of the erstwhile noted gunmen stood his ground. Even Burke the halfbreed, the terror of the San

Carlos Reservation, turned and fled, leaving his charges, the two brave Indians, to fight the battle alone.

Big Bill Smith, the leader of the posse, also disappeared in the manzanita. He was wounded again, the leaden shotgun pellets having torn through the hard muscles of his neck. Now one of the frightened posse, gunless, hatless, running pell-mell, bumped into Smith. Cursing loudly he shoved the man aside, dashing still further into the maze of underbrush,— anywhere to get from the scene of that inferno.

The outlaw Chief had turned his attention to the Indians, by his rapid fire keeping them within the shelter of the rock. Every little while they would stick out their hats and occasionally risk their heads, evidently bent on trying to exhaust his ammunition. The younger outlaw had been covering the posse with long range shotgun fire. The battle was going well.

One of the dying men who lay directly in front of the cabin and right in line with the Chief raised his rifle and fired a wild shot. The younger outlaw, perceiving the danger to his partner, turned to grasp his own rifle resting against the cabin. In a moment the dying man had bored him through the center, and he fell face down upon the ground, apparently dead.

Chris was drawing a fine bead on one of the Indians who had dared to venture his head clear of the rock. This time he felt sure that a dead Indian would answer to the crack of his gun. Again the dying man, gasping his last breath, fired, spoiling the shot and at the same time cutting a painful groove through the bandit leader's eyebrow.

The retreating posse proved to be the agency of fate to turn the tide of battle once more in his favor. The Chief was standing at bay like a tiger fighting his tormentors. A few remnants of the retreating band of gunmen grouping themselves on a distant ridge, started a long range desultory rifle fire which took the Indians directly from the rear.

The air around the rock was filled with screeching lead from their guns. The shelter had become a trap, with the fire from behind and with a man directly in front who applied the redskin's method of warfare, rifle leveled watching for the first instant of advantage. Knowing their man, they now feared him.

Something must be done. A bold move must be made or two dead Indians would be added to the list of the day's killing. An Indian ever runs true to form. He is brave and never quakes even when at a disadvantage. The closing of the battle proved to be as spectacular as anything that had ever occurred in Indian warfare. With ear splitting shrieks, the true war-cry of their race, the two redskins bounded into the underbrush as the shots from the lone bandit's rifle gave a parting salute.

The toll of the Battle of Jim Young's cabin was two killed, four wounded, and three horses slain. It was a sorry day and a fitting climax to the disgrace of the imported gunmen who had terrorized defenceless women by their insulting behavior and their drunken carousals around the stage station at Mill Creek.

Now the bandit leader was alone with his wounded partner and the dead. Not a moment must be lost. Time was precious, and capturing a horse near the gate he returned to where his partner still lay face down on the ground, overjoyed to find that John was alive, tho completely helpless from the impact of the bullet which had pierced his lung.

He groaned, "Leave me alone, I am done for. Just put me out of my misery before you go. That is all I ask. I don't want to be captured alive." There was a clicking sound in his throat and the voice was husky. Chris held a tin cup of cool water to his lips and then, when he had staunched the flow of blood was pleased to note that his friend smiled, tho still pleading for a mercy shot.

"Mercy shot be damned," impatiently blustered the Chief, "you are worth a thousand dead men yet. By night

I will have you miles from this slaughter pen, tucked in a comfortable bed with the best medical aid. You'll be on your feet in a month. Come on man, pull yourself together!"

"Why John, during the Civil War I've seen men walk from the battle line to the first aid station with enough lead in them to sink a ship, and never make a whimper. Grim determination can take a man into Hell and back again. This is our battle today. We have mopped up a bunch of dirty gunmen. Now they'll cease their strutting in these mountains, I'll bet."

Without another word and apparently unfeelingly, he lifted the helpless man from the ground, with an almost superhuman effort placing him on the back of the trembling horse. Then tying him securely he gathered up his firearms and after another last look around to be sure there were none of the posse skulking in the underbrush, he wheeled his horse and was soon out of sight of Jim Young's Cabin.

Now the outlaw leader, with his burden, had reached the higher range of Pine Ridge. He was well above the roads and beaten trails where he might have encountered members of the posse. Turning, he struck due South descending through perilous arroyos, and on down into a rugged wilderness. He had plodded doggedly, the hot midday sun beating down upon him and his helpless burden now delirious from the terrible jolting and loss of blood.

Occasionally the outlaw leader would stop at some mountain brook, forcing a little of the cooling water between the wounded man's parched lips, and again trudging on to the Tulare Mountains. The sun was going down. Still he continued well into the night, guided by the stars to a descent into the Dry Creek Valley above Camp Badger. Here friends and medical aid came to his rescue. The outlaw Chief had saved his partner in a race with death. His iron determination won the fight against odds of a thousand to one.

By late afternoon of that day the dead and wounded had been collected and brought down from the Pine Ridge over the steep winding Barton trail, to the stage station on Mill' Creek. One by one the straggling members of the gunfighter's posse were coming in, stripped of all outer garments, cast off to lighten their burden in the rush from the scene of battle and with not even a gun in hand. They bolted straight for Bill Traywick's saloon and gulped down glass after glass of whiskey in an effort to quiet their maddened nerves, vowing in answer to the questions put to them, that they "had been through Hell."

One beetle-browed ruffian from the Mexican Border became quite loquacious when he described his own personal experience. In his Texan twang he "allowed them there fellers are sho some fighters. I been in this heah business of runnin' down border cattle rustlers and outlaws and thot I'd been in some fighting, but this heah scrap today sho has got my goat. And them railroad detective fellers told us we would have a picnic, that your outlaws were cowards and yellow and wouldn't fight. Somebody's put up a big joke on me sho, and that leader of your outlaws he's some shucks. He's twenty Davy Crockett's rolled into one. I never see'd such shootin' in my life. I say mister barkeep gimme one more jolt of your grog, it's me fer the Mexican Border."

Outside a crowd had gathered around other fag-ends of the posse, some of whom were wounded. Big Bill Smith had arrived. No one noticed the two Apache Indians standing stoically aloof, listening silently to the boasting of several who were assuring the curious spectators that they had been the only ones who had returned the bandits' fire.

A voice interrupted the chatter. It was one of the Indians. "White men damn curs,— no stand and fight." He spoke emphatically. "Outlaws him heap good men. Him leader,— long beard,— all same big Indian Chief." Not another word! The two Indians struck out toward the valley and the railway station on their way back to the San Carlos Reservation.

While boarding the train one of them turned, and surveyed the loungers densely packed around the station. "We no fight brave men. Outlaws him big chiefs." As the train slowly moved out, three cheers were given to the departing Apache Indians, the only two men who acquitted themselves with bravery at the battle of Pine Ridge.

For days there was an exodus of gunmen from the higher reaches of the Sierra Nevada Mountains. Panic stricken from terror and fear of the outlaws they swarmed down into the peaceful valley of safety. The hotel lobbies around Visalia and Fresno were crowded to capacity. "I'm through with that sort of fighting," said one of them. "The railroad played us a damned measly trick. Why, they didn't even warn us that these outlaws were seasoned fighters, men, the equal of any in the world. I am told the older one, the leader, is a Civil War Veteran and a noted Indian fighter and Scout, and we surely know now, he is a cool one and a dead shot. A Hell of a game this is, I'll say. We were just ordered to arrest the robbers and bring them back dead or alive, preferrably dead!"

It was indeed a great shock to have come face to face with the bandits at Jim Young's Cabin. Formerly these badmen hunters had always fought from ambush, shooting before demanding surrender.

All sorts of reports reached the newspapers. Prominent citizens denounced the railroad. The Governor even came in for his share of condemnation, now being called upon to bring out the militia to run down the bandits and also drive out the unsavory characters known as gunmen whom the "Octopus" had imported into the State.

There were many versions of the battle of Pine Ridge. At last it began to assume the proportions of civil strife and it was even suggested that the vast forest regions of the

Sierra Nevada Mountains be set on fire and the bandits smoked out and driven from their hiding places in order to put an end to such disgraceful conditions and dishonor to the great State of California.

CHAPTER VIII

DETECTIVE SMITH ELUDES A TRAP, THEN LAYS ONE.

The wounded outlaw was convalescing rapidly at the home of some friends in the Dry Creek Valley. Every care and attention that loving hands could bestow upon him was given and after about a month he was well enough to be removed to Camp Manzanita, the stronghold of the outlaws.

I paused here in my story to the "Tiger" who had long since ceased to snarl, the diversion of knuckle talking and human companionship bridging the chasm of loneliness in this man's awful prison life.

"How is the story going, Jake?" I asked.

"Very good indeed," he replied with quick taps, "but go on Ed. I want you to get to the point where the outlaws either kill or capture the detective, Big Bill Smith." A laugh in knuckle talk followed. The "Tiger" was revelling in the excitement of the moment and wanted to rush on to the untimely ending of the villain in the plot.

Big Bill and I had many interviews during the long months of hunting that followed, I had told the "Tiger" after the short period of interruption. At times it was difficult to convince the detective that my services were as important as he believed in the beginning. Then I would give him information of the outlaws so accurately that even he, the most suspicious of men, would have to admit that I had something on the best of his spies and scouts.

At such times I would take him to task regarding his agreement to have my friend released from prison, pointing out that unless he did so I would be powerless to bring about the ultimate capture of the bandits. Reference to this part of our contract usually brought on a heated discussion and each time I became more convinced that Big Bill thought he was making a cat's paw of me.

THE TWENTY-FIFTH MAN

Winter had passed. It was already Spring. The mountain fastness had thawed and wild flowers made the hillsides gorgeous with their color. For months not a word had come out of the mountains, regarding the bandits. Everybody wondered what had become of them. Was it possible they had left the region and were now lost forever in some far away part of Mexico? Many hoped that this would prove to be the case. Then something happened again!

The old passenger stage coach from Visalia to Smith and Moores' in the Sierras was near the end of its sixty-five mile journey on an up-grade bordered on either side by thick forests and underbrush. The driver swerved his leaders out of a cut, pulling the horses to a quick halt as two armed en sprang from the chaparral.

"Never mind, Tom, you're all right. Stay on the box where you are," said one of the bandits as the driver curled up his whip in the act of alighting.

"Get out and be quick about it," they commanded the passengers who had jerked their heads inside when they saw guns levelled at them.

Having obeyed instantly they were now ordered to take off their coats and empty all pockets onto the ground, the outlaws urging them not to be alarmed if they were not blood-money hunters. Each passenger was questioned and looked over carefully, all of the time being kept in line by one of the bandits with levelled Winchester. Pocketbooks and tobacco pouches were examined for marks of identification, then the valuables were returned to their owners, who were ordered back into the stage with the assuring remarks of the leader. "We are not robbing men. We are just looking for some of those hunting us."

"Say, Tom," the spokesman added to the driver who had remained like a statue on his box, staring at the ears of his off leader, "You will hear from us again. Whenever you do, stop! So long!"

As the stage rounded a turn on the hill the passengers noticed the two men walking leisurely down the road toward the little settlement of Camp Badger. News of the hold-up was not received until after the return trip, the telephone wires having been cut as a precaution. But when it did come, the citizens of Visalia noticed that strangely enough there was no hasty gathering of posses to hunt down the outlaws this time as on former occasions. The ardor of the gunfighting blood-money hunters had been dampened since it was evident that the bandits had assumed the offensive, breaking their rule of reserving fire until cornered. It was also known that the country they were in offered excellent ambush

Receiving a message from my employer to meet him at Sumner, the junction for Bakersfield, I boarded the Northbound train there, and entered the Pullman smoker. I scarcely looked at Big Bill Smith while proffering my hand. He ignored it, so I settled down in a chair, puzzled. The glint of a six shooter levelled at my head arrested my attention and then I heard his voice.

"Young man, explain how the outlaws knew I was to leave Visalia on the stage they held up near Smith and Moores' Mill," he rasped. "Nobody else knew of my intention so you were the only one who could give that information. If I could satisfy myself that I am not making a mistake," he cursed, "I'd shoot you this minute as a traitor."

The plan had miscarried. For some unknown reason he had not taken the stage as intended. We had made up our minds to capture Big Bill Smith and hold him as hostage for some concessions such as the release of the friend from his twenty years in San Quentin Prison. Also there were other scores to settle and the great detective was to be used as the means of coersion. There must have been a guilty expression about me, but I quickly assumed an air of bravado, laughing outright into his glowering distorted face.

"Lower your gun," I exclaimed. "What are you trying to do, make a grandstand play? Don't you know, man, that I left Visalia on the Northbound train before you did, and couldn't have known whether or not you took the stage? It would have been utterly impossible for me to have given the outlaws information on so short a margin of time. You're suspicious of everyone, including yourself. That's the trouble. Don't you know that if I wanted to doublecross, I could have had you trapped dozens of times?"

"Now I am beginning to wonder if you have forgotten all of our past relations and if this is not just a new plan to sidestep your agreement with me," I concluded.

Big Bill dropped his arm and shoved the gun down deeply into his side coat pocket, but did not remove the hand. He looked perplexed. "You are right, Morrell, I have made a mistake," he muttered apologetically. "I should not put you in the door on such flimsy evidence but," he cursed again, "I am simply amazed to fathom how this holdup was timed to stop that stage, and only for an eleventh hour change of plans the outlaws would have trapped me. It was a damned close call, and I'll look to it hereafter that you or no one else will have any line on me regarding my movements, even an hour before I put them to work." He sat down, stuck his customary black cigar in his mouth and puffed slowly, quietly searching my face.

"You are to come North with me," he added, changing his tone. "Stop at Fresno and tomorrow evening at six join me at the El Capitan Hotel in Merced. I have some work that will keep you busy there for the next few weeks."

He had planned a big task for me, as I learned the following evening in his room at the Hotel. Big Bill maliciously tapped with his pencil a spot where he had placed a cross on a Mariposa County Map. You'll find a quartz mill there, and near it an old cabin or bunk house. Go and inspect the premises," he smoothly remarked. "I want you to draw up a map covering all vantage points where concealment and ambush may be made to command the cabin. Further, I want this map to show plainly the surrounding territory and how bodies of men may best approach the place without detection from within. Supplement this by a written description and your suggestions as to the best method of successfully making this spot a complete man-trap.''

"When you have finished the work and while you are still in that territory I want you to go to Raymond and look up the local records of these two men," he added, handing me a memorandum paper containing some detailed information. "Find out, if possible, the source of their wealth. We know that until the last year or so, these men were absolutely without means, and had to depend upon their daily labor for a living. I have had several men on that job, but each time they reported 'no progress' to me. I am suspicious of the whole matter and I wish you would give it a thorough investigation."

Rapping with clenched fist he went on, his big black cigar fairly aflame from continuous puffing. "Now, Morrell, the time is here when you must make good. It is useless to go further along the old lines, and nothing can be accomplished unless you succeed in decoying these murderers out of their stronghold. This plan will prove your true metal, and finally determine whether or not you are big enough to measure up to the job. By the time you have finished in Mariposa County, I shall have your friend released from San Quentin Prison. With him you must work your scheme across. Once the outlaws are satisfied that it was through you he obtained his pardon, there will be little chance of further suspicion against you."

"Make it plain to your friend from San Quentin that it was only through your playing the role of a detective with me that his release was accomplished. After you are accepted you can put this whole scheme before the gang, explaining how you have learned from me that some of the officials of the railroad company, including the president are coming to

Merced in a private car, to go from there by stage to Yosemite Valley.''

Smith was now fairly alive. His words vibrated with the venom of all he had suffered at the hands of the daring outlaws. This time he felt sure of victory. The hour would soon be here to wipe out all his disgrace. "Show them how they can take the president of the railroad and hold him for a king's ransom and a guarantee of immunity from punishment. You must enthuse them with the idea that this would be a grand climax to their career, since, rather than endanger one hair of the president's head the whole power of the big company would be offered to back any terms to secure his immediate release."

"We can't fight them in their own territory, Morrell, but if you persuade them to come to ours, their doom is sealed. I will concentrate a posse of the best gunfighters that can be found in all the West," he said, giving the cross on the location of the old Mariposa Quartz Mill a vicious jab with the point of his pencil and looking at it all the while as if it were a dagger with which he had pierced the hearts of the train robbers. "Once the trap is set, we can take them there, 'dead or alive,'— preferably dead."

Big Bill reached across the table and gripped my hand fiercely. "Young man, if you lure them there, your fortune is made," he announced.

I looked at him curiously,— almost dumfounded. I had known he was unscrupulous, but I never dreamed that he thought me capable of being a willing instrument to decoy human beings into such a contemplated cold blooded murder trap. Was it possible the man believed me to be an utter fool? Then again I marvelled that he did not note I made not the least protest against this wanton endangering of my own life. He was a madman, obsessed with but one idea, else he should surely have discovered my true identity, and the double role I was playing.

Blind to everything, however, Big Bill concluded his business with me. "When you finish this work, Morrell, you must report at once to me in San Francisco. You will there meet your friend from San Quentin. Then you can both return to the stronghold of the outlaws. We must never meet again in Visalia," he insisted. "Don't even indicate that you know me from now on, because new forces have entered the field there."

"United States Marshal George C. Gard, with a picked posse of deputies from all over the West is at Visalia." Here the great detective paced up and down the floor fairly shouting "Damn him! I hope the bandits clean him and his deputies out! He is just looking for a cheap reputation. When I have everything tightly in hand this ten cent marshal and his hungry gang of gunfighters must butt in at the eleventh hour and try to steal the result of my work. But I will beat them to it, even if I have to set a trap for the bunch and have them shot up." He swore violently again.

I left him, pondering over my next move. It was indeed a bad situation, and in the light of my last experience on the train I was convinced that he would not hesitate to shoot me down in cold blood if I showed the slightest evidence of faltering, or if he suspected that I was other than the tool he believed me to be.

At last I realized that Big Bill was slowly but surely inclosing me within an iron band from which there would be a hazardous retreat,— my end doubtless coming with his final demand that I deliver the goods.

My role of detective had been exciting and romantic. The conclusion was near at hand, but shaking off further feeling of apprehension I retired, and before the sun broke over the plains of the San Joaquin was on my horse galloping at full speed out of Merced and Eastward to the old Quartz Mill in the mountains of Mariposa County.

I would draw the plans and carry on the by-play for a time at least.

CHAPTER IX

THE BATTLE OF STONE CORRAL, TURNING POINT IN THE LONG YEARS OF OUTLAWRY.

The bandit Chief lunged forward and hands high above his head he fell face down upon the ground. A rifle bullet had clipped his spine and lodged in his back.

"His own gun must have exploded," thought John, as he huddled down to determine the extent of the injuries. He was left in doubt only a moment. A barrage of fire from the nearby cabin answered his question with weird music.

"I am hard hit," said the leader, coming to finally. "Retreat, man, and save yourself." But his friend refused indignantly. Again fire burst forth from the cabin, this time shooting out the Chief's right eye and shattering his left hand at the wrist, while stray shots inflicted wounds all over his body.

These added injuries and excruciating pain had the effect of arousing the old war scarred veteran to madness, and like a painracked dying lion, with the good arm he grasped his shotgun and steadying it between his feet, let both barrels go. The cabin was riddled and the gunmen scurried out in confusion. They were so panic stricken that they even ignored one of their number who lay just outside the door wounded in the leg, pleading for a rifle that he might not be left helpless and at the mercy of the outlaws.

The bandit leader again urged his partner to go, insisting that this would be his only chance. He was right, for not a great distance from the lone cabin the posse formed a long semi-circular skirmish line. They reopened the fight from their new vantage point, the outlaws answering the puffs of smoke by shooting whenever a head appeared above the ridge.

The Battle of Stone Corral had come as a rough conclusion to a month or more of intermittent skirmishes between the outlaws on one side and the various wandering bands of professional gunfighters on the other. They had all been imported into the mountain districts of Fresno and Tulare Counties by the "Octopus," in its frenzied efforts to kill or capture the perpetrators of the many daring train robberies committed against its lines.

Long since, the local peace officers of the two great Counties where the feud waged hotly had been relegated to the discard by the managers of the local war, not even being consulted regarding issuing of warrants or the deputizing of these railroad hirelings to give them legal status.

There were so many strangers under various group leaders in the field that United States Marshal Gard from the Southern District of California slipped into Visalia practically unnoticed. He made his headquarters at the Palace Hotel, there being joined from day to day by mysterious looking men who dropped off the trains coming from both North and South, until finally his quota of picked deputies was on the ground.

These men were quite unobtrusive, moving about the lobby, hardly attracting attention, lost in the hordes of other strangers who filled every quarter of the big hotel. The bar room worked over time, loud noises issuing from within, where some of the more boastful discussed openly their opinions regarding the outlaws and their fighting qualities. Local loungers would listen and accept the proffered drinks with winks and smiles, while enjoying the bluster of the badmen.

George C. Gard was United States Marshal for Southern California, a man who had made a reputation as a terror to evil doers along the Mexican Border. Tall, thin and wiry, blue eyed, with sharp acquiline features and blondish hair inclined to baldness, Gard had one outstanding characteristic. He never failed to smile. It was second nature with him. No matter how serious the situation might be or how gloomy the picture painted by a trusted deputy, invariably Gard's smile would settle the question. Cheerfulness and smiling were the passwords that brought him out of every difficulty. George Gard had long watched the feud waging between the imported gunmen and the outlaws up North in the San Joaquin Valley and through the higher reaches of the Tulare Mountains.

Gard was not sparing of his criticisms and had many times openly denounced the methods pursued by the railroad's posses. Big Bill Smith was often the butt of his keenest satire, that at last brought down on Gard's head the bitter hatred of the great detective. It had often been said that Gard's interest in the man-hunt centered solely around the huge reward for the capture of the outlaws "dead or alive."

Prior to his coming to Visalia, Gard had sent a trusted deputy into that place, a man noted for his daring work through the Indian Territories, in preparing traps and running down clues. He had made a reputation hunting the Star Gang in the Indian Territory. This detective, or Deputy Marshal as he was called, had now been a month or more in the district. On the completion of his plans he had wired Gard at Los Angeles, to come North and prepare for the drive.

The Battle of Stone Corral proved to be the fruits of this man's lone silent vigil.

Weeks passed. The Marshal and his deputies did nothing but lounge listlessly around the corridors of the Palace Hotel, until the people became accustomed to seeing them leaving and returning at will. Several nights preceding the opening of the battle, Marshal Gard gave his orders.

One by one the deputies left Visalia after dark. Joining forces in the foothills they stopped at an old deserted cabin which stood in the center of a wheat field offering no shelter to an approaching enemy. All night, the following day, and the next night they kept completely concealed within the cabin. Finally, at about eleven o'clock on the third day, Gard and his deputies were rewarded. Two men, heavily armed had cut into the wheatfield.

Chris, the outlaw leader, had been suspicious from the moment he came in sight of the cabin. He had an intuition akin to that of a hunted animal and sensed danger.

"Let's throw a few shots in there as a feeler," he had suggested, but John, his partner, objected violently, and after a heated argument the leader ignored his impulse. He advanced reluctantly. About the center of the wheatfield, and midway between the cabin and the line fence there was an old half decayed hay pile, almost flattened level with the ground. The leader stopped there and was just in the act of concealing his rifle and shotgun when the first shot rang out.

What a fatal blunder! If he had only listened to the promptings of that inner voice he would not have been trapped and wounded, with now only the dismal prospect of hopeless warfare well into the night, or until ammunition should give out and they would be taken "dead or alive."

Evening was approaching and still the posse doggedly held their ground. All day long, under a broiling sun, Gard's Deputy Marshals pumped streams of lead into the beleaguered outlaws who were lying flat in the wheatfield, openly exposed to every angle of fire.

The wounded bandit Chief was helpless. Thirst was consuming him but not a drop of water to be had. His intrepid friend maintained the fight alone. Earlier in the struggle, the younger of the outlaws had crawled forward from the spot where his partner lay and set fire to the old straw pile. This made an enveloping smoke screen that concealed them from the direct aim of their enemies.

At times Gard appeared to be baffled and commanded his men to move further out of range of the outlaws' camouflage in order that they might direct a cross fire upon the bandits. The manoeuvre proved to be dangerous, because the younger outlaw, Sontag, was in such a position as to blaze away safely at the extreme ends of the skirmish line whenever they emerged into view on the outer edge of his smoke screen.

Finally one of Gard's deputies, a halfbreed Huron Indian, executed a daring move. Taking advantage of a fierce drum fire between the contending forces he crawled inch by inch around the wheatfield to an open space in the rear of the two bandits, here biding his time for an opportunity to put in a death dealing shot.

Sontag raised to a half reclining position, peering out from behind the shield of smoke to watch the skirmish line in the distance. The Huron Indian's rifle cracked, and he slowly crumpled down bored through the back fatally wounded.

Darkness was approaching and with it came renewed hope that all was not lost. The outlaw leader, with a superhuman effort pulled himself together to leave, not realizing how badly his partner had been injured. "Come on John," he urged, "this is our last chance to escape. They will fire at us, but night is good protection and once out of this Hell hole we have until morning to find a hiding place."

In vain he coaxed and pled, but his friend had been mortally wounded, and in turn urged that he go. Then the dying outlaw touched upon the tender subject of the bandit leader's family, insisting that for their sake he must try to save himself. Common sense won out.

Amid gasps the lifelong partner begged, "Just one favor! I can only live a few hours at best. More than likely it will be but a few minutes. I don't want to fall into the man-killers' hands alive and I'm too badly paralyzed to use my own gun. Do your duty." His eyes closed and he waited for the impact of the bullet. But the bandit leader could not bring himself to fire the mercy shot. Ignoring the dying man's request he stood for a moment gazing down upon the pallid face, then turning, with something of the old fire left, stared viciously in the direction of his tormentors. Bleeding and painracked he clutched the rifle tightly and staggered away, the left arm dangling limply at his side.

After the Huron Indian had delivered his fatal shot he cautiously retreated from his exposed position fearing that the outlaws would concentrate their fire upon him. Slowly he worked his way around the wheatfield, rejoining Gard and his men reporting to his chief the success of his venture. Thereupon, Gard ordered his men to stop firing, but only for a moment.

One of the men holding the extreme end of the skirmish line shouted that the outlaws were retreating. Instantly Gard and the rest of the posse joined the man, renewing the battle. Round after round of rifle fire was sent through the darkness at the retreating form, until it was lost to view.

The bandit leader had fallen again, struck by a rifle bullet. This time the good right hand dropped helpless, like the left one, mangled at the wrist. Almost in delirium, the bullet riddled outlaw stumbled to his feet and staggered forward for a few paces then sagging at the knees he crumpled down and lay still, apparently dead.

Random fire below him in the wheatfield roused the sorely stricken man to renewed life and action. Once more he scrambled up, steadied himself and, with a superhuman effort staggered on and away.

The mortally wounded outlaw, Sontag, still lay near the old smoldering straw pile, tortured beyond endurance. Not knowing the true state of affairs, none of the posse dared approach. Besides, they heard shots and feared that some of the bandits' friends might have come with reinforcements. Gard and his men were not running any risks.

The shots the posse heard had come from the center of the wheatfield. The dying outlaw had tried to take his own life, with great effort moving his fingers sufficiently to pull the trigger of a revolver. But, being paralyzed, he was unable to raise his hand into proper position and the bullets only grazed his face, tearing the skin.

He had failed and knew that he must endure the horror of a night of suffering alone and praying for death. The thought that Gard and his posse would come in the morning and find him alive, worse still, take him away to prison, became an unbearable obsession. Then he grew thirsty, feverishly calling for water. The night became cold, almost bitter as it advanced. This made his pain worse, and he cried aloud for help, but none came.

At daybreak, the posse were elated to find one of their quarry still within reach, tho slowly dying. Like big game hunters, some of the more hardened gloated over the catch. One possessed of common kindness heard the indistinct moan for water. He placed a cup to the parched lips and a grateful smile played at the corners of Sontag's mouth.

Like a funeral procession the posse made its perilous descent into the valley, bearing the captured outlaw in the bed of an old mountain cart to the jail at Visalia. The whole town was cloaked in grim silence during the night, awaiting the end of the tragedy. Hundreds of people had gathered around the jail, some of them speculating on whether or not the outlaw was dead or alive.

All day Visalia was rife with rumors, regarding the possible capture of the bandit leader. It was reported that he was mortally wounded. Night came again, and still the crowds were watching. This time they saw the flickering light through the grated window on the second floor. Occasionally it illuminated the features of the tall gray bearded physician, as he bent over the white cot, where lay the dying man, Sontag, his face a mass of bandages with just the eyes visible. But that was enough to tell the tale. They were the eyes of one hunted, driven to death, worn out, suffering beyond endurance.

I had just returned from the old Quartz Mill in Mariposa County to the El Capitan Hotel in Merced, when the news of the Battle at Stone Corral was flashed over the wires. I had finished my work for Big Bill Smith, the detective, and was about to take the train North to San Francisco.

In the lobby of the hotel men were loudly talking over the sudden turn of affairs. I heard the words, "Sontag shot and captured,— Evans the leader, riddled with bullets, escapes from the scene of battle, retreating back into the mountains."

Instantly my plans were changed. An overland train was due Southbound and I raced from the hotel, having barely time to get aboard. I quickly formed a new line of action, deciding to leave the train at Fresno for the purpose of trying to save the bandit Chief. If I could only overtake him before his pursuers, I might then bring him to the safety of the outlaw stronghold. If there was not a chance to save him my credentials would entitle me to the reward. It had always been understood that I should maintain my role of detective until the end of the chase to capture the Chief and claim the head money for his family.

Gunfighters from everywhere were on the escaped outlaw's trail. Public opinion was now strongly in favor of the bandits, hope running high that the leader would not be captured. Satisfaction and some relief was felt over the news that the dying man, Sontag, would not live to disclose the names of others connected with the band, a remote possibility that struck fear into the hearts of some.

Visalia's bar rooms were crowded again with men who had but one topic, the unequal battle between the gunfighters and the outlaws. Some of the more rabid were red eyed from sitting up all night. The saloon keepers reaped a fortune.

Jaded nerves were stimulated by mysterious whispers which came in almost hourly. Ghastly photographs of the dying outlaw on the old pile of straw at Stone Corral were added to the gruesome influence of tragedy. But, contrary to the usual method of expressing emotion, at this greatest of all events the town and even the entire valley, on the surface, were strangely disinterested.

When the outlaw leader retreated from the battle scene at Stone Corral with both shattered arms dangling limply at his sides, his right eye shot out, and his left one swollen and almost blinded, maimed beyond recognition, despite the shot that had grazed his spine and torn the flesh of his limbs, he staggered to the top of the hill out of rifle range. Here he was hidden by darkness from his pursuers but left a trail of blood behind.

Through dry wash and canyon he painfully dragged himself along, unable to reason, guided by instinct only to the higher Sierras. Times without number he stumbled and fell prostrate upon the ground to lie there motionless, arising with difficulty and moving on at each awakening of consciousness. He had no water during the long siege of battle, and the following day when the blistering hot sun of the Mojave desert penetrated even the mountain fastness, his thirst became appalling.

Again and again he struggled to the bed of some old mountain torrent course, dry and baked, digging with his feet, grinding deep holes, but all in vain,— no water. One time he fell and lay unusually long, while a huge rattlesnake kept watch beside him, refusing to inflict further pain by striking. It was the first act of pity shown the doomed, proscribed outlaw, who in agony again regained his feet and reeled away, leaving a sweltering pool of blood as mute evidence of the fight for freedom.

The gunmen were almost at his heels. They had followed the crimson trail, insisting, "We'll get him all right. He's bleeding to death. Either that or he'll retrace his steps. Those water holes tell the story that he can't stand the thirst much longer."

"He's not far from here," one of them shouted pointing out the pool of blood. The others closed in curiously wondering how a man could continue under such terrible odds. They drew back espying the rattler alertly on guard. "If that fellow had struck him we'd already have the reward in our hands," remarked one of the professional man-killers.

Guns were levelled and shots rang out. They had paused only long enough to kill the snake that had withheld its fang from the wounded bandit.

Delirious and maddened by thirst the hunted outlaw tumbled into Wilcox Canyon. His trackers marvelled afterward that such a thing could be possible, for here all further trace was lost. The desperate man had literally rolled down over the top of thick patches of manzanita, blotting out his trail by acres of ground.

Once again the shrewd Indian scout of old demonstrated his marvelous endurance. His mind had cleared for a moment and he realized that he was a leaving a plain trail of blood for his relentless pursuers. He had resorted to strategy and as a result the man-trackers stood baffled on the brow of a hill looking aimlessly around over a sea of manzanita.

This feat accomplished, the old outlaw leader headed straight for a ranch,— the home of a friend at the lower end of Wilcox Canyon. The house stood out ahead of him. He lunged toward the gate supporting himself against the fence for it was latched and his hands were useless. In vain he hurled his body at this new obstacle. Never had he been so helpless or thirsty, and water lay just a few rods beyond! Unable to withstand the temptation any longer, he climbed up the fence, literally falling over it and crawling to the well in an agony of suffering increased by the jolt. He placed his helpless arms around the pump handle, slowly moving it up and down through sheer force of will. The cooling draught of water revived him, and covering up all further traces in the yard, with a last courageous effort he straightened like a soldier on dress parade, and entered the farmhouse.

I had reached Fresno, and feeling certain that I could find the wounded outlaw, made record breaking time in getting out of town on a fast horse, galloping for the mountain trails to the lone ranch in Wilcox Canyon. It was almost night when I passed through Hill's Valley, and as I climbed the mountain road to Squaw Valley, I realized my horse was jaded. The tremendous speed was beginning to tell upon the stout hearted animal.

At Mill Creek I detoured off the stage road making straight for the ranch house of a friend. Just inside of the corral, the poor horse keeled over. Sweat was rolling in streams from his body, while froth tinged with blood came from his mouth. We had long been pals, and with a pang of dread that the race might cause his death, I leaned over him. At the sound of my voice his ears shot back, and he tried to arise. He would have liked to finish the run.

One of the best horses at the ranch was already saddled and waiting, and fearful of being too late to save the Chief, I mounted in an instant and raced out of the corral and away. It was long after dark when I reached Wilcox Canyon. Leaving the horse I crept cautiously toward the old ranch house.

Too late! Hordes of gunmen were there ahead of me. Gard's Deputy Marshals were blustering about threatening those who had dared take possession of the helpless outlaw leader.

The Sheriff of Visalia, with about ten deputies, had made an all day drive to Wilcox Canyon. He had inside information, and taking a short cut had beaten Gard and his gunmen to the lair of the hunted bandit. A boy had been sent in to ask if the old outlaw intended to surrender peaceably. He lay on a bed in the attic, suffering, delirious and maimed, but pulled himself together at the sound of a voice, to inquire who wanted him to surrender.

"The Sheriff of Visalia," the boy had replied.

Visibly pleased that it was not the Marshal's posse from Stone Corral, but his old friend Sheriff Kay of Tulare County, he remarked in a voice which could be heard outside, "I have had enough fighting. Tell the Sheriff to come up."

The Sheriff entered the room, hat in hand and without the slightest fear, walked boldly to the bed, warmly greeting the stricken man. The bandit submitted to arrest, then Under-Sheriff Hall removed the last remaining weapon, an empty six shooter, from the outlaw's belt. Wrapping him in a blanket, several men carried him downstairs, and placed him in the rear of a wagon, just as the panting horses of Gard's posse arrived.

When I came up the weird light from torches played mysteriously upon the confusion of faces. From my vantage point I could hear voices. The Marshal loudly claimed the right of possession, while the Sheriff of Visalia just as stoutly refused to recognize his authority. Heated words were exchanged, weapons were levelled and it seemed a tragedy was about to be enacted to determine who should take possession of the prisoner, a man they chose to call a bandit. I wondered, if after all, his position was not more enviable than theirs.

At length, with grumbling and smothered curses, the gunfighters of Gard's posse and the Sheriff with his deputies and the captive started upon their hard drive to Visalia, pounding along a rough mountain road. About fifteen miles from the town the first streak of dawn straggled over the ridges of the Sierra Nevada Mountains, piercing the chilly air and falling upon the Chief. He was suffering too intensely from cold, dust, and the hard jolting to heed it.

By short cuts I had reached the Valley long before the huddled horsemen surrounding the wagon emerged out onto the plains of the San Joaquin. I had entered Visalia from a different road just as throngs of people were trooping out to obtain the first glimpse of the captured bandit. Many of them looked as if they had just jumped from bed and dressed hurriedly.

The square surrounding the Jail was jammed with excited people. It was strange how fast the news had traveled. Some lone horsemen must have passed the Sheriff on the road, and rushed into town to give the alarm.

The reeking horses of the Sheriff swung around the corner, stopping of their own free will in front of the Jail. Deputies lifted the outlaw from the back of the wagon. In their effort to hold the swooning man carefully they had forgotten to watch the blanket, which fell away from his head, giving the excited crowd a view that made them shudder. It was ghastly. His face looked as if he had suffered for a century, the features being drawn like those of a dead man. His jaw had fallen, his teeth showing through the tangle of reddish brown beard. The black and bloody socket was all that remained of his right eye, and the left was still so swollen from powder burns that he did not attempt to raise it to look at his friends.

Many addressed the Chief by his first name, offering kindly words of cheer, but he was suffering too severely to acknowledge them and only groaned pitifully as his crushed arms were jostled. The crowd fell apart in awe to make clear the passageway, but they did not disperse, even after he was inside. They were shocked, and not one among them would have willingly added to his misery. Silently they awaited reports of his condition, disturbed only by the noisy quarrelling of gunmen over the division of rewards.

The Sheriff kindly placed the wounded man in a cell room across from his dying friend. The same doctor dressed his wounds. The left forearm had been so terribly shattered that amputation was necessary at once. Evidence of blood poisoning had already set in. Reports reached the crowd outside that the old bandit refused to submit to chloroform. Later those, who had remained, learned first that he was resting easy and then that he was asleep and finally they disbanded.

Within a few days the two outlaws were removed to the County Jail in Fresno. John, the younger, was dying and paid little attention to what was transpiring. His glazed eyes hardly noticed the throngs that filled the station, when the two men were taken from the train at Fresno. They were placed in the same cell in the County Jail, but not for long. Sontag, the intrepid fighter, passed out through locked and bolted doors on Tuesday, July 4th, 1893. Death released him from all his earthly cares, a brave man, loved and remembered by thousands, while his partner, the hero of hundreds of battles survived his wounds only later to face a historic trial in a legal struggle for his life.

December 15th, the closing day of the trial slipped around very quickly. The jury had compromised, the verdict being first degree murder, and, as in that State the jury fixes the punishment, the bandit leader was sentenced to life imprisonment. His friends were furious and so was the company, at the upturn of affairs. The great "Octopus" demanded that his life should be forfeited for his crimes, while his friends loudly clamored for his acquittal and complete vindication.

With Big Bill Smith, the detective, and me, things had reached a climax, and I insisted upon a show down. Our original agreement must now be fulfilled I told him.

"I don't say that I will not keep my promises," said the gunman, "but if I should desire to sidestep them, nothing has occurred that could hold me to the bargain."

My eyes must have been glaring, for Smith's attitude changed to one of blandness. Still it was evident that he thought he had made a faithful tool of me, intending to use me further.

"I admit you have worked hard," he continued, "but neither you nor I, Morrell, had anything to do with the capture of the outlaws. Marshal Gard, damn him, and his dirty crew of cheap gunmen have received all the credit for the work we have done, but he will never get the reward if I can prevent it," he concluded with a string of oaths.

The very thought of Gard's name threw the great detective into a frenzy, and he walked the floor mumbling incoherently something about vengeance. Smith never was the same after the day Marshal Gard and his fighters beat him to victory in the capture of the California Outlaws. Finally he stopped, struck by a sudden impulse, and trained his ear on the door. Then, like a panther cat, right hand shoved deep into his side coat pocket, he glided silently to the door and with the free left hand, swung it wide open, evidently expecting to discover someone crouching just outside.

Not the least abashed at my chuckle, Smith closed and locked the door, banged up the transom, wheeled and glowered at me. I had long ago gauged the extent of this man's sinister character. Seldom did his real self ever emerge from behind his stoical mask. His very smile was wooden, often a mere leer or a grimace. Big Bill reminded me of one in whom the "milk of human kindness" had soured. To him the world was a rotten joke and man the puppet and whim of circumstances, not to be trusted. In his eyes all men were scaled by price lists, to be bought and bartered for, according to supply and demand or the rise and fall of the market while woman was a creature without virtue.

Smith upheld, obeyed, and defended the law doggedly, but entirely irreverently, and it was with little surprise that I listened to his new scheme. My horror was stifled for the moment.

"Now, Morrell," he confided, "there is a plan on foot to make it easy for the condemned bandit to break jail. What I want you to do is to urge him to attempt it. We'll fix everything easy for him to escape. That will be your part. I will have men stationed outside of the jail to nail him as he leaves. By this move, I aim to settle two scores. I will have finished with the author of all my troubles, this accursed leader of the outlaws. His escape will cause a forfeiture of the rewards and I will then make a counter claim as having captured the escaping bandit. I do not expect much success in my claim for the reward but I will at least have the satisfaction that Gard and his outfit won't get it."

He removed the heavy hand from its concealing pocket long enough to pat me on the shoulder, adding, "after that the rest will be easy, Morrell. I will take care of you and also have your man pardoned from prison."

Scarcely able to speak I left Big Bill's room at the Grand Central Hotel in Fresno a-whirl with emotion. I staggered up Mariposa Street to a seat in the County Jail Plaza, hoping that the night air would clear my brain of contamination from the atmosphere of such a character.

"So, they are going to bait the helpless outlaw to escape," I thought, "and then shoot him down in cold blood." I had not believed it possible until then that even a man of Smith's type would dare to stoop to such criminal infamy, and resentment over the terrible deed spurred me to instant action. I bounded across the plaza and stood at the door of the County Jail.

Flashing my detective's shield, I was admitted to the old outlaw's cell. "Never fear, I will be ready," he said reassuringly after our whispered conversation, and I left the jail with the intention of not returning again until the day before the one Big Bill Smith, the detective, had planned for the execution of his murderous plot. I had resolved to block him at the risk of my life.

I had finished. The "Tiger's" tapping fairly danced across the bridge of thirteen cells. He was alive with emotion. "I say, Morrell, this is corking good stuff,— a wonderful story. Go to bed, man, take a good sleep. 'Give-a-damn' will be on tonight. He's on the tail end of a whiskey bout and he will sleep like a dead man. We can talk a streak."

CHAPTER X

A FAKE MESSAGE. A JAIL HOLDUP.

"New Orleans Sunset Limited to be robbed fifty miles South of Fresno tonight," read a telegram received at the Sheriff's Office on Thursday morning December 28th.

All that afternoon the Fresno County Jail was the center of unusual activity, of buzzings and suppressed excitement. Every Deputy Sheriff of the County appeared to be on duty and the armory room, being located inside, the prisoners confined in their cells came to the conclusion that strange things were occurring. They could plainly see that all of the officers were busily occupied cleaning and loading rifles, shotguns and revolvers, and speculation was rife among them when a group of heavily armed men filed out leaving the assistant jailer alone.

It was about six o'clock in the evening, dark, drizzling and rainy. I was at the railroad station standing well back from the platform as the big overland train pulled out Southbound. The armed posse, acting on the fake telegram darted from places of concealment clamoring aboard the tank of the engine and the forepart of the express car, all primed and ready for a holdup.

I counted them one by one, and satisfied with the check up hastened toward the jail on my bicycle, stopping only long enough to examine my team on Mariposa Street about two blocks away, then proceeding to a restaurant near the Court House where I had already ordered a meal.

Cutting through the Plaza Park, I set the tray of food down for a moment to strap a belt with two six shooters in it around my body, concealing them under my coat, and tying on a waiter's apron to serve the double purpose of hiding the bulk of the six shooters and making my disguise complete.

In answer to my ring, the substitute jailer peered out through the round aperture in the door, and I knew that he would not have been there on duty if the decoy telegram had not been a complete success. I had gauged my time to arrive about half an hour earlier than the regular waiter, so the substitute jailer, knowing only that a meal was brought each evening to the outlaw, admitted me on the strength of my apron and tray.

After the death of Sontag, the outlaw leader had been placed in a steel cell called the "tank" as an added precaution against possible escape or rescue by his host of friends. But he was allowed to eat and receive visitors in the grated corridor outside.

I was locked in there with him, and it was only possible to carry on a desultory conversation while he ate. Nearly every move could be watched by either the jailer or some of the prisoners. We talked loudly to avert suspicion. Occasionally the Chief's voice would become subdued as he tried to impress me with the fact that something serious had gone wrong, that a whole band of officers had just left heavily armed. The strange doings made him apprehensive.

I dared not tell him, and could not make him understand by my actions that the officers' departure was all in keeping with my plans, so finally, in fear of his attracting attention, I commanded bluntly, "Cut out this nonsense, Chris! What I want to know is, are you ready to go?"

For a moment he seemed to be considering the hopelessness of a life in jail, and then his chin set firmly, the one eye glistening, he contemplated a chance for possible freedom and escape without the sting of more bullets. Silently, as if praying that if the posse were hiding outside the next volley would go true to the mark and end it all, he finished his meal, raised the coffee cup to his lips and gulped its contents, then turning he coolly whispered, "I am ready. Lead the way."

As the jailer opened the door I dropped the tray and dishes on the floor commanding, "Throw up your hands!"

At first the dazed man thought it a joke, then glancing toward the condemned outlaw questioningly he looked into the muzzle of a Colts forty-five which Chris had taken from my belt and was holding threateningly before him.

"Yes, Ben, that goes. Put up your hands and be quick about it," he urged the jailer.

I pushed the confused deputy down the steps toward his office. I thought he was armed, but could not bring myself to shoot when he refused to throw up his hands.

The door bell rang and instantly a series of shrieks came from the hobo wing of the jail as an alarm to those outside. I left the jailer with the bandit leader and sprang to the top of the stairs derisively shouting to the men huddled in the corridor below, "The first one who gives another yell down there is going to cause trouble for the bunch. I'll cut loose and shoot you full of holes."

"This is none of our pie," said a tall evil looking character, stepping forward from the huddled group, a keen edged knife in his hand. "Go on with your work. I say it's fine, mister, and the first gallute that makes a squawk down here again I'll cut him to pieces." He spoke as if he meant it, and I felt secure about that quarter. But the jail gong was still ringing and I feared that our plans might be spoiled.

After looking out through the small slot I opened the door with a jerk, and the regular waiter who had been leaning against it almost fell in head foremost, dropping his tray upon the floor with a terrific crash and standing amid broken dishes and spilled food, trembling as he stared into my six shooter. Then he began to sputter and fume in broken English. Locking the door I caught him by the nape of the neck and pushed him into a cell adjoining the jail office, where I snapped the lock upon him, without further loss of valuable time to explain.

"You'll have to come along," I said to the jailer, and the three of us stepped out together, the escaping outlaw taking him in hand. "Here's your key," I added, locking the outer jail door. "When we release you, return and everything will be found in order. Let the waiter out then. Just keep your head now, we don't intend any harm, but remember we are taking no chances, and see to it that you take none."

I walked on ahead to look after the buggy full of supplies near the church on North Mariposa Street. It was dark. We had been delayed too long in the jail, valuable time was lost and as I approached the Court House Plaza the city lights were flashed on, a big arc flaring directly above us.

A well dressed man stood just beyond looking at me, and believing the plot had been discovered I resolved on a desperate chance, making a move as if to pass him, then wheeling, locking arms, and commanding him to come with me.

"You come along and be quiet," I persisted, shoving the barrel of my six shooter against his ribs, and he moved on mechanically, mincing his steps as if to save his patent leather shoes and emaculate white spats from the mud.

I was astonished after his apparent coolness in leaving the Plaza to find that he stopped on the other side of the street in great agitation, refusing to move another step, half weeping and half shouting, "I am the Mayor of Fresno, and if this is a plot to murder me, it will have to be done right here on the public highway and not in some back street or blind alley!"

I realized then that it was all a mistake and that the man had not been watching the jail. But it was too late to mend the blunder. Also later I found out the reason for his mincing steps. The good Mayor of Fresno had long been a sufferer from neuritis, and I felt gratified when the rumor reached me that the terrible fright he had received on the night of the Fresno County Jail holdup had entirely cured him of his affliction.

When he had stopped I could not force him to move again, and we two stood there and argued, I trying to explain that no harm was intended, not even robbery, but that my partner who was following would not be so gentle if he persisted in refusing to come along. Over and over he kept repeating that he would not be taken to a dark alley, and that the murder must be committed there in the open and in sight of the entire community.

Even as he spoke, half pleading and half weeping, he felt the sudden shock of a second revolver thrust against his breast.

"Move along, and be quick about it, if you don't want your head blown off," shouted the escaping Chris gruffly.

"I am the jailer," came another voice from a third man, "don't you know me? There are no footpads here. One of these men is the bandit, Evans, and you should know better than to trifle with him. There has been a jail-break. These men are only trying to escape before an alarm can be given, and if you walk along peaceably, no harm will come. See, I am not taking any chances. Don't make a fool of yourself, but come on!"

Believing there would be no further trouble with the Mayor, I turned him over to my partner and went ahead to see that the way to the team was clear. But the Mayor began to doubt the jailer's identity after they had gone a short distance and stopped at the next corner, making the new plea that one of his children was dying and that he had been sent out for some medicine. "Won't you please let me go home?" he added, pointing to his house nearby.

The good Mayor thought that this bit of fiction would bring about his release. The outlaw Chief being easily touched where children were concerned turned from his course with the intention of taking the frightened man to his door. But better judgment made him realize too much time was being wasted, and he again started toward the team forcing his captives reluctantly ahead. Still they were some distance behind me.

I was now abreast of the team and stopped short. Two men were standing there, one of them wearing an odd looking raincoat, which was unmistakably part of the regulation police uniform. I dared not retreat, and thinking only of life and liberty bobbed out from the darkness.

"Throw up your hands!" I ordered with gun pointed directly at the strangers.

Both men obeyed, and to my great amazement I discovered that the one in uniform was the Chief of Police of Fresno. The other man proved to be a real estate agent, and they were standing in front of my team chatting.

Was it a ruse or were they ignorant of the true contents of the buggy? They did not leave me long in doubt, for with a jocular remark, pretending that he thought I was a friend playing a joke on him, the Chief of Police started to lower his right arm.

"Put up your hands and keep them there!" I commanded, thrusting my revolver close enough that he could see it. I then took his from his side pocket, and feeling relieved that he was unarmed, turned my attention to the other man.

"What is that in your right hand?" I inquired, uotieing that he held something bulky.

"Just a little money," he stammered.

"Lower that hand! Put it back in your pocket! Now, raise your hand again," I laughed. "Your money is perfectly safe. I am not a robber."

"Then, what in Hell are you holding us up for?" asked the Chief of Police with great control, apparently trying to force me to talk while he sparred for time to act.

"I want this team, and will take it when I get ready. In the meantime you had better shut your mouth and keep those hands above your head," I remarked, with an air of recklessness which evidently did not affect him in the least, for, as I turned to search the other man he made a step backward and wheeled. This quick move brought me directly between the two. Then, like a panther, he sprang upon me, gripping my arms in a powerful hold, and pinning them to my sides above the elbow, as his own encircled my body completely. Now he set up a shouting for help that could be heard blocks away, at intervals vainly imploring his friend to take the two guns from my right hand.

It was a tense moment, and I was filled with fear, not for myself, but for the Chief of Police. He was facing certain death if the positions were not reversed before the old bandit arrived with his two prisoners.

Already my ears had caught the thud of footsteps. I looked helplessly at the officer's gun and my own, both held in my right hand. I moved the left hand over as close as possible, then cautiously swung the barrels of the revolvers toward it.

The Chief of Police was so busy, that he did not detect the move, and I tried again and again, and finally with a tremendous stretching of my arm and fingers grasped the end of my long barreled gun. Releasing it, I reversed the position and gripped it firmly by the handle in my left hand, then turned both guns until the cold barrels pressed against the officer's groin.

"Now, do you see where you stand?" I shouted in order to make myself heard above his bellowing. "See, I can shoot you, and there is no way you can prevent it, so don't be a fool. You thought you had me, but you haven't. Let go, and you will be safe!"

He continued to keep his deathlike grip, and again I warned, "Don't gamble with your life! Let go or I will shoot!"

"If you don't want to be killed, let go! Release me at once! I am not alone. There is a man on his way here who won't take any chances. He'll shoot you on sight, so let go!"

The Chief of Police could not seem to understand, and while I pled the outlaw leader arrived with his two charges. Not recognizing in the officer an old friend of long standing and seeing only that someone held me and that our escape was imperiled, he thundered, "release him!"

The command was sharp and when it had been repeated for the third time without effect upon this brave man, I saw the flash of an exploding gun and felt the arms break their grip. He crumpled in a heap upon the sidewalk.

Almost frantic at the turn events had taken, I leaned over. The Chief of Police was not dead, and raising him to his feet, I begged that he pull himself together and get down the street as quickly as possible. But he was too badly stunned to move, and I laid him down upon the sidewalk again, feeling sure he had received a fatal wound.

The shot had entered a few inches above the heart, tearing across the breast, then through the region of the armpit.

"Now, you may go back to your duty," the outlaw Chief said to the jailer. I was still working over the wounded man, trying to shake him from his stupor.

"Get out," he roared to the Mayor who stood before him trembling.

Accompanied by the real estate agent he tore down the street as if some terrible monster were at his heels. Both of them began crying at the tops of their voices when about a block away, and almost immediately their shrieks were blended with others. Bells commenced a dismal tolling, mingling their sounds with the blasting of whistles. Lights flared up until the town was ablaze.

Now above the clamor and roar, words took shape. I could hear a howl, "THE COUNTY JAIL HAS BEEN HELD UP AND THE BANDIT IS RELEASED!"

Hardware stores were thrown open to the mob of people who were beginning to run in all directions as in a nightmare, pressed by desperate straits. There was not a moment to spare as the angry, seething, brainless mass, armed with guns, shovels, hatchets, hammers, picks and other implements were bearing down upon us.

The high spirited horses strained at their halter rope tied fast to the post. I turned my attention to them, pulling it loose just as a crash of wild shooting came near. Panic stricken they leaped into the air and dashed down the street. It was not within the power of a human being to hold them. At last we had reached a climax, life and liberty swinging evenly in the balance, with death for the old bandit Chief who had gone through so many horrible combats, and for me.

We resolved to make a run for freedom, dog trotting in a South-easterly direction toward the outskirts of the city. As we cut across the intersection of a street, I caught the sound of approaching horses, and with the intention of forcing the driver out and taking the team I bounded into the road catching at the bridles.

Their hot steaming breath moistened my face, and instantly I was conscious that it was my own snorting, frightened team, which had redoubled. I managed to step clear of their hoofs, but the heavy front wheel of the buggy struck. It knocked me down. As I fell the fingers of my right hand involuntarily clutched the trigger of my gun and a bullet tore an ugly groove through the point of my chin. I crumpled to the road and the rear wheel crunched over my left leg.

With his one remaining hand my loyal partner tugged furiously at my clothes, dragging me to a vacant lot. He found an emergency flask in my pocket and forced some of the liquor between my clenched teeth. The stimulant worked like magic. "I am not hurt, just stunned," I shouted, jumping to my feet. "Let's get out of here before the mob tears us to pieces. If we don't run across a team we must head straight for the hills on foot."

In the excitement I neither felt that blood was trickling down my clothes nor that the injured leg was swelling and becoming painful. The only reality to me was that we were taking short cuts through rough fields and over fences to avoid the mob that was coming ever closer.

Again I heard the beat of horses' hoofs and the crunching of wheels. Leaping to the center of the roadway, I grabbed the horse and ordered the driver to jump out if he valued his life.

"Get out of there as quick as God Almighty will let you, or you'll get your head blown off," bellowed my panting friend in an effort to force quicker action.

Somebody tumbled backward from the seat. "Help! Help! Robbers are stealing my horse!" he shrieked running toward a house directly opposite.

Jumping into the cart we turned the horse to the Southeast. He immediately whirled around and faced the gate, refusing to budge an inch. He was a stubborn little mustang and held his ground well, repeating the twisting performance each time I succeeded in facing him toward the South.

What could be done? The unmanageable little brute was eating up our minutes. Time was growing short. Even now the officers must be returning from the fake train robbery. Posses were being dispatched in every direction, cordons of gunmen would soon be on all the roads and trails leading into the mountains. Telegraph and telephone wires were buzzing with messages, and as a last extremity, tho dreading to inflict pain upon a dumb beast I resorted to an old horse trick, firing a shot that just grazed his flank.

He bounded into the air and dashed away at a tremendous speed. Our course led us on a section road between the Sanger and old Summerville roads. We could hear the clatter of horses and shouts of pursuing men on either side as we sped along in hope of gaining the bridge first. It was the only one that spanned the Kings River from Fresno, and if our mustang could hold out against the killing pace at which we urged him ahead, we might make it. Once across that turbulent stream the Tulare Mountains and liberty would be ours.

CHAPTER XI

A WILD RACE TO THE KINGS RIVER BRIDGE.

"The bridge is covered. There are at least a hundred men guarding both ends," I whispered, returning from a reconnoitering trip at the converging of the roads.

On the other side of the river lay safety. To the East if we could but keep going were the Tulare Mountains and friends by the hundreds, ready to provide food and shelter from our pursuers. But of little consolation was that thought at this time, with the rainy season on and the bridge under careful watch. The Kings River had already burst the confines of its channel and spread out over the San Joaquin Plains in wide bayous both to the North and South.

To attempt to ford it was suicide, the least of the menacing dangers being the large morasses of quicksand, which would bury us in the horror of a smothering death.

"Every avenue of escape is cut off," I remarked, "Still, to remain here means capture, and perhaps even death. Daylight will make concealment impossible in this flat country."

"We hold the trump card in the game of hide and seek," interrupted the old Chief, his years of soldiering and scout experience standing him in good stead as on hundreds of other occasions of like emergency. "We know where they are; but they don't happen to know where we are. Our retreat is made to order."

"The Sanger Flume cuts in between this bridge and the road to Trimmer Springs. They won't think of guarding it. The footpath on top is so high in the air that no one could ever climb up the sides to reach it. We can pass over the bayous, along the bottom stanchions of the Flume, and escape by cutting out onto the Trimmer Springs Road far above the place where the posse are located," he continued.

"We have the whole night ahead of us then, because our enemies won't advance any further into the mountains until daylight."

There was no time to waste, so we left the horse and cart, covered with mud after the nine mile run. Hobbling along behind the Chief, for the first time that night I became conscious of a painful limb and the stinging gunshot wound which had made me weak from loss of blood. I had not tasted food since morning, and had really not eaten or slept properly for several days preceding the working out of my plans to release the condemned bandit. The effects of it all were beginning to tell on me but I gained a second wind over the reassuring words and the thought that escape was more than possible.

Every plank and stringer along the course of the Flume seemed to have been nailed in exact position to form a providential avenue of escape for us hunted men. I led the way stopping frequently to lend assistance to my one armed confederate who used his stump almost as skillfully as if the hand had not been amputated. Our progress was painfully slow, still we inched along. A slip would have buried us in the sluggish waters. Then with an almost superhuman effort we struggled to solid ground, released our grip and walked off, forcing our way through the low hanging hard wood branches of tangled manzanita, which tore our garments and scratched us at every step.

Completing a long hard journey through the brush, so peculiar to the lower foothill regions of California, we almost tumbled out upon the road leading to the little mountain camp of Trimmer Springs. As we continued, nearing the snow line of the Sierra Nevadas, the rain which had fallen steadily all night changed to stinging sleet and it became bitter cold.

My companion, who was scarcely more than convalescent and whose muscles had grown soft during confinement in jail, became very tired. My wounded chin continued bleeding, with every step the pain in my leg increased, but we dared not stop for even a moment's rest. At last a light, piercing the almost impenetrable darkness which precedes the first streaks of dawn, filled us with renewed courage.

We swerved toward it, and without a knock, I pushed open the door of the little mountain home. I must have looked like some strange apparition, drenched to the skin, mud bespattered, and covered with blood. The several men and women who occupied the room stood up in amazement as the glare of the lamp fell upon me.

In the strained moments that followed I took in the situation. A young woman, — pale, emaciated, dying, — lay upon a bed at one end of the room. I offered an apology for the intrusion and backed out.

"It is only a couple of miles to the next ranch," the man of the house whispered, following me to the door. "By the time you arrive, the folks there will be up preparing breakfast." He closed it gently, and again facing the cold biting rain and sleet, we trudged silently upward.

The darkness brightened, gradually lifting, and in the early morning light another ranch loomed up. The welcome odor of frying bacon greeted us, and with the usual mountain hospitality the lady of the house warmed a basin of water for my face. We were urged to sit down and enjoy the good meal.

True to the custom of the mountains, the ranch folks did not show the slightest curiosity about us, neither asking for name nor destination.

After an hour's rest we departed for the fastness of the higher mountains beyond and more certain safety, thanking them for their kindliness. At about eleven o'clock we passed the straggling Trimmer Springs settlement, but continued until we reached the home of an old friend of the outlaw leader.

The mother of this home, a very highly intelligent woman, who had been a nurse, expressed alarm at the neglect of my torn leg and wounded chin. Dressing these carefully and prescribing some medicine for a raging fever, she insisted that I should be put to bed. From the room in which I lay, almost delirious, I could hear talk about blood poison setting in, and then I knew no more. We had made nearly forty miles in our escape from the jail, eluding hundreds of man-hunters. I was completely worn out from the gruelling chase and needed rest, but longer delay might endanger our safety and against many protests by our friends, the Chief bluntly ordered that I be awakened.

Exerting all of my will power, I dressed and stumbled into the living-room announcing that I was ready to leave. I could not eat the steaming food so kindly placed before me. The rest had only intensified the pain and suffering. I was just able to mount a horse when the time arrived to start and then I crumpled limply in the saddle and allowed him to follow as he pleased in the rear of the Chief and the guide.

"We are going toward Secate Mountain," I vaguely heard my partner remark. "We can work over into the Dinky Creek Country and shake off posses and trailers. There you can rest safely before we attempt the hard journey South to our old stamping grounds in the Mineral King," he concluded.

My mouth was swollen and I could not reply, tho aware that ill luck appeared to be stalking our movements. We had scarcely started on the upward trail into the higher mountains when rain began to fall again, and cold howling winds swept the rocks, beating against the pines,— danger signals of a coming winter blast.

It pursued us along the zigzag course so swiftly that the accompanying sleet and ice were carried horizontally into our faces, cutting and bruising them. The horses were blinded. Still they exerted every effort to keep going. We soon realized that further progress would be suicidal and stopped to figure out our next move under a group of white conical forms. They proved to be snow covered firs that showered us with crystals as they bent under each sudden gust.

"On a spur of Secate Mountain there is a hog ranch,—a winter feeding station. It is the only place now, if we can reach it," our guide suggested, his voice scarcely audible above the storm sounds. "This will be a real blizzard before it ends, and you can at least stay there in safety until it is over. No posse will be able to get into these parts for some days to come."

Without another word the guide started again and we fell in line. Even to this day I have never been able to connect the incidents of that trip. Somehow the poor, forlorn, ice covered animals pressed ahead, and the next I recall, we had drawn up to a lonely shake cabin, entirely enveloped in snow.

We were soon gathered around a log fire within. After gulping down a cup of steaming hot coffee, I was placed in a "shake-down" and wrapped in warm blankets. Rays of sunlight piercing through the chinks and crevices of the old cabin aroused me. I realized that it was morning and I had slept soundly.

My wounds were not so painful, and the swelling was much reduced. I felt that there was no further occasion to worry about blood poisoning, and throwing off the covers sat up and looked around, asking what had happened to our guide.

"Oh, he left long before daylight," laughed the Chief as he turned from his place near the fire. "Led the two horses back over that trail in hope of reaching the ranch before anyone should discover either him or the animals missing. He also wanted to go while it was snowing so that his tracks would be covered."

Tho hardened to all sorts of rough travel, I shuddered. Still, he had done well to go then, for after a couple of hours of sunshine, the storm started again, lasting for three days and nights. Had he remained it might have been a week before he could have made his way back,— possibly longer if the snow began to drift.

For the time being we were secure from even the wide encircling movement of the posses, who, if they were near, would have to seek shelter themselves. Thus, through the vagaries of fate, the terrible storm contributed to our advantage. I was fast recovering from my wounds, and would soon be equal to any emergency.

Lost in the intensity of the story, I had forgotten the mechanical operation of the knuckle voice spanning the distance of thirteen cells in the dungeon. I had been again living over those mountain adventures so vividly photographed upon my memory, and the knuckle tapping of the "Tiger" shocked me back, with a rude awakening, to the fact that I was doomed to darkness for the balance of my life and would never again know sunshine or mountain air, snow covered forests or fields of wild flowers.

My companion of solitary had gone through too much of prison life to have any sentiment left. He was a perfect practical stoic and in quick, jerky, nervous tappings demanded that I tell him how Big Bill Smith, the gunman, my detective employer, took the shock.

Back in Fresno, I told the "Tiger" as I renewed the story, excitement was terrific when the quickly organized posses realized that we had slipped through their cordon to the safety of the higher mountains. The bridge and every road leading to it had been so carefully guarded all night that Big Bill and his railroad forces were sure we did not have a chance.

When the truth came out they said he stormed and raved and then his determined features became more set under the great black mustache that had twitched so convulsively when he realized that he had been double-crossed,— his murder plan foiled by me, whom he believed a willing tool. Worst of all had been the news leaking out to the world that I was once a detective for the defence and his private operative.

Big Bill never acknowledged defeat, and after the first shock assumed an air of easy indifference. He inwardly gloried in the belief that sooner or later both of his enemies would be captured and, in addition to revenge upon the outlaw Chief who had so skilfully eluded the death plot framed for the night following the one on which the escape took place, I also would be made to pay.

He could have murdered a man and kept it within the law. I had saved the life of the same man and was therefore proscribed. He must have felt even a little secret pleasure in the fact that he had distrusted me at times, perhaps regretting only that he had not shot me in cold blood the instant his suspicions were first aroused. Big Bill's shrewd, weasel-like eyes seemed to grow narrower, and he became more silent and reticent, patiently biding the day when he would be able to mete out his own peculiar form of justice.

The County officers agreed that the most exasperating feature of the whole affair was the fake train robbery. Many of the citizens tho they did not know the circumstances which had prompted my act, expressed sympathy and hope that we would escape.

After investigation and temporary imprisonment of friends of the bandit in the search for an accomplice, it was finally agreed that the County Jail holdup had been engineered and executed by me alone,— a single handed job. Gunmen and hirelings of the "Octopus," proclaimed me a daring outlaw. Among the excited crowds on the streets they endeavored to arouse a lynching spirit, believing that we would surely be brought back within a few days.

"I don't want any weak-kneed men about me," said the Sheriff of Fresno County as he chose his assistants from among the flower of all the posses that had taken part in the earlier man-hunts. "I will not return until I bring the fugitives with me," he added as the picked man-trackers started for the mountains followed by pack trains of supplies.

"It can't last long. The old outlaw leader won't be able to stand up under the pace I'll set for him. Six months imprisonment in the County Jail must have taken the wire out of his muscles, and added to that the loss of his sighting eye and one hand will make his race for freedom uncertain. Loyalty will prevent Morrell from leaving him. So, if we get one we have them both," the Sheriff concluded.

The faithful little animal that had aided us in our flight to the Kings River Bridge walked into a livery stable in a nearby town the following day and was turned over to the newsboy who had feared that the outlaws intended to steal his horse. Then came wild rumors that we had been killed and our bodies were to be brought in by the posse. Every time the telephone rang in the County Jail it meant a new story and a crop of absurd tales.

Friends and foes stood in groups around the streets and in the Plaza. None could work,—none could compose themselves. The gunmen and company forces had made unsuccessful attempts to convince them that lynching would be the proper fate for the bandits. Then they prepared the ropes themselves, which some from among their numbers would use if we were returned alive.

What would the outcome be? We, the hunted men, did not know, and cared less, for in our desperate straits it was necessary to forget the future and live from day to day. For the present, at least, we felt measureably safe, snowbound in the warm shelter of the shake cabin near Secate Mountain.

The people of the lower valley regions were anxiously watching the progress of the man-hunt. It had taken on an entirely different complexion from anything that had occurred in the past. This time large groups from the main posse were directed to advance into the mountains in a fan shaped formation with the intention of making a drive upon the whole section of territory North of the Kings River, to force us from cover.

On January First, the only night that it had not rained or snowed since the search began, some of the scouts of the posse saw a light descend from the brow of a mountain, disappearing in a gulley. The next night the light was there again and did the same thing. These watchers learned that not far away in a high brushy mountain, seamed with deep ravines and canyons, there was an old cabin which had been unoccupied for years.

In the midst of a blinding storm, a large detail of the posse started out to locate it. Over rocks and through brush they trooped along the slippery dangerous route, where the rain had converted every little arroyo into a torrent. The darkness was so complete that none could see even an outline of the man before him. They halted only once for a hurried exchange of words, and then advanced out into a clearing, attracted by the light of a log fire flickering through the chinks and cracks of a cabin.

The leader of the posse brought his men together, whispering a last hurried instruction to each of them. Then from tree to tree and from rock to brush heap they crept stealthily finally splitting up and drawing a deadly circle about the cabin that stood out sullenly in the darkness and rain.

These trailers were adepts in the game of manstalking. It was to be a surprise attack at daylight.

CHAPTER XII

A BLOODLESS BATTLE AMONG THE CLOUDS.

There was an alarmed shriek of a hog startled out of a heavy sleep by an intruder in his burrow. This was followed by pandemonium as hundreds of others joined in the clamor. Then came the sharp challenging of the hog dogs, a cross between the Siberian bloodhound and shepherd, specially bred and trained to perform a man's duty of herding and protecting the hogs from wild animals. It was indeed a frightful chorus.

The vigilant Chief caught the first sound and awakened me with a tap on the shoulder. We listened attentively. "I can tell by the barking that it isn't a lion, timber wolf, or anything that steals hogs or harms them," said the shrewd mountainer. "It's gunmen and we are trapped, so be cautious!"

One of the posse taking up his position to the South of the cabin had stepped upon a sleeping hog.

"Put out the fire, Morrell!" commanded the chief.

I was in the act of throwing a bucket of water upon it when he stopped me saying, "No, no, my God, man, don't do that! Put it out gradually, a few tin cups full at a time. Give them the impression we are asleep and the fire is just naturally dying down."

We waited about an hour and nothing occurred. Then again the Chief's long training in Indian warfare proved to be our salvation. "They won't attack until morning unless we start it or they see us attempting to escape. I think I know the situation. We are completely encircled," he observed, "but we're going to break the line and it must be done under cover of darkness or never."

"We will crawl out and locate one of the men," the old bandit leader continued, "measure the distance between him and the next and there cut the circle midway between the two. It is our only chance. We have just one shell for the old rifle so fire must be reserved. Let the man-hunter start the trouble if he sees us.''

It was a desperate chance, the only one, so having good eyes and whole arms, I took the lead, dropped flat upon the floor, gun in hand thrust out before me, inched the cabin door open and pushed myself belly fashion out into the deep slush.

Our progress was slow and the suspense so great that I jumped involuntarily upon detecting one of the posse crouched under a tree for protection from the cold, bitter rain. He was squatting in front of me, and so near that the barrel of my rifle had almost touched him. Was it possible that he was faithless to his duty, or perchance stealing a few cherished winks of sleep? Still, his position was so uncomfortable that this seemed unlikely. The phantomlike, sinister figure annoyed me.

Speech was out of the question now. The Chief crawled close beside me and I gave him a warning tug, then, directing all further progress by hand pressure, we moved in a parallel direction to the menacing ring until about midway between the crouching man and his neighboring picket. There we cut the line, continuing to propel our bodies along with a knee and arm movement. About half an hour later we began sliding downward in the snow at the abrupt ending of the table land.

The suspense was terrible. I felt uneasy about that crouching figure, because I had a suspicion that he stared at us with wide open eyes. Perhaps he wanted the honor of killing us single-handed and might now be only a few paces behind. In my mind I conjured up all sorts of plans for a battle without ammunition.

We looked around, jumped to our feet stealthily and departed. There was no more time to be lost if we were going to make the most of our opportunity. As we forged ahead the snow became heavier under foot and the rain grew worse, turning into sleet, thus creating more obstacles to face. A rushing roaring sound made us stop short, and just in time for we were on the edge of a vertical precipice of solid, massive granite, sheer and naked except for a few pines growing out of small crevices that were not large enough to give even a foothold to a human being.

Hundreds of feet below rushed a mad torrent, forcing its way along the impassable gorge, a fretting mass of white foam, the treacherous Kings River. It seemed as if nature had just newly rent the mountain mass assunder to obstruct our retreat.

"I guess it's all off," commented the Chief. "You know what the Kings River is, a devil's caldron. Years ago that river nearly cost me my life."

We were too dejected to discuss our terrible plight. We had broken through the dead line of man-hunters without so much as a scratch, only to be confronted now by one of nature's death traps, and wet and storm beaten we stood there looking vacantly into nothingness.

At last aroused to action, I began to edge myself Southward along the frowning cliff as if impelled by a strange influence. Automatically my companion followed. Nearly an hour later, my feet munched down into a yielding substance. "A sandbar," I whispered cautiously to the Chief who had slowly picked his way along behind me.

We were on the brink of a turbulent river, and examining more closely I found that from this point a riffle crossed it. "She's bank full and ice cold but I'd rather take a chance here than turn back to certain capture and very likely death."

"There is hope if we can keep to the riffle," declared the Chief, plunging in after me and holding onto my shoulder. I grasped the gun with both hands on the barrel, using it as a prop against the force of the heavy current.

Scarcely half way across I made a false step and would have been swept down to my death if the old Chief had not held me with all his strength until I regained my footing. Our effort in fording the river had taxed us to the limit. Drenched and cold benumbed from the ice chilled water, on the other side we dropped to the ground exhausted. As we lay there our clothes froze upon us, and realizing that we would die of exposure even before the posse discovered us if we remained, I staggered to my feet and helped my companion to get up, urging that it would soon be daylight and there was little time left in which to make our escape.

The first streaks of dawn were already showing above the higher range. Turning, we confronted another wall,— not from the top this time, but from below. "Heaven's name, what next?" exclaimed the Chief in despair. "Now we are blocked again, and after all the risks too."

My heart seemed to stand still as I stared upward. This was a real obstacle, for cold and bare to a height of several thousand feet the peaks of the Secate Range, with their treacherous rocky crags, frowned menacingly above us, — granite almost perpendicular, and so slippery that even the snow which had fallen steadily for days could not stick.

Neither of us ventured a word, but with a silent understanding as if impelled by the same thought, jaded and encased in sheets of ice, we started the dangerous climb of the glacierlike mountainside. It was particularly hard on the Chief and I had almost to drag him along. We climbed higher and higher, not daring to look down, and only halting occasionally, where a scrub oak or pine or a sharp ledge offered a moment's footing, so that we might beat loose our stiffened garments.

We seemed to have been hours feeling our way up the zigzag route of crevice and jagged water course, full of frozen bodies of ice. Digging our toes in here and there, and straining our muscles to the limit, by sheer force of will we struggled at last to the top of the range, again falling, this time among the protecting crags. Mute, semi-conscious, we lay there, while unobstructed the early morning sun beat down upon us, thawing out our ice crusted clothes and bringing warmth into our shivering bodies.

"We can see the cabin from here," I called back excitedly having crawled over near the edge of the peak to look down.

"Can you make out any of the gunmen?" my companion laughed, drawing close to me with evident interest. "Your eyes are good on distance. Mine used to be until I lost one of them."

"I see them crouching, and from their strange antics, they're exchanging signals," I continued.

Just then, one of the leaders stood up waving a handkerchief. Instantly a circle of blue smoke, formed a screen around the acre of ground. In another moment, the echoing and re-echoing of the sounds of firing reached the top of the mountain.

"The battle is on," grimly remarked the old war scarred veteran, "and they're fighting with a deserted fort. The enemy has retreated."

It was a vivid picture spread out below us in the early morning light — mute evidence of the fate we had just escaped. The sun rising higher had now cleared the mountain barrier. Its beams flooded the table land below, casting back reflections from the rifle barrels, as the air cleared about the encircled cabin, and before another fusilade started.

Volley after volley of rifle fire was wasted in an effort to force the bandits outside. It lasted for hours and the flimsy shake cabin must have been full of rifts and holes, when again the signal cloth was hoisted.

It ceased, and looking like a huge blacksnake, the circle compressed itself sending forth another burst of fire from closer quarters.

They must have been able to look clear through the cabin now, for the man who was evidently the leader stood bolt upright, and throwing caution aside advanced upon the place fearlessly. The skirmish line broke then, and the man-hunters soon gathered in groups around their leader, evidently discussing the new turn of affairs.

The man-trackers were plainly disgruntled as they scattered around the shot torn cabin, seeking telltale tracks of our miraculous escape. Finally one of them must have discovered those made by our sliding bodies during the night, for a number of the posse started on a run to the edge of the table land. There they picked up our footprints which led on down to the brink of the precipice where we had stood trembling in the blackness of the night before.

From this point the foremost of the trackers detoured along the downward steep defile which had providentially opened the way for our escape. Now the full complement of the posse started on a dog trot to the banks of the Kings River. There they stood huddled together, gazing long and hard at the turbulent, rushing water, then raised their eyes to the wall-like side of the icy mountain, seeking evidence of our possible retreat.

The Sphinxlike mountain told them nothing. Could their quarry have dared to risk their lives in a hazardous attempt to ride the rapids of the Kings River to safety below? It was unthinkable that the wary old bandit, hero of a thousand hair breadth escapes would fall into such a trap. He knew his Kings River too well for that. Still, the tracks ended at the water. Was there a chance that fox-like he had redoubled? Acting on this lead as a solution to the baffling problem, the posse spread out in a long skirmish line, beating back up the mountainside to the table land, there to renew the search for a clue to our escape.

The man-hunters had lost in the chase, and cheated of their quarry retraced their steps down through the rugged defiles of the mountains to food and shelter at Trimmer Springs.

"That's over," grunted the Chief. "We don't have to worry about them for a while. The Mineral King and Camp Manzanita are far to the South, and we must make it through the White Deer Trail Country."

I knew what that meant. Facing a mob of gunmen would have been more preferable. We were setting out through an almost uncharted mountain territory. No one had ever heard of its having been traversed before in Winter time, and we were without supplies having had neither food nor water since the previous night.

"This sunshine is only a lull in the storm. It will prove of short duration. Look to the Southward. What do you make of that black cloud?" asked my partner, shading his one eye with the remaining hand as he studied the sky.

"A mountain fog bank; an aftermath of the spent storm,—nothing more," I assured him.

"You're wrong!" He shook his head emphatically. "We'll have bad weather by nightfall, worse than any so far, and we'd better be on our way before we freeze or starve to death."

"All right. If you feel equal to it," I said, swinging out in the lead, breaking a path to the Southeast over snow gulleys and bald mountain sides,— assisting him through almost impassable moraines, and ever becoming more aware of the fact that he was not the daring campaigner of former days.

At even our great elevation, when the mists in the valleys below would lift, ranch houses were visible, tho scarcely more than specks to the naked eye. They sent a thrill of renewed strength through my whole being. "It is a consolation to know that we are at least near human habitations," I finally exclaimed.

"Distance is very deceptive in these mountains," came the ready reply from my companion, "and even if we were near, it would do no good. The man-hunters must be made to believe that we are held secure in the upper ranges, perhaps frozen to death there. On this account we must shun all settlements.''

These words were not very encouraging and when the short day ended with a cutting wind sweeping through our scanty clothing, chilling our tired, unnourished bodies and bringing a mountain blizzard in its wake, I heartily wished that I had obeyed my inner promptings and made straight for the valley below. Instead of that, with blue lips and chattering teeth, snow and hail beating mercilessly down upon us, weary, half frozen, and lost, not knowing which direction we took, ready to drop at any moment, we literally felt our way along, seeking a shelter from the storm.

The man-door to solitary had opened. Shuffling of feet and the sound of a bumping body cut short my knuckle talk to the ''Tiger.'' Gibbering screeches broke the silence. I jumped from my station near the back wall of the cell, to the door, peering out into the dim light to see what was happening. Manhandling was going on up at the other end of the big gloomy solitary room.

''Shut-up!'' shouted a voice, tho only faintly it percolated to me. ''Shut-up, damn you or I'll crack your head for good.'' This time, the bull-like bellow of the enraged prison guard could be heard reverberating through the building.

There was no mistaking the sounds now. Chortling voices were in chorus. One screamed above the din and racket. ''See, see, Barney, the 'Chink' has got me! Bit me on the hand! Oh God! Give me that club! Let me at him! Step away there, I say, look out; I'll fix him, the dirty 'Chink' dog,'' and amid the shuffling of feet and groans I could hear the dull thud from the impact of a bludgeon.

''Hold on there, Jim, don't do that,'' another cried. ''What in Hell are you doing? Don't you know, you can't kill a 'Chink' like a white man in prison? The Chinese

Consul General in San Francisco will have you by the neck, and if you raise Hell for the old man by bringing on a mess you will get in trouble. He will never cover you up where a 'Chink' is concerned. I tell you, man, let go. The Warden will raise Hell!''

The very air vibrated with murder, and tho the "Tiger" and I had known most of the red Hells of prison life, somehow I felt that this scene represented strange doings.

I had been through all such manhandlings, myself the central figure. Still my impressions never registered the same while undergoing gruelling brutality as when compelled to listen in silence to some other victim's groans. I gripped the bars of my door in rage, began to see red, and the next instant would have shouted out my defiance against this wanton savagery, but was jerked back to my senses by the sound of our own prison warder shouting, "Here, here, what in Hell are ye men doin'?"

He was a fiery Celt, full blooded and bull-necked, with a temper like a jackal held at bay. He had a cruel leering mouth with short thick teeth almost worn to the gums, tobacco stained and altogether formidable, and was the worst man on the San Quentin line, feared by the other guards and so hated and despised by the convicts, that the Warden had hand-picked him for solitary. He was the autocrat over us two of the living dead; and tho I had escaped an open encounter by never giving him the excuse to measure his bull strength against mine, in my very soul I knew he was biding his time to reek his insatiable hatred upon me.

Time and time again, with catlike tread, he would sneak along in the shelter of the cell wall and stand near my door, motionless and hardly breathing, often as long as an hour, then, when his addled brain conceived that he might catch me in some unalert act he would jump out and stare in at me, his glinting red eyes showing clearly the half suppressed insanity of the man, and his steaming breath reeking with the fumes of alcohol.

His thundering shout to the other brute guards brought me to earth and a sense of my own danger. I trembled in every limb like a weakened child when I realized what I had escaped. Had he heard my voice I firmly believe that the solitary would have been turned into a shambles.

"Get me my mouth gag! Lay off yer hands of the 'Chink,' I say! Who in Hell is boss here? Me or yous? Tomorree mornin' be the Eternal, I'll have yez all before the Warden!" he bellowed. "I'll let yez know I'll not have such indacencies committed in my department. 'Give-a-damn' is boss here and no brutalities goes unless some cons starts the rumpus first with me personally."

In another minute the poor Chinese victim was mouth gagged and I could hear his body hit the back end of the cell. Then the door closed and the lock was snapped; some more wrangling at the man-door, as "Give-a-damn" threatened his fellow freemen, and again solitary resumed the old familiar death-like silence.

The "Tiger's" tap was calling me. His first words sounded terribly harsh in my ears. "I'm sorry, old man, that you were interrupted by this most unseeming exhibition,'" he rapped cynically. "But I trust that you noted the humane and admirable conduct of our precious warder in chief,— a most charming gentleman, to be sure, a shining example of the refining influences that are creeping into our prisons."

"Also, did you note that he made it plain he would not tolerate or permit brutalities to be committed *in his department?*' That is, unless some damn fool con first started the rumpus with him personally."

I was almost angry with the "Tiger." His unfeeling words annoyed me. Still, I should have remembered that he was long ago case hardened to all such unholy things, and the mere matter of brute man-handling now meant little to him,— just ordinary routine of prison life.

Our surroundings were vile. Our food was filthy. The one meal every twenty-four hours had even become monotonous. Only men by force of will could live on such an unnatural diet. We had no books to read. Our very knuckle talk was banned as a violation of some absurd arbitrary rule. The world so far as we were concerned practically did not exist. It was more a ghost world. We were the buried alive, the living dead. Solitary was our tomb in which on occasion we ventured knuckle talk like spirits rapping at a seance. So the poor "Tiger" was not to blame. The inhuman jail had made him what he was. His prison guards were brutes, and under their treatment he had to harden into a brute in order to live.

They called Jake Oppenheimer the "Human Tiger." Some cub reporter coined the phrase that has long out-lived the man to whom it was applied. And yet in spite of his prison-made brutishness, during all the years of our knuckle tapping that I spent with him in the loneliness of the dungeon, I ever found in the "Tiger" all of the cardinal traits of upstanding manliness. He was faithful and loyal to the core, he was brave, he was patient, he was capable of the extremes of self-sacrifice. I could tell many stories of this but will not take the time.

I purposely refrained from commenting to the "Tiger" upon his callous remarks over the shocking brutality that had just been committed, fearing that I might cause an estrangement between us. Men in prison are supersensitive. A look, sometimes an idle passing word may cause a deep wound that will take years to heal. It was days before I could compose myself to continue the story, and then only after the poor "Tiger" had urged me piteously to give him the conclusion of our struggles through the storm.

"All right, Jake," I finally agreed, "but I warn you, another upset like the one I have just experienced will end the story of the California Outlaws."

Once more I was back in the mountains, out in the cool biting air, living the life of a freeman, tho an outlaw with a price upon my head. The human derelict, the outcast who was tapping sound talk, bridging the distance between thirteen cells, was only a shadow man. The real man was living in the past.

CHAPTER XIII

THE LOVE OF LIFE. LOST IN A MOUNTAIN STORM.

Another step seemed out of the question. We were giving way to the numbness of a freezing death, and were ready to sink down in the deep snow when again something happened.

All through my life this strange, uncanny power has come to my rescue in the darkest hours. It brought me out of the desert when I hadn't one chance in a million for my life — lost and aimlessly wandering, bone dry, my tongue swollen ready to burst the confines of my mouth, my brain reeling, — mad and delirious. I have stood, the target for a leaden hail of shotgun fire, only to disappear without a wound. In strange lands it has made me feel at home. Lost in the interior of Australia in long stretches between sheep stations, it has brought me to safety as true as the needle responds to the North Star.

As a boy I had been engulfed in a mine explosion. All about me men were dead. I never received a scratch, and old miners said I bore a charmed life. Now, in this last extremity, when death was so near, that guardian angel of my fate once more took me in hand.

I stumbled against a shelf of rock slanting out from the mountainside. Underneath I found an aperture large enough to admit a man crawling on all fours. Calling to the old Chief who was stumbling along behind me, I leaned down to enter. "We will, at least, have shelter from the storm in here. Follow me," I shouted.

"Be careful there! What are you doing?" feebly cautioned my partner holding me back by my coat.

The old one eyed fighter was game to the core for, even in this, his last extremity he ventured the bantering remarks, "I say, young man, you'd better knock on the door first. That place may be occupied by a sullen mother bear or a mountain lion who would just naturally resent intrusion."

From a pocket he drew out a match and, as I jumped clear of the opening, reached in and brushed up a pile of dead leaves. Lighting them, he took a commanding position on the rock above. The smoke was drawing inward, heavy, circling clouds of it, indicating that there was a vent which would assure us of good air. When we had waited long enough to be certain that our cave was uninhabited, wet and shivering we plunged through the dark entrance, feeling our way to the warm back wall, where we soon fell into an exhausted slumber all unmindful of the storm that raged unceasingly without.

I was the first to awaken, roused by a sense of suffocation. "We must have slept through a full night," I thought. Still it was dark. Groping my way to the entrance I found it blocked with snow. Pushing through the solid bank I discovered daylight and a raging storm that drove me back to shelter to dream and sleep some more. There was nothing else to do. We had not even a bite of food and advance was still impossible.

The next time I looked out the second night was almost ended. It was dark and bitter. Sheets of snow were driving with hurricane force across the bald face of the mountainside. Now the old bandit was feebly moaning something inarticulate. His bones were aching and the pangs of hunger were gnawing at his vitals, telling the grim story of privation and near death.

Soon he was fast asleep again. I could not sleep. The pain from the gunshot wound and the injured leg was troubling me. The next was the third night in confinement with neither food nor water. Morning followed with some little abating of the storm, but it was still impossible to venture out.

Our plight desperate we prepared for another night, the fourth, eating snow to quench a burning thirst and wondering which would be preferable, death by slow starvation within the warm shelter of a mountain crag or a drive against the raging elements with scarcely a chance of reaching safety. It was hard to resign ourselves to the former. Something must be done! Come what would we must start the following morning!

Bright warm sun was shining. We had beaten the spectre of Death, and weak and aching, our mouths so swollen and sore that we could scarcely speak, we tumbled clear of our shelter. Once more I began my dogged task of breaking trail to the Southward, my companion staggering along at my heels.

Our halts were frequent and unable to refrain we consumed handfuls of snow to slake the burning thirst, but we kept going until sunset, then threw ourselves down bodily in the snow to rest. The glaring whiteness had changed to deepest gold, while the stillness was unbroken by even the slightest rustle, and we looked at one another, curiously wondering over the contradictions of life.

"That's the spot we are making for," grunted the Chief pointing toward a high table-land to the Southeast, visible through the falling night shadows below us. "Somewhere over there lies the Upper Mill Creek Valley. To the West runs the Lower Mill Creek," he added gesturing with his one arm, "and somewhere along it the posse will strike their trail Southward."

"The Kings River, into which it empties, is back of us. From here we must work our way down the mountain to the higher reaches of the Lower, and then on into the Upper Mill Creek where we will find friends, food, and shelter," the Chief concluded.

I repeated the last three words after him thoughtfully. They sounded strange, but like a magic spell spurred me on to renewed effort, and again I continued my task of trail breaking for a half fainting man.

Struggling, stumbling, plowing through deep snow, sinking to our knees and sometimes even falling, we broke out at last upon the bank of the lower portion of the roaring Mill Creek. Here a discussion followed. Something told me plainly to go directly down into the valley for food and shelter, even tho it meant a possible clash with the gunmen.

The Chief was obdurate, and insisted that we should climb to the Upper Mill Creek Valley, following the course of the stream. His judgment in the past had always been unerring, and blindly I gave way, once more trudging on ahead.

The day was gone, turning cold and gray in the paling light. Gusts of wind began a merciless crashing through the trees, threatening to break them off at the ground and tumble them down upon us. A new storm was coming and unless we soon made the Upper Mill Creek Valley our plight would be worse than on Secate Mountain.

Now we stopped, baffled. We were facing a sheer impassable precipice, the dividing line between the Lower and Upper Mill Creek. White foamed, the tumbling waters of the falls sent up a deafening roar.

"We are miles from any habitation, and nothing remains but to trace our steps back and down into the valley," I suggested weakly. "The posses are stalking us in every direction now, but I'd rather take chances with them than remain here."

The Chief nodded, too tired to speak, and followed me.

The wind was terrific. Blinding sheets of snow beat into our unprotected faces, changing now and again to biting rain and sleet as if to harry us to the very depths of our souls. The worst of the winter was on!

Stumbling along trying to break a trail I had failed to keep a watchful eye upon the Chief. Glancing around quickly I discovered that he was no longer with me. My repeated calls were unanswered, and I retraced my steps for some distance almost falling over his limp form, snow covered and cold.

"Just a little further," I coaxed, urging him to get up, shaking him, and trying to lift him.

"I'm all in! Let me sleep! Go away and don't annoy me, I say! Let me sleep for about an hour and I'll be all right again! Go on ahead! Keep on breaking trail! I'll be up with you in the matter of an hour. Don't be foolish, I say! Damn it, I'm worth a thousand dead men yet!" The Chief muttered the last words so low that they were smothered in a heavy, deep breathing, and I realized what it meant.

He had lost control. The man who had gone through hundreds of battles, whose muscles were made of iron, had succumbed to weariness and was already in the sleep that precedes the slow freezing death. His terrible wounds and the jail were telling their tale.

I tried to lift him bodily, but was too weak and dropped him, falling myself in the attempt. For a little while I dragged him over the half covered trail I had just broken. Then I became aware of added dangers. The storm which had now assumed the proportions of a gale was lopping dead limbs from the trees around us. It was also bitter cold. Something would have to be done, or we would both perish.

Then I began prodding my partner to exasperate him, trying to goad him to rebellion, feeling sure that if I could once arouse the old veteran, his notorious quick temper would bring him to his feet. With an oath he sprang up, the fighting man overcoming bodily weakness. Blindly he struck at me.

When I had him thoroughly enraged I jumped behind him raining blows upon his back to urge him forward, and in this fashion we covered a short distance down the course of the Lower Mill Creek. But the snow was so deep that two men could not travel through it together. It was impossible for me to do both, break trail, and push the dying Chief before me. My strength gave out. We both pitched headlong and were soon almost covered by the drifting white mantle.

How long I lay there, I will never know. It might have been but a few minutes. My conscious mind was slipping. That part of the mind which urges the man eternal to let go, give up, surrender was gaining control. It was prompting that the cold unfeeling snow was just a warm bed, that the elements raging about were merely cooling Summer breezes, and that sleep, most refreshing sleep was mine for the taking.

I struggled hard against this death dealing narcotic of my senses. There was still life enough left to combat the opiate which was preparing me for the long sleep and again that silent monitor, the shepherd of my fated career assumed control. I became rebellious and fought against my deadening physical consciousness. Now I was cursing, loudly shouting invectives upon the elements. Then I saw Big Bill Smith glowering over me, taunting me in my helplessness. The shrewdness of the man-wolf hunted to his last lair was upon me. I gloated inwardly as I planned my attack.

I would show this yellow, swaggering " nine points of the law bully" what a real man was. Feeling around in the snow I grasped the old rifle that I had dragged with me all through the struggle and bounded to my feet like a panther, ready to fire. My senses cleared. I was alone except for the huddled figure in the snow.

A bright light was shining upon him. Alert and full of hope I realized the storm had spent itself. The snow had stopped, the light was a cold winter moon that had just topped and cleared the range on the other side of Mill Creek. In another moment I was dragging the helpless man through the snow. Common sense told me that the love of life was mine and I should save myself, but I could not steel my heart to leave a brave man alone and helpless, a prey to the timber wolves.

Then I remembered the one shell resting snugly in the old rifle. I smiled at the thought that at least I would defeat the wolves of their prey alive, but could not bring myself to fire the mercy shot. As if ringing in my ears I heard the oft repeated slogans of the old Chief when encouraging another fallen by the wayside to get and keep going,—"You are worth a thousand dead men yet! Where there's life there's hope! Never surrender, never give up!" the catechism of a brave man.

Pulling off the old coat, the only one that I had to protect me, I gently wrapped it completely around his head, hoping that the warmth from his breathing would help to sustain life long enough until my return. Then I left in search of help, drawing on every fibre to the limit and quickening my trudging pace through the snow, fearful lest prowling wild animals might get the scent of quarry before I could return.

A crackling of manzanita made me stop short! "The stealthy tread of a panther or the posse," I thought, looking off to the right of me.

On the top of a jutting ridge something stood clearly outlined in the moonlight. In a frenzy of joy I bounded to a position of easy range, grasping my rifle tightly with stiffened fingers.

It was a young steer, a stray yearling that had been lost in the storm, and resting the rifle barrel in the fork of a stunted tree I took aim. This time, a new horror appalled me! My fingers had frozen in a clenched position and would not move.

Prodded by fear and desperation, I shoved the tips of the fingers of my right hand into my swollen mouth, trying to soften and warm them and break the deadlock. Again I made ready to fire. There was only one shell which must go true to the mark if we were not to be lost.

The finger moved. I fired. The young steer sank slowly to his knees then rolling over and over fell limp almost at my feet. I was no longer a man. Demon-like I fell down upon the warm, lifeless bulk, knife out ripping at the jugular vein until the warm blood gushed forth. My mouth close to the wound, gulping the thick hot fluid, I drank deeply.

A feeling of energy surged through my shrunken body with this first nourishment in five days. I thought of my fallen friend, and placing my sombrero under the geyser of blood filled it to the brim and staggered back along the trail to the prostrate form.

I tried to shake him to partake of the blood before it coagulated, literally kicking life and consciousness back into him with the toe and heel of my boot. I next raised him to a sitting position, holding the hat to his swollen lips. He drank a little and then tried to fall back in the snow again.

Now I was furious and shook him until my own teeth rattled. He called out, "Where am I? What has happened? I feel cold."

"Wake up, man!" I shouted. "Where is your old time grit — the fire that has whipped so many others to action? You are lying down on the trail like an old woman. Another hour and you will be finished. Here," I urged, "drink this blood quick before it freezes to a lump in my hat."

Again holding the rim of my sombrero scoop fashion, I let the fast cooling liquid fall down his throat. He was a gritty man,— one in ten thousand, "the Last of the Mohicans," and to my great relief he called, "I say Ed., they don't make them like you any more. The molds are all broken. Give me your hand. Help me up. If I'm to die, I'm going to die walking, and when I fall again let me lie with my boots on facing my enemies."

Urged by the fear that our strength had been so sorely tried that the effects of the nourishment would not be lasting, we started off at head speed working against time down the Valley of the Mill Creek toward the lower region and the settlements.

When we passed the spot where the yearling lay, I realized the fate that my partner had been spared. A pack of snarling, snapping, hungry timber wolves were devouring the carcass.

The battle for life was still evenly in the balance. A new storm was on. The wind which had died down a while veered to another direction bringing in its wake snow, sleet and rain. Again I was in front, this time feeling my way ahead. The blizzard had wiped out the light of the moon. I could not see. In places the drifts were high. Pushing through one of them I dropped shoulder deep into a snow covered gully, a feeder that emptied into Mill Creek.

"God Almighty! what next?" I heard the old Chief exclaim, as I clambered out on the other side.

Half the life was taken from me by this new and unexpected accident. Already I was chilled, my vitals shrinking up within my body. Teeth chattering I called, "For God's sake, man, come on. If I fall now I am done for."

Going up and around the treacherous water trap my partner joined me. He placed his arm about my body, in his feeble exhausted condition even striving to help me forward. Racked and shivering I struggled on. It was unbelieveable that human beings could stand so much

We had covered miles, working down the Valley of the Mill Creek toward human habitation. A light finally flashed before my eyes, much like a vision through the snow, then a cone of heavy smoke. Lunging toward it we tumbled almost headlong upon a large shelter tent on which the light from a fire within shadowed human forms, and we knew it was tenanted.

"The posse at last," said the old outlaw dejectedly.

"Well, what of it?" I asked. "It is suicidal to go on and there is at least a chance here. Let's capture the place!"

"How?" questioned my companion as he leaned against a fallen tree. "We have no ammunition."

"An empty gun, with your reputation is enough," I exclaimed. "We can make them prisoners. Take them by surprise. I'll make the dash at the front. If there is opposition, you challenge from the back of the tent. How will they know we are without ammunition?"

Crafty as the old scout had been, his mind was not working clearly. "You're right," he whispered, "it can be done. Give me time to get to the rear, before you make the play."

Strained moments followed as I watched the war scarred fighter stalk to his position at the back of the tent. Satisfied that he was at last ready and waiting for action on my part I covered the entrance with my empty gun. A dog sounded the alarm from within, and a man opened the flaps peering out into the darkness.

Inside I saw a woman with a baby in her arms, and lowering my rifle I addressed the man in a friendly tone. In another moment the Chief joined us and with our host we stepped inside. Hot coffee, beans and dry bread were given us before we had time even to ask for help.

We found the people friendly, a bond of sympathy from common origin springing up between us when they discovered who we were.

"I was always faithful to duty, worked for years as a foreman of section gangs for that railroad," the man remarked. "They discharged me without any explanation. I later learned I was accused of expressing sympathy for the ranchers of the Mussel Sleugh. Our last hope was to treck back into the mountains and try to start life all over again."

A feeling of pity surged through me when the riddle was cleared away regarding the reason why this little family were living in a flimsy shelter tent during one of the worst winters that had ever been known in the Sierra Nevada Mountains.

I asked the distance to the first ranch.

"About half a mile, but there is no one home. The man who owns the place is well fixed so he takes his cattle and goes down into the lower valleys for the winter. He made me a sort of caretaker while he is away," the husband mumbled half apologetically.

"Didn't he offer you the chance to live at the ranch during cold weather?" I quizzed.

"No sir," said the wife, drawing herself up, "and if he should do so now I would stay here and freeze to death, rather than be under compliment to such a man."

"Let me have that key," I commanded sharply, jumping to my feet.

Roused from his position on the bed where he was lying the Chief insisted, "That's right, Morrell. We'll take possession of the ranch and these good people must come along. I know him well and he needs such a lesson at this."

The husband stood near the door looking foolish when he heard the strange order, but the woman, the mother, was made of different metal. With eyes brightening and cheeks crimsoning she laughed outright, "Won't this be a joke on that old skin flint?" Wrapping her baby comfortably she followed us out into the heavy snow.

The ranch house proved to be a substantial place with every comfort to be found in the homes of the mountain stretches. Tho fires had not been lit during the winter, to us famished men it seemed warm and comfortable. Our new friends busied themselves, fires were soon aglow and a hot meal was prepared from the well stocked larder.

It was growing late and we needed sleep before daylight. Tucked away in a warm bed we forgot the misery and struggles of the battle just fought for life across the bleak stretches of the White Deer Trail in our escape from Secate Mountain.

Before leaving in the morning the Chief ordered the family to occupy the ranch for the rest of the cold weather, gruffly warning that if they failed to comply in every detail he would return and take things in hand again. Also he gave them a note for the owner in case he should come back before the warm weather. It was brief and to the point.

"Sir:"

"You have violated the hospitality of the mountains. In every ranch house through hundreds of miles of the Sierra's the latchstrings are always out. Having denied these people the shelter of your unoccupied ranch, in defense of the code of white man and Christian we assume the right to act."

"They are to live here during the winter months. If you should return and countermand our order, this is notification that you may expect a visit from us. We will wipe the ranch and everything you possess off the map along with other reprisal upon you, personally."

"Signed"

"The California Outlaws"

I turned and waved as we crossed over a ridge in the mountain which would close the view behind. The baby held securely in one arm, with the other the mother shook her apron as a farewell signal until we could no longer see her.

It was well past noon before we dropped down to rest and to eat the substantial lunch which had been prepared by the friends of the preceding night. Having finished, we quenched our thirst at a mountain brook, and tho longing to find some excuse for remaining, forced ourselves to move on.

This was indeed a pleasant contrast to our condition for the past five days, lost in the snow far above the tree line, and it is not to be wondered at that we revelled in the change, becoming our former selves again for the first time since the jail hold-up.

The Chief was now able to assume command of the retreat. He was well acquainted with this country of low, stunted pines, and led the way. Once he stopped, motioning me to his side and pointing to the Southeast. "Over there and down is Squaw Valley" he exclaimed. "We must make good time in order to pass that place before dark. From there we will go to the Mill Creek stage station where you can reconnoiter. If there are no men of the posse around we can secure horses and make a rapid night ride down into the Valley. We will go about fifty miles out of the course, double our tracks, and return to the mountains, avoiding any possible clash with the man-hunters."

"In another five days we will be in the Mineral King,—then Camp Manzanita, home, and rest." The Chief's voice had the ring and tone of the man in command. He was himself once again, and I felt a new man equal to anything.

CHAPTER XIV

CAMP MANZANITA, STRONGHOLD OF THE OUTLAWS.

A gentle rap on the door, followed by a voice aroused me from a death-like slumber. "Breakfast is ready and the bath is waiting," called the lady of the house.

I groaned as I tried to pull myself out of bed. My injured leg would not work. We had made a long trip on horseback from the higher mountains, and were now down in the San Joaquin Valley in Tulare County at the home of a friend of the Chief, a very prosperous citizen. What a strange contrast to the rough cabins and open forests which had been our only shelter for weeks!

We had made a back-track from snow line to valley comforts in a night. Once more the old Chief had used his wits in a daring move to shake the posse from our trail. Every foot of the San Joaquin Valley was hostile territory, and it seemed an act of madness that we two hunted men should venture down out of the protecting mountains.

But the Chief was noted for his originality in making whirlwind moves. His fox doubling antics had baffled the best man-trackers for years and this last daredevil whirl was in keeping with his uncanny power of strategy. Coupled with that, his long years of Indian scout trailing caused him to do things that might appear acts of the highest folly. He was a born leader of men, and organization and obedience to orders were a fetish with him.

Spurred to action by the thought of a bath in a white porcelain tub, I forgot my aches and pains. In another hour we two men who had presented ourselves in the middle of the night, clothes torn, wet, and bedraggled now stood in the library shaking hands with our friends, dressed in warm winter corduroys and heavy topped laced boots. We had new forty-five Colt revolvers strapped about each of our waists in belts lined with shells.

Two Winchester repeating rifles, also new, and a high powered field glass were resting on the library table. Near at hand was a military pack, which included two blankets, two raincoats, rifle ammunition, a first aid emergency kit, a water canteen, and six days rations, all supplied by friends and sent to this home in anticipation that we would make a drive here.

Not the least important was a large sum of money, which our good friend turned over to the Chief, suggesting that he thought it might be well that he have a receipt in the Chief's handwriting as proof that he delivered the money in case some accident should happen.

All of these things out of the way, we felt that we were almost on an equal footing with our pursuers.

Early in the morning the lady of the house had gotten rid of the servants on some excuse, sending them in a carriage to the town with the remark that they could "make a day of it."

Breakfast over, we again took possession of the library, there relating in detail our experiences of the Fresno County Jail hold-up and the mad chase through the mountains.

"A two weeks record of your exploits by the press," said our friend pointing to a pile of newspapers. "Perhaps you would like to get that version of your escapades. I never thought it possible that you could have broken through the line of man-hunters which hemmed you in, North of the Kings River."

We scanned the press reports, headlines being particularly interesting. One of the big San Francisco dailies made a special feature of the great man-hunt. The first paper had in bold headlines, "DARING JAIL HOLDUP. BANDIT EVANS ESCAPES," another, "PURSUIT SETTLED TO A PERSISTENT SEARCH," again, "THE OUTLAWS ARE NOT CAUGHT YET. PURSUERS HAVE NOT HAD SO MUCH AS A GLIMPSE OF THEM;" "OUTLAWS IN CABIN ON DINKY

CREEK, FIGHTING IS EXPECTED SOON;" "BANDIT CHIEF EVANS STATES THAT HIS GRIEVANCES ARE WITH THE RAILROAD AND EXPRESS COMPANY AND THAT HE WILL BROOK NO INTERFERENCE FROM ANYONE."

Another read, "HOT ON THE OUTLAWS' TRAIL. SHERIFF SCOTT'S POSSE CROWDING THEM HARD. OUTLAWS' PURSUIT AN UNRELENTING MAN-HUNT."

The most interesting was the report received about our escape from the hog camp on Secate Mountain. "A volley meant for the outlaws sent into a lonely mountain cabin. The fugitives had flown. Footprints of the two men show plainly in the snow miles to the East of here."

It continued, "Posses stealthily approached the cabin, the door was ajar. The guide ran back whispering, 'They're there now. Come out and you won't be harmed. The cabin is surrounded,' shouted the leader of the posse. No word from within. Winchester bullets tore through the shakes. The place was empty, but they found the remains of a fire a couple of days old and long footprints of the men they were hunting, and traced them down to the river."

I had read aloud, and the Chief laughed with our host as he told the story of the real escape from the surrounded cabin. "Those footprints must have been long," he commented. "They were made by the full length of our bodies sliding stomach fashion in the snow. That sentry who watched us pass him evidently did not tell that we went by, as he had given no alarm. They took good care not to mention the great battle the man-hunters fought with the empty cabin before they approached it," he added laconically, "nor about walking on a hog and setting the whole camp squealing. We would have been foolish to wait until morning to be shot up by them after such a noise and with the hog dogs sounding the warning."

That was enough. I could read no further for supper time arrived almost before we realized it, so pleasant had been the day. Partaking of the substantial meal we departed in the rear seat of a carry-all which was ready and waiting at the door.

The host, our friend, took his place in front and with reins grasped tightly whirled the horses around and out of the driveway, cutting into the main road. We were soon going at top speed Southeast through the valley.

We had reached the mountains again and it was nearly dawn when we stopped at a ranch in Three Rivers on the Kahwea. Pulling into the corral the horses were unhitched and taken into the barn. There the owner of the ranch joined us, evidently a little nervous lest somebody should discover that strangers had arrived at his place.

We felt safe, now almost within the region of our old stamping ground. After night had fallen again the friend who had brought us here returned down into the valley. The parting was commonplace. Hands were held in silence. Men of the West show little emotion, no matter what the sacrifice, or how great the deed done in behalf of a friend. It is passed with a curt word, or mayhap the shrug of a shoulder. We never saw him again; — the old Chief has long since passed to the Great Beyond — but I have often wanted to meet that man and talk over our wild night ride.

"Now we can relax in peace," remarked the Chief. "We are among friends, and should the man-hunters think we are in this section they would never expect to find us tucked away between clean sheets in a warm bed in one of the most comfortable homes of Three Rivers. This is really the first breathing spell since the jailbreak."

"Guess what time it is," I called. Warm sunshine was flooding the bedroom.

"It must be all of eight o'clock," ventured the Chief.

"It is eleven, and you have slept ten straight hours," I laughed turning the face of my watch toward him.

"Come on, you boys, your breakfast is ready and waiting," called a voice up the stairs. It was the mother of the ranch house, one who had cooked us many a good meal in the past, a wonderful woman and a staunch lifelong friend of the Chief.

We needed no second invitation, and were soon at the breakfast table. Nothing so much as a siege of privation and hardships such as we had gone through, makes one appreciate home cooking.

We spent two wonderful days and nights with our friends,— days that spelled much needed body building. On the morning of the third, just before dawn, we were up, had breakfast, and with packs adjusted left Three Rivers while it was still dark, plunging toward the higher reaches of the Mineral King.

It was nearly noon when we stopped to rest and eat the lunch which had been prepared by our friends. The Mineral King is a noted beauty spot of the Sierras. Some day it will be discovered by the tourist, and will be catalogued as another wonderland to compete with the Yosemite along with the Kern and Kings River Canyons. I had spent a great deal of the time wandering through the Mineral King, but never until now did I realize the marvel of its grandeur. From where we sat we could trace the Kahwea thousands of feet below, like a silver ribbon, winding and unwinding through gorge and valley. Opposite, only a few miles away, bulky structures of solid granite shot their pinnacles and castellated turrets high above into the dome of blue, throwing back weird shadows upon the mist cloud between us.

I have seen such dream cities in a desert mirage. Visions in the Mineral King change with minutes. You will never see the same wonder picture twice. It is a region of miracles. To old mountaineers given to folk lore fancies, the place is enchanted. Too soon was I jerked from my reverie, pulled back to raw realities by the Chief.

"I say, Morrell, one would think that you didn't have a concern in life,— that you weren't an outlaw with a price on your head and gunmen stalking your trail ready to shoot you down. You have missed your calling. You should have been one of those vagabond artists who sit like a graven image, or a lazy Indian looking at nothing from sun-up to sun-down. Do you realize, man, that the day is half spent and that we still have the toughest piece of country between us and the Valley of the Dry Creek? It will be nightfall before we reach the General Grant Park. I doubt even if we will be able to get across this country tonight," he concluded.

I knew my partner too well to question the truth of his remark. He was a noted mountaineer, the greatest "single footed hiker," as they used the phrase in the Sierras, who was ever known, and it was common knowledge that he could outdistance a horse from sun-up to sun-down. None knew his prowess better than I did. I had been a great walker myself, but this man could walk the very life out of me, and then laugh at the end of the trail. I had visions of a gruelling day before me as he swung to the lead in our drive across the Mineral King.

It was ten o'clock the same night when the big dogs of the ranch in the Valley of the Dry Creek challenged. Our call was answered and a command to let us pass shouted at the dogs.

With hardly a hand shake, I dropped into a chair exhausted. The Chief's predictions were true. It was the toughest walk I had ever made.

This ranch was our mail station, and supper was hardly over before the Chief began sorting out letters, hundreds of which had accumulated during the past weeks. One of the younger boys proudly occupied himself opening the more important under the direction of the old bandit leader.

I was too tired even to glance at my mail. I went straight upstairs to bed, not entertaining so much as a thought of danger,— something which is ever uppermost in the mind of a hunted outlaw, a man with a price upon his head.

We left the home of our friends on Dry Creek, under cover of nightfall and a fresh storm, which fast grew to the proportions of a tempest. We zigzagged up the mountains, at times plodding through snow which was more than three feet deep, finally coming out upon an old abandoned road.

"I have my locations now," said my partner, his voice husky. He gestured toward the closely netted manzanita, chaparral and scrub oak which made a dense, impassable thicket of the mountainside.

"Morrell, you'll have to walk in my footsteps," he cautioned. "It is unsafe for us to leave tracks here. Brush them out as you follow me."

"They won't be able to trace us if you keep to your work," he concluded, waiting for me to catch up with him. Then his unerring ear caught the faint sound of tumbling water.

I followed him as he plunged off the road and to the right. In a little while we were on the banks of a creek into which we stepped, wading knee deep upstream for almost a mile, and coming again upon the old wagon road. The water was very shallow where it crossed, and I was cautioned to keep to the center as, above all, no trace should be left at this point.

We still continued upstream for another half mile. Snow was falling heavily, and with a feeling of safety in the assurance that our tracks would be well covered we walked out of the cold stream, turned to the West, and groped along the edge of the impassable mass of thick manzanita, seeking a weak point.

"Here it is," I shouted, dropping to my hands and knees and crawling under the low hanging branches. Finally I was able to stand erect in a trail of blazed chaparral about two feet wide. It was one of the four blind trails to Camp Manzanita cut by the outlaws years before.

THE TWENTY-FIFTH MAN

Reaching the cabin I shoved the door open, struck a match and lit the large coal oil lamp which had been standing in readiness on the big table for nearly a year. I turned to welcome the Chief as he entered, then closed the door behind him. The fireplace was filled with dry tamarack wood and the sound of crackling embers soon made us comfortable.

"Camp Manzanita, home and safety at last," the tired old man sighed. "There is no more cozy retreat in the country, and it is stocked with enough food to last for six months."

"Three o'clock," I said, whistling in surprise. "We have been traveling all night. Get out of your wet clothes and I'll prepare a meal.

In a little while the Chief opened the door again, remarking, "This storm looks like the real thing, and even if it continues only another hour the jig is up for the man-hunters. Daylight will give less trace of us than the Pacific Ocean does of the course of a vessel on its surface."

While eating the meal the old Chief again half audibly mulled over the words, "We are safe at last," and then lapsed into silence.

I shook him. He was almost asleep at the table. He had hardly eaten enough to satisfy a child and complained loudly of drowsiness. In another minute he was fast asleep in his bed. I had noted for some time since his recovery from the last terrible wounds received in battle that many changes had occurred in his disposition. Ever a light sleeper, quick and alert to the slightest sound he would spring instantly to action, the trained man of war always on the defensive in the protection of his life.

For years these characteristics had been intensified through the terrible tragedies in his later life. He was a hunted man, an outlaw with a price on his head, with every man's hand turned against him and his wariness had been almost supercanny. He would never accept anything for granted. A random footprint might hold him fascinated as he analyzed it for signs. A strange sound would halt him in the midst of an animated conversation, or the rustling of a bush would arouse him from deepest slumber. He had always been inexorable in his vigilance.

But now everything was different. The bullet which rested at the base of his brain had worked strange magic in this marvelous man. He became shiftless. His indifference to danger almost bordered on madness, and this particular night the sounds of his heavy breathing could be heard outside.

I don't know how long I had been asleep. A strange noise awakened me. The light from the blazing logs in the fireplace was still strong enough to make out every object in the room. I glanced toward my companion to see what effect the unusual sound had upon him. He did not stir.

As hunted men are wont to do when startled I lay perfectly quiet watching, waiting. This time I could not be mistaken, and sitting bolt upright with Colts 45, I watched the door. "If the posse have followed," I thought, "there is not a chance of waking the Chief now before the battle starts. To make a sound will warn them that we are ready. Would they send one man-hunter ahead to scout?" I speculated.

If they came even one or two at a time I could handle them. There was no other entrance, and in the dreadful suspense that door appeared to open a dozen times. Then came a noise, like a crew of men at work wrecking the cabin. A sliding sound near the fire-place followed. "There's a man coming down,— it's a human form," I thought, and on my feet in a second I sprang to a commanding position, ready and waiting for the encounter.

A terrible clatter, and something emerged from the flames, leaping across the room and landing full upon the Chief asleep in his bed. It was impossible to fire without endangering his life.

Two changeable eyes, glittering and glaring like live coals shot glints of fire at me from the black mass which formed the body. It was not a human being but a wild animal. I wondered helplessly what would happen next. If the old man continued to sleep he would probably not be harmed. If he moved he might be torn to pieces.

Gun poised, awaiting developments with my hand on the trigger, I stood baffled. "If it would only spring at me and break the suspense," I thought. "If it might move just a little from its present position, I could venture a shot."

It appeared to be a mountain bobcat, and knowing that it would attack upon the first move, I urged with all my will that the Chief would prove as good a sleeper tonight as he had been since the jail break. But the Chief stirred, the weight of the body had awakened him.

"What in Hell is the trouble?" he demanded.

I was ready to fire.

Now he was looking at the black object. "Stop!" he cried loudly, and I lowered my gun at the command.

"What are you trying to do? Don't you know this is poor John Sontag's cat? Don't you remember, he brought it here when it was just a kitten? I wonder what has become of the bear-cubs. I hope they are here still. But they must be big and I suppose by this time have gone back to their natural state."

"He certainly looks like a wildcat," I laughed, relieved, and then approached with the intention of patting him on the head.

But the big black cat hissed and sputtered threateningly, leaping toward the fire and making a scratching retreat up the sheer face of the chimney. We did not see him again until the following night when he entered in the same manner and at about the same hour, curling near the Chief and remaining there until daylight when he again made an exit up the chimney. Fire held no terror for that cat, and the visits became nightly, his resting place being always close to the old Chief. He could not be persuaded to enter through the door or to allow us to touch him with our hands.

Camp Manzanita, the stronghold of the California Outlaws, was located in section thirteen of the General Grant Park of the National Forest Reserve, a wild, inaccessable place in the far reaches of the Tulare Mountains. The main approach to the region was through the Valley of the Dry Creek. From the Mineral King the route to Camp Manzanita was across a rough stretch of country, little traversed except by the most experienced mountaineers.

Camp Manzanita was a veritable fortification with four blind trails entering from East, West, North and South, cut through a dense, tangled mass of manzanita and chaparral, the higher growth being low hanging tamarack trees. The cabin proper was built against the sheer face of a mountain ledge, with its chimney jutting out of the center in such a position that the smoke from the cabin fire was lost in the folds of a large tamarack tree at the top of the rock.

A dense clump of scrub oak around the front of the cabin completed the camouflage, while an endless supply of cool fresh water from a mountain brook flowed past the door.

It had remained undiscovered through all the years of the man-hunt. It had defied detection by the best mountain trackers in the employ of the "Octopus," who had made every effort to discover and destroy the rendezvous of the outlaws.

After the Camp had been completed and the blind trails cut to four avenues of escape, the younger outlaw, Sontag, who later lost his life at the Battle of Stone Corral, had ingeniously created a man-trap for the gunmen. Near the entrance to each blind trail he planted a dynamite mine, the contact wires from each leading up to a central post of observation. There the battery controlling the mines was located under a spreading tamarack tree, which commanded a view of the entire surrounding country, making it impossible for a posse to approach without being seen by the lookout in the station.

It was an ideal position of defense, but a death trap for those within if the invaders succeeded in penetrating the blind trails beyond the mines without detection. This condition made our situation critical. There were only two of us now, and we could not maintain a lookout.

The lookout station was exposed to the harsh winter weather, making it impossible for one man to perform sentry duty for any length of time. The old Chief was too weakened from his wounds to stand exposure, so everything depended on our tracks being covered to Camp Manzanita.

Toward evening of the third day the storm which had waged fiercely since our arrival, had spent itself, and for the first time we made a careful survey of the country outside and the trails, detecting nothing out of the ordinary. Night came with a visit from the cat.

The Chief stared into the fire, while I read aloud to him. A brushing sound in the manzanita outside brought me to my feet, Winchester rifle in hand. We listened mutely as the sound grew nearer.

"Camp Manzanita has been discovered," said the old man in a low whisper. "Put out the light, Morrell, and dampen down the fire."

Working swiftly I did as directed. Then we waited.

"They're hunting around outside, but haven't located the cabin," I remarked, creeping toward the door and slowly pulling it open an inch at a time. I peered out. Then I saw it,— live game not more than ten feet away!

I raised my Winchester to fire, whispering to the Chief who was now beside me, "at last we will have some fresh meat."

"Don't shoot!" he shouted, grabbing my arm excitedly. "It's one of Sontag's cub bears. I can tell by the way he acts. He's grown up too."

There was a scraping sound on the chimney. The cat had left by way of the fire and almost instantly appeared outside, jumping onto the bear's shoulders as he scampered into the darkness.

"Well, what do you think of that?" I exclaimed.

"Now I know I was right," declared the Chief. "The cat and cubs were raised together and they have evidently continued the friendship."

"Strange he's out in the dead of winter. Must have been hibernating so near that the odor of food aroused him from his sleep," he concluded as we closed the door.

We were still upset from the nervous strain, and the least sound brought me to my feet all through the night. Upon investigation in the morning I discovered the bear in his burrow across a little ravine just opposite our door. He came out to look me over but refused to make friends, even a ham bone failing to bring him close. When I tried to approach him with it, he growled a challenge.

Nevertheless he seemed to recall vaguely the upright standing animal. He once had a master, but in cub days recognized only one, the dead outlaw who alternately teased and petted him or fed him choice morsels of food. He would never know another, tho his recollections of man made him tolerant of us two strangers who had so rudely disturbed him and his black feline companion in their winter quarters.

The cat and the bear were inseparable. We discovered that the wily cat did all the hunting, and when not engaged in that pusuit nestled snugly between the wide shoulders of the bear, even when he strolled out from his burrow.

One day I called the Chief to the door, pointing toward a tree. "Watch that cat," I exclaimed, "this is something new."

In one of the higher branches he pounced upon a large bushy-tailed squirrel, dragged him down to the burrow and dropped the limp fur-covered object at the bear's nose. He ate it while the cat made another foraging trip, continuing the same antics until the bear had sufficient food.

Later we observed that this was a daily occurrence, and that the bear lazily depended upon his agile companion for provender. The two wild creatures afforded great amusement, and many an hour we outcasts whiled away in the shade of the cabin door studying the strange communal life of two different species of the animal world.

We spent weeks resting and relaxing in the quiet security of Camp Manzanita. The Chief had recovered some of his former vitality and my wounds were now entirely healed. Undisturbed we waited for a storm, hoping that it would be as heavy as the one endured on Secate Mountain.

There was business outside of our fortification, and we dared not undertake a journey unless certain that all traces would be covered by fresh falling snow.

The country was in a fever of excitement over the County Jail holdup, while on trees and bulletin boards all over, blazoned descriptions of me. State, County and railroad offered tempting rewards for my capture dead or alive, and now we were both proscribed.

"Hello, Ed.," tapped the "Tiger," when I had finished about two straight weeks of knuckle talking. "You mentioned that the old bandit Chief said that John Sontag, the younger outlaw, had two cub bears before he was killed at the Battle of Stone Corral. Now, in your story you only mentioned finding one at Camp Manzanita. Can you tell me what happened to the other?"

The phlegmatic "Tiger," true to form, had put another one over. "I say, Jake," I laughingly tapped, "damned if I know and I care less. But, as a point of information, I suppose the two youngsters had a falling out and as humans sometimes do, agreed to disagree, and perhaps youngster number two departed from Manzanita for pastures new."

The "Tiger," fearing he had nettled me by his senseless question, rushed into the breech with a streak of knuckle tapping. "Ed. if you could continue this story for the next twenty years, solitary would be a paradise. The past few weeks have gone by like a couple of hours."

The "Tiger" was right. The doom of solitary seemed less appalling since we of the living dead had established human companionship through the kindly boon of knuckle tapping. These past two weeks in solitary had been particularly fortunate. "Give-a-damn," the boss warder, had been drinking continuously and slept right through his entire watch.

I welcomed these bouts with "John Barleycorn," for they tended to make our autocrat of the solitary lazy, and indifferent to duties. I often speculated whether he was a better man drunk or sober. Still, there was little choice between these two states. Half drunk he was a man-stalking demon continually seeking the least excuse or justification for a man-handling bout. Now, while the story lasted, I prayed that he would keep really drunk, and the "Tiger" reinforced that hope, urging that I lose no further time.

"On with the story, Ed., I say,— on with the story and let joy be ours in the silence of the 'City of the Living Dead'."

"Now Jake, this will be a surprise," I tapped. "I am going to take you into familiar surroundings."

CHAPTER XV

A BANDIT IN THE ROLE OF A COLLEGE STUDENT.

"A room and private bath? Yes sir," said the clerk of one of San Francisco's leading hotels, looking at the name, "Charles E. Bolten, El Paso, Texas," on the register. "Front" he called. "Do you wish to go to your room right away, Mr. Bolten?"

"Yes sir," I nodded my head as I spoke.

"Room 245, one of the best in the house. Boy, take Mr. Bolten right up to his room." The clerk was obsequious but not overly observant. I had been in that hotel and had spoken to this clerk not more than six months before. Was it possible that he failed to penetrate my rather flimsy rakish attempt to ape the typical college student's foppish clothes and cap?

In another moment I followed the bell-hop with my two grips into the elevator. Dropping his load in room 245 he bowed his way out, then reopened the door and ingratiatingly asked, "anything else, Mr. Bolten?"

"Yes," I answered, going to the door and producing a silver dollar, which I placed in his outstretched palm. "What is your number?" I added.

"Fourteen, Sir!"

"All right, fourteen," I drawled. "I will need good service. Fourteen will be my lucky number. Say, hold on, — come to think of it fourteen is my lucky number," I called after him. "I won a bet on the races a short while ago. He was a rank outsider, but number fourteen on the card."

The bell-hop leered a half quizzical laugh. "All right boss. I trust I'll be a lucky fourteen. I play the races. How about a tip? You look like a live one."

Nodding my head up and down and closing my right eye in a knowing wink I slowly shut the door, and turning the dead latch securely, I was immediately transformed from the spoiled son of a supposedly wealthy father to a hunted outlaw with the bearing befitting a man who carries a heavy head-price.

I made a quick survey of my apartment. There were two large windows opening on a back street. It was only a drop of about ten feet to the roof of an extension of the lower part of the hotel. From there it would have been easy to lower myself to the alley for escape.

Unbuckling a heavy brace of six shooters from my waist and removing a coil of rope from one of the bags I placed both on a chair near the window. I then took a 38 short barreled Colts from the bag, and placed it under my pillow on the bed. These precautions attended to I felt free to refresh myself with a hot bath.

Again dressing completely I jumped into bed to rest, worn and tired from my many hardships. I was soon sound asleep.

It was a long way from Camp Manzanita to San Francisco, but the trip was necessary. The desired snow storm had come. We had waited patiently for it. Leaving in darkness with the flurries of snow and sleet striking against our faces, we pushed our way through from one of the blind trails and walked at a lively pace down the mountainside toward the Dry Creek Valley, laughing and joking almost lightheartedly.

In a short time we arrived at a ranch house. The table was quickly set with the choicest preserves and dainties that a good mountain housewife knows how to make. It was a welcome relief from camp diet, and the cold night air and strenuous walking had but sharpened our appetites for the tempting meal.

We retired very late, after telling some stories of our escape to Camp Manzanita to a group of friends who had gathered around us. The first streaks of dawn were brightening the horizon before I slept, but we had a long day of rest ahead.

The following night darkness again obscured our movements, and we took the straight route to Eshom Valley.

"I will leave you there," I had remarked to the Chief, "and you must return to Camp Manzanita. I am going on to San Francisco."

Altho we had gone over every detail of my trip before we left the stronghold, now that the moment of parting was near the Chief blustered out, "Morrell, this is madness. It is not safe. Let us call it off and wait for Spring, then go instead to Mexico! There we are both at home and know the country like a map. Besides we have friends there. Once in the mountains of Chihuahua, we can laugh at the power of the 'Octopus'."

Thinking that he had persuaded me, he rattled on. "The whole State knows you now, and San Francisco is in turmoil over the County Jail holdup. Yesterday you saw the papers our friends had saved, filled with descriptions of you. Besides, the blood-money men think we have fled the mountains and it is only natural they will watch San Francisco. Don't make the trip now. It's bad business," my partner concluded.

Ignoring his plea, I called attention to the fact that the last letter to San Francisco had definitely arranged for a meeting. "You know I must not disappoint our friends. The plans for our departure are already under way, and it is necessary that I go there to complete the final program."

The Chief became silent, realizing that nothing could now move me from my purpose and we trudged along until almost in Eshom Valley. We heard the sound of horses' hoofs, and stepped off the road to wait.

A man drove up to us. He quickly leaped to the ground and placed the bridal rein in my hands with scarcely a word lest someone might be lurking near.

"Don't take any chances during my absence," I reminded the Chief in a whisper, bounding into the saddle. "Go back to Camp and rest easy until I return." The old man bowed his head slightly.

With a handshake I rode away through the long stretches of the foothills to the plains of the Tulare, where lay the greatest danger of detection. Down from the sweeping slopes, down from the snow and cold to a mild climate and beds of grass and flowers, my horse beat out his pace, crossing meadows and fording streams that were familiar, and by daylight I had reached the outskirts of Visalia and the home of a friend. There I slept and rested until dark. After supper I ventured out on a pilgrimage to the old Chief's home.

The place cast a pall over me. It was in a state of decay, bullet scarred and neglected, battered and torn by invading posses and blood-money men. The family had deserted it and were now scattered. In an effort to re-establish her father's reputation, the eldest daughter over whom the first battle was fought was starring in a play in San Francisco called "The California Outlaws."

It was indeed lonely and I left immediately on my ride across the great Valley of the San Joaquin and thence to Sunflower Valley in the Coast Range Mountains. As the night wore on I regretted having gone to the old homestead. Try how I would I could not cast the shadow of the tragedy from my mind. It made the long journey doubly oppressive. The haunted feeling of the pursued did not leave me until I reached my destination, where food and shelter and a supply of costly clothing awaited me.

I was among friends again. The sensation was so strange and new after the days at Camp Manzanita with only the companionship of the wounded man, that the time sped by too quickly. I was loathe to leave.

Once more the old hunted feeling returned with the urgency of the business ahead. From the home in Sunflower Valley I was driven in a round-about way to the railroad where I boarded a night train for San Francisco, with grips and fashionable clothes suitable to the role I was now playing. I had reached the hotel in safety.

I thought I had slept unduly long. The door rattled slightly as if someone were outside tampering with the lock. I jumped to my feet and, buckling the six shooters around my waist, with rope ready I prepared for a leap through the window.

The sound passed to the next room. It was only the night maid making her rounds. I drew down the curtain and snapped on the lights. It was seven o'clock. Locking my grips and taking a last survey of my general appearance I left my room and strolled leisurely down into the lobby, where I dropped into an easy chair and scanned the evening papers.

The daring exploits of the outlaws were no longer being featured, but on the second page of one of the papers I found an article which caused me much amusement. Tho in San Francisco, the story ran that I was almost trapped on the outskirts of Hanford in Tulare County — that this very day I had shot and nearly killed a local character who had been accused of laying a trap for my capture.

I laughed, feeling assured that they had not yet suspected my presence in San Francisco since harrowing tales were being recounted about my exploits many miles away. I looked at my watch, dropped the paper and sauntered from the hotel, boarding a Market Street Car.

From Seventh, I walked South to Howard Street. Stopping at a restaurant and picking out an unoccupied table, I ordered a meal. A suspicious looking stranger, dark and glowering, seated himself opposite me at the same table.

In the looking glass on the side wall, I could see that he was stealing quick, furtive glances. I prepared for action. He might well have been a detective. My head-price was indeed alluring.

I grasped my gun with the right hand under the table and waited for him to make the next move.

"Good weather we're having, but it looks like rain," he ventured.

I drawled out some reply in monosyllables, on my guard and carefully studying every move and gesture. In another moment he had buried his face in the evening paper, giving his order to the waiter in a rasping impatient voice.

Relieved at this new turn of affairs I relaxed the grip on my six shooter and commenced to devour the food. I was hungry and had a man's appetite. The meal over I edged sideways past the stranger, still alert and ready if he contemplated a surprise move.

Nothing occurring I was soon in the street again and inwardly remarked, "it is dangerous for strangers to become too familiar with a hunted man." I forgot the incident, trying to find numbers in the darkness.

Finally I located the right house. At first there was no response to the bell. Between each ring I paused, waiting and listening for the sound of footsteps. When none came I leaned down and looked through the keyhole. Unquestionably there was someone standing near the door. I rang again. It opened a crack. I gave the name of a certain person, and it opened wider.

The head of a dark squatty man peered out as if to examine me more carefully. I asked again for the man I had come to see, and without saying a word he shook his head in the negative, backing and preparing to close the door in my face. I pulled a shining silver dollar from my pocket holding it up to view along with an envelope.

"Will you deliver this note when the party returns?" I said, almost laughing aloud at the comical expression on his face as he snatched the money first and then the envelope from my hand. He nodded and shut the door without having spoken a word.

I was satisfied with my evening's work and craved adventure, and adventure it was indeed. I was next sitting in the first balcony of the theater where the melodrama called the "California Outlaws" was being played. I had gone there from the house on Howard Street and had worked my way through the lobby filled with people, daring even to run the risk of identification.

A beautiful young lady sat at my right. She was about twenty. Her escort was a dignified elderly gentleman, undoubtedly her father. I studied them carefully and then looked at my neighbor on the left, a tall thin man with a crane-like neck and a large Adam's Apple which danced up and down when he was amused.

Between this comical figure and the girl, I was kept so busy that I lost many of the high lights in outlawry as the play progressed. The cast was a good one for the audience was thoroughly aroused to a high pitch of excitement. Now I was all attention. The jail holdup was in progress.

The beautiful girl at my side gasped occasionally, at times whispering words of admiration for the hero to her father. When I again looked toward the stage the actor who was impersonating me had held up the jailer. Just as he released the old outlaw Chief, throwing her reserve aside the girl impulsively shouted in a voice that could be heard almost above the loud applause, "Oh, daddy, I could kiss that young man! He is my ideal of a real hero!"

I don't know what force impelled me to do it, but without a thought of the danger and consequences, seeing only the drollery in my mad impulse, I looked squarely at the young girl. "Miss, the opportunity is here! You can kiss me right now!"

In all the months of the chase I had never been so reckless.

"How dare you? I have half a mind to have you thrown out of the house," she hissed, wheeling back, hand poised ready to slap me in the face.

Coming to my senses quickly, amazed at what I had done, I slid out past the tall man. My head-price loomed up sobering me as I retreated from the crowded house.

"More than fifteen hundred people in that place, and no doubt most of them would be pleased to have the reward!" The thought sobered me. "What if that very girl should suddenly penetrate the hidden meaning of my remark? Dire results might follow should suspicion center upon me from those idle words. San Francisco would become the center of an exciting search for the youngest member of the California Outlaws."

Walking in the cool night air I realized this incident might have cost me my liberty and even my life. I vowed from then on to attend strictly to the business which brought me to San Francisco, not daring to call even upon the Chief's daughter,— a meeting which I had looked forward to since the night I left Camp Manzanita.

The experience had sobered me. Once more I was the shrewd, wary outlaw, a hunted man with a price upon my head. From that moment I worked seriously during the rest of my days in San Francisco, shrouding all of my movements in secrecy until I had everything accomplished, including the chartering of a three masted steam schooner for a two year's cruise covering the ports of the South Sea Islands and the Coast of Australia. Final arrangements were made to have the boat taken down to the Santa Barbara Channel, there to lay off shore waiting for our arrival from the Sierra Nevada Mountains.

I left the overland train at Goshen, and instead of taking the customary Visalia local I disappeared at the junction as if the darkness had consumed me. A few hours later I was on a saddle horse, riding over the rough roads to the foothills.

I sounded the signal from one of the blind trails at Camp Manzanita about a week later. No reply came. I anxiously repeated the signal. Could it be possible the old Chief might have been captured, perhaps killed! Might the posse be in possession of the Camp, biding my return? I would not approach without the signal.

A long time passed. Then I heard a low sound,— his welcoming answer to my night call. I plunged up the blind trail, and bolted through the door. The Chief gave me a hearty greeting. "You have come at last," he sighed.

"Yes, I am here. Is everything all right?" I asked in alarm, noticing that my companion looked haggard and worn,— another evidence that he was not the man of days gone by. The silence and loneliness of the cabin had weighed heavily upon him. Now he began to pull himself together, inquiring eagerly regarding my trip to San Francisco, and becoming visibly happy as I explained that the boat would be waiting in the Santa Barbara Channel.

Enthusiastically I mapped our future. "We can safely slip out of the mountains," I said. "We'll make our getaway to foreign lands by boat, bidding 'good-bye' forever to Camp Manzanita in the Sierra Nevada Mountains, and last, but by no means least, to the 'Octopus.' Then we can start life all over with a fair chance to make good."

While chatting, I prepared a light meal, and when we had eaten and cleared away everything I opened out a map of Australia upon the large table. We discussed many points regarding the proposed journey, and becoming happy and carefree again, the Chief congratulated me upon my success.

"You have gone to San Francisco and returned. You passed safely through the mountains and Visalia which are infested with man-hunters. Having accomplished this I know you can successfully carry out the escape. Once on the wide Pacific Ocean we will forget the hardships of the Tulare Mountains, and man-hunters and blood-money men will become a thing of the past." The Chief was himself agaiu. His words had fire and snap to them, and happy, we both retired, I to a well earned sleep.

Again camp life assumed its old monotonies, and the bear and cat played on, frolicking away their winter time. We two outlaws partook of the same spirit of abandon, fresh hope giving us a new interest in living. Without the slightest apprehension, bright and early one morning we made a foraging trip into the outside world, far from the old cabin with its blind trails and sheltering manzanita.

CHAPTER XVI

THE FIGHT AT SLICK ROCK.

Breaking out of the chaparral and entering a little clearing at the rear of a ranch house far down in the foothills from our stamping ground, the Chief and I, heavily armed, stood in the shade of a barn. We were waiting for the answer to a low whistle which I had just given, a signal call well known to all the mountain ranch people who were our sworn friends.

There was no response. I gave the call a second time. In a moment a large black and tan dog, one of the species that has made this region of the Sierras famous, poked his nose inquiringly around the corner of the barn. He sniffed suspiciously as if to say, "Well, what is your business?"

The Chief spoke to the dog. "Go back to the house and tell your master friends are here." He used the master's name, and the dog stepped clear from the corner of the barn, without the least show of fear walking up and nosing us both. Then he turned and ran to the house.

In a few more minutes a young man about twenty, the son of the rancher, came running toward the barn. "Hello, Mr. Evans, how do you do?" he exclaimed, extending his hand. "The kids were fussing in the house and we did not hear your call. Dad went down to Visalia Saturday and we are expecting him to drive in most any time now. Ma is expecting you and has 'second breakfast waiting.' We all sure will be glad to have you. Ma says some other ranch folks from over Sawyer Canyon way are to drop in here on their way back from Sunday meeting. They all want to see you and Mister Morrell. Everybody thought you had left the country without a chance to say 'Good-bye'."

Here he was interrupted in his voluble greeting by a bunch of tow-headed kids who made a united drive upon the bandit Chief. He was their God and hero. They clamored about him like a band of wild Indians. The Chief was evidently touched. Tears moistened his cheeks. He was thinking of his own children, his boys and girls, and the happy home now broken up forever. It was the one tender spot in the composition of this man of iron. He could close his mind to every appeal. He was obdurate and relentless to his enemies, except where this chord of human sympathy would be touched through thought of wife and children.

Of many such instances, one stands out strongly in my mind. It was in the early part of the hunt. A noted Pinkerton detective, now a man up in years, had been sent into the mountains to play a lone hand at the game of bringing down the outlaws. He was utterly without fear. A long record in the Civil War as a Secret Service Agent had stamped him as one who bore a charmed life.

Our friends, the ranch people of the mountains, spotted him on his first appearance. He carried a pack on his back and was alone except for the company of a white bull dog that stalked at his heels. The mountain people quickly dubbed him "the man with the white dog."

The reports which came to us regarding his movements and actions at last warranted attention. The old outlaw Chief quickly sensed danger. There was nothing of the blood-money hunter's attitude and boisterousness about this silent character. He became a sinister menace, just the kind made to order for trail pot-shotting.

Late one afternoon "the man with the dog" was trudging along a mountain road. The Chief and the younger outlaw Sontag stepped from behind a clump of bushes with the command to halt.

He instantly shot his hands above his head. Sontag relieved him of his pack. A careful search of his clothes revealed no damaging evidence. He did not carry even a

THE TWENTY-FIFTH MAN 181

pistol, and stood motionless, never changing a muscle of his face while the younger outlaw made ready to open his pack.

Head erect, looking straight up the road, he did not deign to offer the least defense when the now enraged outlaw flashed a Wells Fargo sawed off shot gun before him, damning evidence of his true role — a Wells Fargo Man and a Pinkerton. In war the fate of a spy is death. The Chief as an old soldier, knew what to do.

He fairly blazed in anger. "I have some sympathy for professional man-killers, blood-money hunters who will take chances and risk their lives openly in pursuit of their game, upstanding men with guns in their hands asking neither fear nor favor from their quarry when caught in their own trap," he hissed. "But you!—You are the scum of the earth. You are a jackal that creeps and slouches in the wake of the kill."

"Get down on your knees, you damned coward, and make one prayer. Let it be a real one because it is going to be your last," commanded the Chief.

The two outlaws stepped to one side, and held a whispered conversation. There was not one chance in a million for the captured Pinkerton. The Wells Fargo sawed off shotgun had sealed his fate. Sontag, the younger outlaw, drew his Colts forty-five and stepped within easy range.

"Wait a moment," called the Chief. "I am a soldier and even a spy has rights which must be respected."

He ordered him to stand up, and the stranger arose from his kneeling position, face ashen white.

"Have you a last message?" asked the old outlaw. "Is there any one that you want notified of your death? It will be the only evidence left of your existence. Before morning the timber wolves will have devoured everything of you, even to the heels of your boots."

"I do not know you, but I take it that you are Chris Evans, the bandit." The Pinkerton was speaking now.

"You mentioned that you were a soldier. A soldier salutes you, a soldier of the Civil War. As a soldier my first instructions were blind obedience to orders. I have never been found guilty of breaking that ironclad rule of war. True, I am a Wells Fargo Man, a Pinkerton as you say, but I am here in these mountains in obedience to orders, just as I went through the Civil War, in blind obedience to orders."

"It is not true that I am 'a jackal skulking in the wake of the kill.' My orders were to come into these mountains and bring about your capture, alive if possible, dead if necessary. It is not true that I aimed to shoot you down in cold blood. Never in my life have I shot a human being in the back. I am getting to be an old man and money rewards would not tempt me now to do that which I have never done in all my life."

"You have taken me redhanded all right. Little would it profit for me to defend myself on the score that I had plans slowly working out which could prove that I did not contemplate your ruthless slaying."

The Chief was studying him.

"I would not offer this in the hope of gaining your mercy," he continued. "If my life is the forfeit, well and good. It will be lost in the line of duty. That is all. Yes! I have one request. I want to write a message and I ask you as an old soldier to see that it is delivered."

The Chief nodded his head slowly, remarking, "your message will be delivered, have no fear."

The old Pinkerton drew a letter pad from an inside pocket of his coat and wrote swiftly with pencil, not exhibiting so much as the tremor of a hand. With bowed head he gave it to the Chief who read it slowly,— a last message to his wife and family, closing with the words, "My time has come. I die with thoughts of you, my loved ones."

That message saved his life. The two bandits again stepped a few paces down the road. The man stood upright and motionless still waiting.

"I can't bring myself to do it, John. It would be different if he whined for mercy. He is brave to the core and besides he has a wife and loved ones. Damn it, man, where is your heart?" The Chief was plainly agitated. "This is bad business and not the work of brave men. You are brave to a fault but your anger blinds you to the real spirit that is in you."

The younger man was furious, and muttering something about when the tables would be turned, remarked, "Mercy does not belong to the code of Pinkertons. But all right! All right! Have your way!" he concluded. "'He who fights and runs away lives to fight another day!' This old codger is laughing up his sleeve at you. There are many more Wells Fargo sawed off shotguns than this one. He will have another on the up stage and his next experience may be his answer by way of pot-shotting you from a trail," he chuckled.

The younger outlaw turned on his heel and walked down the road, leaving his Chief alone to settle the difficulty with the Pinkerton captive as best he might. This he did in his usual decisive manner. Picking up the sawed off shotgun, the Pinkerton Man's symbol of destruction, the old bandit mumbled something incoherently about tyrants, autocrats, and the "Octopus," then turned and smashed it against a rock on the side of the road. That done he flung the broken weapon down over the lower mountain into a hollow ravine filled with dense chaparral.

After eyeing the silent rigid figure the Chief spoke in a well controlled voice. "I noticed you had a small bible in your pocket. Put your hand down and produce that book."

The man did as directed.

"With that bible in your right hand swear to God that you will leave these mountains the moment you are released and swear that you will never again return, or in any way aid or directly assist in the attempted capture of us men. Swear to that," said the Chief, "and you will be free to go your way."

"The man with the white dog" made a pivot move to the right and clicked his heels. Hand raised in military salute, he held the position for a moment, then placed the little pocket bible to his lips and kissed it. "I swear to my God on the bible that I will faithfully keep this oath."

With that he extended his right hand toward the bandit leader.

The Chief eyed him questioningly for a moment. He hesitated, then stepped forward and clasped the out-stretched hand. They were enemies no longer.

The tragedy had been averted. Two outstanding high lights had saved the Pinkerton from death, the touching farewell message to loved ones and the man's iron determined grit. Coupled to that, he was an old soldier. The stern bandit could not withhold mercy.

When the thought of family, a child perhaps, would change his whole attitude toward 'a man-stalker out to kill him, it is little wonder that this group of 'kids' at Slick Rock could so completely take possession of him. The mother of the ranch was calling and we entered the house. The Chief was almost carried along bodily.

It was Sunday morning and, as the boy had said, "second breakfast" was all ready and steaming on the table. We had come a long way from Camp Manzanita and were hungry, but this was a meal I never ate.

There were two strangers in a mountain cart on the brow of the hill. One of them stepped out and stood talking to his partner. Levelling my field glass, I recognized both men. The one in the cart was a murderer awaiting trial from Fresno, a well known dead shot, released on probation from the County Jail under agreement, it was said, with County and Railroad Officials that he would bring the quarry back with him. This meant death.

I recalled that a great deal of indignation had been aroused over the cowardly pact between "a criminal murderer and officers of the law," and it was common gossip all over the San Joaquin Valley that prominent citizens had hoped the bandits would "send him down out of the mountains to town in a dead wagon."

The man standing in the road was a fitting crony, a braggart who had created cheap notoriety for himself by issuing challenges to fight me single handed upon our first meeting, regardless of time or place. He took great trouble to advertise this, posting notices on trees, barns, and in every conspicuous location he chanced to pass, until it became a joke throughout the region of the Tulare Mountains.

I forgot the savory food. The very devil boiled in me as I glued the field glass to my eyes and watched the movements of these two human vipers. The game was now assuming a new meaning. At last it was life for life, and I determined that mine should be sold dearly.

For the first time in my career the thought of man-killing was in my heart. I was losing all bounds of restraint at the sight of this monster, a red handed slayer in the guise of a peace officer. He was out to ransom his cowardly life at the cost of mine,— that man who now sat quietly in his mountain cart.

His pal I regarded with contempt only. I resolved to give him a lesson that would terminate his cheap bravado for all time. Passing the field glass to the Chief I casually remarked that the two on the brow of the hill were the very men with whom we should welcome an encounter. I had already adjusted my rifle, and was preparing to charge from the ranch house when the Chief urged me to be careful. He remarked that in all likelihood they were only two innocent mountain men, and that if I made a blunder it might mean a disturbance and possibly "bad blood" among our friends.

I was well aware that my partner had recognized the men and was concerned only in my safety, so ignoring his ruse and disregarding the pleas of our friends, I sprang through the doorway.

The ranch house was in a basin. Above it the road, at times hidden from view by manzanita and chaparral, skirted down along the side of the ridge. It flattened out and ran horizontally for a short distance on Slick Rock, where a stream of water crossed it, and on about fifty yards, coming abruptly to a sharp angle and being lost to view where another ridge overlapped.

The man in the cart started down the road as I stepped from the ranch house. His pal, who had climbed out on the brow of the hill jumped across the line fence and was ambling slowly toward a pile of rock thickly covered with manzanita.

I was now at the corral gate. Our friends had tumbled out of the house in excitement over the approaching gunplay. The Chief called after me to be careful, that if I attempted to go up the mountain toward the road the man in the cart would have me at his mercy. I had no intention of falling into the trap, my plan of battle having matured quickly.

For an instant the cart was out of sight, then appeared again coming down the ridge at a lively clip. My sharp whistle rang out as a challenge.

The man in the cart did not stop, nor did he apparently look, but it was plain that nothing had escaped him. He intended to keep going this time. It was evident that this was not his style of fighting, tho on the surface he had an advantage over me.

I planted a rifle shot across the horse's head. It leaped and bounded, again being hidden from view by a sheltering patch of manzanita. He made no effort to stop. Rather, taking advantage of the momentary concealment, this crafty man-killer stood upright in his cart, lashing the frightened horse to greater speed with the end of the lines.

There was no longer occasion to doubt his identity, and I raced up the hill to the road, gaining the top in time to see him go dashing down toward Slick Rock, still standing and excitedly beating the horse. He was far below me before I reached the road.

In a kneeling position, I took aim firing my first shot as the cart careened through the stream. Luck, blind luck was on the side of the man-killer. The lunge of the cart spoiled my aim tho it was a close call, the forty-five ninety barely clipping his spine.

My second shot was a long drawn bead and a last chance. I fired high, cutting the top of his hat just as the horse plunged through the gap. He was lost to sight. That part of the battle was ended.

I turned my attention to the self-advertised gunfighter. He stood rooted to the brow of the hill, gaping in open eyed amazement at the little panorama of war enacted below him. At the top of my voice I bellowed that it was his turn now, and charged up through the broken field of the ranch, scarcely pausing to hear the warning of the Chief as he called, "Look out there Morrell. You are poking at a hornet's nest. That fellow will potshot you from his rocky barrier."

The "dualist" was watching me with a rifle hanging loosely in the crotch of his arm. Believing that I was going to charge straight up, he moved back into the shelter of the rocks and manzanita. This was just what I wanted, and about fifty yards from the top, I crouched down, skirting rapidly in a parallel direction to the left under the base of the hill out of view and away from the range of his rifle.

Here I rested safely, gaining a second wind before finishing my man-stalking game. I signaled to the Chief who stood down near the corral where he could watch the man in the rocks above. His hand wave told me the way was clear, and I charged parallel in a flanking movement to cut off his escape, from a point where he least expected it.

The sun was shining brightly. Something flashed into my eyes. It was a reflection from his rifle as he moved quickly. The "bad man" was gone. He had retreated at least three hundred yards, and was still on the run down the other side of the mountain toward the creek. He was now plunging through it. I fired, dashing the water into his face, and like a frightened jackrabbit he stopped and looked back over his shoulder.

"How about your challenge, you dirty man-killer?" I shouted.

He did not wait to hear more, but ran on.

Now the spirit of the chase was in my blood. I resolved to give him a taste of real gunfighting and prove him the coward that his boasting deserved. In scurrying from the ranch house, I had agreed to meet the Chief at the home of friends near Sulphur Springs if anything happened to separate us, so there was nothing to interfere, this bright Sunday morning, with one of the most laughable man-chases in the history of the Sierras.

He was zigzagging, now running wildly, clearly at a loss which way to go. He had his choice, straight across the range, up it, or down it. At last he took the latter, plunging down through thickets of manzanita, with every little while a bullet from my long ranged Winchester screeching a strange sound to his ears as it whizzed by.

I played with him, teased and tired him, drove him over rocks and rough ground and through dense thickets of scratching manzanita and chaparral. Behind, and all the time just a little above him I could see every move. Hour after hour he worked his way down the brushy mountainside heading toward the stage station at Dunlap and dodging in and out to avoid the spattering lead which hit about him.

My fire frustrated his every attempt to hide under the clumps of bush for rest. The man was wild-eyed, panting for breath. He had cast away his rifle. All caution was gone. Heedless of the tearing manzanita he now plunged head foremost through the thickets, his pace quickened every little while by more random shots.

Climbing to a high ledge of rock where I could overlook the entire mountainside below me, I took up an easy position to rest and watch the antics of my frightened game. My ammunition was nearly gone, but I still had enough left to use for a parting salute.

These last I directed with careful aim, striving to knock him over by a leg shot, but he was ever a moving target and hard to hit. The sun was setting and darkness would soon put an end to the struggle. I ceased firing and watched him as he disappeared far down the mountain and out of sight.

After separating from the gunman I had pursued all day, I found that I was very tired, with throat and mouth parched, and hands and face scratched. I left my resting place to skirt across the range toward Sulphur Springs. Near the place agreed upon to meet the Chief, I dropped down and took a long drink from a little stream. Refreshed by the cool water I was able to go on at a quickened pace.

In another hour I opened the ranch house door. Inside the room was well lighted and I saw the Chief with some friends. A look of relief showed on their faces as I entered. They had waited all day and feared for my safety.

All stood up to greet me. Some were concerned, for I did look like a man seriously wounded. My face was smeared with dried blood from scraping and cuts, my clothes were torn, and I was exhausted.

Sympathetically the Chief urged that I have my wounds dressed and go to bed.

"Let me wash. There is nothing wrong. Go to the table yourselves and I will join you in a few minutes to prove that I can eat my share of that chicken dinner," I declared.

They had promised it, and had waited all day for my arrival. I did not disappoint them either, for I had been on a long chase without any food since the night before. During the meal I related the story of the bloodless battle, which caused roars of laughter. It was later confirmed when a mountain man drove up to the house, stopping long enough to tell how he had passed one of the man-hunters busily washing his clothes and bathing in a creek.

It was called "The Battle of Slick Rock," and a lurid story came out in the metropolitan press. It recounted the glorious exploits of brave peace officers in a battle with the bandits which lasted all afternoon, stressing the point that they did not retreat until out of ammunition. The word came from the posse that one of the outlaws was badly wounded. It closed with a glowing account of the bravery of the gunmen.

Most important to us was the fact that the man-hunt had started again with renewed vigor. After weary weeks which filled the posses with doubts and misgivings, we were definitely located. Once more the mountains swarmed with blood-money men, and time after time we barely escaped with our lives until people began to say that we wore armor and if not, then miracles were at work.

The "Tiger" was calling. "Let me interrupt you for just a moment, and this time don't laugh at me, because I am serious. On the level, Ed., did the old 'man with the white dog,' the Pinkerton detective, keep his oath?"

"That fellow Sontag was a man after my own heart. He had the right idea. Dead Pinkertons are the only kind that ever kept their word, to my way of thinking," he gibed.

All detectives were an anathema to the "Tiger," and I understood the drift of his remarks. "Well, Jake," I tapped, "I'm sorry to disappoint you. 'The man with the white dog,' the Pinkerton, proved as good as his oath. Sontag was wrong and the Chief was right. He left the mountains and never returned. More, I understood that he even resigned from his work as a detective. The blow was too much for his pride to endure."

The "Tiger" was in his old humorous mood again. "Oh well, Ed., I'm not going to question your word. I suppose there might be at least one exception to the common rule even with detectives, but I never heard of one until now. Go on with the story and I promise not to interrupt."

CHAPTER XVII

A MINER'S CABIN AT SULPHUR SPRINGS.

We were on our way back to Camp Manzanita after my strange encounter with the two gunmen. We had stayed all night with our "host of the chicken dinner" and had left early in the morning with the firm intention of making straight for our stronghold to get under cover before the drive of the gunmen. It was sure to follow since we were once more definitely located in a region where they had never expected us to be.

Acting on a sudden whim the Chief had suggested that we detour in order that he might pay a visit to his old friend, a miner, a little way down the canyon from Sulphur Springs. I mildly objected, pointing out that we needed every hour of daylight to cover the distance to camp from where we were.

"It is rough country," I said, "and we should not lose any time crossing the range to Dry Creek."

"Oh that's all right, Morrell," he responded, "I can go through this part of the mountains with my eyes shut. Daylight or dark means little to me. Besides, I want to see my friend Jim, the miner, before we leave the country. I want to repay a kindness that he did for me in the beginning of the man-hunt. He saved my life at the risk of his own. I couldn't leave the mountains without bidding him 'good-bye'."

I forgot my opposition when I witnessed the greeting between them. The miner, now up in years, was standing at the door watching us approach, two men heavily armed and apparently strangers. The Chief stopped before him. His face lit up with a smile.

"Chris!" he exclaimed.

"Jim!" returned the bandit.

In another moment the old miner had affectionately placed his arms about my partner, excitedly shouting, "By the almighty wildcats, come in, come in! This is the happiest moment of my life. I thought you were thousands of miles from here. You know, Chris, I am getting to be an old man. Only last week I finished digging my grave over on that little knoll. I love these mountains and I want to rest here when I die."

"They told me you had lit out for Mexico, and I couldn't blame you. I know what you have been through in your feud with that damned 'Octopus.' It nearly broke my heart when I heard the news. I felt hurt to think you would leave the Sierras without a last farewell with me." He stopped speaking. The Chief was interrupting.

"Jim, Jim, enough of this. You know I could not leave that way. Here, have you forgotten your manners? Why don't you shake hands with Morrell?"

I had stepped inside and was suspiciously eyeing a stranger crumpled up lazily in a chair facing the log fire. Holding Jim's hand, I asked pointedly, "Who is your friend?"

Jerking his head around, the stranger measured me from the toes of my boots to the top of my head. I did not like his face and mentally registered the thought that we would not be friends.

Here the Chief took a hand. "Jim, I thought you were alone, and I did want to have a few hours with you. This man is a stranger to me." There was meaning in his last words.

The old prospector looked foolish for a moment. He was clearly not at ease. "Oh, this fellow is all right. He has been here with me for nearly a week. Helped me out a lot down at the claim," he half apologetically explained. "He is real, and an old timer who knows the mountains from the British Northwest to Yucatan."

As if to cover his confusion under the stern gaze of the Chief, he turned toward me. "I say, Morrell," he bantered, "By Gad, here's a chap that can take your measure. You have been a globe trotter, we all know that."

"See if you can put one over on this fellow. Get up, Mac, damn you," he shouted. "Now here are the two men you wanted to meet."

He felt relieved that he had broken the ice so smoothly, and again glanced at the Chief explaining, "I have told Mac so much about you that he's fairly wild to get acquainted. In fact," lowering his voice he went on, "he told me he'd like to make partners with ye, that he is under cover himself."

The old miner was virgin gold and took every man at his own estimate and Mac, to use a prospector's phrase, evidently assayed well "in the panning."

My suspicions were aroused that the old man was handling "fools' gold" when he continued, "Mac is all right, but he has one fault that I don't like. He drinks too much. Saturday he left to go over to Camp Badger for supplies. He got drunk and forgot about his errand. Just popped in here this morning. Now he has a big head and is crawsick to boot."

Mac was standing in a half upright position against the chair in which he had been sitting, and when the old prospector had finished, sheepishly stuck out his right hand.

Wishing to cut short the old miner's embarrassment I grasped the hand, resolved to play the string out and see what this unusual stranger was planning and why he was here in these mountains at this time.

He stood the first test, answering grip for grip. He was no mean adversary and I calculated that he had clearly deceived the old miner. He was playing a part. I satisfied myself then and there that this man had not been drinking. There was no evidence to warrant the old miner's explanation of his absence since Saturday, and I wondered why this newcomer resorted to lies.

THE TWENTY-FIFTH MAN 195

The Chief made no attempt to acknowledge the meeting, stepping outside instead and motioning for me to follow.

"What do you think of him?" my partner asked curtly.

"What do you think of him?" I countered, using his own words.

I had touched upon a sore spot with the Chief. He abhorred direct questions. But I had him in the door and there was no other alternative.

He began to speculate. "Morrell, if this fellow is all right and old Jim is not deceived in him he is made to order for us. We need a man who is an absolute stranger in these parts. We can use him to do a piece of work right now that will save the possible compromising of some others who are under cover. You are very seldom wrong, Ed. Tell me what you think of him."

My mind had already been made up, but I was fearful that my companion might do something rash if I gave him my conclusions. I wanted to put "Mac," as he called himself, to a real test.

"Oh well, he may be all right," I drawled cautiously, "but he has some of the ear-marks of a Pinkerton. Bide your time. I will get under his armor plate before this day is over. We are creating undue suspicion. Let's get back into the cabin. Then you suggest that you want to chat alone with old Jim, and I will invite him to take a stroll outside with me."

The poor old prospector was plainly nervous when we re-entered, but the Chief instantly switched his demeanor, clapping him on the shoulder and remarking, "I say, Jim, we have only a short time to stay and I want to have a chat with you alone before we say 'good-bye'."

Turning, my partner looked inquiringly toward the man, Mac. He took his cue and, adjusting an old battered hat, stepped outside. I followed.

We walked in silence for nearly half a mile. He was playing a waiting game, bent on making me talk first. I was of the same mood so the duel of silence continued.

I had left my rifle at the cabin. He noted that I had also unstrapped my belt with the two Colts forty-fives, resting in their holsters. This move nonplussed him. I was apparently without weapons, tho not unmindful that he carried a six shooter strapped at his waist. He glanced furtively at my right arm, the hand of which was thrust deeply into my side coat pocket.

To put him off his guard I removed my right hand and casually placed the left one into the other side pocket. This movement did not escape his attention. It had the desired effect, breaking his silence. We were near a steep ravine and had stopped to look down.

"I had pictured you a different man, Morrell," he remarked.

"Is that so? Why?" I countered after a short silence.

"Oh, well," he continued pleasantly. "I thought you were older, a man quite up in years. I formed my conclusion from newspaper descriptions but now I see you are young and," he ventured hesitatingly, "of course you are reckless, otherwise you would not be so damned foolish as to leave your firearms back there and out of reach. I am on the run myself, and I don't propose to be caught off my guard," he volunteered confidentially.

Ignoring the well driven thrust evidently aimed to smoke me out I loosened up and waxed confidential, assuming a mien of well feigned anger over the thought of being stigmatized as a tyro in the role of an outlaw.

"Don't be so damned sure of yourself, stranger," I ejaculated, blustering out heatedly. "It is true I am young in appearance, but I'd like to let you know that I have had some experiences in my young life. You think I am unarmed, which proves to me that you are not so keen as you would like to have me believe."

"See, Mister Mac, I've got you covered right now." I was pantomiming. I wheeled like a flash, both hands thrust deeply into my coat pockets.

Looking down he stared mutely at two short thirty-eight Colts revolvers, barrels extended about an inch through a hole in each pocket.

I had played my trump card and won. Watching his face, I noted a quick transformation. It plainly revealed he thought he had my gauge, and his next words verified that deduction.

"Oh here, Morrell, I didn't mean any harm by what I said. I knew that you were a hunted man with a price on your head and only wanted to put you onto yourself. But I see now that I was mistaken. That is a new wrinkle to me. By God man, this is the first time I ever saw such a line-up. You sure are a walking arsenal, a second 'Billy the Kid,' or I am a liar."

Mr. Mac had the admiration stuff at his finger tips, still he little reckoned with my real calibre. I had been over too many wooden bridges and a few iron ones thrown in for good measure to be fooled by this slick character, and dismissing further blandishments I impatiently waived my hand remarking, "Oh well, I'm glad that you don't take me for a fool. Sit down and tell me something about yourself. You know the Chief and I 'are from Missouri,— we've got to be shown.' Lots of would-be badmen come up here in the mountains wanting to join our band, but very few have ever made good."

"You look like the real thing to me," I continued. "Show us that you are all right, and we'll talk business," and again displaying a growing confidence, I told him that we were about to make a drive for Mexico and were now planning to pull off a last big train robbery before leaving, adding that we wanted one or two more good men to help put the job over.

I had at last played my master stroke. Mr. Mac swallowed hook, line, and sinker. He proved himself a real actor. I sat spellbound as he disclosed a red career in a history of crimes committed against the law along the entire Western Border. He concluded with sinister insinuations that he had not only "killed his man but many men."

This was acting indeed and I was amused to see that he really thought he was putting it over. I clinched our little by-play, exclaiming, "Mac, you'll do. Here is my hand. Consider yourself one of us. Shake!"

He was satisfied that I was utterly his dupe. We were friends. That is, he thought I was, but time would tell. I determined to put this blustering pretended badman to an immediate test. When we stood up to move away from where we had been sitting, and while he was facing me with his back toward the West, my eye had caught the flash of the sun on a rifle barrel not more than a mile back, and just over the top of a ridge.

I kept my man's attention distracted while furtively studying this new situation. There were at least forty or fifty men in the posse trooping over and down the ridge. They were following hot upon the trail that we had just made in coming to old Jim's cabin. No further time could now be lost. It looked like "Hell was going to pop" this day.

With a great show of confidence I shouted, "Come on, Mac! Let's get back to the cabin. I want you and the Chief to become acquainted. He will be tickled to death when he finds that you are a real man, one of our own sort and one hundred percent."

Locking arms I tugged him quickly down the trail to old Jim's cabin. The two men were indulging in a confidential chat which was interrupted by our unexpected return. "Here, Chief, stand up and meet a real man" I exclaimed. "Old Jim, our friend, certainly deserves credit. Mac has been over the coals and wants to join us. I haven't time now to tell you all, but he has come clean with me. He's the very man we've been looking for." I gave my partner a glance inferring that he be on his guard. It meant that our new acquaintance was a mountain spotter and a dangerous one.

The Chief caught the drift of my pantomime easily falling into his part. He countered with hand outstretched to the new member of our band, smoothly remarking, "I'm sure glad to hear what Morrell tells me. This shake means that you are one of us."

Old Jim, the miner, was now on his feet clapping the backs of both men as he loudly declared, "Damn it, Chris, I am happy the way things have turned out. I was afraid you and Morrell might think I took too much for granted in bringing about this meeting and pushing Mac upon you, but I know a man when I see him and no yellow hearted galloot ever fooled old Jim, the Miner."

While the three men were talking, entirely unaware of me, I had buckled on my belt and six shooters and carefully examined my rifle in preparation for quick action. This done, I curtly commanded, "there is no more time for conversation. Just get a move on yourselves!"

"What is up?" demanded the Chief, puzzled.

My next look answered his question. I was now working on code. His alert eye was reading my signs. In plain language they meant, "The gunmen are already on our trail. They will surround this cabin within ten minutes."

That was enough for the wily Chief and without showing the slightest trace of excitement he drawled, "you are right, Morrell, we have overstayed our time. We have wasted the day, and night will soon be upon us."

"Jim," he continued, "won't you come a pace with me?" Rifle in hand he stepped out ahead with the old miner and walked swiftly down the trail toward Sulphur Springs.

Mac, our new partner, was clearly out of the running, well aware that something strange had transpired during the last few minutes in the cabin, but unable to fathom its import. He had tried to read my face while I signaled the warning to the old bandit leader, but it was too much for him. Manifestly this Pinkerton had met his match, and not wishing to give him further time to form a counter plan of action I hurriedly suggested, "Come on Mac, let's get out of here. Where is your rifle?"

He mechanically walked over to one corner and picked up a brand new gun. He mumbled something under his breath as if registering a mild protest at being so suddenly taken off his feet, and we left the cabin together. My partner and old Jim, the miner, had already crossed Sulphur Springs and were climbing the ridge on the other side.

Just as we joined them I glanced over my shoulder to the cabin which nestled below us on a little flat the other side of Sulphur Springs.

The sight startled me at first. Gunmen, a small army of them, were swarming out onto the flat, getting ready to form a death circle around old Jim's place. I gave a low warning whistle. To the Chief it meant, "Get ready!"

Then I crouched down, pointing toward Sulphur Springs and the flat beyond. My reason for the sudden departure was now plain. Old Jim and the startled Mac were a picture to behold as they watched the strange doings below them.

Rifles poised to shoot, the posse filed Indian fashion, slowly closing a circle from the rear, out of sight of the door. Not a word was uttered until the Chief broke the silence. He was speaking to Jim, his friend. It was a few hurried words of farewell, and then he took command.

"Go back to your cabin as quickly as possible. Go as if coming from work at your claim," he told the old miner.

"Be discrete, Jim. Don't say or do anything rash. They might cause you lots of trouble."

While this parting was going on I had been watching Mac. He was lying flat down on the ridge drinking in the scene below him. His face was ashen. This Pinkerton was indeed between two fires. How could he ever prove to the posse that he was one of them after the battle started? Again, how could he continue to play the part of a badman under the scrutiny of his two desperate confederates, outlaws, men with prices on their heads? The least show of "the white feather" and his life would be the forfeit.

My next move startled him out of all semblance of composure. It was as if I had been reading his very soul, an answer to his unspoken words.

"Chief," I said, "you have but one eye and one arm. This makes you now only half a man. Besides you are getting old, and if we are compelled to make a quick retreat the mountain would knock the life out of you before you could reach the other side."

Ignoring the quaking Mac I went on. "It's a Hell of a note! After all the experiences of the past these gunmen don't exhibit the slightest fear of us outlaws. They have forgotten Jim Young's Cabin. They have forgotten Stone Corral. All that means nothing to this new band of 'fire eaters.' Today they are out for scalps and blood-money. Well, we will give them a run for both, Chief. What say you?" I looked at him meaningly.

"You know I am a dead shot. Mac tells me he has been under fire himself and that he also is a dead shot. Now here's what I propose. Chief, you slowly work your way up the ridge. Be sure to keep out of sight while you are going. Sit down on the top and take it easy while you wait for us. Mac and I will crawl back down until we are within easy range of the posse."

"See, they are breaking up," I added. "Now they are talking to old Jim." I was watching them through my glass.

"Big Bill Smith appears to be brow-beating the old man. He is shaking his fist in his face," I laughed.

"I say, Chris, old Jim is fighting back too. The damned old fool has forgotten your orders. They'll surely take him down to jail if he keeps on. Now he's walking to his cabin with two of the leaders. The rest of the posse are picking up our trail. They'll bunch down at Sulphur Springs."

"Now, Mac, get ready," I commanded. "Grab the Chief's shotgun, and let's go down the trail. We'll open the battle with a belch of buckshot, repeat the dose and then turn on the rifles. We can easily account for a half dozen of them and maybe more while we are retreating back up the mountain. Safeguard your rifle ammunition. Stop and take deliberate aim each time. 'A shell a man' must be our motto. I'll prove to you that I am more than a 'kid!' Come on now, and show me what you can do!"

It was the last straw. Caution thrown to the winds he bolted, flinging his rifle on the ground before the Chief and stopping for a moment to plead, "For God's sake, Mister Evans, this is too much for me! Let me get away from here before I am killed. If I hadn't been drinking I would never have made such a mess of things. Drink is my curse, Mr. Evans. Drink is my curse. Please let me go and I promise you before God and man I will never drink another drop for the rest of my life."

"All this damned stuff started in a saloon down in Visalia. I was working at Miller and Lux's Ranch and had saved up a couple of hundred dollars. I got a lay off to come into Visalia to buy some clothes, and instead went on a drunk. When I get loaded up I imagine I am a bad-man. They were talking about you men and I made a boast that I would like to join you. Some fellow gave me a note to old Jim, the Miner. He said, 'Go see that man. He is a friend of Evans and you will have no trouble in joining the band.' I went out and bought a new rifle, a six shooter, and ammunition and here I am between the devil and the dark sea," he concluded. "I am no fighter, never was, and never will be, and if you don't let me go before the battle commences this day's foolery will cost me my life."

Of course the Chief was all unmindful of the part this slick Pinkerton was playing. He had not the opportunity to study him that I had while away from the cabin up the trail where I had discovered the posse trooping down upon us. I little wondered at him as he impatiently waved his hand in an attitude of disgust, curtly commanding Mac to go out of his presence.

"Get up the trail and away from here as quick as Hell will let you, and mind that you don't attract those gunmen down below, else I will deal with you as you deserve." Mumbling something about "cowards and would-be desperados," he turned and adjusted the field glass to his one eye to examine the group of gunmen down near Sulphur Springs.

The shrewd Pinkerton, Mac, instantly moved over the brow of the ridge out of sight of the posse, taking advantage of the momentary deception that he had practiced upon the Chief. He ignored me, avoiding my direct gaze and levelled rifle, until he heard my low warning command, "Lie down flat on the ground where you are, and don't move until I am ready to deal with you. Unless I change my mind in the next ten minutes I am going to use you as a breastwork while I fight that posse down below. If you were a real man I could overlook the fact that you are a Pinkerton. You are not only a detective but you are yellow to the core."

Groveling on his stomach, face white with fear he moaned, "Oh God, Morrell, surely you would not kill a man in cold blood. I am no detective, and if you kill me you'll have the blood of an innocent man on your soul."

"Shut up, damn you!" bellowed the Chief, lowering his field glass.

"I say, Morrell," he looked at me impatiently, "what is all this about? Why are you wasting your time with that damned skunk? What is the matter with you anyhow? The first thing you know we will be surrounded in a ring of fire. Surely you do not aim to go down there and face this army of gunmen. There is not one chance in a million. Besides, have you forgotten the ship in the Santa Barbara Channel?" He lowered his voice so the Pinkerton could not hear the last remark, raising it immediately to ejaculate.

"You started this mess on Sunday morning by your escapade at Slick Rock. You have brought down every gunman in the mountains upon us, and instead of escaping at once from here to throw them off our track, you are wasting precious moments which may cost us our lives. What do you want to do now, Morrell?" he shouted jumping up rifle in hand. The Chief was riled.

"Why, you know what I will do as well as I know what you must do, and that is, get out of here as soon as possible." I spoke cautiously, fearing to exasperate further the quick tempered old man.

"All right," he grunted. "That's settled. Now for the next move. Dry Creek or Eshom Valley, which is it?"

"Dry Creek, of course. Don't you know that they will have a wide sweep at us if we make a drive toward Eshom? There is no protection whatever in that direction." Cutting short further parley with the Chief now that I had him in the right mood, I stepped quickly toward the crouching Pinkerton, Mac.

Kicking him with the toe of my boot I shouted, "Get up from there you cowardly skulking timber wolf! If it were not for attracting the posse, I'd fill your carcass full of lead. It is such as you that hound hunted men to murder. Walk out there ahead of me, and if you attempt to bolt I'll stop you quick enough."

The Chief interrupted further talk, grasping me by the arm and speaking calmly, "Oh Hell, Morrell, can't you see that bonehead is harmless? You are fooling away precious time. Let him get out of here as quick as possible. He has had the scare of his life. It will be a lesson that he won't forget."

"What makes you think he is a detective?" he quizzed.

I did not answer the question. We were now topping the range ready to drop into Dry Creek Valley out of sight of the posse. Cutting onto an old corduroy road I ordered the Pinkerton to halt. He stopped and elevated his hands. Cold perspiration from the heavy pace we had set dripped from his forehead. His eyes were bloodshot. He was terror stricken, altogether presenting a miserable spectacle. Perhaps he thought his execution time had come.

Resting the rifle in the crotch of my left arm, with my right hand I jerked loose a six shooter, forty-five Colt. Aiming it straight at his heart I hissed, "Mr. Mac, you're a Pinkerton, damn you. I had your measure from the moment old Jim, the miner, tried to alibi for your absence on Saturday on the score that you were a drunken loon. I know where you were between Saturday and today. You were over at Camp Badger telephoning a confidential report to your boss, and you were there on Sunday when the message was phoned about our fight at Slick Rock."

"But you weren't drunk enough to tell old Jim the news you heard about that battle. You had a reason, Mac," I went on, ignoring the Chief, who was now all attention. "You thought you were dealing in a streak of good luck when we two men popped in at Jim's, especially when you discovered that the Chief's partner was young and reckless. You played your part in the cabin well, Mac," I pressed on. "You managed to cover up your real true character from the Chief here," I inclined my head toward him. "But the Chief did not witness the transformation when you and I left the cabin."

"You're a fine actor, Mac," I drawled, "but I had you puzzled and guessing some when I did not bring my rifle and six shooters along. Oh yes, I know you took me for a tyro all right, but as smart as you are, you fell into my trap. That was a good tale you spun about your career of outlawry, and you thought you put it over, hook, line and sinker."

"Mac, you may be a well trained Pinkerton, but Pinkertons are as helpless as babes in these mountains, because they haven't the Indian eye trained to pick up approaching gunmen. You did not get onto my play when I picked up the posse, and were fooled when I rushed you back to the cabin. Now, you know the story."

"You are my prisoner and at my mercy!"

"Chief," I turned, "this fellow is dangerous. He is the type of villain who would not hesitate to shoot a man in the back, kill in cold blood; and I have half a mind to drop him here in his tracks." The Chief was a quick man. Action was instant with him.

"Morrell, the posse are already topping the hill. If you do any reckless shooting here they will locate our position. Either let this man go now or bring him along until we are out of range. I will not delay any further." He brushed past and was soon trudging up the road.

The Chief had left me in a delicate position, because if I released the Pinkerton there he would join the searching gunmen within an hour. To avoid this I decided to drive him toward Eshom Valley, and before discharging him I sent home my concluding warning.

I want you to go right into Eshom Valley. Just as soon as you do this, leave these mountains at once. If you are reckless and still remain then do it at your peril, for, as God Almighty lets me live I swear I will get you within a week. I will feed your rotten body to the first band of skulking coyotes."

THE TWENTY-FIFTH MAN

"Now go, and keep going straight ahead of me until you strike the brow of the hill over there. Then see to it that you hike for Eshom Valley and do just as I have told you." Giving him a poke with the barrel of my rifle, I started him on a double quick dog trot for the jutting brow of the mountain beyond.

The Pinkerton was still going fast as I watched him out of sight from the top of the mountain overlooking Eshom Valley. That was nearly an hour later. I had enjoyed the discomfiture of the shrewd man-spotter and would have indulged in a lot of fun at his expense had time permitted, but the posse, a small army of gunmen, were spreading fan-shape all over the ranges.

I dared not risk longer delay. The Chief was down somewhere in the basin of Dry Creek. I must find him before dark. In a little while I came out again on the old corduroy road, intending to go to a ranch house where we always received supplies, ammunition, and mail.

This old road lay parallel to the regular stage road, tho some distance away. I heard whistling, and darted behind a clump of bushes. Then I recognized one of the boys from the ranch.

I gave a low call.

He stopped and looked around.

I stepped clear from the bushes almost at his feet and asked, "What is the trouble? Are you looking for me?"

"Yes, Mr. Morrell," the boy spoke up. "Ma sent me on a pretense of going to the store at Camp Badger. Our house is surrounded tho we are not supposed to know it. Because of this she felt sure you and Mister Evans were somewhere about. Ma knew I could find you. She told me to stay out until I did and tell you to keep away."

Hurriedly, I ordered the boy to continue to the store at Camp Badger. On second thought I stopped him saying, "Here, take this money and buy whatever things your mother is short of at home. Be sure to carry back plenty of bundles. The posse surrounding your home might get suspicious otherwise. Be cautious, boy, or you may bring trouble to your own door.''

He smiled. ''Don't fear, Mr. Morrell. Ma is too slick fer them man-catchers. She would take my head off if I showed the white feather. Anyhow we boys up here in the mountains hate detectives.''

The boy went on, apparently to carry out his errand, and I don't know why I returned to the corduroy road. I continued along it hoping to meet my partner, not even dreaming that any of the gunmen were in the immediate vicinity.

Evidently the posse which was now surrounding our friend's ranch was large. They had flung out scouting parties all down through the Dry Creek Valley. A short distance behind where I had cut into the old road two were lying in ambush entirely concealed. I strolled on leisurely then paused for a moment.

One of them saw me just ahead. He was a dead shot and raised his rifle with the intention of boring me.

''Don't shoot,'' whispered his companion excitedly, tugging at his arm. ''That is not Morrell. He is one of our own men. It is Edwards I tell you.'' Continuing, he struck down the rifle barrel. ''If you shoot you'll have to face a charge of murder, and you haven't even a warrant of arrest in your pocket for protection. I tell you, Bill, you'll get into trouble if you don't look out.''

''It is Morrell,'' the other man-hunter insisted, jerking his rifle loose and looking up to take aim again. I had disappeared, and in telling me of the incident later on they said it seemed as if the earth had swallowed me.

I was not conscious of their presence, but for some freakish reason, the very moment they were arguing, I had changed my mind about traveling further along that road and had walked from the center to the side across from where they were stationed. There I ducked into the maze of manzanita and chaparral which covered the entire bottom of Dry Creek.

It was dark when I met the Chief, and he predicted that it would be snowing. As if to confirm his opinion the temperature dropped to a biting cold and heavy snow began to fall. We trudged along never before so anxious to reach Camp Manzánita as we were that night.

CHAPTER XVIII

A QUICK RETREAT TO CAMP.

"We have raised a hornet's nest," the Chief remarked gloomily. "Times have changed. The mountains are swarming with man-hunters of a different type from those imported by the railroad long ago. These new ones are real trailers who know their business. They are particularly dangerous. They have adopted our own methods. To have expert trackers dogging our steps is no joke, and we can't take any more chances. We must get under cover within our stronghold tonight."

He appeared to be gloomy, and for the first time in many weeks my easy indifference gave way to feelings of danger. Try how I would I could not shake off the thought of capture or possible death. Then a prison cell became photographed upon my mind as if the hand of destiny had placed a mirror of the future before me.

Suddenly the battering and booming of rifle fire interrupted. The sounds echoed and re-echoed against the mountain wall.

"Do you hear that shooting down below?" the Chief muttered, panting and puffing from the hard climb. "The gunfighters have split up and they're firing from every direction. I hope they will kill off each other. The newspapers will then get a true account of their wonderful bravery." He fell silent again, and neither of us spoke until we reached the creek through which we were to wade before taking the blind trails to camp.

"Let's not go there tonight," I said, stopping short in the water. "This snow won't last long enough to cover our tracks. The man-catchers can't be far from us now. If they hit one of the blind trails they'll be inside of the dead line before we know anything about it. Once inside, our stronghold becomes a death trap for us."

"I'm tired," the Chief groaned.

I stopped to plead with him.

"It is impossible for me to go another step. Besides, the snow storm will blot out every evidence of our tracks."

"Man, do you hear? I am dead beat out," he went on. "You have the endurance of a mountain deer and you're without the bowels of compassion."

He was childlike at this most critical moment of his career. Battle had surely left its marks on him, for he was utterly changed. His alert cautiousness had gone to the other extreme.

"During the entire history of man-hunts the posse has never penetrated so close to our camp," I persisted. Then I tried to appeal to his pride urging that it would be a crime, since the time for our escape was so near, to allow the secret hiding place to be discovered, and that too by ruthless gunmen.

Even now our boat was waiting off the Santa Barbara Channel. "Why not start immediately to make our way toward it? Let us leave Camp Manzanita to be found in years to come, perhaps by some lone hunter," I urged. "How much better that would be than for us to guide the blood-money men to it. They will destroy it."

He again moaned incoherently.

"If you are really too tired to help throw the trackers off, go to Eshom Valley and hide in the home of a friend," I continued. "That is not far from here, and you won't find any posses there. I will jump a horse, and make a quick night trip into the lower sections of the foothills. I will show up down there and draw the posse from this district."

"Leave it to me, Chris, I'll do the trick. Take a grip on yourself, man. We must do it or lose everything through one foolish act."

"I am too tired," he declared finally. "My blood is like ice water in my veins. I will freeze to death if I don't get under cover soon."

I relented, realizing that further urging would be hopeless. Since the jail break I had made a practice of humoring the Chief. He had gone through enough to kill any other ten men. So, with a heavy load tugging at my heart, and premonitions of danger dogging my footsteps I plunged ahead, again taking the lead. We were soon within the confines of Camp Manzanita.

Jumping from bed the following morning I looked at my watch. Eleven o'clock! Could I believe my eyes? Was it possible that was the correct time? It was dark in the cabin. Just a faint, murky light seeped through the window at the rear. I dressed quickly and went outside.

Our mountain fastness was completely enveloped in a dense, impenetrable fog bank, dreadful, silent, stifling, a cold, consuming veil. Through it appeared huge undiscernible forms, weird looking, even ghastly, and it was a long time before I could determine that they were only familiar objects distorted by the vapors.

I turned back to the cabin dejected, feeling as if that fog were an augury of evil, harbinger of coming events that would soon cast black shadows before us. Never had I been just like this. Never had the serious side of life presented until now, and I could not fathom it.

I had lived in the great outdoors, thoughtless and happy, but instantly everything changed. I became nervous, suspicious and uneasy.

"It must have stopped snowing shortly after we came in last night," I remarked noticing that my companion was awake. "Of course the man-hunters would have been here long ago if they had found our trail, so I am hoping for the best."

He laughed, insisting that we were safe within the camp. "Why, Morrell, what has happened to you? Has the excitement for the past week jarred your nerves? Those trackers could not hold down the bush during the storm of last night. I'll bet you anything you like, they are at Camp Badger enjoying the comforts of the bar. It's a dime to a dollar half of them are drunk by now."

The old Chief's words were reassuring. Nevertheless I could not shake off my agitation so easily, and we breakfasted in silence. The meal over I commenced to unwrap a bundle of late papers we had brought back to camp. I finally found a full page by one of the San Francisco staff writers. It recounted his experiences with some of the mountain people, who were thought to be friends of the outlaws, and analyzed their "strange" characteristics.

"The posse had charged up the mountains close behind the outlaws," I read. "Their route brought them past the home of old Abel, 'a hog raiser' they would call him in the mountains."

"The aged man approached the door cautiously as the officers of the law arrived at his cabin. 'I can't understand why them fellers allers comes this way,' he remarked in an annoyed plaintive tone, hobbling outside."

"'Why, them desperadors just met me a-piece down the road yonder. They made me lite and walk while they went on to ride and tie clar up to my place. I sent 'em down to Ben's cause I know'd three men with guns were thar, and I thot sho they'd take 'em. And do you know them fellers there never did nothin' but let the desperadors go?'"

"Old Abel didn't raise his eyes from his boots except to flash a quizzical glance at the officers."

"'It's no use a-talkin', it won't do to have such men runnin' round terrifyin' an a-scarin' us people. It's a fact, Mister officer, I'm afraid to talk about him, 'cause I killed the bandit Chief's partner in a fight nigh onto twenty year ago,' Abel continued dramatically, 'and I'm sho if he hears about me talkin' he'll come back and bump me off fer that killin'.'"

"'Why, the leader of them desperadors says when he went away, "Abel, do you see that pile of rocks on the off side of yo' doah? Well it 'ndn't be much of a trick to call a man out and kill 'im from there." He wagged his head meaningly. "So I darn't talk."'"

"At last he repented, seeming to have a complete change of heart as his quick, furtive eye caught a glimpse of his oldest son, tall, lean and sharp faced, returning from a long trip back into the mountains. Old Abel agreed to find Morrell and the outlaw Chief, at the same time cautioning that the vengeful pair would put an end to him if they should not happen to be captured."

"'I don't care,' he remarked resignedly. 'Abel and all his family are on the side of law and Government, but my boy will have to take you to him. I 'udn't go up there for a hundred dollars,' he drawled. 'I'm sorry for the outlaw's widow that's to be, and his children, but I'm a man that allers tries to do his duty'."

"As the posse trooped out with the lanky son in the lead, old Abel was still mumbling to himself about law and order, good government, brave peace officers, and cowardly bandits."

"Old Abel and his family were so well acquainted with the mountains that they claimed even the roads told them tales. Night came on cold, with a drizzling rain. Old Abel's son, the lanky blond youth was leading the posse to where Morrell and his partner, the outlaw Chief were basking in fancied security, now that his father was on the side of law and order."

"He was not very talkative, but occasionally when stopping to let the posse rest, while he stood gazing fixedly at the toe of his boot, digging a hole in the snow with his heel, as was customary with old Abel's family generally, he would tell of a few day's spent with the fugitives miles back in the mountains. He claimed that he had even shown them which trails to take to avoid cabins and Indian settlements."

"Finally the stoop shouldered guide pointed out an old deserted place where he insisted the outlaws had cut peep holes in the cabin to command approaches from every direction."

" 'It would be pleasanter if the weather was nicer,— but we'd better not waste any more time,' old Abel's son finally remarked, when the posse discovered that the outlaws were not there and never had been."

" 'Well they said they were comin',' exclaimed the fair-haired guide, giving no further explanation regarding why he had brought the men such a great distance. It was later learned that the bandits were faring well in the opposite direction, while the posse consumed time and wore themselves out in useless effort."

"Returning," the article continued, "they found old Abel busy around his cabin, his face fairly beaming with satisfaction. 'Hello,' he called out from behind his brush fence. 'Have you boys got them elusive desperadors?' "

"Old Abel was fond of reading the newspapers, and had made a special effort to acquire for use such words as 'desperadors,' 'bandits' and 'elusive,' always trying out his parlor vocabulary on the various posses that came his way, at other times referring to the fugitives as 'them fellers'."

"Now the Abel family agreed that it was wrong to mislead the officers, and the younger brother who had just popped in from nowhere was requisitioned as a guide. 'Take these brave peace officers to where them desperadors is hidin,' the father urged."

"Tho only about seventeen, slight, undersized and pale, he knew the mountains. They started without delay. Staring at the toe of his boot the boy told the men that he had spent many months each year since he was a child alone on the hog ranch where he did his own 'chuckin,' herded the pigs and drove off mountain lions and bears, claiming that he was even too small to hold a gun then, but that he had his mountain hog dogs.''

" 'I carry a gun now, right enough,' he added proudly. 'All the Abels kin shoot. It comes kind o' natural to 'em'.''

"This youngest Abel was in the act of driving the officers to a cabin a great distance up the Kings River where he said he had found suspicious looking tracks. They had trudged over the rocks for miles when young Abel suddenly stopped, taking a seat upon a bowlder. He too had a change of heart and confessed that he was tired of this sort of thing, misleading good peace officers and taking them away from the bandits as his father and brother had done, that he didn't intend to do any more of it.''

" 'They ain't up in this country atal,' he said. 'They're down 'cross the river near Dunlap way where I took 'em myself, living in a camp that was fixed for them a long time ago'.''

"He was on their side now, and tho he had led them a long tiresome trip, the posse still followed him, silence being unbroken except for an occasional drawl by the boy. 'The Warren's have gone to town, or the Simpson's must ha' come home yesterday,' he would comment, for like his father and lanky brother, he too thoroughly understood the language of the trails.''

"Passing a school house the guide stopped short, insisting that the outlaws were hidden there. Surrounding it and searching in every nook and corner, the officers were disappointed. Their quarry was not within. The young Abel's faded eyes dropped even lower than the toe of his boot under the Sheriff's scrutiny. 'I thought they were there sho' he stammered and would say no more.''

"Returning to old Abel's home the posse were assured by him that he was still on the side of law and order.

'There must be something wrong when them desperadors stand off good men that way,' he remarked, bidding the Sheriff and his men 'good-bye' and staring solemnly at the toe of his boot."

"Stories have been passed about that the Abel's are unpopular anyhow, the other mountain people claiming the old man's hogs are too dog-goned short-eared for any honest man's stock, a stout pair of shears being a ready agent for the accumulation of pork, when a crop on the ear is the mark of ownership."

"But old Abel seems to hate hog thieves, expressing loathing for any manner of stealing. Abel's brother, who made the holding up of railroad stations a specialty found no favor with the old man. 'Bill generally gets caught, and anyhow he's the only Abel that ain't honest that ever was and I disown him for any brother of mine,' he often said."

"It was claimed that old Abel used to get the mountain people worked up about hog stealing. He would lead his neighbors far into the mountains after thieves, but they never caught any, returning always to find that the Abel's had plenty of hogs while they were poorer than ever."

"At such times, the hog men would talk about lynching, and when they did that stealing always stopped for a while."

"One unfortunate day, Abel and his elder son were put in jail on the claim of a man who said they had stolen pigs and that he proposed to prove it. The Court and jury were not convinced. Still it cost the Abel's all they had to get out, landing them back in the mountains broke and destitute except for an old Winchester rifle which it was claimed no one would have picked off a waste heap."

"The magazine was lashed to the barrel by a piece of rawhide. The stock was wired in place. 'We got a box of shells somehow,' said old Abel, 'and began shootin' our way back to fortune'."

"He claimed they killed forty deer with that one box of ammunition, and that his lanky son hauled the carcasses down into town selling them for meat. This made it possible to buy a new rifle and other necessities. Then, they were lucky enough to see a big brown bear across the river. 'We got forty dollars out'n him and that started us back on the road to wealth. Now, we've got horses a-plenty and hogs and lands again,' explained the old man."

"Needless to say that the two Abel offspring followed the posse back to Fresno," the article continued, "where at the Sheriff's office they brazenly asked for the pay due them for guiding the posse over trails that had never been traveled by the outlaws, through rivers they had never crossed, and to cabins they had not stopped in. It was even asserted these crafty mountain youths had spoiled every chance the officers might have had to capture the bandits."

The old Chief laughed heartily at this new story of the mountain people. Terrible tales were spread by certain members of the posses and gunmen, about those assumed to be friendly to us. The Chief knew that old Abel was a consummate actor, and delighted in playing a part before gunmen and even interviewers. He quickly assumed a dialect in their presence to create an impression of ignorance, and told wild stories which were readily believed by people hungering for them.

The "Tiger's" tapping came again to interrupt. "Tell me something about the mountain people Ed.," he asked.

"Well, Jake," I rapped back, "many of the old timers came there after the gold rush of '49, many others were driven there from homes on railroad land. Still others had made the mountains a final resting place after a life long nomadic career. Most of them were descendants from excellent families of the far East and South."

"All possessed a common virtue, generosity and open hospitality, the only unwelcome guests being man-hunters and gunmen. True peace officers were respected by the mountain people. Blood-money hunters, imported by the railroad, were heartily despised. They felt a keen enjoyment in spying upon these hired thugs."

This question had been rankling in the "Tiger's" mind for sometime. My few words of explanation evidently satisfied him, for he asked me to continue.

"All right, Jake," I hastily replied. "This part of the story is going to be exciting, so get ready for the fireworks."

CHAPTER XIX
THE FALL OF CAMP MANZANITA.

A rifle cracked sharply! I dropped the paper and sprang to my feet, Colts 45 in hand.

I had been reading to the Chief, and did not notice him cross the floor and open the door, stepping just outside. There he had raised his good hand above his one remaining eye as if to penetrate the fog and look over the Dry Creek Valley far below.

I don't know why he did this. On a clear day it was even impossible to see outside of the dense inclosure except from the observation post under a tamarack tree high above the Camp.

With the report of the rifle my partner wheeled and fell into the cabin, striking the door-jam with his head. He dropped upon the floor face down, to all appearances lifeless.

"Well, old man, you've got your final shot at last," I murmured, believing him dead, but not daring to lean over just then to pick him up.

Grasping a sawed off shotgun I stood a little to the side of the door waiting for the first man to enter. So far as I could determine the one who fired the shot must have been crouched against the cabin wall waiting for some sign of life before taking another chance.

I could just distinguish the bear's burrow across the way. He verified my suspicion that strangers were near, scampering inside followed by the cat.

Something stirred. I held my breath. There was a shuffling movement. It was the outlaw Chief who sat bolt upright shouting, "They're surrounding us!"

"Are you hard hit?" I asked, still holding my position, shotgun poised and aiming at the door.

"Hard hit, Hell," came the angered reply. "Get ready and come on," he shouted, jumping to his feet and bounding through the door, his short carbine rifle grasped tightly in his good right hand.

I was too amazed to answer. He leaped into the stream which supplied our water and trudged knee deep in the center of it, up the mountain side. He was completely concealed from the flat ridge to the East of the cabin.

"Are you going to stay there and be trapped?" the Chief called, looking around only once and continuing on up to the sheer face of the mountain wall. Then he turned abruptly to the right.

I knew that he had reached one of the blind trails despite his terrible wounds, and felt sure that I would find him there bleeding to death. It seemed strange that he had escaped without being fired upon. I was baffled, not knowing then whether it was just one man or a couple of hundred gunmen. They might be down to the rear of the cabin reserving fire until I should come out.

Taking advantage of the silence I hurriedly strapped on my cartridge belt and six shooters, loading my pockets with extra ammunition for the rifle. Then, I crept as far as the corner of the cabin to search for footprints of the man who had pot-shotted the Chief. I even held my hat out and edged it up and down, hoping to draw his fire.

At last I peered out. Through the fog bank I could see nothing moving, and suddenly the import of the Chief's warning that we were being surrounded was clear.

With the first streaks of dawn a posse of about twenty-five gunmen had picked up our trail of the night before far down in the valley of the Dry Creek. All forenoon they had persistently dogged our tracks finally reaching the creek where we had last traveled. There, our footprints ended abruptly.

Some keen mountain tracker among them tried to solve the puzzle, concluding that "the fox had doubled on the hounds." The running water could tell no tale. The snow was flush to the edge of the stream. Not a mark showed on the other side.

The posse strung out along its course, seeking evidence for a new point of contact. Finding none, the leader ordered his men to follow, and jumped into the creek, again heading down toward the valley. At the end, where it emptied into Dry Creek, they halted and without the least evidence of discouragement wheeled about and trudged upstream until they reached the spot where our tracks were lost. Here they started all over again. This time they turned abruptly and followed the creek up the mountain, searching along every foot of the way.

One man, out in front stopped and held up his hand for caution. He was looking down at the telltale footprints where we had left the water. The chase was now on in earnest. The posse strung along Indian fashion, zigzagging in and out until confronted by a solid wall of manzanita.

Here was a new mystery. The night before we had made a beaten trail up and down in front of this thicket seeking the main entrance from the East. We had covered nearly half a mile, doubling and redoubling until it was impossible to determine where we had entered.

The man-hunters spread out before this natural barrier with orders from the leader that each man should force through from where he stood. One of them accidently pushed his way into an opening. He had stumbled upon the blind trail which led in from the East, right up to the back of the cabin.

Camp Manzanita was discovered! The lucky gunman crept cautiously forward until he reached the sheltering rock below the back of the cabin. He was not more than fifteen paces from the corner and directly in line. Hearing voices and the familiar laugh of the old Chief he had taken up his position there deciding to keep the secret that he alone might have the honor of killing the outlaws.

THE TWENTY-FIFTH MAN

It was a shot from his rifle which had dropped the Chief. It was he who had made the bear hasten to his burrow. If I had gone to the slide window at the back of the cabin I would have seen him hurrying back down the trail to join the rest of the man-hunters.

If I had only known the real situation I might have acted differently. My crafty partner apparently sensed it when he jumped up urging me to get out before the place was completely surrounded. I had wasted a great deal of time.

The cordon of gunmen were already crawling in from the East. They would soon have me within a circle. Not hesitating another moment, I leaped through the door. Unlike the wary Chief, I ignored lurking dangers, taking the foot path out on the open flat above instead of the sheltered stream.

I was about to turn to the right to the blind trail over which my partner had retreated. Bloodstains clearly marked the way. A banging crash brought me to a standstill. A volley from eight or nine shotguns, only twenty or thirty paces away, had been turned loose upon me.

The posse were gathered planning to encircle the cabin and seeing a moving object through the fog bank, had fired. I was stunned,— glued to the spot, a comical looking sight now. For an instant I stood there like a scarecrow with the crown of my hat ripped off, clothes torn to shreds and rifle stock shattered by the impact of the lead. Pulling myself together, I then leaped over into the stream. They all believed me dead.

The noise attracted the man who had shot the Chief, and he ran to the rest of the posse shouting, "I got the old man all right. Knocked him over with my first shot. He's in the cabin dead."

"Well, if you got him, we killed Morrell escaping up the mountain side," the others boasted, "and our next move is to surround the cabin in case any more of the band are there."

I had reached the blind trail up which my companion had fled. It was spattered with fresh blood and I thought bitterly that I would find him dead somewhere on the ridge.

Still in a fury of pain from the burning flesh wounds upon my body, I located a place high above the death circle of the posse. I crouched, whipped out both six shooters and fired downward in an effort to make them believe an army of outlaws were there. Again and again reloading, I kept up the fusillade. Now I turned my battered rifle upon them, this time aiming carefully in the direction where I believed they were hiding.

The gunmen were by this time well inside of the mined section of the blind trails. I knew they were out of harm's way, and resolved to give them a real fright, one that would strike terror into their hearts for the remainder of the day and possibly prove the means of allowing us an opportunity to escape if the Chief might still be alive.

Retreating up to the lookout station under the tamarack tree, stirred to still greater action by my pain, I kicked frantically at the snow on the box which concealed the batteries leading to the mines. Jerking the lid off I pulled upon the lever and jammed it down hard.

I listened for the reverberating shock. Nerves tightened to the breaking point I released my hold, straightened up and stared blindly down into the fog bank. Nothing had occurred!

The mines had not been tested in over a year. Could it be possible that wood rats had worked havoc, gnawing the wires and spoiling the contact?

There was still another alternative. I recalled the mine directly beneath me, under the lookout station. Its wires led up the blind trail ending in a separate battery on the ridge above. "I might still give them a parting shock" I thought as I rushed up the trail.

Here again the battery was out of order. Time and the elements had made them useless.

I no longer felt the pain from my flesh wounds. An overpowering dread of what might have become of the Chief had possessed me. I worked my way over the ridge, still guided by the trail of blood. I knew that the man who had done the shooting must have fired with deadly aim and nerved myself for the ordeal.

A figure crouched on a log ahead. It was the old Chief. He presented a pitiful sight. A deep groove had been cut in the top of his head terminating in a blood blister about the size of a hen's egg. He rubbed it with his only hand. The stump rested upon his knee. Blood from the lacerated face which had struck against the cabin door in the fall, and from the rifle wound trickled down his beard, carmining the snow at his feet. His left eye, the one remaining after the Battle of Stone Corral, was red and swollen, painfully injured, I noted as he raised it to glance at me.

"What are you trying to do, bring out the whole United States Army?" he snapped angrily.

I did not reply and the Chief was silent for a few seconds.

"Did you get any of them?" he finally added manifesting some interest and not being quite so irascible.

"I hope so," I said, smiling my relief that he had not been fatally hurt, and for the first time seeing the humorous side of our forlorn condition.

"What are you laughing at?" he shouted. Then patting the egglike lump he commanded irritably, "Burst this, burst it, I say it's burning the top of my head off."

"The gunman who shot you there was surely aiming for the big reward," I parried. "That was a close call. You're a lucky man."

"Oh, is that so?" he blustered up showing something of the old time fire and snap. "I'd like to have you know, young man, that 'all is fair in love and war,' also that 'a miss is just as good as a mile'." Then he cursed violently.

"Cut this blister, I say! Cut this blister before I go clean out of my mind."

I gently punctured it with my knife, and the blood made a red pool at his feet. I washed the ugly wound with clean snow, venturing a remark that his career was evidently not to end by the gunshot route. If the big fory-five ninety had struck but the fraction of an inch lower the top of his head would have been blown off. It seemed a cowardly act to take such a mean advantage, but murder even becomes legal when the victim is an outlaw and his pursuer a blood-money hunter.

We were ready to move on. Our one time safe retreat lay wrapped in a veil of fog below us. "Good-bye, Camp Manzanita, good-bye forever," I muttered aloud, dwelling prophetically on the last word. I knew that we would never again see Camp Manzanita.

Our stronghold had been discovered. The place where we had spent so many days in safety, where we had always found food and shelter after a weary chase was lost to us, and sadly following my companion I became obsessed with a feeling of dread.

Night was falling as we retreated from the scene of the day's disaster. Still, danger stalked in every direction. The mountains were swarming with gunmen. Death lurked on every trail, and we were compelled to plow blindly in unbroken mountain fastnesses, groping through the impenetrable fog to seek out the location of some friendly ranch house. We were lost!

The Chief had lost his sense of direction. For the first time in his life, that almost superhuman instinct had failed him in this critical hour. The mountain fog was too much and we floundered on aimlessly, trusting to our wretched fate in the hope that it would lead us to a haven of rest.

The night of struggle seemed interminable. Would it never end? The hours dragged on as centuries. Now the Chief complained pitifully that his head was bursting with pain, and to crown our misery he confessed that he was going blind. "Can't see, Morrell! Lead me," he called.

Taking his arm and trying to lift the weight from his body I encouraged, "Come on Chris, trust to me. I will find a ranch. See, it is getting daylight now," and as if in answer to my hopeful words, we stumbled into a line fence. In another moment I located the barn. It was the home of a friend down at the lower end of Eshom Valley, many miles from the scene of our late encounter.

We tumbled through the ranch door into the living room where the family were seated at breakfast. They jumped from the table in alarm, the younger children badly frightened. We were so bedraggled, wet, and covered with blood that none of them recognized us until the Chief spoke.

"Chris!" excitedly shouted his friend, the father of the family. "You have been in a fight, for God's sake, man, are they on your heels? Surely you wouldn't bring the gunmen down upon my home to endanger the lives of my wife and children?"

"Be quiet, Charlie! This occurred yesterday afternoon." The Chief spoke calmly. "We were lost all night in the fog and the man-hunters are miles from here, I suppose in as bad a plight as we are." Then again he added, "You should know better than to think that I would bring man-trackers to your door."

"Forgive me, Chris," his friend muttered, brought to his senses by the outlaw's mild rebuke. "You know I couldn't blame you for anything you might do in your desperation. You have been through Hell, and now you are wounded again. Where is this thing going to stop?"

"I say, Lucy, hurry and get some hot water ready," he called to his wife. "These men need our attention."

Turning compassionately to me he asked, "Morrell, are you also hard hit?"

"Sit down in that chair, Chris. Let Lucy wash your head." He was examining the Chief's wounds. "My, my,

— another inch, man, and all would have been over with you."

I had stepped to one of the windows facing the East to look out. The sight gladdened my heart and made me forget the terrible ordeal of the past day and night. A high wind was blowing downward from the upper ranges, sweeping the dense fog before it to the lower foothill country. In its wake was coming a snow storm of blizzard proportions. I watched it for a few moments. The ranch was now enveloped in the drifting flakes.

Turning, I said to the Chief, "Our luck is breaking for the better. It is snowing outside and if it keeps up our tracks will be completely wiped out in another hour. Then the posses can look in vain. They have had the last sight they will ever get of us."

We washed off the marks of battle and dressed in clean clothes supplied by our host, then ate breakfast and tumbled into bed as if nothing unusual had ever happened in our lives.

We had gone to hide among our friends. The ship that I had chartered was waiting in the Santa Barbara Channel, but since the State was now again in uproar we dared not go directly to it.

We vanished. The press loudly thundered for action denouncing the baffled posses and gunfighters who had so nearly trapped us "in a little cabin hidden under a beetling cliff." There was great excitement for a few days, and then once more the chase settled down to the same old condition of stories, rumors, and counter rumors.

The time came at last when we decided to leave the Sierra Nevada Mountains forever and make our way to the vessel. We lay concealed in an old shed on the outskirts of Visalia, wet and hungry, waiting for darkness.

My leg which had been injured on the night of the jail holdup in Fresno had weakened first, and then given out completely. I suffered excruciating pain aggravated by a high fever. It seemed as if a complete breakdown would occur at this most crucial moment of my life, and at the very time when I needed every ounce of strength.

Being younger and stronger than the Chief I had always tried to shield him, struggling against terrifying odds, carrying extra loads, sleeping out in the snow exposed to the elements, braving winter blasts for days, and leading the posses in wild chases from places where the Chief was safely resting. I believed I had been built of iron until now.

With the coming of night my partner fairly lifted me to my feet, helping me slowly and painfully over heavy roads, his one arm encircling my body. We were making for a ranch a few miles South of Visalia. There friends would be waiting to give us every care. From here we were to ride on horseback across the great San Joaquin Plains and to the Coast Range beyond.

But we were still North of Visalia. The rain was pouring down and in our extremity we made our way toward the old outlaw's home which was near and occupied by people whom we thought friends. It was a great risk but we were compelled to take the chance.

We returned to the house which had been the scene of the first troubles. A welcoming light gleamed out through one of the back windows. I was staggering and stumbling, and so weak from hunger and suffering that I virtually fell in through the door to a chair in the dining room.

The caretakers, husband and wife, looked at us alarmed. The unexpected visit was a complete surprise, but whether pleasant or unpleasant I was then too exhausted to determine. The woman placed extra dishes upon the table and urged us to take some food.

My partner answered questions in monosyllables. I was too exhausted even to speak. Gulping down a cup of steaming coffee like a famished man, my head dropped upon my arm and I fell asleep.

The Chief aroused me, and between alternate spells of sleep and shakings I made a feeble effort to eat. Revived a little by the stimulating effect of the coffee and food I jumped to my feet exclaiming, "Come on, Chris! Let's get out of here while the going is good." My old spirit of alertness had returned for a brief spell, and I insisted that we leave, that we were "selling our lives for a shoe string."

"Go to bed," said my partner after listening to me patiently, relieved at the signs of a change for the better. "You are badly used up. A couple of hours of rest will prepare you for the rest of our journey." He was in his own home now and leisurely walked over to a rocking chair, disregarding my code signals of danger and settling himself as if to remain for the night.

I bluntly protested that I was all right and that we should not stop another minute. "Who knows but we are being surrounded right now?" I asked.

This did not phase him. He stubbornly insisted that he would not move an inch until I had slept.

I gave in at last. My power of resistance had again dwindled away. Still I agreed to rest only on condition that the Chief would remain awake on watch and allow no one to leave the house.

He had not been suffering the physical pain that I had endured for days, and completely refreshed by the hot food he promised to stand guard and awaken me sharply at two o'clock in the morning. War trained and trustworthy, he had always been even more vigilant and wary than I and so I felt the deepest confidence in him. Placing my life in his hands I retired for that brief period of rest which would make it possible to go on to safety,

CHAPTER XX

AT THE END OF THE TRAIL.

The bright sunlight shining in through the uncurtained window awakened me from a heavy sleep. Forgetting my crippled leg I jumped from the bed to look outside. I believed that I must have been dreaming and that it was not possible I had slept all night.

I staggered back amazed! The place was surrounded by a horde of armed men. My brain was muddled. When it cleared I thought of the Chief. Had the friend for whom I had risked everything failed me in these last critical hours?

My confusion changed to anger, and determined to know the truth I brushed the curtain aside with my rifle. I took in the living room at a glance. The Chief was in front of the fireplace. He appeared to be asleep. The caretaker's wife sat opposite watching him and apparently had not retired.

Her husband was gone. He had evidently slipped out some time during the night to give the alarm. They were traitors and had sprung the trap!

But why was the Chief sitting in his chair asleep? Could it be possible he was unmindful of the danger that hemmed him in? This was unthinkable! He was one of the shrewdest men who ever baffled a posse.

A terrible thought flashed into my mind. Had the Chief connived with these two professional spies to bring about his surrender and to peacefully wind up a spectacular fight in a lost cause? It was unbelievable! It was monstrous!

A fury bordering on madness possessed me. My decision was quick. I would end it all. I aimed my rifle at him.

Hearing the metallic sound of the hammer clicking into position the woman jumped to her feet, screaming and loudly imploring me not to shoot. She thought the gun was pointed at her. It was an evidence of a guilty conscience.

The loud noise did not disturb the Chief, who slumbered on heavily. My mind cleared. I had the solution to the whole damning plot. He was drugged. Now all was plain. These two human rats had doped the Chief's coffee while I slept. Then the man had slipped out and given the alarm.

The Sheriff of Tulare County took command, and during the night he had posted hundreds of armed men around the old homestead until by daylight a cordon of steel hemmed us in.

Visalia was once more in the limelight. It was humming with excitement. The alarm was spread broadcast and people began pouring in from miles around. Men, women and children drifted toward the old place. Business and school were suspended for the day.

Tragedy hovered in the air. People stared at the neglected and forsaken place which had once been a happy home. They looked at the broken down fence, a mute testimony of many inglorious retreats by man-hunters. The historic barn where Oscar, the badman, had been killed was ripped, torn and battered by bullets. Altogether the place was forbidding.

We had always so successfully eluded the posses that hundreds of our friends outside hoped the officers were on a wrong clue.

The professional gunmen of the railroad were now arriving. Special trains were bringing them into Visalia in carloads. Marshal Gard, the hero of Stone Corral, was on the scene brandishing a highly polished rifle which had been presented to him by the citizens of Southern California as a token in recognition of his bravery. He had taken charge totally ignoring the constituted authority of the Sheriff of the County.

I could hear loud words and hoped that the division of authority might bring on a clash. The confusion would work to my advantage.

Some man near the fence shouted, "A woman is being tortured inside that house!"

The woman had screamed again. As if in answer to the man's words, she kept it up.

This time I aimed my rifle at her ordering her to "shut up on penalty of death."

The noise half aroused the Chief from his heavy unnatural sleep, and vaguely recognizing me he mumbled an indistinct greeting, then dozed again immediately. This time I shook him, finally using a wet towel to break the stupor.

The dazed man was slowly coming to his senses. I jerked him to his feet demanding the truth from his own lips. I had sacrificed and suffered, exposed myself to dangers, faced death a hundred times for this man. It was almost incredible that he had failed me at the end of the trail, with our boat just a few miles beyond ready to carry us out upon the high seas to a land of peace and safety.

I could readily understand that life now meant little to him, scarred, bent and broken with only a few years at best to go, but it was appalling, unbelievable that he had failed to think of me at this moment, young and healthy, with everything to live for. I had planned my future. In a distant land life looked big and beckoning. Now all was lost.

"Damn you, man!" I shouted. "What have you done? You insisted that I lie down for a few hours giving me your sacred promise that nothing should occur to endanger us. Here I find you sleeping in a chair drugged, your caretaker gone, the house surrounded. Look, I say! Look out through that window!"

He jumped! He was awake and himself once more. The sight of hundreds of armed men, thousands of people, brought him fully to his senses.

"Heavens, man," he exclaimed, "what has happened? I have no recollection of anything. It seems not more than an hour ago since you lay down. You said something about drugs, what do you mean? Still I feel funny. My head is bursting. Ah, yes, now I have it! I recall everything. That devil's witch there," he continued, pointing at the woman, "urged me to take another cup of coffee after you retired. It is the last I remember."

He scanned my face questioningly and then muttered "God! — Man —" and paused again as if thinking, then went on, "No,— No! Surely you do not believe me capable of willfully contributing to this trap,— if you do, have your revenge. Shoot me where I stand!"

Once more the Chief was the man of old, brave to a fault. He would die before he would defend himself where he might be in the wrong. I relented. His generosity of nature had brushed away my black thoughts. Relieved I extended my hand. "Chris, I forgive you, but I can't help believing you are not the man of other days. If you were you would never allow such scurvy people to betray you."

"I will take charge here," I added. "Go back to the kitchen and cover the rear. Reserve fire until an effort is made to charge upon the house. This woman has been a party to the scheme of treachery," I went on. "She sat beside you all night without an effort to awaken either of us. Let her stay inside and take the consequences. If a battle starts and she is killed, her life will be the forfeit for the cowardly work of her husband."

People were still coming, most of them friends. They were unaware of the plight in which their presence had placed us. Not one of them would have knowingly done anything to hinder a dash for liberty. But still they kept coming. We dared not shoot.

Hour after hour passed while we watched and waited hoping that they might tire and go home.

THE TWENTY-FIFTH MAN 235

There was a stir among a group of officers near the gate. A young man approached with a note. I now heard his timid rap on the door and gruffly commanded him to come in. As he entered heads were thrust forward and the crowd surged toward the fence as if to burst into the yard in their anxiety to see what was going on, or to get a look at the outlaws if they were really there.

He held a paper toward me in a trembling hand.

"Put it on the table. Step to the corner of the room and face the wall," I ordered, refusing to take it.

After seaching him for firearms I brought a chair over telling him to sit down and keep looking at the wall. I then turned my attention to the message. It was addressed to the Chief from his old friend, the Sheriff of Tulare County and appealed to his honor to surrender and avoid bloodshed.

I passed the note to him without a word, returning to the front room and paced up and down like a caged animal. Occasionally I stopped to peer out into the crowd, wondering if they would never disband.

The Chief stepped to the door. He had read the note. "There seems to be nothing left to do but surrender," he remarked dejectedly.

"All right!" I shouted, thinking rapidly. "If this is your final word let's ring down the curtain! Take the woman and go out through the front door. I will hold this man here. He had no business interfering in the trouble and carrying notes to dangerous places for money. If they start fighting and if he gets out alive, I can assure you he will never again put his head in the halter for the sake of a few paltry dollars. I refuse to give up without at least trying to escape. If successful I have life and freedom. If not, I will abide by the issue." I turned on my heel with the final remark, "Go, if you like!"

He was not affected by my cutting words and commenced pleading with me. He refused to surrender alone, insisting, "You have one of two things to do,— face death or surrender and bide your time for another fighting chance. You are young and I am old. My race is run so it makes little difference either way."

"There is a chance that you can escape after we surrender. At worst they can't give you more than ten years for the jail hold-up. There are no other charges against you. Perhaps public opinion will turn in your favor. Remember, we have thousands of friends. You may even get a light sentence, but you will be young when you leave prison and nothing will be hanging over your head to force you out of the country. You are too young to sell your life so cheaply. Be reasonable and let us both face the ordeal together," he urged.

I was silent, and he left me to think it over, returning occasionally to offer some new suggestion.

At last, after hours of hopeless waiting, I gave up the thought of trying to escape thru that dense mass of people closely packed around the place. Yes, the Chief was right. There was not one chance in a million here, but there might be many between my surrender, the County Jail at Fresno, and the big State Prison of San Quentin. There were friends who would have to help me if I demanded it. I would bide my time.

The Chief was still at the back window of the kitchen staring dumbly at the mob. "You are right, Chris," I called to him. "I haven't my head about me. To refuse to surrender will only cause needless killing. There is lots of time between now and my trial. Another fake train robbery, and I might leave the County Jail as you did."

"Write a note to the Sheriff of Tulare" I added. "Invite him to bring the under sheriff and come in." They were both friends of ours.

The Chief wrote hurriedly, "Dear Sheriff: Come to the house and bring Hall. We want to talk. No harm will come to you. We are willing to make terms with you and no one else. When you reach the gate, Morrell will step outside to meet you as an evidence of our good intentions." He signed it, "Chris."

I handed it to the messenger, directing him to give it to the Sheriff. From the window I observed that men gathered closely around the two officers, strongly objecting to their venturing into such a trap.

"If they don't kill you, they'll hold you as hostages and we'll then be forced to give them freedom," I heard one shout.

"I know my men," the Sheriff insisted. "That note means just what it says and if they won't surrender not one hair of our heads will be harmed. They won't hold us, either. We'll come back safe and sound, without so much as a scratch."

The two officials brushed everyone aside, stepping through the gate and walking toward the house. The scene must have been dramatic, judging from the silence and straining of the mob. As I opened the door and stepped out to meet them, loud gasps were audible.

The Sheriff took my hand in a hearty clasp. We spoke in whispers and then entered the house together.

"I knew I could not be mistaken," shouted the Sheriff. He had discovered the Chief sitting in a chair by the fire, his back turned to the door. He placed his arm about the shoulders of the old war scarred veteran, patting him affectionately.

"Chris, you are one of the bravest men who ever lived, and this is just what I expected. I knew you would not fire upon your old neighbors. I am your friend, and I'll also be damned if I'd allow any of those gunmen to shoot into this place."

I was silent. The scene was intense. With the fire of a soldier blazing in that one remaining eye the old man dragged himself erect. Standing at attention he saluted the Sheriff as he had his commanding officer, General Sherman, many times in the days gone by. It was indeed a pitiful ending to so stormy a career.

"My life has run its course," he spoke slowly and tremulously. "I am a broken old man and have nothing to ask for myself. You are an officer sworn to uphold the law, and tho it might be possible to stretch a point for me, I would not desire it. I am ready to meet my fate."

"However I have a last request to make, Sheriff." Motioning toward me he added, "There stands one man in a million. He is fearless, brave, and loyal to the core. He is not a criminal in any sense of the word. He would die this instant for what he believed to be right and just."

"For myself I ask nothing," he went on after a pause. "I am ready to humble myself for this friend, however. What I ask is your promise as a man that you will at least defend him against those bloodthirsty hirelings, railroad thugs who are my enemies. I know they intend to stir the town to madness in an effort to form a lynching party."

"If you give us a square deal and will see to it that Morrell gets a fair trial we are both ready to surrender," the Chief concluded.

"I swear that I will defend you both with my life, and with my right hand extended in reverence to God I promise that I shall use all of my power to see that Ed. Morrell has a fair and impartial trial." The Sheriff was a man of his word. Shaking hands without speaking, we four slowly filed out of the house.

The waiting thousands greeted us with loud shouts. We had given up without bloodshed. Bells and whistles were shrieking, adding their din to the general excitement. We made our way between the lines of people crowded closely

THE TWENTY-FIFTH MAN

together in an effort to see. Hundreds of friends tried to force through to grasp our hands and offer words of encouragement.

Glancing casually over the sea of faces we noted that the few who bore dark expressions stood out in strange contrast. They were professional man-hunters. This pleasant ending to the long chase had cheated them of the big reward.

I had heard of the undying hatred that Big Bill, the detective, bore me for outwitting him in his murder plan, and felt sure these sinister characters would not fail to stir up trouble among the lower element. They would try to arouse the spirit of mob violence.

We entered the County Jail. The doors clanged to ominously behind us. This marked the final act of a drama that had held the State in a grip of excitement for years. It concluded one of the most spectacular epochs of outlawry in the history of the country, and for me it was prophetic of a new chain of experiences strange and terrible.

Outside in the town of Visalia subtle forces were at work. Information reached the Sheriff's office that Big Bill and a gang of railroad gunmen were busy gathering a mob to lynch Morrell and the old outlaw Chief as well.

Every little while trusted deputies glided swiftly up the steps and into the Sheriff's office at the jail, making reports of what was going on in the town. It was learned that the rope was ready and the mob were to act under the guise of a vigilance committee. They had agreed upon a signal. Three short taps of the firebell would be the order for storming the jail.

This mob who styled themselves regulators of law and order centered around Visalia's Spanish Town. Money was distributed freely among them. The sinister leaders dropped an occasional word which acted as a firebrand among the drink sodden ruffians until at night, when the lights flashed on, the babel and discord of the mob had become deafening.

Now they no longer confined themselves to the disreputable section of the town. They congested the main streets in confusion. A loud rumble permeated even the air I breathed in my cell. I could hear the cries and the clatter of horses' hoofs as the peace officers tried to scatter the crowds.

So much money had never before been in evidence there. Men who were known not to posses a five dollar piece at one time, carried pockets full of gold. They spent it lavishly in the saloons and dance halls of Spanish Town which seemed a-crawl with the dross of humanity.

Whiskey was poured like water. Thousands were saturated with it. The air was reeking. Its pungent odors were everywhere. Howling, cursing, drunken fighting were added to the bedlam.

The law abiding people, fearing the hopelessness of the situation, had timidly retreated to their homes and awaited the outcome from behind bolted doors and windows. The vicious, drunken mob was in possession of Visalia, surging aimlessly through the streets, shouting wildly, frenzied and delirious, lacking nothing but leaders to drive them into crime.

Time was ripe for action. The desired effect had been produced at last. The leaders, cold and calculating, showed themselves amid the throngs of drunken men, haranguing and loudly urging that the outlaws be brought to justice, insisting that crime must stop, that the outraged citizens of Tulare County should be avenged upon Morrell. He had defeated justice when he released the bandit Chief from jail, and he had terrorized the community.

Hundreds of friends moved about through the mob protesting, insisting that this disgraceful exhibition did not represent the true sentiment of law abiding citizens of Tulare County. Their voices were lost amid the shouting of the roughneck leaders who were loudly bellowing, "Here's the rope boys, we'll lynch them!"

The insane drunken mob were at last beyond control!

CHAPTER XXI

"JUDGE LYNCH," THE AMERICAN MOB.

The fire-bell tolled out three short taps, sinister, cold, prophetic. There was breathless silence, then the mob bore down upon the jail. They stopped short before the long stone steps that led up to the main entrance.

They had noticed the barrels of many guns leveled at them from grated windows.

For a moment this show of force had a calming effect. Maddened men even recognize danger of death. Those frowning rifles meant business. Then again from a safe distance the leaders of "Judge Lynch's" court blusteringly demanded admittance, all the while cursing, pushing, prodding the cowardly insane mob to attack.

One bull-throated, malignant character bellowed, "Get a battering ram! Damn them, we'll cave in the jail door! Somebody get some dynamite!" shouted another. "We'll blow out the front of the jail! Let's make a clean job of it tonight. Hang all the cut-throats and save the County unnecessary cost of trial."

Some one pushed his way through the dense mass, crying at the top of his voice. The mob listened. Had he come to assume command? They wavered slightly, undecided. This time they heard.

"They've gone!" he shrieked. "Slipped out the back way with the Sheriff, headed for Goshen in his buggy!"

"We'll lynch them yet!" the mob wailed.

A man jumped to the front. "By God, they have tricked us, but we'll get them yet! They haven't much of a start. Come on men, come on!"

Buggies, carryalls, all sorts of vehicles merged into sight so quickly that it seemed they must have come through the air. Men on horseback rode out swiftly in advance. The mob surged through the streets in a rush for every livery stable in Visalia. Hundreds of horsemen were soon trooping out of town in wild pursuit.

Two muffled figures, strangers in Visalia, left in a buggy carrying a heavy coil of half inch manila rope. The night air was filled with the crunching of wheels and the pounding of horses' hoofs. The lynchers sped along. They were gaining on us.

In strange contrast to what had gone on all day outside in Visalia, everything had been silent and commonplace within the jail. The Sheriff sat in his private office cool and composed, while messengers brought him news of coming trouble.

Finally one said, "I tell you, Sheriff, this mob means business, and unless you can call the best fighting men of the town to your assistance we will be hopelessly outnumbered. Every gunman and badman for miles around is here. I never before saw so many strangers in Visalia, and bad characters every one of them. The jail can't hold out against them."

"We have plenty of rifles, shotguns, pistols and ammunition," remarked the Sheriff after some deliberation. "I am going to make this place a fortress. Do you hear that 'phone working? I am calling up all of our citizens, deputizing them over the wire and demanding that they report at once." The Sheriff impatiently waved the men aside, ordering them to go out and mingle among the people.

"Get the names of the agitators, do you hear?" he shouted. "If you haven't a list of every one of them tomorrow, consider yourselves discharged."

Citizens were now hurrying to the Sheriff's office, rifles in hand. It was like the gathering of a clan. The reports kept coming in that Spanish Town was a seething mass of drunken men. A prominent judge of the County had entered the jail. Now, he was talking to the Sheriff in his private office. His voice could be heard outside in the corridor.

The Sheriff soon entered the jail proper. He stopped at the cell of the old Chief. A whispered conversation was held before he stepped over to me to say that Chris would abide by whatever I should decide to do.

"I want to tell you frankly, Morrell," he added, "there is no hope of holding this jail against the mob. But I have given my oath to protect you men with my life, and by God I mean to do it! Now, if you want to stay here and see it through, I am ready to fight to the end. You will be released from your cells. I will return your rifles and ammunition."

"What else had you in mind, Sheriff?" I inquired.

"The mob hasn't started to advance, and if you would rather leave this jail and go to Fresno I think we can make it in my carry-all. I have the best team of horses in Tulare County. They are waiting, hitched and ready, in the alley at the rear of the jail. We can put up a running fight of it if we have to, but I know we can be well out of Visalia before our escape is discovered. If the lynchers overtake us in the open, they'll get a warm reception. Neither I nor my deputies will desert you while we are able to fire a shot."

He had spoken in a commonplace tone, but I knew the man and knew he meant it. I knew Sheriff Kay's word was his bond. He was utterly fearless, and loved by all in Tulare.

Tho most concerned, I had felt the least agitated of any man in the jail that night. I had never feared death. I had been mysteriously snatched from its jaws so many times that even now, when the mob was howling for my blood, ready to strangle the life out of me merely to satiate a mad desire to kill, I did not waver for a moment.

"Sheriff, I have no intention of holding you to that promise given in my behalf today," I continued calmly.

"That is too much to ask of any man, least of all one in your position, the father of a family, with a wife and mother dependent upon you. No one who has red blood in his veins would permit the sacrifice. My partner and I will not hear of it."

The Sheriff did not interrupt me.

"Place me in the same position I was at the time of our surrender," I continued. "Give me my firearms. I am no longer an outlaw. Neither is Chris Evans in the light of coming events. Tonight the 'Octopus' is the criminal. They have deliberately sent their cowardly agents here with orders to inflame the mob. Big Bill, the detective, wants my scalp, because I balked his murder plan."

"The professional gunmen are bent upon violence. They are the offenders. They are now openly breaking the law. Your only duty, Sheriff, is to return our firearms. We will fight for our lives, and I am also ready to defend the law against that pack of cowardly criminals with the last drop of blood in my body."

He shook hands with me through the bars. The grip silently cemented a life long friendship. It would have been a strange sight to anyone who might have seen,— a proscribed outlaw with a seething mob of madmen already hungering for his life and the Sheriff of a great County of the State of California, one of the bravest peace officers who ever lived.

The Sheriff gave the order to the jailer to release us. We stepped out into the corridor. There our firearms were returned, and following the Sheriff the Chief and I silently filed out through the back entrance of the jail. He told us that the immediate surrounding territory was all right as he had posted pickets to keep away suspicious looking characters who might be spies.

At the end of the alley leading to the jail a deputy sheriff signalled that the way was clear. We joined him near the team accompanied by another deputy and also the Sheriff of Fresno County, making five including the old Chief and myself.

As if sensing some unusual condition the high spirited horses leaped from the dark shadows of the narrow lane to the street, turned to the right and we were soon lost to Visalia in a dense cloud of dust. The Sheriff himself was driving. He was a noted horseman and we covered mile after mile without once breaking the gait of the fast traveling team.

"It looks like everything is all right," the Sheriff finally commented. "I telephoned orders to have relay teams at two points between here and Fresno and we're breaking all speed records now."

"By Jimminy," he finally declared laughing, "I'd like to be back there in Visalia tonight. It will howl as it never howled before when that crazy mob learns we have given them the slip. I see my finish as Sheriff of Tulare County too," he added with no apparent regret at the price to be paid for the night's work in defence of law and order.

A horseman rode up, jerking his foam covered animal back on its haunches. "I have raced nearly ten miles," he panted. "A mob of several hundred crazy fiends will be upon you in less than half an hour if you continue along this road. Drive East into the foothills," he wheezed. "Throw them off your tracks and by morning you will be North of the Kings River on the old Centerville Road. Then we'll bring a strong body guard from Fresno to your rescue. You can't fight them off. Not a man of you will escape alive."

The Sheriff had stopped his team, and leaping out listened with head turned and hand cupped behind his ear. He evidently heard nothing, for he again jumped back to his seat and leaning over the wheel coolly announced, "I'll keep on this road straight to Fresno."

"Your orders are to return South until you meet the advance guard of the mob," he told the deputy. "With the compliments of the Sheriff of Tulare County say to the lynchers that I am on the main road North with my deputy, also the Sheriff of Fresno County and the two prisoners.

"Tell them that we are five determined men heavily armed and sworn to uphold the laws of the Counties we represent. You may add that the two men they want have their own weapons, and will fight to the last breath in their bodies and that we also will defend them with our lives."

"If they insist upon breaking the law in spite of this, say that I challenge them to come on and suffer the consequences." The team struck out on its chase North as he called back to the deputy, "Deliver that message correctly to those night riders."

"Your wage of battle has been accepted, Sheriff, and I guess there will be fireworks all right," I called out from the back seat of the carry-all.

There was a high moon, bright and clear. It lit up the landscape. I could make out figures of horsemen far to the rear. The Sheriff pulled his team to a stop, again alighting.

"By the Eternal, men, here they come," he exclaimed with a soft whistle. "Jump out and get ready all of you."

Inspired, perhaps by the remarkable courage of the Sheriff, we coolly watched the advance column of raiders approaching. It was a strange new experience, and both the Chief and I were amused. We had a faint suspicion that this mob lacked the hearts of real men. They were cruel and at the same time cowardly. Their appetites had been whetted by the desire to commit a loathesome deed. Most mobs are like this, but none can compare with the liquor inflamed.

The leaders saw our carry-all standing in the middle of the road as a barricade. They must have realized that true to his word the Sheriff's prisoners wore neither handcuffs nor Oregon Boots and that both were armed.

Even the most notorious of them conceded that the outlaws were dangerous foes and up to this moment had not believed the Sheriff would turn us loose. They had again been foiled in taking us at a disadvantage, and the great, black, serpent-like mass stood still. The Sheriff knew what was wanting, and before anyone could asume the role of leader he advanced up the road a few paces, stopped and faced the menace. It was breathing as but one, acting and thinking as but one,— the mob, a primitive monster.

He shouted in a commanding voice, "I am the Sheriff of Tulare County, sworn to uphold the law and by the Eternal God, I mean to do my duty."

Not one of them spoke. They stood panting and waiting, a band of terror stricken, hungry wolves.

"My prisoners are armed and free," the Sheriff continued, "and I am ready to fight by their side until the last one of us drops. But, I warn you that for every life you take we shall exact a toll of ten to one."

There was a ring to his voice, and the mob knew he meant it.

"I know most of you, and I warn that there will be tragedy in many homes before the sun rises. To those who escape in this night's work I swear that you will dangle at the end of ropes in the jail yard at Visalia."

The Sheriff moved back to the protection of the carry-all. We five stood ready, waiting. The three officers were on one side of the team, while the outlaw Chief and I were on the other side.

My partner spoke in low whispers, not even audible to our defenders. He had been strangely silent until now. I could tell by the lion-like shake of his head that the old war scarred veteran had once more scented the smell of battle. It was in his blood, and now since the cause was just he could no more resist the urge to fight than defy the law of gravitation. He was again the intrepid leader.

I felt his power when he asked, "I say, Morrell, how do you stand? Is your nerve all right? We must do some real shooting tonight."

"Chief, I am with you," I replied. "This old Winchester of mine will drop them like ten pins in a bowling alley."

I was ready, waiting, nerves and muscles in a tension. At first a rage of anger overpowered me. Then I began to grow cooler and cooler each moment. I knew that the full strength of the mob had arrived. The moon grotesquely magnified their numbers into thousands which stood out like a black shadow against the brightness of the country road.

"Why didn't they do something, why not come on?" The suspense was aggravating. "What power held the grim hand of death for me, perhaps for all of us? When would it make the forward plunge?" I thought.

There was a stir. The leaders seemed to be advancing, but suddenly they turned their horses and went to the rear of the main body which was blocked solidly in the center of the road.

Like automatons each rank as it was exposed to front view leaderless, followed the action of the first line. True to the history of mobs which are always cowardly in the face of danger they were retreating South back toward Visalia from whence they had come. They were lost to view in a cloud of dust. Every man had gone, and relieved the Sheriff turned his attention to the horses.

Ready to start, he stood. waiting with the other officers at the side of the carry-all. The Chief and I were quite a few paces from them. The chivalry of the California Outlaws who had so long roamed the Sierras' unmolested was again being tested that night. We were armed and free to fight our way to liberty under cover of darkness. Our ship was waiting to take us to the far ends of the world. Should our honor compel us to sacrifice liberty and be sentenced to penal servitude for life under a Medieval system of torture in the fetid air of a prison?

I walked up to the Sheriff holding out my weapons in token of surrender. The Chief followed almost upon my heels.

The brave officer broke the silence. His words were stressed by great emotion. "I am the happiest man in Tulare County tonight. Boys, jump to your seats and let's get out of here before the crazy mob changes its mind."

A tragedy had been averted. The fair name of the State had been saved from a disgrace, which would have cast reflection even upon the Nation and all of its free institutions.

The sun was up, and the people of Fresno were moving about in the early hours of another day, when tired and covered with dust the team halted before the portals of the County Jail. We filed up the steps in silence. A strange feeling came over me. Just three months before, in that very place I had committed an act of outlawry. Here I was back in the same jail from which I had taken the old Chief, after holding it up single handed.

"I was strangely calm," I rapped to Jake, my silent listener. "Perhaps I did not clearly realize what was in store for the future. One thing I know now, however, is that the black curtain of destiny fell upon me that day when the jail door banged shut, closing the career of the youngest member of the California Outlaws."

"Tough luck," tapped Jake, in the home of the living dead. "Your last words speak volumes."

"Say Ed.," he continued, "what became of the cat and bear at Camp Manzanita?"

"They trapped the cat," I replied," but they never found the bear. One day they brought the cat to my cell in the County Jail. The moment he was released a dark streak passed through the air and alighted on my shoulder hissing and sputtering. He had never before allowed me to touch him, but things had changed. He appeared to sense a common bond of fellowship in our dual captivity."

"He dug his claws into my clothes, clinging like a lost soul to the last refuge that was dear to him. I could do nothing to help the poor creature, and after about an hour's struggle they chloroformed him and took him away. I was later told that the wild looking pet of the outlaws had been placed upon exhibition at the Midwinter Fair in San Francisco. It was said that a mint of money was made from him."

CHAPTER XXII

RAILROADED TO PRISON.

"Life!" angrily thundered the judge.

It rang in my ears. Vaguely, I was conscious of the terrible meaning of that one word of the Court.

My doom was sealed. It had come at the end of a long harangue by the magistrate who, at this solemn moment, took occasion to drone out a moral diatribe on my evil, criminal career.

"Let your fate be an example to other misguided young men who might be tempted to emulate your career of outlawry. The sentence of the Court is that you shall be confined at the Folsom State Prison to hard labor in the rock quarries for the balance of your natural life!" The judge hurriedly left the bench as he uttered the last word.

That last word, "life," concluded one of the most farcical trials in the history of the great State of California. In the language of the jail I was "kangarooed." It was a damnable mockery of justice.

Two Deputy Sheriffs clutched both my arms with firm grips. I was still standing rigid, staring up at where the judge had been, the man who had so cold bloodedly taken away my life. I was dumb, inarticulate.

It had come suddenly, at the end of two long months of incarceration in a steel tank of the County Jail. I was confined strictly incommunicado, not being allowed even the privilege of having one friend admitted to give me the help of a cheering word. I was denied every right including that of consulting with counsel.

I had been treated as one awaiting execution. A special death watch sat at my door day and night. This time the "Octopus" and the County officials determined that I should roam the mountains no more.

They feared an attempt would be made to release me. They knew I had hundreds of friends, and suspected that many accomplices were ready to risk an attack on the jail. It was rumored that they would do this rather than take the chances that I might break down through the long sieges of third degree torture and confess all.

It was figured that the unknown members of the band of outlaws would prefer to attack the jail rather than to have their names become known. The patrolling guards challenged every stranger that approached. Nobody was allowed to come near, unless brought in by officers and detectives. The deadlines were secure.

For two months my case was shrouded in mystery. Hardly a day passed without strangers being ushered into the corridor to stare through the bars of my cell door. Some would give me hard looks then turn away shaking their heads and saying, "No, he's not the man."

One day a detective heatedly insisted that I was the man. "We know he is because we've got the facts. If you identify him our case is complete. We can prove that he was in your town on that night, and was seen leaving the vicinity of the crime."

But the man he had brought to identify me shook his head emphatically.

"Good God!" I thought, "Is it possible they are trying to frame me for a murder charge in order to hang me?"

Attempts like this were innumerable. Some were grotesquely funny.

A middle aged woman gaudily dressed and jewel bedecked, brazenly declared that I was one of two robbers who held up the Yosemite stage. "He's the man who took the rings from my fingers and tore my flesh," she screamed.

After waiting patiently for the half hysterical woman to quiet down I asked, "Madam, pardon me, when did this occur? What month and what date?"

"Oh, you know well enough what date, you brute! I wish I had been a man with a gun in my hand that day. I would have fought you alone, because you were a brace of dirty cowards. A rope would be your fitting end if I had my way."

But I insisted, "Madam, you are unreasonable. You are dishonest if you refuse to state when that crime occurred. I can prove you are wrong out of your own mouth."

She began to fight back. "If you want to know, it was last September. But that won't do you any good. I know you are the man and I will swear to it in court. To be exact it was on the fourteenth. But,— oh, you know the date all right. It's just like your kind to play a part. You're all innocent until you are caught. I would like to be on your jury. I would send you to prison for life." Her voice ended in rasping jerks.

Now it was my turn. I was smiling. "Lady, I am sorry that I cannot offer myself as a sacrifice. It might satisfy your desire for revenge, but truth compels me to say that it would be physically impossible for me to have been present at the scene of this stage robbery on the date which you name. I was in Chicago at the World's Fair and I have unquestionable proof of this fact."

Two long months were spent in an effort to break me down or pin some crime against me that would bring me to the gallows, but all failed. I resisted every effort of the shrewdest and most brutal man-handlers to crush from me the confession of some fancied or unsolved crime through the terrors of the third degree.

"Oh, Morrell, we know it all," the baffled man-handlers often shrieked. "We know every one of you. They called you the 'Twenty-Fifth Man.' We have your history complete. We know, of course, that you're not half so bad as you are painted. You're young and the older men have taken advantage of you."

"We have five or six captured and already locked up in the Kern County Jail. Only yesterday two more were caught and are now held at Visalia. We even have several of your band locked up in the other wing of this jail. We have as many as a half dozen confessions, and if you don't look out they are going to beat you to it."

"That jail holdup won't stand hard against you. We can get you off with a light sentence. Now be sensible and come clean. Tell us all you know and we promise that you will be protected."

"There is lots of man in you, and it's a damned shame you ever got into such bad company." Then instantly such cajoling would be reversed.

"By the living God, Morrell, you'll never go to trial. You escaped us at Visalia just by the skin of your teeth but you can't do it here. If you don't confess and come clean, and if you persist in this stubborness, before long some night you will be jerked out of jail and will be found in the morning hanging from a tree in the Court House Plaza."

About a week before my trial one of the oldest detectives in the employ of the company fought it out alone with me. This was to be the last effort. All day he sweated and fumed and at the end exasperated and broken down by his Herculean effort he gave the final blow.

"Morrell, I have finished. Here are my last words to you. Help us bring the rest of these outlaws to justice. Help us stop further depredations and crimes against the railroad. Come over on the side of law and order and you will be rewarded. I promise you on my sacred oath that you will get a light sentence. I have already been assured by the District Attorney and the Presiding Judge of the Superior Court that you will receive only seven years, with a recommendation for future clemency. Once that is done I can promise that you will be given a pardon within two years."

THE TWENTY-FIFTH MAN 255

He had finished, then lighting a big black cigar he puffed it excitedly while waiting for my answer.

"You are wasting your time. I have often told you and I'll tell you now as final, that I have nothing to say. I am sorry I could not take advantage of your flattering offer, and all that deprives me of this, is that I haven't the information you seek."

He stared at me blankly, then jumped from his chair hurling the half smoked cigar across the room. "All right," he hissed, "I have finished with you. Now listen to what will happen within the next week."

"You are going to get the quickest trial in the history of this State. To be exact, it will not consume any more than an hour's time to get the jury, and to try you and sentence you. That sentence is to be life in the sunbaked rock quarries of Folsom. And as God lets me live I swear you will be hounded to a convict's grave."

His face was livid with rage, but I laughed at him. I thought he was merely indulging in a huge joke at my expense. I calculated it to be the concluding harrowing climax to the terrifying ordeal through which I had been in the past two months.

I felt secure in my constitutional rights, and knew they would give me the extreme penalty of ten years for the crime I had committed. I had held up the County Jail and released an outlaw prisoner. The maximum penalty for that crime was ten years. I was young and healthy. I could live it out, and through good conduct and strict obedience to prison rules my credits would entitle me to be released from prison in six years and six months as a free man without a shadow over my future life.

That night I rested contentedly in my cell for the first time. "The future is not so black after all," I thought. "Surely I can live through six years in prison and then, freedom once more." But I did not think of the Chief of Police and his pistol.

I had been caught in the maw of the criminal machine. My life would be used as grist to be crushed in its ponderous wheels, then cast upon Society's Criminal Scrap Heap. The "Octopus" had marked me for the sacrifice and the court officials of the State were willing tools. My condemnation would wipe the slate clean. I was to pay the price for all the depredations committed against the big railroad company.

Two months incarceration and they had failed utterly to pin a major crime against me. Now the jugglery of law would serve to make one.

In the escape from the Jail I had held up the Chief of Police who stood near the team in which we were to retreat back into the mountains. I had taken his pistol to prevent him from shooting me. This was robbery in the strange interpretation of the law used against me.

Therefore I was tried on the technical charge of robbery, convicted, and sentenced to life.

The large courtroom where the mummery of a trial was enacted was packed to the doors with a motley assemblage of people many of whom were manifestly servitors of the "Octopus." On the other hand a great proportion were sympathizers and friends. The balance was made up of citizens who were open minded and desired only that I be justly tried upon the charge of holding up the County Jail and aiding a prisoner to escape.

The speed with which the machinery of the court moved amazed even the spectators. Before I had entered, the jury box was filled with twelve men "good and true." God save the mark! They were professional jurymen hired at so much per day to acquit or convict at the behest of their employer irrespective of evidence for or against the accused.

Our American Jury System has long outlived its usefulness, but of all its countless defects none have equalled the abuses perpetrated through the infamy of the Professional Jury System. Sinister and terrible it has been used as an instrument of tyranny and it has done more to disrupt and make a mockery of justice than all other anti-social evils. It has weakened and broken down the majesty of the law. Through the medium of a "braced" jury powerful and wealthy criminal law breakers have found easy refuge and escape from condign punishment while the poor and friendless are crushed without mercy.

At the time of my trial and speedy condemnation the "Octopus" was all powerful in the State of California. Its control of the State's Machinery and Courts was notorious, and it was commonly bruited about that the big company appointed its agents in every office from Supreme Court to Poundmaster.

The grim comedy of the trial consumed about an hour. The jury had filed out to deliberate. The people who packed the courtroom were speculating whether or not they should remain to hear a verdict.

The written verdict of "Guilty as Charged," must have been prepared beforehand. It could not have been executed in so short a time, for the jury were back in the box in less than five minutes with the foreman answering the question of the clerk, "Gentlemen, have you arrived at a verdict?"

"We have," monotoned the spokesman.

"Gentlemen of the Jury, what is the verdict?"

"We, the Jury, find the defendent guilty as charged."

The Court was now speaking. My guardians had lifted me to a standing position and all I heard was that conclusion, "You shall be confined at hard labor in the Rock Quarries of Folsom State Prison for the balance of your natural life!"

I was pushed from the courtroom to the corridor through a side door banked around by deputy sheriffs heavily armed, who fought their way through the crowds. They brandished guns and threatened everyone who made the slightest attempt to approach.

Outside I was shoved into a buggy and hurried to the railroad station through side streets. The big Overland was waiting. A mob of people were struggling with the police to crowd onto the platform for a last glimpse of the doomed outlaw.

I was hopeful for a moment. There were many friends in the throng and I wondered if they had come to attempt a rescue. Then in an instant I was secure within the coach helpless, "Oregon Boot" on my left leg and both hands heavily manacled.

As the long train pulled out of the station I could hear the farewell calls of friends bidding "good-bye." It sounded to me like a funeral dirge as I left the world, speeding toward the dark shadows of the hideous beyond that confronts a life convict.

Big Bill, my implacable enemy, followed me clear to the entrance of Folsom Prison. His great black mustache fairly bristled.

"One word before you go, Morrell," he said. "If I live a hundred years and you endure your torture that long I will make every day of it a living Hell on earth for you, and my last revenge will be complete when I hound you to a convict's grave!"

I did not reply to Big Bill's horrible threat. I was already being pushed through the main entrance gate of the notorious State Prison at Folsom, a man-killing jail known as the private lockup of the "Octopus." His threat to hound me to a convict's grave was not a mere idle boast. I knew the man and knew his power. His evil genius had demonstrated that he could railroad me to prison, and I felt that if the past two months were any criterion of what the future would be, I could liken my fate only to a cornered rat at bay. I might fight back and snarl a little, but my inevitable end would be death by slow torture.

My senses reeled for a moment. I had seen a picture of the past. Was it possible that this man might have crossed my life as a nemesis, and at the end of the trail had fate ordained that he was to be my executioner? The irony of bitterness seized me. Why had I not removed this slimy brute from my path? He had many times been at my mercy.

The "Tiger's" staccato raps indicating a laugh interrupted my story. I knew I was in for a gruelling and it little surprised me when he asked, "Say, how about that Sheriff of Visalia? Didn't he promise to do everything in his power to see that you were given a fair trial, eh?"

"Hold on, hold on," he tapped, "not so fast! Hear me out! I want to show you where you made your first fatal blunder. Your surrender at the house was all right. You couldn't help yourself there, altho I think I might have done differently."

"When the mob turned yellow on the county road you were armed and on equal footing with Mr. Sheriff," he continued. "That was your time. You should have fought it out then and there. Ed, the chivalry of the California Outlaws has gained you nothing. The proof of this is that you have been through Hell and everybody has double-crossed you including your brave, heroic Sheriff."

The poor "Tiger" could scarcely be expected to understand the spirit that dominated us men in our feud with the "Octopus." Our code was not his code. To him, the Sheriff of Tulare County represented simply a minion of the law, his natural enemy. It profitted little that I told him the Sheriff had been a life-long friend.

Still I tried to explain that the Sheriff was helpless and could offer little assistance to overcome the power of a great railroad company arrayed against me.

But for the "Tiger's" tragic ending in years to come I could have proven to him that the Sheriff was a real man. He had been successful in business and when my pardon was announced made the splendid offer to start me all over again in life. His message to the prison said, "I want to be your friend, Morrell. Let me help you on the road to complete rehabilitation."

CHAPTER XXIII

FOLSOM, THE JAIL OF THE "OCTOPUS."

In prose and poetry Bret Harte and other famous Western writers have immortalized the beauty and grandeur of the low lying foothills of California. No mountain range in the world has foothills just like the Sierras.

For a few short months during the rainy season the hills are mantled in deepest green. A change comes then with golden hues. The California poppy brightens the landscape. Again a change, and all is turned to sombre brown.

Night and morning a heavy mist hangs over the foothills weird, enchanting, and then the sun burns relentlessly down upon the parched earth. Travelers have cursed the inhospitality of the region and its scorching long Summer months.

On the very site of the State Prison at Folsom the Gold Miners of '49 had camped. Here on the banks of the mad turbulent American River, they had dug frantically for gold. Little did any of those early Argonauts dream that there, in years to come, would be located a charnel-house of sin and misery, a great American Jail. Had they known they would have shunned it as a place marked by fate, obsessed and damned.

Nowhere in America is there a jail built like Folsom. Its physical appearance is frowning and terrible. Its buildings are low-squatting, resembling the lines of a bull dog. They are made of solid granite.

The prison proper rests upon a flat piece of table land which is tucked away between two ridges that slope abruptly down to the banks of the rock-lined river. There are no walls around it. Folsom needs none.

Below the prison the American River flows. It serves as the front wall. No convict dare approach it with thoughts of escape. Death lurks in its choppy, boiling water. On the other three sides gatling-gun posts stand high above the landscape. These are known as the outside deadline. Nearer in are two other deadlines, composed of "pill boxes," rifled horse-guards and foot-guards.

Within these death lines creatures in stripes pray or curse, as they choose, while they slowly drag out the stunted measure of life that the law has left them. Convicts at Folsom were never told not to escape. The gun guards welcomed every attempt. It was called "the blood sports" there.

Nothing is so pleasing to hardened game stalkers as a moving target. The standing order to the guards of the line was to ask no questions, to wait for no explanation, but shoot to kill. And the bloody history of Folsom has amply testified how these brutes carried out the order with unerring aim.

Folsom has made a blood-curdling, terrible history. Convicts not hardened to endure its slave racking toil and tortures have deliberately faced the guns of their eager executioners or mayhap have blindly hurled themselves into the rushing waters of the River to go down at least to a more merciful death. Such tragedies were common at the time I entered Folsom.

One took place that very day. A poor, half demented Chinaman had wandered from his work in the stone quarry down to the edge of the River. Without even challenging, a guard had fired from a frowning cliff above. The poor victim toppled over into the River desperately wounded, but fortunately it was at a spot where he did not come in contact with the rushing current.

At that moment the Captain of the Guard happened along. He was an ungodly, unfeeling, ruthless man who cared less for a convict than for a mad dog. He brutally gave the order to two convicts to jump in and pull out the drowning man.

That order in itself would have been very humane, had he first taken the precaution to command the guards not to fire.

Hundreds of convicts cheered as the two men bravely faced death to save a fellow prisoner. But the scene was turned to one of horror in a moment. The guards had deliberately fired upon the rescuers.

The hyena-like shrieks of hundreds of convicts brought the cowardly Captain of the Guard to his senses. Quaking with fear that he might be killed by the hammers of the quarry workers he shouted frantically and waved his hands to the murderers above him to cease firing.

They were loathe to release their kill but had to obey the commanding officer. The brave convicts tho wounded had brought back the man. He was dead.

The business of handling "fresh fish" at Folsom could be summarized only by one word, DISPATCH! The moment I was received my shackles were struck off.

The Chief Deputy, one of the three who had brought me to Folsom, handed the key to my "Oregon Boot" over to the Captain of the Watch, I had told the "Tiger," continuing with my story.

An orderly quickly unscrewed it and the thirty pounds of steel, which I had worn two months were removed from my left leg. That Hellish instrument made its marks and scars wherever the heavy weight came in contact with the tender flesh.

In exactly one hour from the time I entered Folsom, I stood at attention before the Turnkey's Office. My head was shaved and I was garbed in the hideous ring around, wide band stripes, the badge of shame allotted to a convict. While I waited there in my misery, sneering guards and scowling petty officers would pass and stop for a moment to eye me up and down curiously.

THE TWENTY-FIFTH MAN

Then, a grey haired officer, presumably one in authority issued an order. "Take him around by Liberty Gate to the front. The 'Skipper' wants to deal with this fellow."

In a little while I stood in a large, elaborately furnished office more like the reception room of the Governor of the State. The orderly had clicked his heels, saluted, and left.

I waited in silence for the Warden to turn. I was before none other than the autocrat of the "city of the living dead." He too had been a great railroad detective for the "Octopus," and as a reward for faithful service had been given the position of Warden of the big Folsom Prison. It was a well known fact that he was still on the payroll of that company, while enjoying the high salary of his office at the expense of the taxpayers of the State.

He was a mean, irascible, shriveled natured brute without the least vestige of the milk of human kindness in his soul. He was feared, hated and despised by even the lowest convict within the deadlines of Folsom. He had come with the building of the place, and like the prison, had made history as black as Hell.

He was a man about five feet eleven inches tall with a large, protruding paunch and a heavy jowled face. Bulging, blue sacks beneath the red scalding eyes almost concealed them, denoting the alcoholic sot that he was. Altogether, the Warden of Folsom Prison measured up to his reputation.

I watched the pendulum of the clock swing slowly to and fro. In the dreadful silence its tick was like the sound of a hammer blow.

This old thief catcher, the Warden, was trying the well worn police trick of silence and inattention, and not until he felt that the desired effect of nervousness had been produced did he arise from his swivel-chair and look at me for the first time.

With both hands shoved deeply into his trousers pockets he remarked sneeringly, "So, they've got you here at last! You're that bad man from the Tulare Mountains!"

He was fiercely biting on the stub of a big black cigar and his lips were heavily stained from its juice. He glared at me for a moment then walked across the room. "Morrell, come here and look out of this window!"

With a lofty wave of his hand he shouted, "You will notice that there are no walls around this Hotel to obstruct the beautiful view of the foothills. A pleasant place indeed! It is really a fact, however, that some of the boarders at this HOTEL try to leave without checking out through the office!"

He had turned and was again glaring at me. "Now, Morrell," he rasped, "I am going to extend a special privilege to you. Whenever you get tired of my HOTEL accommodations," repeatedly accenting the word "Hotel," he continued, with a threatening leer upon his face, "you are at liberty to go. You can walk right off the grounds."

"You can go East, West, North, or South; but, by the living God," with clenched fists and flaming eyes he hissed, "I reserve the right to stop you." As an after-thought he added, "That is if I wish to enforce that right."

For the first time since I had entered the prison, I now gained complete possession of my faculties. I had heard much about this brute Warden and of how poor quaking convicts had groveled in fear under his blustering tyranny.

I was fresh from the mountains, full of red blood, upstanding, and afraid of no man. I looked furtively around the big office. It was unthinkable that he was alone. Still I could see no one else.

"This man is a coward," I reasoned. "Surely he must have a gun over there in the drawer of that big desk. If I can get it in my hands he is at my mercy. What is to prevent me from forcing him to take me out of the prison beyond Liberty Post? His guards would not dare fire upon me, and endanger the Warden's life,'' I figured on.

A moment's silence ensued. He was very near me. I could smell the hot fumes of his alcohol tainted breath. Was it possible that this craven hearted paltroon had sensed my plan? It seemed so, for he quickly stepped away and touched a button.

An armed guard was standing in the doorway in a moment.

The Warden grimaced a savage look at me, then turned and in jerky words ordered the guard to keep that station until he told him to leave.

This man was no mean adversary. He was shrewd and cautious,— much like a guard at a zoo in charge of wild animals, he took no chances. But what was most humiliating to me was the knowledge that this man was silently enjoying my discomfiture.

He evidently had had many such experiences before. He had measured my guard and in the vernacular of the street "had beaten me to the punch," and the galling part of it was that not a word had been uttered. Like deaf mutes we had pantomimed the parts and each understood the other.

The next open move was up to me. Baffled I switched. I must now use caution. "There is surely some vulnerable point in this ogre's armor plate,'' I thought.

"Warden," I spoke at last, confident that my new line of attack would bring results. "I am only a boy. True, I have been sent here as a life convict with a notorious record. I don't ask for your personal interest other than that which you accord to the most friendless convict in the State."

"All I ask from you is a square deal,— nothing more. Just give me a chance and I'll prove that I'm not the bad man they have painted me to be. I am willing to work hard and perhaps in a couple of years you'll realize that what I say is true."

Now he was openly laughing at me. Yes, it surely must have been a joke for he continued to laugh outright.

I was puzzled and amazed. I did not understand the man. He made me look foolish. I roundly cursed myself for daring even to think that, for a moment, I could strip my heart to such a monster. I instantly regretted having done it. It would have been better to remain like a stoical Indian in his presence, concealing my real face with an outer mask as hard as steel.

During all my long years in prison that was the first and last time I ever committed such a folly. I did not then know the true significance of the terms "a man-killing jail," "a Mediaeval Prison" with a stone age warden in charge holding in his hands the power of life or death over his defenceless victims.

The wards of the State were not sent to prison to be reformed, but rather to be crushed and broken. Some would fill convict's graves and others would be released to go forth and pollute the social stream after having been made dehumanized brutes.

Yes, this Warden was right. My little heart-confession of good intentions if given a chance must have sounded strange and absurd to his ears.

He spoke again, almost mimicking my concluding words. "You know Morrell," he countered, "I am a 'We're from Missouri' man. Words don't count nothing to us. I've got to be shown! Words don't prove nothing. See?"

"But now, just to show you I'm a good fellow I will give you that chance."

As I was being taken from his presence he called back over his shoulder, again half laughing, "Say, Morrell, by Gad that was a good speech you made. Some old ex-con' must have given you that, you have got it down so pat.

Better write it out and send it to me in a letter. I will have it read before the next meeting of the Board of State Prison Commissioners. We will incorporate it in an appeal to the Governor for an immediate pardon. You are altogether too damned good to be in here among us bad ones. You could employ your time better robbing trains down in the San Joaquin Valley."

He was so pleased with this run of sarcasm that his face became red from laughter, and I in turn, sensing the joke, also laughed for the first time in months.

In another hour I was ready for work, being marched down into what was known as "the lower prison," to a place called the stone yard. There I was turned over to the man in charge. He was a huge giant and wore a terribly dirty suit of faded blue. His right cheek bulged as if he had a large rock inside. It was a cud of tobacco.

His capacious mouth was wide and loose and whenever he talked it emitted a spray of tobacco juice. There were several hundred convicts in his charge, all life timers and so-called desperate characters. They were the stone cutters of the prison.

When this man spoke, he shouted loudly so that all of the convicts could hear. "What be your name?" were his first words to me.

When I told him he jumped back a few paces, finally delivering a ponderous speech. "Oh ho! So you're Morrell, huh? I should have knowed as much. They allus sends me the hard biled ones. I get them all,— I get them all."

"Ye're tough when ye come t'me first. The 'Skipper' knows his business when he sends ye t'me. I came here with him when the prison was first built. I'm the man that breaks 'em all."

Sweeping his hand in a majestic wave around the circle of stones, he went on so every one could hear. "Look ye,

Mr. Fresh Fish, Mr. Bad Man from the Tulare Mountains, yer kind is all here together like Brown's cows,—train robbers, bank robbers, burglars, arson fiends, wife murderers, rapers, porch climbers, common thieves,— and every one of yez' cut-throats into the bargain. I get yez all, because I'm the right man in the right place."

"Oh ye're tough when ye come all right, but within a week after I get yez, I have ye catin' out of my good right fist like sucklin' babes. C'm on with me an I'll show ye yer task."

He led the way to a large bowlder that stood to one side and out of line of the circle of stones with the towering derrick standing in the center. A convict runner had handed him a point and a four pound hammer.

I had already noticed a heavy plank leaning against the bowlder with cross pieces nailed on as cleats. Holding out the point and hammer for me to take, he ordered me to get up on that rock, and at the same time with a motion of his big forefinger he warned, "Morrell, pick out the center and keep busy with that hammer and point. Yer job is to dig a hole down through the middle of that rock. Mind what ye do now. Don't move from that spot without first givin' me the sign. If ye do the gatling-guns will be turned on ye."

"Do ye mind that last? I say the guards have their orders. Ye might ha' ben' a good shot when ye was fightin' honest officers of the law, but up over yer head in those gatling-gun towers are men who are sharp-shooters, and their orders are to 'shoot to kill'."

"Now ye have heard me through," he concluded, "an' ye can do as ye like. From today ye can work, root hog or die. Here in this place the divil takes the hindmost."

CHAPTER XXIV

LIFE IN A MAN-KILLING JAIL.

The stone cutting yard of Folsom Prison and its huge derrick were located in the center of a basin shaped piece of ground. High cliffs almost surrounded the great circle. They were bristling with towering gatling-gun posts.

Into this basin the sun poured its unrelenting heat laden rays from dawn until dark. Scarcely a breath of air stirred the hot fetid atmosphere at any time. To me it had seemed like a devil's cauldron where boiled the tortured souls of the State's condemned. In this spot all of the prison's most desperate convicts labored, men who were regarded as being utterly outside the pale of the law, having not the vestige of a right that might he respected by the State's cruel task masters.

There they bent to their hated toil, damned and damning from the first stroke of the hammer before the sun began to burn deep into that bowel of Hell, to the final shriek of the giant sirens, which announced the end of the day's weary drudgery. As the night shadows crept over the foothills of the great Sierra Nevadas, the long sinuous line of striped creatures dragged its tired way up the dusty road that led to the other fiercer Hell behind the steel barred gate, the cells within the prison house. Soon the sweat smelling mass of humans begrimed, dirty from the day's wretched, life killing labor, would be lined up in the stifling mess room to partake of the evening meal. It consisted of vile unsweetened "bootleg coffee" black as coal tar, dry coarse bread, and a dish of watery unseasoned beans.

Just a few minutes were allowed to gulp it down, when the blow of a gavel annouced the termination of the unappetizing mess. As the line filed out into the cell house it fell into fragments, each striped creature madly rushing for his crypt of stone. Then pandemonium broke loose, caused by the loud jar of banging cell doors and the doleful tolling of the prison bell, which announced the lockup and "all is well."

This was followed by a death-like silence, broken only by the catlike sneak of the night watch, patroling the tiers to see that the discipline of the jail was sacredly obeyed. Of all the Folsom horrors none equalled the torture of the long, hot sweltering night endured by each convict in his unventilated tomb.

Even in San Quentin's dungeon I could live again those Folsom jail days listening once more to the groans of tortured, tired souls, the curses of prison made brutes.

The convicts of Folsom were accustomed to watching the iron being burnt into the heart of some victim marked for crushing. This does not mean that they were calloused or indifferent to the misery of others so long as it did not strike personally. It was the usual, the commonplace.

As a body of men, they were at all times anxious and willing to sacrifice even themselves if this could lighten the burden of sorrow for an unfortunate who was being slowly crucified, perhaps for a violation of some absurd prison rule, or bending under a heavy load of work. To witness these Spartan deeds was enough to prevent one from losing faith in the brotherhood of man. It brightened the gloom of the jail with a halo that was Christ-like.

The daring deeds of the California Outlaws had long held the convicts of Folsom in a grip of interest, and the day I entered, the big prison was alive with buzzings. Old convicts, hardened to the brutalities of the jail, ominously shook their heads and openly predicted that my life there would not be worth a nickel. Some of them had felt the power of the "Octopus," but their deeds against the giant monopoly were mere child's pranks in comparison to what I had done. No, they could not figure that I had one chance in a million.

THE TWENTY-FIFTH MAN

When I climbed to the top of the great bowlder, hammer and point in hand, the two or three hundred convict stone cutters stopped their work as one man to stare in open-eyed amazement at this new and unheard of spectacle.

At first their sense of humor made them laugh. Then they felt ashamed and became angry. Loud shouts of protest burst forth. The stone yard was in near mutiny. I glanced up mechanically to the towering cliffs above me. The guards had turned the guns downward waiting, ready to shower the place with lead.

The big bull foreman was now bleating commands with the most horrible imprecations and oaths I had ever heard. "Sound yer hammers men, every mother's son of yez or be the livin' God I'll raise my hand for lead!"

That was enough. The cowed convicts knew what he meant. It had happened many times before. There were always stretchers in the tool house ready to carry the victims to the dead house or the hospital. There was not an ounce of sentiment in the soul of the Folsom Jail. The warders were brutes and the convicts in order to live had to harden into the semblance of brutes.

The moment the big foreman had his mill of misery grinding again with sullen order restored, he marched over within earshot of the ten ton bowlder upon which I was standing, puzzled and nonplussed about what to do. Waving his gorrilla-like arm in the air, he bellowed up to me, "Hi you, Mr. Fresh Fish, you g‑‑d d‑‑‑‑‑‑‑d outlaw crook, what do you think this place is anyway, a school fer makin' sky pilots or d‑‑‑‑‑‑d high toned bums? Get down on yer marrow bones and make that granite dust fly, or I'll send ye to the dungeon for sixty hours stretchin' on the derrick."

Crushing had commenced on my first day in Folsom. I was truly a marked man. I thought of Big Bill, the detective's last words to me as I commenced my senseless work upon the granite bowlder.

The day finally ended. I was weak from hunger, not having broken my fast since I left for the State Prison. I staggered into line. A convict behind me was talking in a low whisper. I glanced at him. He was a stranger.

"Don't turn your head," he cautioned, "or you'll get the derrick tonight. Just listen and let me do the talking. I know the ropes and can fool the foot-guards. They're watching your every move and will grab you at the first bad break. You're a 'fish' and don't understand. All they want is the first excuse. Morrell," he whispered, "you're in for Hell. It's common talk they'll do you up before your stripes are dirty. Next Sunday in the yard I'll tell you who I am. Don't lose your head. Keep a stout heart."

"Here's a piece of news that will make you feel like a new man," he added. "You are already in on a get-away. You have been accepted hands down by every one in the plan. In less than another month the work will be finished. I can tell you now it's a walk away. In the meantime don't turn a hair. Don't allow the prison dogs to get you rattled or you won't have enough life left to go a hundred yards outside of the dead-lines." He stopped talking as we filed through the man-gate.

At last the steel door banged in my face. I was locked in my cell for the night, but not alone. I had a cellmate.

I staggered over and sat down on the edge of my bunk. My convict mate still stood at the door, peering out, silent, listening. Then he jumped quickly to one side. The inspection guard which followed the lockup gang stood and glared through the wicket. Satisfied that there were two live convicts within he went on to the next cell to do the same thing.

Knowing we were alone the young man who was to share my misery became instantly transformed into a new being. His face lit up with a smile. The silent dogged expression had left it. As if acting a role, he pompously extended his hand. "I take it that, as a fellow boarder of the Hotel de

Folsom, your name is Morrell. How I know is that I just had a lengthy interview with 'Spud,' the Captain of the Guard."

"This affable gentleman assumes that I am a 'stool pigeon' acting in his employ. Only today he gave me my instructions. 'Frenchy,' he said, 'you have been a good boy. Now I want you to do a real piece of work. I am going to put Morrell in the cell with you. Try to make a friend of him. Do everything in your power to gain his confidence. If you can get him talking about the California Outlaws your future is made. If through you we can get a line on the other bandits still at liberty and they are captured, I promise you a pardon from the Governor'."

" 'In the meantime you will have one good meal a day on the side. Now Frenchy lets see what kind of metal you are made of'."

"So, Morrell," Frenchy went on, "you will understand that I am a real Simon pure, 'stool pigeon,' and like the dicks and the District Attorney in a third degree I warn you that anything you might say of a damaging or incriminating nature will be used against you."

We both laughed, but not aloud. I was learning fast at Folsom. Tho the psychology of the jail was subtle, terrible, still it held me fascinated and I resolved to play the game adroitly, since it was wits pitted against wits.

The first Sunday at Folsom with liberty in the yard was a revelation to me. It was the one day of racking life in the jail that the prisoners were free from the malice and tyranny of the guards, and unless an overt act by some reckless convict was committed we were left comparatively free for about five hours.

The prisoners, in general, showed their sympathy for me with unstinted measure. Hundreds had shaken my hand, but I was watching, eager to find the man who had furtively spoken to me in the line. At last a stranger approached, not the man for whom I was looking.

Biding his time so that no one would hear, he whispered in an undertone. "Morrell, just follow me slowly over to the blacksmith shop. Make it appear that you are wandering about aimlessly, only keep your eye on me."

There were nearly thirteen hundred convicts in the yard, but I never lost sight of that man. In and out through the crush I worked my way, and finally stepped inside of the blacksmith shop. As I entered a convict closed the door.

At least eight or ten men were in the big room. One of them was swinging the bellows at a forge. Perspiration was pouring down his face.

I sensed that something quite unusual was going on. There was an atmosphere of apprehension, belying the careless attitude of the men.

One with a large pair of tongs had now lifted an iron pot from the glowing coals. It had been heated to a sputtering white. Holding it out at arm's length he rushed across the room and entered an adjoining one. The door was quickly closed.

The man who had spoken to me in the line stepped up and extended his hand. "Morrell, you are one of us. Would you like to see something funny, a joke on the 'Skipper'?"

He took my arm and we entered the room where the man had disappeared with the red pot. I have never been easily taken off my guard, but the sight I beheld that morning in one of the most notorious man-killing jails on the North American Continent baffled me for a moment.

At least a half dozen men were in there, all busy. I noticed the one who had the pot was carefully pouring the molten metal into clay molds, while others were frantically working, chipping off rough burrs from shining new coins. Twenty-fives, halves, and dollars were strewn in little piles on several tables.

This was a money mill! They were making counterfeit coin!

My new found friend answered my unasked question. It was biting sarcasm. "You know, Morrell, the State works us hard, but pays us nothing. They steal our labor from us but that is not robbery according to the ethics of Society and the constituted law."

"Now, you know, all work and no pay makes Jack a bad man, and convicts are no exception to this inexorable rule."

His words were not lost on me. I looked at him sharply. How strange they sounded. He was evidently a man of education and I was receiving my first real lesson in the mysteries of the jail from him. The underworld was unfolding. There in a grimy prison the man had given me the first weapon that I might use in later years to confute the champions of so-called modern penology and the creators of that pseudo-science, criminology with its bastard spawn, that diabolical den of torment, mischief, and damnation, the American Model Prison System.

My new friend continued, "You know, Morrell, in this country you can't do anything without money, and since the State robs us of the fruits of our labor to which we are morally entitled, necessity compels us to resort to a like means to supply our wants. Since the State is a barefaced robber it would surely be unreasonable to expect the wards of the State to be any better."

"Then again, we have heard that there is a great complaint over shrinkage of money in circulation, and that the United States Mint is working feverishly night and day, trying to meet this pressing demand."

"Now, look at this in the proper light. Really, don't you think that we should be rightly regarded as patriotic citizens, by our industry helping to save our beloved, paternalistic Government from going plumb to Hell?"

As I said nothing, he went on, "You will say this is not good coin, and there are others who will condemn it as counterfeit. Granted! But look at it! Satisfy yourself that this is at least a work of near art! See, it has the true color, weight, ring, and feel and the only thing in which it differs from the coin of the realm is the quality of the material of which it is made. A mere bagatelle,— only exacting folks would object, such as the Chief of the Secret Service Department, or other unreasonable connoisseurs."

The other counterfeiters laughed at the witicism of my friend.

Somehow I mechanically grimaced in order to conceal my complete astonishment. I was amazed when I thought over the incongruous situation Of all the places that the wildest stretches of the imagination could invision in which to locate a counterfeiting plant, surely a big State Prison should be the last. Yet here it was in full operation and right under the eyes of the "bull dogs" of the law, and as far as I could determine carried on openly and with perfect impunity.

The underworld and its life are full of strange complexities and contradictions. Nothing operates directly. Everything postulates upon indirection. Few understand this enigma. Even those who approach with the intention of studying crime flounder hopelessly in the attempt to unravel its puzzling mysteries.

Its terminology is even perplexing and vague. For instance a tall man is called "shorty," while a short, fat, stocky fellow is called "slim." I have often heard a two hundred pound man called "skinny." On the other hand I have seen men in prison who were notoriously reticent and morbid scarcely ever speaking a word called, "windy," while their opposites, blatant and loud mouthed were dubbed, "silent Jimmies."

But life anyhow is full of contradictions and the underworld is only a part of it.

I wanted to learn more about the counterfeiting plant so I plied my friend with questions. "Tell me, how you can get away with this?" I asked. "It all seems so unbelievable."

"The hardest things, Morrell, are sometimes the easiest and this happens to be one of them. If it weren't for the 'stool pigeons' in prisons the convicts could steal the uniforms off the guards' backs and they would never know it. It takes brains to cope with brains and the only brains in American Prisons are those clothed in stripes."

"This batch of money we are making will be in San Francisco by next Wednesday. We have been operating for nearly a year. That bull-dog faced guard that you saw outside near the door is the meanest brute on the line, but he is the ring. He used to be a rounder in Frisco and off duty he's a square shooter and all right. We got him appointed on the guard line through a Frisco pull. He has played a part since he has been here and now the old 'Skipper' and 'Spud,' the Captain of the Guard, think he is the devil incarnate. They point to him with pride for some weak kneed guard to emulate."

"The blacksmith out there in the other room works on Sunday and 'Spud,' the P.K., picked our man for special duty to watch this place. We are safer in here than in the most inaccessable regions of the Sierra Nevada Mountains. After dark tonight this trusted man-killer of the Warden will carry the coin down to the town of Folsom. It will leave on the first train in the morning, shipped to Frisco by Wells Fargo. It's a dollar to a dime some of these newest coins will be in circulation within a week."

When it was all explained I understood what my friend's idiomatic language meant, "that the hardest things were often the easiest." It is a well known truism in the underworld that the safest place to hide as a fugitive from justice is to be securely locked up in some jail, and these counterfeiters plying their trade seemed to be no exception to this rule.

My first Sunday in Folsom had so far been one of thrills and surprises. It was all new to me. I was now sitting over in a corner listening to the whispered conversation of this man who had come so suddenly into my life.

"Morrell, if blind luck is in our favor I figure you won't be here more than three weeks. You will have finished your life sentence in the shortest time on record in the history of this prison. A tunnel is being dug in the cell block. It is now over two thirds finished. We are already attacking the foundation of the outer building, and when that is done we can go."

"Now here's where you come in. There are about fifteen in the plot. All you will have to do when you are given the tip is to commit yourself and be thrown in the dungeon. The punishment cells are right back of where the tunnel is being dug. There is a space of at least six or seven feet under those cells. By releasing the supports of the foundation we can let the floor drop down in a matter of about an hour's work, then it will be out through the tunnel and away. We will have all night and until six o'clock the next morning before the escape in discovered. In that time we should be far from the guns and guards of the Folsom Jail."

For the first time in my life I realized what it meant to be lifted from deepest misery to the heights of joy. My brain reeled with emotion. Then I saw the face of Big Bill, my persecutor, the man who had crushed me to the level of a beast, who had sworn to hound me to a convict's grave.

That night Frenchy, my new cellmate, was plainly not at ease. He lay on his bunk watching me furtively as I paced back and forth. Long afterward he told me he thought I was suffering from what they call in prison, "the life timer's spell," that awful period of the first days of a man condemned for life.

"Just a minute, Ed.," called Jake, "we have all heard about the counterfeiting plant, but I did not know how it turned out. What happened to it?"

"It blew up with a bang, Jake," I tapped. "The leak occurred somehow in San Francisco, and the United States Secret Service Agents traced the 'queer' to the last place of all places on earth, Folsom Prison. When the Government men showed their hand to the great Czar of the jail he nearly had an epileptic fit."

The Warden blustered and thundered around his office like a mad bull, I had explained to Jake. Now he accused the agents. They were enemies who were trying to frame him. "What the Hell?" he shouted, "What the Hell do you men think I am? Do you take me for a Simple Simon in charge of a home for the feeble minded? By Gad, this is a JAIL! Do you hear? This is a JAIL! Do you know who I am? Well, I'll tell you! I'm the Warden here, and I have had thirty-five years experience with Wells Fargo!"

"Do I understand you right, counterfeiting United States Coin in my Jail?" Now the pompous bleary eyed stifler of convict hopes was laughing loud and long. The joke was too much for him.

"Say, Mr. Secret Service Man," he drawled between spasms of laughter, "in my career as a detective I've had pretty tough stuff put up to me and I'll admit some of it was put over, but not much of it,— not much of it, take it from me."

"As Warden of this prison I've had some of the slickest cons that ever donned the stripes try to pull the bunk on me, but it don't go! Here's my reputation. It will show you whether I know my prison or not."

"Wherever two cons gather together, there am I. That's me, Mister, that's me! Now, what's your next move? I'm waiting, shoot!" A student of human nature would have fathomed that the Warden was bluffing. He was manifestly not at ease. No one knew better than this autocrat that he was not the man of old in his particular line. It was common talk inside that he was drinking himself to death, and depended solely upon his under officers to manage the prison.

The Warden was not left long in doubt. The Secret Service man was more than a match. "If you do not permit us to search this prison and make a proper investigation we will leave and return soon with a search warrant. It may sound funny to your ears, eh? But nevertheless the Federal Government happens to have just that power."

"Now, let's get down to business," he continued. "I am not only making the charge that counterfeiting is going on here, but I stand ready, as well, to prove it! More, I can take you to the very spot in this prison where that crime against the Government is being committed."

The Warden leaped from his chair like a panther, crushed his black sombrero down over his big head, then grabbed his Bill Sykes club, a part of his walking equipment that was known to every convict in the Jail.

"Come on," he shouted, "Come on! Bottle up any more of this chatter! Let me see your cards! Take me to a counterfeiting plant in this prison! Let me see it with my own eyes and I'll write out my resignation to the Governor within ten minutes by the watch!"

The two Government men and the Warden hurried out of the office and down the long stone steps of the Administration Building. The Warden's armed body guard followed at his heels.

The four men trooped up the road to the horse shoe circle of the prison proper. They were now standing before the Captain of the Guard's office. "Spud," as the convicts called him, was at his door eyeing the Warden queerly, and now and then measuring the strangers up and down. This P.K. knew his Warden inside and out. His first glance had told him that the "Skipper" was fuming with rage and he wondered what it was all about.

He did not have to wait long. The Warden was jeering at him in rough sarcasm. Deep within his ratty brain he was already formulating a mode of defence in which he would make the Captain "the goat" in case these slick Government men "had something up their sleeves."

"I say, Captain," he grimaced. "This is a pretty kettle of fish! This man here, tells me that we are running a counterfeiting plant in our prison! Making bogus coin, do you hear? Making bogus coin!"

"Oh, say, wait! I forgot, I should have introduced you! These two gentlemen are Secret Service Agents and they are going to show you and me where our money making machine is located! Eh, by Gad, what do you think of it? And it's not the first of April either." Now the Captain in his turn was working on his funny bone. He too was laughing, and not to leave him alone in his mirth, the Warden joined in the guffaw at the expense of the two silent visitors.

"Captain, where is your blacksmith shop?" inquired the older of the agents. "I have already wasted too much time here. I want you to take me there at once!"

"Spud," the Captain of the Guard, indicated by a jerk of his thumb and led the way across the yard. Entering the big blacksmith shop, the Secret Service men, ordered all of the convict workers from the building. That done, they whipped off their coats and commenced the search.

The two Secret Service men more than made good their claim. In less than an hour from the time they entered the shop they had dug up and spread to view the damaging evidence, molds, tools and metals, and a large quantity of coins in every stage of making. In fact, they had found a complete counterfeiting plant, the whole paraphernalia of a money making machine.

The old Stone Age Warden, the "Skipper" of Folsom Jail, staggered from the building the picture of a miserable, broken man. He seemed to have aged twenty years in the space of a minute. The bodyguard and "Spud" were holding him. Otherwise he would have crumpled to the ground.

They half carried their limping burden back across the yard, seated him in a chair in the P. K's Office, and gave him some water. Slightly revived, his first words were, "Blow the big whistle for general lockup!"

"Phone for my carriage," he groaned. "Take me to my house. I feel I am a very sick man. Gad, it is too much, and my reputation! This is the hardest blow of my whole life! But wait, but wait," he lamented, "I have the toughness of a cat with nine lives."

He heard someone 'phoning for the doctor, the prison physician. It sent him into a near epileptic fit.

"No, damn you, no 'prison croaker' for me!" He was now shouting, fairly himself once more. "Telephone to Sacramento for my physician, do you hear?" He was glaring at "Spud," who shriveled under the accusing eye.

"Oh, I'll be better by tomorrow. Then I'll take charge. Here's what I get for trusting a damned bonehead like you to run the inside of this prison."

"Clean all of the derrick cases out of the dungeon. Get it ready! I'll fill that place with every con working in the shop over there. I'll drag the lives out of them on the derrick until I squeeze the truth from every zebra mother's son of them."

His carriage had stopped at the door, and as they lifted him bodily to his seat, he still continued gibbering about what he'd do to everybody when he got on the job and took the reins of government into his own hands.

The law of compensation was at work. This unfeeling autocrat, who had crushed hundreds of poor unfortunate convicts without the slightest evidence of pity or remorse, for the first time in his long bloody career was feeling the irony of rebuke. It had humbled him to the dust, vain man that he was.

The news of the finding of a counterfeiting plant in full operation in the second largest Bastille of the State of

THE TWENTY-FIFTH MAN

California, discovered by two Government men from Washington rather than by the vigilant officers of the prison was by far the biggest joke of the season, both inside and outside of prison. It was the greatest thing that has ever occurred to show up the assininity of our whole American Model Prison System.

The "Tiger" was laughing. The quick taps indicated that he was laughing hard. "That's the best prison joke I ever heard, Ed.," he finally called. "Don't tell me any more. Everybody knows about the week of black Fridays when the poor Folsom convicts were crushed on the derrick."

"Go on with your story. I'm anxious about the tunnel plot for escape, tho I know it must have been a failure else you wouldn't be here tapping on the wall like a ghost. True, we are only shades of living men anyway. I have never seen you and I don't even know what you look like. When your story is done I want a good description of you, the color of your eyes and hair, about how much you weigh and how old you are or rather how old you look after these years of Hell. In fact, I want everything Ed., because it seems I have known you a million years."

I rapped back a good laugh. "All right, Jake, but I warn you that your description of yourself will never stand up with mine."

"Now, if you promise not to interrupt again I will try to tell you the most interesting part of all, the rest of my life in Folsom."

CHAPTER XXV

TORTURE, A FINE ART AT FOLSOM.

Over four months I worked day in and day out with that four pound hammer, trying to dig a hole through the center of a ten ton bowlder, going to my cell at the end of a long day with bursting head and eyes aching from the glaring sun.

As the time dragged out I had ceased to be an object of curiosity to my fellow prisoners. They now passed with a casual stare at the Ishmaelite fooling away his time on the top of a bald rock. Life was too strenuous in' that man-killing jail. Too much was happening from day to day. Clubbings and shootings came in rapid succession. One mere convict and his troubles were soon lost sight of in the seething maelstrom of strife and the groans of many.

In the years that have come and gone, I have often tried to analyze my feelings during the four month's time I suffered on the top of that rock, exposed to the broiling sun. I have endured the extremes of excruciating pain from direct man-handling torture under every imaginable phase of brutal prison routine, but there was no torture more appalling to me than that which I suffered in those first months of my life sentence at Folsom.

Only a man with the distorted brain of a devil incarnate could have conceived the cunning idea or have hit upon the plan to single me out as an object for such humiliation and torture as the Warden of Folsom prison had done. His orders to the foreman of the caldron of Hell were, "Put that train robber on top of the big bowlder which stands outside of your circle there! Make him work without a stop from morning until night. If he rebels or gives you even so much as a scowl stretch him on the derrick until he cries for mercy. But don't kill him, I want him to drag out a few long miserable years before we plant him on the hillside under the little white cross. Keep him on top of that rock for the next year if it takes him that long to dig a hole deep enough so that I can't see him from this window in my office."

"By that time I will have conjured up a new mode of torment for him." Those were his orders and it looked as if they would be carried out to the letter. But fate again intervened. My good angel of mercy saved me at the moment when I felt that my sanity was ebbing away.

The State Engineer in charge of all operations visited the prison. He came close to my rock and was staring up at me curiously. He had asked the foreman what that convict was doing up there.

This shrewd task master evaded the direct question but finally admitted that I was there through special orders from the Warden. "He's a bad man, Sir! He's a bad man!"

The State Engineer had turned his back in disgust. He was now calling and I could hardly believe that I understood him correctly. "Come on down from that rock!" he repeated.

I obeyed.

"What are you doing up there?" he asked.

"I don't know," I replied, holding my hand against my burning head.

"You don't know?" he queried.

I answered, "No!"

Interested he asked, "What is your name?"

I replied respectfully.

"What is your sentence?"

"Life, at hard labor!"

"How long have you been on that rock?"

"Since the day I came to this prison. Four months even, sir!"

"Have you ever been punished?"

"Yes sir! Every day since I came to this place, every day of my four months,— there on the top of that rock."

Taken back he hurried to explain, "I don't mean that way. Have you ever been sent to the punishment dungeons or, in other words, have you refused to perform useful labor?"

"No sir, I have not! I have never even been given the chance."

"Are you willing to do useful work? Do you suppose you could learn to cut stone if you had a chance?" he finally asked.

I told him that I was willing to work. More, that I would try hard to learn to cut stone. Further, that I would do anything that was right to prove that I was not the bad man the foreman had called me.

In the next instant he had wheeled upon the big blustering braggart. "Put a gang of men to work at once splitting up this bowlder so that it cannot be used hereafter for such a despicable purpose. The law of the State does not permit a human being to be treated in any such manner. I consider this an outrage and I shall report it to the governing body, the State Board of Prison Commissioners."

"Start this man as an apprentice and show him how to cut stone. Those are your orders and I will give the same to your Warden."

Turning, he looked at me compassionately. His were the first kind words that I had heard from a freeman. They had softened my heart and I humbly thanked him.

I stood at the rock listening to my convict instructor for several days. Then an inspiration came to do my best and prove my worth by mastering the trade of stone cutting which usually takes four years, in the same length of time that I had spent in worthless effort on top of the rock. I worked tirelessly, accomplishing in four months what I had set out to do, and at the end of that time had an apprentice under me.

I then learned that my energy had been taken only as an added evidence of my criminal viciousness. Now the order had been passed down from the tyrant on the hill to commence crushing in earnest. I was soon subjected to increased espionage.

Life and everything else was upside down in prison, topsy-turvey, distorted as reading in a mirror.

The blow fell at last. It started with a guard accusing me of having stepped out of line when I had not. It had come at the end of a long hard day's work just as I was about to pass through the man-gate. One of the foot-guards, club in hand, dragged me from the line.

"Spud," the P. K., was standing at his office door waiting. It had all been arranged. Reckless, indignant I never flinched before the scowling tyrant, and hardly knowing or caring what I said I called the guard a "liar."

Two man-handlers were now holding me firmly by both arms. "Spud" was shrieking, "Oh, you're starting trouble, uh, even before your stripes are dirty? By Gad I'll do for you! Calling a freeman a liar, uh?"

"Take him away, take him away! Give him fifty hours on the derrick!"

I heard no more. I was being shoved through the man-gate. At this time in Folsom ten hours on the derrick caused the near death of any man. He had to be made of iron to stand up under it.

I only knew about the derrick from hear-say, but if it proved to be one half as bad as convict victims had told me, then that brute Captain had sentenced me to death. "Good

God!" I thought. "Fifty hours hanging by the wrists in the derrick!"

This meant hanging five hours a day,— ten days to complete the fifty hours,— the rest of the time being spent on the cold stone floor without even a blanket to cover my shivering body. The food for that period would be a few ounces of dry bread and just enough water to slake my burning thirst once every twenty-four hours.

It was fiendish, hellish, unbelievable, and I had still to learn what they did to men on the derrick. Here my imagination ended, but I had all night to think it over for the torture would not begin until early morning. This first night in the dungeon would not count in my sentence.

The torture chambers in Folsom were located in what was called the "back alley." They were boarded off from the rest of the cell houses. In there the groans and moans of the victims were lost in empty air.

I was one of ten convicts to face the punishment machines the next morning. They told me this number was not anything unusual. It was about the average complement day in and day out the year around at Folsom.

My cell door was the last of the ten opened. The freeman in charge gruffly ordered me to step out. The bright light of the corridor confused me for a moment and then I saw the horrifying spectacle of nine unfortunate human beings all dangling from the ends of ropes. They were suspended each one by a block and tackle, from a balcony above their heads.

Two convict assistants helped the freeman perform his gruesome work. My arms were extended backward and then a pair of handcuffs were snapped upon my wrists. One of the convicts began pulling the rope which was attached to the handcuffs, drawing me slowly upward. When my heels were just off the floor the attendant made a move to tie the rope fast to a cleat on the side of the wall, but he was brushed aside by the dungeon warder who grasped it with both hands and with the full weight of his body gave it a savage jerk.

It was cruel, unmerciful! The weight of my body caused the steel of the handcuffs to cut deeply into my wrists, as I swung limply at the end of the block and tackle. Now he released an inch or so of slack until I had again regained a steadying position, the tip toes of my brogans resting on the stone flags of the dungeon corridor.

Satisfied that he had me just where he wanted me he made the rope fast to the cleat and then stepped back. Glaring fiendishly he spoke for the first time. "Damn you, if I had all your kind in here for just thirty days I would wipe out the crime of train robbery in this State forever!"

I had a constitution with the toughness of iron and perfect health, but could I possibly endure this for two and a half hours, the morning stretch? My head was tilted downward to the level of my waist, forced into that unnatural position by my arms being trussed up backward and held tightly by the cruel handcuffs.

My first sensation was one of reeling drunkenness, caused by the blood rushing to my head. I had not received a bite of food since twelve o'clock the preceding day and was weak and nauseated.

There was a cold splash of water. It revived me, and I half consciously made out the form of one of the convicts playing a hose upon me. He stopped when he observed that I was coming to. Full of pity he whispered encouragingly, "By the heavens, Morrell, you're the first man who has ever stood that in the history of Folsom. They usually go out in ten minutes. And you never whimpered."

"Say, what has the 'Skipper' against you anyway? You're a fish on the derrick and he's handing you the limit on the first stretch. Only cons who try to escape get that. Here, take a drink of water. Keep a stout heart and you will be down in twenty minutes."

I had been hanging two hours and ten minutes! Unbelievable!

I had registered only the first sensations. All the balance was a blank to my conscious mind. But now, since I was revived again, each awful minute dragged out with the seeming slowness of centuries. Warm blood was trickling down my arms from my lacerated wrists. I had bitten my tongue while I was unconscious. The blood had coagulated in my mouth. My breathing was slow and heavy, but I still managed to struggle on to the end of that eternity,—twenty minutes.

The warder had returned and ordered the dungeon tenders to commence releasing. The convict who had so mercifully played the hose upon me, stepped to my derrick. While he was in the act of taking me down the free man shouted, "No, by God, not on your life! He was last up and he is going to be the last down."

This meant little to me at the moment, but before they had finished releasing the other nine unfortunates I realized the coveted boon of which this unfeeling monster had deprived me. More than ten minutes were consumed before the last man in line had staggered drunkenly into his cell.

Gripping upon my will I braced myself, when the weight of my body was released and the handcuffs taken off. I was the first man who ever walked upright from the derrick after two and a half hours of torture.

Men usually dropped limply to the floor and crawled on hands and knees back into the dark shelter of their cells, after even the mildest torture on the derrick, moaning piteously from their bruises.

On the seventh day the prison "croaker" was called to the dungeon. Alarmed, the convict attendant had brought him to my derrick. I was undergoing the afternoon stretch. Blood had been dripping from my kidneys for two hours. Both of my shoes were soggy from the warm fluid. It had stained even the flagstones beneath me.

THE TWENTY-FIFTH MAN

The convict runner told me afterward that large blue black circles had formed around my eyes while the rest of my face was ashen white. "Morrell, I sure thought you would be dead in another ten minutes if that 'croaker' hadn't ordered you taken down," he said.

The "croaker" had not come on a mission of mercy, but rather from curiosity to see the notorious outlaw convict who had been specially marked for a quick ending by the "Skipper" of Folsom Jail. Prison "croakers" at best do not stand very high among convicts, but this man, parading in the guise of a physician, a healer, was a dishonor and a disgrace to the medical profession.

Next to the Warden and "Spud," the Captain of the Guard, he was the third most hated man, cursed and reviled by every convict in the prison. Sober, he was cold, cynical, and mean. Drunk, he had the temper of a raging bull, and would hurl anything within the reach of his hand at the first defenceless convict who might approach him.

The drinking bouts of the "Skipper" and the "croaker" were common talk throughout the big prison, and often during one of these protracted sprees they would have a falling out. Then they would not speak for a couple of months, and during that time the "croaker" resorted to all manner of spite work to aggravate the Warden.

On this occasion, while I was still hanging in the derrick, he looked me over carefully with a mock show of sympathy. Wagging his head back and forth he gave several "Ahems" as a mild protest against such extreme brutality. He then ordered me taken down and placed in my dungeon cell, leaving instructions that I was not to be hung up again until released from his care.

At the end of three days the torture was resumed. It took me thirteen days to do my first fifty hours on the derrick at Folsom.

I had offended against the all powerful "Octopus," and try how I would I could not square myself with the prison authorities. Feeling more than ever the hopelessness of my plight, I wondered when the tip would come that the tunnel was ready for me to escape by way of the dungeon.

Another month had passed, and still no word. I became restive. I could see that my guards were now preparing for a new trap to put me to the torture again. Then I was lost sight of for the moment in the general excitement of the prison.

Folsom was stirred to its very foundations. One of the biggest plots for a prison break in its history had been uncovered. A new scandal had broken out and the Warden was once more in disgrace.

The newspapers of the State were openly denouncing him for allowing desperate convicts to dig a tunnel under the prison, big enough to drive through with a horse and wagon. It had been discovered just in time to prevent the escape of a large body of the worst men in the prison, they said.

Next to unearthing a counterfeiting plant at Folsom this tunnel, right under the eyes of the vigilant keepers of the confined, almost proved to be the finishing blow to the Warden. To me, it was like my death knell, but I soon forgot all of my own troubles in sympathy for the poor unfortunates who were involved in the plot. To a man they were nearly crucified on the derrick. Folsom had degenerated to a shambles. It was a horror and a nightmare.

Somehow, I managed to struggle through my first year's incarceration in that mad sink hole of perdition. Many stretches of torture on the derrick had caused me to become wily and prison sly. Old hardened characters styled it "con-wise." I now no longer showed the iron in my composition. In order to live I must beat the game. I acted the part of one crushed and broken, all the while boiling beneath with vengeance.

The foot-guards plied me with curses to aggravate me to rebellion, but I turned a deaf ear to all such revilings.

THE TWENTY-FIFTH MAN

I was biding my time, plotting from an unheard of vantage point. I had been frustrated in several attempts to escape, the last of which nearly proved to be my ending.

The "Angel of the Prison," as the convicts called her, the Warden's wife, had saved me. She had overheard her husband planning to allow me to make the get-away. He had secretly stationed guards outside to shoot me down in cold blood, and she sent the information through another convict, to warn me against my peril.

They waited for days and, when I did not fall into the trap, gave the signal for my arrest. Two foot-guards dragged me from the line and forced me through the door of the P. K.'s office. The Warden, "Spud," the Captain of the Guard, and about a half dozen other underling officers and guards were in the room.

Spread out on a table was a complete bicycle uniform made from a suit of blue. It had been filched from the guard's quarters by Frenchy, my cellmate, "Spud's" private stool pigeon. It had been cut and made to order in the tailor shop by one of my best convict friends.

The get-away would have been absolutely sure. It was all planned that I should escape from prison on a bicycle. This was possible on any Sunday, because large numbers of people came on excursion parties and all used bicycles. Disguised, I could mingle freely with them, pick up a wheel from the stack at Liberty Post, and ride away.

This plot was revealed through the treachery of another prisoner, a man who had proved a weakling and decided to profit by my misfortune.

I was put through a soul crushing third degree in that office. The Warden thundered that he would murder me if I did not confess how I came into possession of the guard's clothes.

I stoutly protested my innocence, insisting that I was framed. But this had no effect. I was battered and beaten by the burly man-handlers and it was long after midnight before they gave up the struggle.

Frothing at the mouth the Warden ended a tirade of curses. "By God, if you don't tell, then all right! I'll finish you this time."

"Take him away and give him the chloride of lime cell!" he commanded. "If he lives through that he'll hang his mother before he'll take another dose of it."

I finished the rest of that night in the dungeon, bruised and battered from the devil's prodding that had been given me in the P. K.'s office, and now I was to get the chloride of lime cell. Only two other convicts had suffered that ordeal in the history of the prison, and I wondered what the outcome would be. I had heard terrible stories, and knew that it beggared the terrors of the Spanish Inquisition.

I had already lost faith in man and was now even losing faith in God, and by the time my tormentors opened my cell door I was so blind with anger that I welcomed the sacrifice. I vowed that if the accursed fate, which seemed to pursue me with such an unrelenting fury, would let me live on, I would willingly sell my soul to the fiend incarnate, the very devil himself, for a temporary power to turn upon my enemies and rend them to pieces.

Before the open door of the torture chamber, two powerful guards held my arms pinioned from behind. I could see the white coating of lime inside of the cell. It had been spread evenly upon the dungeon floor at least three inches thick.

One of the guards was freely sprinkling it with water through a hose. A white mist from the exploding chloride of lime was filling the cell. They shoved me inside in another instant and closed the door with a bang.

I clutched my burning throat with both hands, then reeled and fell to the floor. That only brought me closer to the volcano of fiery death. Struggling frantically I scratched at the jutting stones of the dungeon trying to pull myself to my feet.

I then staggered, groping blindly until I hit the door. I pounded upon it with my bare hands.

Cramping pains tore at my bowels. My breath grew hot. It had the intensity of molten lead. My fingers, hands, and arms finally became numb, and paralyzing shocks stunned my brain. Had I been offered a draught of deadly poison in that awful agony I would have drunk it with gratitude,— anything to escape further torture in that lethal chamber of Hell.

The black hole seemed at last to revolve. I felt my position slowly reverse. It now appeared that my head was down and my feet up. Then I started to whirl and as if obeying some terrific centrifugal force I was shot off into space.

The door was opened and a guard reached in with a long hook and dragged out my limp body. The dungeon tender played the hose upon me. The cooling water stifled the burning fumes and slowly brought me back to life.

The whole gruesome deed hardly consumed six minutes in actual time, but I had been dead for ages. Two guards laid hold of my legs and dragged me back to the cell where I had spent the night.

What I suffered for the next ten days beggars description. The delicate mucous membrane of my mouth and throat was seared and burnt. My eyebrows and eyelashes were gone. I could not speak above a whisper. Physically I was a wreck, and the day I left that dungeon to report again for work I was a changed man. The iron of hate had branded my heart.

Henceforth it would be plot and counter plot. I lived on solely for vengeance.

The end of my second year was near at hand. I worked with unflagging energy to spin the scattered threads of my spider web so that they would encompass the prison. This time I was determined that nothing should fail me. It was to come with the suddenness of an earthquake. I had picked upon one reliable man. He had been released and I had sent him to friends outside.

This man had faithfully carried out his part. Rifles and pistols and ammunition were already cached in the foothills near the Folsom Prison, awaiting the word to be brought in at night and planted inside the deadlines. The plan of prison mutiny was complete. Trusted men stood ready to perform their part.

My confederates outside were to cut telephone and telegraph lines, isolating Folsom Prison in the foothills from the world. The signal for assault was to be given at ten sharp on a Sunday morning when all of the prisoners were out in the upper yard.

The P. K.'s office was to be taken quietly and "Spud," the Captain of the Guard, was to be forced to 'phone the Warden and bring him there on a ruse. That done, the two were to be led to the first gatling gun tower and ordered to command surrender.

While this was going on, expert rifle men among the mutineers were to get into commanding positions to cover the tower and open fire in case surrender was refused. A like procedure was to be carried out from post to post until the entire guard line was taken.

When the prison was captured, the real work would commence. The tables were to be turned. The former tyrants would be our captives, and the Warden, Doctor, Captain, and several extremely brutal guards were to be given a speedy trial by court-martial, and undoubtedly their sentence would be death by hanging. What an irony of fate that they should be taken to the death house and executed on the State's murder machine, the prison gallows!

CHAPTER XXVI

A PRISON TRANSFER.

A prison Judas betrayed the mutiny plot. A black cloud hovered over Folsom. Once again fate was operating. The beam of the scale hung evenly balanced.

The shocking prison brutalities had, at last, released forces that were now almost beyond control. Like a spark of fire in the dry tinder of a vast prairie, winds of hate were fanning the flames into a raging inferno which would consume the author of its being, the hated Warden of Folsom Prison.

He was horrified and baffled. His stunted mind would not allow him to believe that his dread torture machines had failed him. He, the unfeeling judge and executioner who had made convicts grovel in fear and tremble even at the thought of breaking one of his ironclad rules, was now fast losing control.

The discipline of the prison was breaking to pieces. His brute guards were becoming untrustworthy. Even "Spud," the Captain of the Guard, was growing lazy and stupid as proven by the many prison intrigues and near escapes which had occurred in the last year. Now had come the crowning horror of all. A plot had been hatched right under his nose. Twenty-five of the most desperate men confined were to act as leaders and drive the fourteen hundred others into open mutiny. They were to blow the prison off the map, and the irony of it all, he, the Warden, was to be the first man marked for slaughter.

He shriveled up in fear this time. He forgot his "Inquisition machines." They were for the moment lost in the thought only of how he could quickly be rid of his convict plotters. He must resort to an emergency transfer! It was imperative. No time should be lost. Hidden dangers engulfed him.

His drink-sodden mind cleared for the first time in several years, and he was sobered by the revelations into the semblance of his former self, a man of action. For nearly an hour he sat at the long distance telephone in his private office, calling up the members of the State Board of Prison Commissioners to come at once to the prison and hold an emergency meeting.

Saturday afternoon the State Board of Control arrived and almost immediately went into secret session, where the Warden briefly laid the facts before them and urged that the twenty-five ring leaders be transferred early Monday morning to San Quentin Prison, as a precautionary measure for the safety of Folsom.

Alarmed over the shocking disclosures, the governing body ordered the transfer. The Warden was relieved. A burden had been lifted from his shoulders.

Henceforth, this would be a lesson to him. He would mark time and watch his step. From now on all officers and guards on the Folsom line would feel the brunt of his fist. Further, he planned a careful weeding out of every man who had shirked his duty and he even calculated how he could discharge his man, "Friday,"—"Spud," the Captain of the Guard,— who had been with him for years.

A happy thought came to him then. "If I can only get rid of the Captain of the Guard and in his place substitute a different calibre of man, I might take advantage of it to announce a new policy and blame all of the past upon him."

"By softening up a little, I might re-establish myself as a popular Warden." The light was breaking. Cowardice and fear were stripping the man of his iron. His torture machines had failed him in commanding respect. To a man the convicts hated him. He would therefore resort to cajolery.

Monday morning the dead routine of the prison began. The convicts were being counted out through the man-gate.

They were filing slowly to their hated tasks, the work of the day. Marked men were jerked from the line. Twenty-five of us were soon standing to one side, and as the end of the line passed clear we were ordered back inside.

There we were commanded to strip naked and each man was given an old pair of pants, a shirt, and brogans. We were not allowed underwear or stockings.

A long bull-chain was dragged into the corridor. It had cross chains with handcuffs at intervals of every two feet. "Spud," the Captain, pushed me to the front end handcuffing my left wrist to the first cross chain himself.

That done, he walked over and singled out another man, bringing him forward and repeating the operation. We two convicts were to lead the line. The man was my trusted lieutenant, one of the principal ring leaders in the prison break which was to have taken place on the next Sunday.

My heart sank. It was the first suspicion which had crossed my mind that anything had gone wrong. This was a complete surprise. I felt whipped and beaten. Nothing seemed real. The world was only a phantom and I but an atom of dust just floating aimlessly.

At last the twenty-five were handcuffed to the long bull-chain. Then several guards commenced to attach leg irons, heavy shackles, to the right and left leg of each pair of men in line. That done "Spud," the Captain, shouted an order to march. He was leading the way through the man-gate.

Once clear of the prison, about fifteen foot-guards with clubs strung along on each side, and we started out of Folsom and down to the railroad.

Work had stopped. Hundreds of convicts were watching, wondering what was going on. A heavy coach was waiting at the railroad. The engine had steam up, ready to go. I dragged in, the others following, and then the doors were slammed and locked. Guards with rifles were stationed at each end. We were next moving out of the prison and it was soon lost to sight.

I left Folsom after two years of living Hell on earth. I had entered just two years before, only a boy verging on manhood, clean of body and clean of soul with none but the kindliest of impulses, holding not a mean thought against a human being in the world.

Just two short years had come and gone, but I had lived and endured an eternity of suffering and wrongs. My life was completely changed. Bitter hatred was boiling in my heart. It rankled and seared my soul. Inwardly I cursed man-made laws and even the law of God. Liberty now meant nothing to me. I lived merely for vengeance and hated the fate that balked my plans for revenge.

At any other time but now I would have welcomed the transfer as an act of divine mercy, because San Quentin was not the lockup of the "Octopus," and there I might redeem myself for a life of future usefulness. But now all was changed. I wanted to remain at Folsom. I hungered for the clash. I wanted to hear the sharp crack of the rifles and see men in blue coats and brass buttons fall. If the day went against us I would have welcomed death because I had reached the end of the trail.

"That is all," I rapped to the "Tiger." "You know the rest about my transfer from Folsom to San Quentin, the riot in the Jute Mill and later the treachery of Sir Harry which resulted in my second life sentence, this time to the dungeon."

The weird, incessant tapping of the knuckle voice had stopped. I had waited all afternoon, wondering why the "Tiger" failed to bombard me with his usual unexpected questions. Then again, I wanted him to make some comment on the long story. I was disappointed. He said nothing.

Several days later I heard the familiar call, "tick, dash, tick tick tick tick tick;" then "tick, dash, four ticks,"

"Ed.," in knuckle voice. He went on, "Are you a fatalist?" Amused at the "Tiger" and wishing to draw him out I asked, "Why?"

"Only this, your story has me guessing. If there isn't anything in fatalism I can't understand why your life has been spared through all those harrowing experiences. There is either something in it, Ed., or life is one of the damnedest jokes that was ever perpetrated on a human being."

"But we will talk about that later," he went on. "Tell me what became of the old outlaw Chief?"

"He too was sent to Folsom, but the Warden never allowed him outside of the cell house building. He was given light duties tending a gate near the hospital and was not permitted to mingle freely with the convicts. The Warden feared his dominating influence upon them. He might lead them to attack the prison. He had been an old soldier and knew how to command men."

"But the 'Octopus' was not idle," I continued. "Other men in the San Joaquin Valley and the mountains who were under grave suspicion of being members of our band, were railroaded to prison on trumped-up charges of crime. One in particular, a very good friend, the owner of the ranch where I had eaten the chicken dinner after the battle of Slick Rock, was arrested on a charge of robbery. He was given twenty years in Folsom, a victim of injustice through the hatred of the 'Octopus'."

"Another man was given fifteen years. The agents of the railroad had framed him. He was innocent of the unmentionable charge and died of a broken heart in prison."

"Later on, the proprietor of the notorious 'Hole in the Wall' in Visalia's Spanish Town, was tried on a charge of train robbery and given a life sentence. Many other men under suspicion, fearing the long mailed hand of the common tyrant, had quietly left the country forever, ringing down the curtain on the last act in the aftermath of the history of the Mussel Sleugh.''

Solitary was a bitter place. The "Tiger" thirteen cells away had kept me from insanity, and I had done the same for him, yet the very taps by which we conversed, tho scarcely audible to the most alert hearing were an infraction of the rules. Our guards were mere elemental beasts. The place was unthinkable. The outside world was dead. We were buried alive, and still the "Tiger" and I talked about anything and everything.

We might speculate a week over what, to people in a living, moving world, would be but a triviality.

We were cursed and reviled for our rapping, but that did not stop us. We continued it, delving into every conceivable subject. Then we again grew restless. The "Tiger" had been showing remarkable growth, reaching out for greater avenues of knowledge. Still, his feeling of suppression became much akin to mine.

Our life stories had been told and it was now necessary to find something new to stifle our misery.

"The magazine business! Let us publish one," I knuckled to the "Tiger."

"Good!" said Jake. "Let's call it 'The Mental Utopia'!"

Once again we were feverishly busy. The "Tiger" took charge of the advertising, introducing a new and humorous method. He also had short stories and illustrations with the sporting news. I handled special columns, editorials, treatises and essays on philosophy and travel.

We had so much work blocked out that, on the day of issue, when the "Utopia" came off the mental press, it would take nearly a month to exchange it through the medium of the knuckle voice. But that even grew monotonous in time.

The darkness, the small space I had lived in so long, the foul air, all began to pall upon me. From every corner the

THE TWENTY-FIFTH MAN

demon of insanity leered at me, again maliciously waiting for my fall.

The crisis was at hand. I had fought against the inevitable for months. Then something happened.

Freemen, strangers, had visited the dungeon. Through the bars of my cell door I could see "Give-a-damn," the warder of solitary, shaking hands with one they called the new Warden. I heard the words, "the new Administration."

It was the first intimation the "Tiger" and I had that the old crew of prison brutes had been kicked out in disgrace. Convicts always fear a change. "A new broom sweeps clean."

They were now at my cell. In another instant "Give-a-damn" had pulled the new Warden to one side. "Look out for that man," I heard him say in a whisper. "Don't take any chances with him. Never trust your face near the door. He would jab your eye out with his finger if he had the chance. That's the man, Morrell, who has the firearms planted somewhere in this prison. He was sentenced to life in here, and he refuses to give up the guns."

"Yes! I've heard all about him." The new Warden was speaking. "And I know all about the guns too. Wait until I get the ropes of this place and have a little time to look over the ground. I'll find out all about this prison plot. I brought the model of an overcoat here when I came to San Quentin. I'm having several made from the pattern. When I get ready to use that coat, if there are any guns planted on Point San Quentin I will have them within three weeks or I'm a liar."

He was evidently talking loudly for my benefit. I looked him over more closely. He was anything but prepossessing, slight of build, about five feet seven, with dark, swarthy features. A drooping black mustache concealed his mouth. He had one eye.

I gave him his name instantly, the "Pirate." It stuck to him to the end of his bloody career at that prison. All in all he was the most ill appearing man we ever had in San Quentin.

"Give-a-damn" opened my door and ordered me to step out.

The group of men eyed me strangely. I must have looked like an apparition to them. My matted hair almost concealed my face. My beard was getting long. My old clothes were tattered from constant wear through the months in the dungeon.

"Morrell, from all I hear about you, you must be a pretty tough customer," the Warden said.

That introduction boded evil for me. I did not reply. Nettled he went on, evidently bent upon creating an impression for the benefit of the others.

"So you wouldn't give up the guns, uh, and you have them planted down here in the prison? All right, I will make a try at finding them. I'll be up to see you in a few weeks when I get my sea boots on. I don't think you're comfortable here. I'm going to put an overcoat on you. It will keep you nice and warm. It might cause you to feel different and maybe tell where the guns are."

"In fact, I know it will. If it don't, then you're a devil and I'm a piker." "Give-a-damn" pushed me back in the cell.

When I was alone again I called up the "Tiger." But he had overheard the loud talk of the new Warden, the man I had nicknamed "the one eyed Pirate." More, he had seen him. The Warden had gone to his cell to look him over.

"I don't think much of him, Ed., and if my judgment of Stone Age Wardens is worth anything, I guess fate has handed us a rotten deal in this new shuffle. I am afraid we are in for a racking time, and it might be well that we cut the talk until we see which way the cat will jump."

The poor "Tiger's" knuckle talk now sounded gloomy to my ear, and I thought of the fearful story he had told me of his life. Everything he had done had seemed to be against him from the first. Even his premature birth was the result of a tragedy.

He had never gone to school. He worked on the messenger service when but a child. He was just a boy when he came under the ban of the law for resenting an act of injustice. He was charged with assault, having shot the superintendent of the messenger force, and refused to take the stand to vindicate himself. It would have brought the name of a young woman into the case. This was his novitiate course in the honor code of the under-world.

His silence brought down upon him a long sentence in jail. There he was molded by specialists in crime, who expounded warped, distorted concepts of right and wrong to the boy. He learned that law and the minions of the law were his natural enemies, to be circumvented and opposed. Hardened jail companions had told him it was right to commit perjury in defence of an under-world friend, and that death was the proper ending for traitors.

He went back to the under-world after his release from jail. Next time he faced the court on the serious charge of robbery. He had really taken no part in the crime. Four men had been arrested. One of them turned traitor, and in order to have his younger brother saved from prison he unfolded a tale to the District Attorney. It was perjury. He confessed that the other two men and himself were guilty, but that they had his "kid brother in wrong" and that he would "come clean," testify for the State and also tell who the fourth man was if he were given the mercy of the Court. He then gave the name of Jake Oppenheimer as the fourth man.

Poor Jake was the first tried. The other two youths were forced to sit silently by and hear another man sentenced to fifty years on perjured evidence. They dared not speak in his behalf, as their own guilt had not yet been determined. Everything went black before Jake's eyes, a boy of eighteen given fifty years!

Then, he remembered the honor code of the under-world. Fifty years, life, forty years, and ten years completed the judges' work for that day, closing the lives of four young criminals, three of them equally guilty,— himself, innocent.

"How strange!" he thought. "If the law were just our sentences should at least have been uniform."

The poor "Tiger" questioned me, "Why should a judge show leniency to a man who is a partner in crime? Does the fact that he trades his damaging evidence for the conviction of the other, make him less criminal and dangerous to Society?"

"He is a Judas any way you can put it, and the only difference between the ancient and modern one is that the betrayer of Christ committed suicide. Treachery is treachery the world over," he said, "and I just echo the cry of nations when I say, 'death to all traitors'!"

His under-world training now bore fruit. He had entered Folsom Prison to serve his fifty years. He was there on trial before the bar of public opinion of that miniature world behind prison walls. The very knife which was to vindicate the "code," was thrust into his hand.

The traitor who had condemned him to fifty years penal servitude without pity, felt his impending doom. He too had been given a knife. It was a fair duel, the knives being drawn at almost the same moment. A few flashes from the gleaming blades and the informer lay gasping. His life's blood stained the stone flags of the prison yard.

Jake was now sentenced to life imprisonment, making life and fifty years. The victim of a distorted concept, the code of the under-world, indeed faced a tragic future. Having committed a crime in Folsom he was this time remanded to San Quentin. His arrival there was a signal for persecution.

"Break his spirit or kill him!" That was the order given. He had now run counter to a guard. He was sentenced to three months of unmerciful treatment in a dungeon. When released he was once more framed and thrown back into the dungeon.

The sinister voice of the jail again uttered its disapproval of Jake's forbearance. The ready knife was thrust into his hands with the encouraging words, "Be game and strike back." And the guard who had started his downward dungeon career was the next to fall under the upraised hand of Oppenheimer.

The prison howled its approval into his dazed ears. The gallows were cheated a second time for the victim lived. Jake was sentenced to the dungeon for the balance of his natural life.

They now called him "The Tiger of the Prison Cage."

CHAPTER XXVII

THE BLACK TERROR OF SAN QUENTIN. THE REVELATION.

My cell door banged shut. I was left alone, and writhing myself across the floor an inch at a time, with the edge of the sole of my right shoe I rapped out on the wall a message to the "Tiger."

I was fearful that he might rebel. He had heard the loud talk and the man-handling down in my cell. I urged him to keep quiet.

A new horror had struck San Quentin. History, as black as Hell was now in the making.

The "One Eyed Pirate," the Warden just appointed, had introduced a peculiar looking torture machine which was later known as "the Bloody Strait-jacket" of San Quentin. The "Pirate," however, always insisted upon calling it his "Overcoat," or at odd times, when he was mad, just "the Jacket."

I was the first victim to be crushed in its constricting folds. My agonized groans and the smearing of my blood were its baptismal at San Quentin.

It had come at the end of a short raspy interview with the "Pirate." He had returned to solitary as he promised he would do on the occasion of his official rounds of the prison.

He shot right to the mark. "Morrell, I understand you are boasting you have the firearms safely hidden down in the prison,— that nobody but you knows anything about them, and that you defy the authorities of the State to find them. You are biding your time playing a waiting game in the hope you will wear down the prison officials and make them believe you are innocent. After your release, then the fireworks!"

"Briefly, that is your program, is it not?"

I did not speak for a while, just listening on to the strange turn of affairs. This "new fish" of a Warden was threshing out old history. When he concluded I politely remarked, "The matter that you are talking about is closed. I have already received my trial on that charge. Five judges heard the evidence and condemmed me to solitary for the balance of my life."

"Oh, is that your alibi?" he ejaculated. "Well, it is a good one so far as it goes, but I am here to tell you it doesn't go far. Get this in your mind squarely, and be sure you get it right. Those five judges might have been all right in their own way, but now you're looking at a man who has the power of those five judges rolled into one, and as such I am going to try this case myself all over again."

"I have brought with me the means to enforce my orders. Before I begin you have one chance to redeem yourself. Surrender the firearms and I will see to it that your sentence to this place for life is revoked. More, I will wipe the slate clean and restore you to good conduct where you can have the same opportunity as any other prisoner in San Quentin who is serving a life sentence."

The "Pirate" gave me twenty-four hours to think it over, and they were now opening my cell door to make good his threats.

I gazed at it with curiosity. It was made of coarse heavy canvas. It was about four feet long, and had brass eyelets on the sides, four inches apart. On the inside of the jacket were two canvas pockets.

It was in the hand of "Give-a-damn," the warder of solitary. In his other hand he held a coil of new half inch manila rope. Extending the gruesome thing out before him, with an oath he ordered me to put my hands into the pockets. That done, he wrapped the canvas folds about me and inserting the rope through the eyelets, began lacing it tight across the back.

This accomplished, he jerked me off my feet, flung me face down upon the floor. He braced his foot against my back and pulled the rope still tighter, until my breath came in short hard gasps.

He called to one of his assistants to take an end and help him cinch. The two men tugged on the rope with all their might, until no more slack could be forced from the canvas shroud. Then "Give-a-damn" tied it fast in a knot, rolled me over on my back and stepped outside.

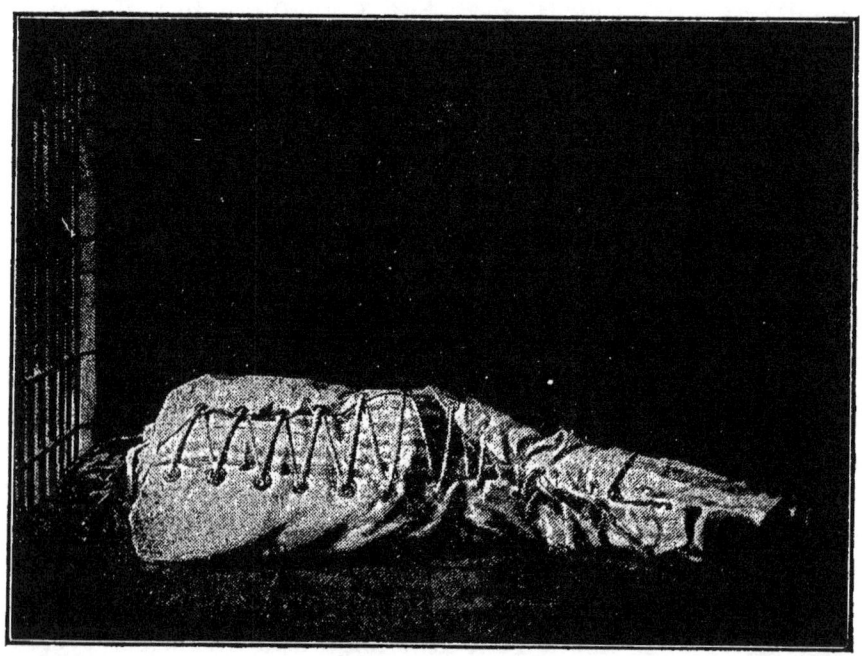

Ed. Morrell, Jack London's "Star Rover."
in the San Quentin Strait-Jacket.

Before he closed the door, the "Pirate" coolly remarked, "If he wants to talk within the next forty-eight hours, release him from the jacket and telephone to me. That's all."

From the day I had entered Folsom, the jail of the "Octopus," until now, I thought that I had run the whole gamut of man's inhumanity to man. The lingering horrors of the derrick were still fresh in my mind — the nights of misery in a dungeon, lying on a cold stone floor without a blanket to cover my shivering body. The chloride of lime cell was terrible, but too sudden to register sensations of pain. Only its aftermath of broken health and twinging nerves remained in the stuff of my memory.

Man-handlings, clubbings, and third degreeings were mere incidents of my prison life, a part of Folsom and later of San Quentin. I shall never forget the long night of insanity spent with seven others in the stone cell, filled with water to our necks, listening to the groans and the pleadings for mercy of the other unfortunates, or the months endured in the bare solitary cell as black as night, punishment for my part as one of the leaders in the Jute Mill Mutiny.

At last came the greatest tragedy of all, when I was framed on the San Quentin gun plot. I had not forgotten the prodding with pick handles, and the slow torturous third degree in which we were taken from the dungeon singly to the Captain of the Yard's Office. After that came the long wait thirty-six days in the dungeon on bread and water, fastened to the wall by a three foot bull-chain attached to my leg with a shackle, then my trial and sentence to solitary for the balance of my life.

But now a new chapter of harried and frightful experiences was about to start. We moderns look back at the dark ages with horror. We shiver when we think of the cruelties inflicted upon the victims of the dread reign of the Spanish Inquisition, and the shuddering brutalities of Chinese pot-heading, their lopping of ears and the chopping of hands and feet of condemned criminals before death; the Malaysian's turgid methods of blood vengeance, pouring oil on the kinky wool of their victims and setting fire to it, placing a large rat inside of an iron basin and tying it to the captive to eat its way through the unfortunate's body.

The awful history of tyrants, Hindu, Persian, and Egyptians; and blood curdling accounts of the terrible

Turk, and the black Czars of Russia have come down to us. France, Germany, England and Italy, all have their history of fiendish tortures. England's shocking jail system, from the days of the first feeble attempts at amelioration by that sainted man, John Howard, to the present has made its victims cry aloud to Heaven for mercy; but from remotest times these iniquities were perpetrated openly and without shame that the world might see.

Not so our American Model Jail System. It hides its depravity and soul crushing deeds behind drab stone walls, away from the light of day and in the bleak gloom of a dungeon where the poor defenceless mortals may shriek out their agony alone and unheard.

It has been often said that "the master knows less about the scandals of his own home than his neighbors." The adage aptly applies to the citizen of this country when it comes to the question of knowledge of our public institutions. His ignorance is amazing, because he knows absolutely nothing about them or their management. The American Prison System, with its red record of jail horrors, is a closed book of mysteries to him, and if it were not for the few feeble voices of heroic souls that are now and again raised as they come out of the jails in this country, not a word,— not a protest would be heard.

"The one-eyed Pirate's 'Overcoat'," the bloody straight-jacket of San Quentin prison, that instrument of Hell, in its black terror outrivaled even the horrors depicted by Poe in the "Pit and the Pendulum." Jungle travelers have described the awful agony of a native victim being squeezed to death by a giant boa-constrictor. It is all too terrible for the human mind to contemplate, but even this inconceivable spectacle must pale before the death terrors of the jacket.

I had not been in it fifteen minutes when pains began shooting through my fingers, hands and arms, gradually extending to my shoulders. Then over my whole body there was a prickling sensation like that of millions of sharp needles jabbing through the tender flesh.

Next a feeling of horror seized me. I must try to burst the canvas folds ere the devil's trap would choke out the last breath of life. In a superhuman effort I pitched my body upward and over, rolling against the opposite wall from the one where I had been tapping to the "Tiger" with my foot.

I now kicked frantically with my heavy shoes and at last succeeded in tearing a shriek from my suffocating lungs. With a bound, "Give-a-damn" was at the door.

"Shut up, damn you!" he shouted. "If you want to talk, the Warden is ready to listen. Hey, Mac, bring the gag, and I'll bottle up any further noise." In a few more minutes, another misery was added to that torture. "Give-a-damn" had roughly forced a gag, made of heavy sole leather, into my mouth, tying the bands securely around my neck.

Hour after hour I endured the pain and as the time passed the anguish became more and more unbearable. I slept neither night nor day, and how slowly my torture went on when all was silent in the prison! The hours dragged as if weighted with lead.

Now a new horror came. The bodily excretions over which I had no control in the canvas vice ate into my bruised limbs. My fingers, hands and arms grew numb and dead.

Thus I suffered incessantly for four days and fourteen hours. At the conclusion of that period the Warden ordered "Give-a-damn" to remove the jacket.

Released from its pressure I attempted to gain my feet, but was too weak. My limbs were temporarily paralyzed. After a time, mustering all my strength I reached a sitting posture and finally managed to drag off my saturated clothes.

What a sight I beheld! My hands, arms and legs were frightfully bruised. My body was shriveled like that of an old man, and a horrible stench came from it.

Crawling to the water bucket I bathed the stinging bruises and washed off the smearings of hardened blood where the ropes had cut unfeelingly into the flesh. And then, entirely exhausted I sank down upon my mattress, covered myself with a blanket, and did not arise from it for a week.

During that time all the horrors of my fated life trooped unrelentingly through my dazed mind. "How unjust, how diabolical are the circumstances that have swept me from my position as a free acting agent — that have brought down such terrible tortures?" I pondered.

It had come with hurricane force, unexpected and therefore the more malicious. Innocent, was I to be literally destroyed a victim of circumstance?

In sympathy the poor "Tiger" tried to call me at the risk of the jacket.

I did not stir from my straw tick, but roundly cursed his tappings. By this time I was in open rebellion against the world. I was on the verge of a great upheaval. I had reached the turning point, that stage where I would sink forever into the abysmal depths of despair, or be reborn a new being with a realization that my sufferings had all been for a purpose, that it was necessary for me to go through this veritable Hell upon earth in order to have awakened in me the consciousness of a great inner power, a philosophy of life that would make possible a great future.

I had been roughly transplanted from a free and easy environment to a prison Hell,—to the most fiendish tortures, finally to be confined in a dungeon for the balance of my natural life. And that was not all. Here I must endure the bloody strait-jacket, the "Pirate's Overcoat" created especially for me. My sanity had been spared for what?

Until now I had always felt that there was a way out, but the strait-jacket had brought me complete despair. I did not then know that some people are called upon to pay a terrific penalty in order to bring out a true understanding of their inherent goodness; that forces of destruction in the form of intense suffering must be brought into play until the old self is annihilated especially with those who come here to perform a mission, perhaps a great service to humanity.

A doctor would have pronounced me dangerously ill. As I ponder back I can say that I was only dehumanized with the fire of a dungeon-made demon burning at my vitals either to consume me and leave but the dregs of human ashes for a mad man's padded cell, or to recreate me and give me the understanding of that great spiritual power necessary for the unfolding of my higher self.

I slept. How long I can never determine. It might have been weeks for all my warders cared. They were concerned only with the fact that their charge was locked securely in the dungeon.

Mine was a strange sleep. I seemed to be awake and yet I was dreaming. I was conscious of the nearness of friends, a host of them, and yet no living being could enter that dungeon save my natural enemies.

Suddenly I felt myself being led. Voices commanded me and I did their bidding without hesitation. Without fear or protest I performed many daring feats and passed thru unimaginable tests of bravery. It was like going thru the rites of a weird initiation.

At last came the most terrible ordeal of all. I stepped into a punishment room. Big Bill Smith, my detective employer, was there, gunmen who had hunted me for my head price were also there. The Folsom Warden who had heaped upon me the wrath of a giant railroad monopoly, the "Pirate," "Give-a-damn," Sir Harry, prison rats and "stool pigeons" and in fact everybody who had harmed me was there. All of them were being tortured, racked by the punishments that they had used in an effort to crucify me.

Before I went to sleep I was seething with hatred for every one of them, cursing them, vowing vengeance. Strange to say now I looked at them with deep compassion instead of hatred. Contrary to that venom which seethed within me at the mere thought of these brutes in waking mood, I was pained when I gazed upon their suffering. Then came the strangest reaction of all. I went to work releasing them. With a great intensity of purpose I madly tore at the fetters that bound them in their misery, and worked with a terrific speed releasing them from their suffering. I did not stop for breath until I had freed all of them.

Then a new marvel occurred. I woke from my comatose state and opened my eyes. I had been in deepest slumber, a death-like swoon. There were two distinct phases in the return to life from this trance-like sleep, first that of the sense of mental existence and then of physical existence. Could it be possible that I had awakened in another world?

Now, a mad whirl of intoxication possessed me, grim and terrible, as all sensations appeared swallowed up in the thought that I must have left the old withered frame in the dungeon. I had been sick, sick almost unto death, and darkness again intervened and I slept much, that is, if I could dare call it sleep.

The black gulf beyond disappeared. Now I was conscious of a great joy. And then there stole into my fancy, like a musical note, the thought of what sweet rest was mine. I was no longer in the dungeon, no longer in the big prison. San Quentin had vanished. The bay which had washed its foundations expanded out into a vast ocean whose rolling billows were mountains high, the sun glancing and shimmering on their crests. It was a glorious sight.

All this changed in a moment, for very suddenly there came back motion and sound, then again sound and motion and touch. A tingling sensation pervaded my frame as I heard a voice, far, far away at first. It rang from the depths of infinite space, but a space bright and luminous.

It seemed to speak plainly, almost in my ear. "You have learned the unreality of pain and hence of fear."

"You have learned the infutility of trying to fight off your enemies with hatred," the voice went on. "You have seen that your sword of defence was double-edged, cutting deeply into your own vitals rather than overcoming the evil which has been working against you."

"From today a new life vista will open up, and you will fight from a far superior vantage point. Your weapon will henceforth be the sword of love, and as time progresses and your power unfolds, this new weapon will cut and hew away all evil forces which now oppose you. And to prove the power which envelopes your life in this dungeon, even the strait-jacket will have no terrors for you. It will only be a means to greater things."

"Your life from now on must be a work of preparation, and when the time is ripe for your deliverance you will know it. The proof will be a power to prophesy to your enemies, not only the day of your ultimate release from this dungeon but also from the prison, when the great Governor of the State in person shall bring your pardon to San Quentin. Peace and love is yours!"

Slowly I opened my eyes. This time to the dungeon proper, but I was no longer conscious of the miseries of the past. I was a new being. My poor shrunken hands did not tremble and the spasmodic twitching of my mouth and eyes had ceased. It appeared as if the strength of a million men were concentrated within my frame, but I was afraid to stir lest it should prove a vagary of a distorted mind and the fantastic ecstacy of the moment be lost.

Then came the great unfolding, an easement of mind immeasurably sweet. The dungeon was no longer a place of horror to me. It was the crucible of fate and I was to be reborn. My brain was as clear as crystal and my ears had become receptive to sounds far below the power of human register. I was conscious that I was not alone in my cell. An unquenchable faith possessed me that a higher power had come to my rescue, and most marvelous of all, that power was from another sphere than mine.

Its very presence sent strange vibrations through the building. It re-echoed back to me in weird sweet tones and I was fearful lest it should be heard loudly reverberating over the whole prison. I instantly jumped to my feet, holding my ear against the barred door intently alert for the first evidence of the approach of guards. But solitary was as silent as death.

Now all was changed for me. Within the narrow confines of that cell I would create a world of my own. Henceforth, not a single moment would be lost in idle, drooling retrospection. I would shut out the demon of hate. Unfolding I would attract great agencies which would help me meet the crisis I knew was at hand, the big test.

The one-eyed "Pirate" had returned. I must again face the terrors of the jacket. For a moment a feeling of weakness swept through my being as I looked once more upon that instrument of horror; but only for a moment. My fear vanished instantly. A new light was shining in my eyes. The "Pirate" noted it and was amazed to see that I was smiling. It riled him to hot anger.

"Oh, you're smiling are you?" he shouted. "Then, by God, you must like it, uh? All right, all right, let's see what I can do to change that smile. If I mistake not, you will be shrieking within the next half hour."

In less than ten minutes I was trussed so tightly in the jacket that the canvas casing nearly stretched asunder. "Give-a-damn" had rolled me on my back, slammed the door and snapped the lock and left me alone.

For nearly half an hour my heart pounded incessantly. The cords in my neck were bulging out ready to burst. My breath left my body, forced grudgingly through my throat in sharp, hot gasps. My eyes were emitting sparks of fire. Now, I had a strange sensation in my feet. I was obsessed with an hallucination that my toes were crumpling into hard knots.

Next, my feet were rolling up as if being wound around a spool. This sensation continued until I could feel the knee joints breaking to the tightening twist. Then it stopped. I was praying, and before the prayer had ended, as if in answer to that appeal for help the pain had ceased.

I was already in the stage of belief that my mind was one thing and my body another, and that the intangible self could control the physical. I started concentrating upon the willing to death of my body.

It was not as Jack London described my "little death," not a willing to die of first the toe and joint by joint and bit by bit the rest of the body, but the entire body at one time.

There came a pounding and smashing of the heart followed by a sense of suffocation similar to the experience of being buried alive,— compressed in a sand pile. The world fairly reeled, a blurring dizziness was upon me, and darkness. Then flashings of light danced before my eyes.

It lasted only a few minutes again followed by smothering. Next a stillness swept my body such as might precede the unconsciousness of a drowning man. Now my heart apparently stopped beating and there was nothing but blackness. I was asleep, at least physically; dead to all appearances; oblivious to sensations yet mentally awake.

There was a period of brain enlargement, an expansion of time and space, a receding of the walls of my cell and even of the outer walls of San Quentin, and leaving my old painracked body laced tightly in the dungeon strait-jacket I bounded away, no longer held to earth but on a quest through space and an eternity of time.

Now the universe tottered about me with a loud resounding crash and I awoke a life convict in solitary, tightly laced in the strait-jacket. The noise! What was it?

Only the "Tiger" knuckle tapping from cell one.

It had been but a short time since my jacketing. Still, I had traveled through the ages. I tried to go again, so pleasing had been the sensation of bridging space. But that sound, like the blow of a hammer upon my senses, held me earthbound. Would he never cease? It seemed not, and with a wrenching agony tearing at my foot, I loosened the muscle sufficiently to tap out a message with the sole of my shoe.

"I am all right Jake," I said. "Don't knuckle talk again until I call you. It may be days, but don't alarm yourself. I am working out something, an experiment. I'll tell you all about it later."

I don't know whether or not he replied. The peaceful, uninterrupted slumber came again, and once more I was out and away from my dismal dungeon enclosure.

The next I heard was the rasping voice of "Give-a-damn." He was peering in at me through the cell door, while talking over his shoulder to the "Pirate."

"I don't know what to make out of him this time, Warden. He's in there like a badger in its hole. Every time I bulls-eyed him he's been asleep. He has never made a murmur since about the first half hour that he was jacketed. He's a queer nut and the divil himself can't understand him."

Ignoring "Give-a-damn's" remarks, the "Pirate" ordered him to open the door. He stepped inside and prodded me heavily with the toe of his boot to arouse me, thinking I was asleep. He then ordered "Give-a-damn" to bring the bulls-eye.

Flashing the strong light down into my face he carefully examined me. A white foam covered my mouth. Otherwise there was nothing unusual and I appeared to be asleep.

Nonplussed and acting on some whim he ordered "Give-a-damn" to cut the ropes. This done I was rolled out of the jacket.

I opened my eyes, but could not stir my body, and I lay there staring helplessly at the "Pirate."

"Well, I don't see that smile on your face that you had three days ago, when I put you in the jacket. You will soon come around to my way of thinking that this 'overcoat' is a world beater!" His words were cruel, but there was evidence of a tone of relief in his voice when he found that I was not dead.

Backing out of the cell he stood near the door for a while, silent, thinking. He finally turned to walk away, but on second thought stopped and spoke loudly to "Give-a-damn," intending that I should hear.

"Watch him carefully and when you think he is ripe for another bout telephone me and I will be here to start the tussle all over again. I want to see if he will meet me with a smile next time. If he does I will keep on pounding along these lines until I turn that smile into a devil's grimace."

Alone, I tried to survey the wreck. I was utterly helpless and nothing but a mass of bruised flesh and bone. Still my heart was strong and a feeling of buoyancy soon overcame even the weakness of flesh. Now, I could stir and in another moment or so I was feebly crawling to the back end of the cell feeling for my water bucket.

My poor crippled fingers first refused to respond to the thought impulse from my mind, but only for a second. One by one each finger opened like an old rusty hinge. Both hands were soon in action and I then rinsed my mouth free from the froth. I was dry and parched from thirst. Yes, that was the trouble! I was choking for water!

I greedily gulped down the full contents of the bowl, and tumbled back upon the old straw tick, relieved. I was enjoying perfectly normal slumber within a few minutes.

And now I heard voices again, felt the presence of friends and seemed to be literally carried from the dungeon and out beyond the prison walls. This time I was permitted to view the cesspools of iniquity — the jails of the nation, the jails of the world. I saw the big penitentiaries, lock-ups and police stations, County jails and juvenile institutions, horrible, inconceivable, some of them much worse than old San Quentin, all of them bad. I saw hundreds of thousands of human beings in idleness, being educated in new and unique ways of crime. They were taught nothing constructive and just drifted in and out of prison at a tremendous expense to the taxpayers. But this was not all. There were a million or more free men dependent upon crime for a living, ranging from the judges down to the policemen and petty clerks and court officials. I could see where billions were being expended each year on the cost and loss of crime. And honest taxpayers were paying for the upkeep of a system the infutility of which has been proven through a century or more of experiment.

The revelation came right here, the vision upon which I was to build the system which I have chosen to call "The New Era Penology."

First I saw the criminal court of the future, concerned only with proving the innocence or guilt of a man. When his guilt was determined I saw him remanded to a central station for examination both mental and physical. Next I saw him in the vocational training department. In all or some of the tests he might be found wanting — very often illiterate, and a man who would never get anywhere if left to himself.

There was a court of equity working in harmony with the zone court to determine the damage done by the lawbreaker in order to fine him an amount sufficient to cover restitution and costs involved in the court procedure of his case so that the taxpayer would not have to bear the burden of the cost and loss of crime.

Then marvel of all came the vision of the jail of the future. I saw the jails of the nation leveled to the ground. I saw the practical operation of the Honor System.

I saw vast tracts of unoccupied waste land dotted about the country. I saw men from the jails of the nation emptied out upon them. They labored, and beneath their hands sprang up great industrial reservations.

Some of these reservations were devoted entirely to the care of extreme cases of deficiency, abnormals, morons and criminal imbeciles. This covered about thirty to forty-five percent of the jail incarcerated.

The others were for the physically and mentally fit, that vast portion most often driven to crime through economic stress. These institutions were run on a basis of fair and equitable competition with the outside world. The prevailing rate of wages outside was paid the inmate, making possible his employment and an earning capacity to pay his fines, his board and to care for his dependents.

What a contrast to the dark and loathesome cells, the dungeon and condemned pens, the disease ridden atmosphere, leg irons, chains, whipping-posts, walls, guns and brutal guards! What a contrast to the two extremes in the prison of today: either idleness, or brutal convict contract labor where the prisoner is robbed of the fruits of his toil becoming a slave for the term of his sentence.

The men were self-governing in this institution. The public opinion was as strong there as in the outside world. It held in check those who might be inclined to do wrong. It functioned for good.

More, there was no force used. If a man refused to work he did not eat, since he had to pay his own board. There was no sentence arbitrarily imposed upon any man. He automatically sentenced himself, being released when he was fit and ready, not as an ex-convict but as a state trained pupil, not in disgrace, but to go out into the world with head erect an honest self-supporting citizen.

Prior to this new and startling experience I had been a light sleeper in the dungeon, and when I awoke I marvelled. The "Tiger" told me they had taken off the jacket the day before. I had been asleep nearly twenty-four hours.

My quick return to strength after the racking torture of the jacket removed all fear from my mind regarding the new faith that a power divine, enveloped my life here. Truly I was a new man. The future now looked big and beckoning.

This was the beginning of a series of wonderful revelations.

From that time, the attempts to break me are too many and terrible to relate, but I endured in spite of them, feeling no hatred, but ever happy and smiling at the most excruciating pain, because I heeded the message given to me in darkness and torment. I had learned the power of love, and tho I could not give up any guns, the "Pirate" in turn could not do me to death. The dungeon no longer represented to me a place of damnation and torment.

Wonderful to relate, I now found that my mind and body were entirely separate. A further proof of this came with the most appalling torture of all I had endured.

The "Pirate" had returned to solitary "with fire in his eye." His patience was being worn to a shred and he showed it in every action. Tho little given to swearing, nearly always cool and calculating, this time he hurled oaths at "Give-a-damn" to pull the rope and break it if he could in the effort to take up the last vestige of slack.

In that siege in the jacket I weathered the storm of one hundred twenty-six continuous hours of constriction. It was the longest torture ever inflicted on a convict during the reign of the bloody strait-jacket in San Quentin.

They cut the ropes and rolled me out. That time, even the Warden, brute that he was, stirred by a sudden whim of pity called for a jar of vaseline, and with his bare hands smeared it over my blistered body, parboiled white from uric acid burns.

Even in that extremity I did not in the least heed the racking torment, because the supremacy of mind had been fully established. I was master of my body. More I could now also direct the mind to leave my body entirely and roam at will, for after having once established the line of least resistance, the way became easier and the extent of my experiments ever greater. And from the brutal jacket and the dungeon Hell I learned to project myself into the living, breathing outside world of today, witnessing events and telling the "Tiger" about them.

I was present during a shipwreck, just outside the Golden Gate, heard the cries of women and children, saw them swallowed by the sea; and while I stood upon the deck of the ship, one man adjusted a strange apparatus and floated safely away as the vessel sank beneath him. In later years I had that device patented as the "Morrell Life Saving Suit."

This wreck was an actual occurrence as I afterwards found out. It happened on the very day that I had left my body encased in the strait-jacket in San Quentin's dungeon.

At other times, unbelievable as it may seem, my mind was projected outside of the dungeon, playing a part in the lives of people I was later destined to meet, some of whom were to aid materially in my rehabilitation and freedom.

I had become master of self-hypnosis, suspended animation, call it what you will, and I believe I am one of few mortals who ever expressed the claim that intelligence endured, or that there was any continuity of thought or knowledge of time and events while in this state.

During my many sieges of torture in the jacket, nothing occurred in my dungeon cell of which I was not aware, tho absolutely dead to physical feeling or pain, proving conclusively that my mind was ever in control.

I was indeed the "Star Rover" of the ages and Jack London's book but mildly touches upon that prison life of mine, leaving the most amazing phenomena unwritten, the most wonderful of my travels and doings untouched. He called those experiences, "the little death." I prefer to call them "my new life in tune with a power divine."

CHAPTER XXVIII

A DOUBLE JACKETING, A PROPHECY.

"Guns or curtains!" shrieked the "Pirate." "You'll come across with those guns this time, or by the Eternal, I'll kill you in the jacket!" He had come to the dungeon, almost before daylight. His face was livid, his one good eye burning red. The man appeared not to have slept all night and I wondered if he had been drinking.

His expression, "guns or curtains," meant that if I did not tell where the firearms were hidden I should be murdered in the jacket, then rushed to the hospital from whence I would be buried in order that my death might go down on the records as occurring through natural causes.

"Well I guess it's to be curtains, 'Pirate,' for I have no guns," I calmly replied.

My unruffled demeanor and ever working smile threw him into a rage. Almost frothing at the mouth, he grimaced. "Then, to make an extra good job of it we'll have a double jacketing!"

Contrary to his usual visits to the dungeon, he was accompanied this time by the man whom they called the prison physician. The convicts knew him only as the "croaker." He was ordered to make an examination of my body.

"Give-a-damn" stripped off the dirt encrusted clothes, which I had worn since my condemnation to the dungeon. The prison "croaker," made a solemn but cursory examination of my wasted body with its parched brown skin ridged and sore infested from the repeated jacket lacings.

"Oh, he'll stand it all right," he muttered. "Heart action's splendid. Yes he can even stand an extra long bout! You can't kill him in the jacket, Warden!"

He stepped back to allow "Give-a-damn" action. That unfeeling brute, the worthy lieutenant of the "Pirate," brought a heavy double blanket into the cell and slowly wrapped it around my body, for the purpose of avoiding too many marks and bruises in case of death, and also with the intention of making the jacket fit tighter about my shriveled frame. My muscles were mere strings and every bone stood out under the dry parched skin.

Two strange guards were now assisting "Give-a-damn." In pulling on the rope they man-mauled me all over the dungeon floor. "Give-a-damn" braced his heavy foot against my back, and with the aid of the other two men tugged and jerked like a stevedore pulling upon a heavy hawser.

Puffing for breath, and with beads of perspiration dripping from his face "Give-a-damn" made fast the rope, then announced boastfully, "I fixed him now, Warden, as snug as a bug in a rug."

"Roll him over!" commanded the "Pirate." And as I lay there crushed to a pulp from the tightening pressure of the jacket, somehow I managed to smile up into his face.

The "Pirate" was beside himself. He could not understand the smile. Somewhere in his back mind there must have lurked a fear that this smile was a warning sign of his defeat. It made him furious and he shouted, "This is your last chance, if you don't come across, I'm going to give you the limit."

Then, bending low over me until his black face almost touched mine, with voice softened he coaxed, "Now, Morrell, listen to me! Don't be a damned fool! Why be crippled in the jacket? You know you won't be squealing on anybody, because you're the only one who knows where those guns are planted. Besides, I'll let you have six months in the hospital on the best food in San Quentin. More, I'll be your friend. Now, be reasonable and say the word and I'll cut the ropes myself!"

I made no reply to his offer. There was none to make since I had no guns, and enraged at my silence, he flung off his momentary guise of sympathy.

"Well, since you don't come through, you start your bout right now, and by the living God, if it takes me ten days you'll stay in the jacket until I kill you."

"Bring on the other jacket," he shouted to "Give-a-damn" who, with keen enjoyment rolled me around the dungeon floor as he put another strait-jacket over the one I was encased in, lacing this up the front.

Then came the sharp needle-like sensations shooting through my fingers, hands, and arms. My head grew hot and feverish and a burning thirst seized me. I had never been laced so tight, but I struggled hard to maintain the carefree attitude and keep smiling, tho it seemed the pounding of my heart must surely burst the heavy jackets.

I vaguely heard someone suggesting that they were laced rather tight, to which the "croaker" replied, "The Hell they are! Don't think for a moment that will affect him, and if it does, why not? He should have been dead long ago!"

At this, the Warden leaned over me and tried to insert his finger under the rope. Not finding so much as an inch of slack he flatteringly commented to "Give-a-damn," "I must take my hat off to you all right! You know your business! I wish I had more men like you on the line! San Quentin would be a place where angels could abide."

Then glacing into my face he became frenzied with indignation. My lips were moving and he heard my faint voice, husky from the squeezing, as I made the proposal, "'Pirate,' you're so sure you are going to kill me, let's have a little sporting wager for the last time! You note I am smiling at you. If I do so again, when you take me out of the jacket will you give the 'Tiger' a sack of tobacco and some papers?"

Disconcerted for a moment he started to run from the cell as if fearful of trusting himself there longer. Then turning back he growled, "You're mighty sure of yourself! Getting religion, uh?"

"No," I replied, still smiling, "but I just happen to possess more life than you can crush out of me. That's why I made the wager, and if you were even half a man you would snap it up, since you have all the cards stacked against me. You can give me a hundred days if you like, and I'll still be able to smile, even laugh at you!"

"I've put the limit at ten, Morrell," he guffawed, "but three or four will fix you with a double jacketing!"

"Then if that's your opinion you should accept the wager. It will cost you only five cents," I remarked.

He raised his foot menacingly over my unprotected face, and in blind rage would have carried out his brutal purpose had not "Give-a-damn" pulled him toward the door.

He stepped outside and paced to and fro in the corridor. At last getting a hold on his temper, he again came in and stooped low over my prostrate body.

"I say Morrell, by the gods you are a wooze," he ingratiatingly remarked. "I'll show you I'm a sport. If you are alive ten days from now, I will pay that wager provided you can open your eyes and give me even the shadow of a smile, much less a real smile!"

Then, evidently not daring to trust himself another moment for any further taunts, the "Pirate" jumped out of the cell and the door slammed to with a bang.

I was alone and in another ten minutes the world began to sway and whirl. Would my guardian angel desert me now in this, the supreme test of all? My heart, instead of beating to seconds was apparently stroking off one beat to the hour. The gap in time between seemed interminable.

Fearful that the conscious mind would not release its grip and let me go, for a moment I felt that I must shriek out to my tormentors and beg abjectly for mercy. Had I done so, all would have been lost. The supremacy of my higher self would have been vanquished. All of my work would have toppled down.

The thought of defeat, with the victory of the "Pirate," was enough! It stirred me to an exaltation unbelievable! Like the raging elements suddenly lashed to silence my physical being quieted down. I no longer felt the slightest pain. My breath eased off from the steam-like rushing sensations of a moment before.

More, I was obsessed by the sure belief that the jackets were being stretched by a force outside of myself. And the uncanny marvel of it all was that not my subconscious mind, but my physical workaday senses clearly registered this fact!

I was now in a greater quandary than ever. Hours, definite hours were passing, still no change, only complete easement from pain. I positively registered that the jackets which encased me were abominably loose. To prove it to my alert, ever questioning mind, I freely moved my arms and hands in the pockets within the jacket. More, I rolled around on the dungeon floor.

Then came a happy thought. It would make a sure test that the persistent physical me was in control, and that I was not laboring under a superinduced hallucination. I would rap a message to the "Tiger."

I counted each tap with the sole of my shoe, and then waited for his answer. Hungrily, I glued my ear to the wall. Yes, the "Tiger" was knuckle talking, and I could understand.

"For God's sake, Ed., don't pound so loud with your foot. It sounds all over solitary. If 'Give-a-damn' hears you, he will go down there and club you to death. They want to kill you anyhow, because they think you are in league with the devil. How in the name of Heaven are you standing that torture? I overheard the 'croaker' whisper to the 'Pirate' that you wouldn't live five hours.''

The "Tiger's" knuckle tapping now seemed far away, as if coming from the lower depths of a mine. I could make out some of it, a sound word here and there. Then the noise became confused like the tickings of hundreds of clocks, all beating time together.

It was maddening beyond belief. Somehow, I conceived the idea that if the rapping did not stop it would deprive me of peaceful slumber in the warm, comfortable canvas shrouds. I was very tired, and oh, how I wanted to sleep!

Now, I was out of my jackets bending down looking at my body. A great pity welled up within me. I felt the urge to watch and safeguard it with the vigilance of a sentry.

I stooped low to listen to the regular breathing, but the "Tiger," that infernal spectre, would he never cease tapping? And now, lest his noise should awaken me from coveted sleep, I determined to go and tell him to stop it.

During my periods of self-induced hypnosis I had often anxiously desired to project myself into that dungeon cell of the "Tiger." I wanted to go there and visit him to see what he looked like, to observe closely his condition and to note some definite thing which he might be doing in order that I could later offer him a real test of my power. But I had failed utterly. A force over which I had no control invariably led me out and away beyond the walls of the prison to travel through space with the speed of lightning, perhaps to some strange distant land where the people dressed in odd clothes and spoke in guttural languages.

Again, I might view seas, desert islands, rivers, with here and there flashes of the tropics and black slaves, only to return in the space of a moment to scenes more homelike, and to people whom I knew in my world of living realities.

San Francisco always held me spellbound. There, I flitted in and out through highways and byways of the big city, sometimes stopping in Golden Gate Park to watch the throngs moving about.

People riveted my attention. They were different than I had always believed. By some uncanny power it was possible for me to look through and beyond them. I could not understand it! I was fascinated!

Human beings automatically divided themselves into distinct groups before my eyes. I found that each one possessed a different odor. If it were pleasant, fresh, good to smell, that person's face invariably wore a happy smile and a bright suffusing light surrounded the head. Those who emitted an obnoxious and fetid odor had faces almost obscured by dark shadows, and these latter I learned to call "the people of the dark shadow."

I have spent whole days in San Francisco, wandering about until night-fall. To me these were the most glorious times, because of the myriad lights of the big city. I liked to elbow my way through crowds on Market Street, but not for long, so many appeared to be unhappy. They affected me strangely.

One time I entered a large and beautifully lighted church. I was drawn there by the sounds of the organ. The congregation were standing, singing a hymn; and fearful of disturbing them in their devotion I stole along through the main aisle looking for an empty seat.

I found one beside an elderly woman, up near the railing. She was singing in a rich well-trained voice. All through the service I was conscious of her presence, and registered how happy she made me feel. Still, I did not lose a word of the pastor's sermon or any of the wonderful singing of the choir, and I felt that I wanted to stay there forever. To me, that church was a shrine of peace and love.

In my wanderings from the "Jacket Hell" of San Quentin, through the guidance of that force which controlled my actions, I always avoided places of evil, shunning people of "the dark shadow"; and seeking out those in whom love abided.

And now at last I was up in the "Tiger's" cell. He had quit knuckle tapping and was lying upon his back on his old straw tick.

I stood inside of the cell, but near the door. My first impression was of horror. There on the sodden mattress lay the wreck of what had been a man, a mere sack of bones, reminding one of a shriveled corpse burnt black from the desert suns.

His hair was matted and he had a shaggy beard. I could see his eyes shining like two black coals. But the face! It was in shadow, and the odor from his body was overpowering. It smelled like a neglected stable. It made me sick and nauseated and I wanted to leave the place, but could not go.

The tragedy of the "Tiger's" life was now plain. The law's charnal house had engulfed him in its sin. Burning hate had cluttered up the channels to his higher self. I desired so much to help him, but a yawning chasm lay between.

In spite of the repellent barrier, I made a superhuman effort to touch him but could not. My feet would not move and my hand refused to obey the command of my will.

The "Tiger" was muttering something and now and then I heard my name and the word, "jacket," and plainly the remark, "They will kill him, sure! He can't stand it! The double jacket will fix him!" Then came a string of imprecations upon the "Pirate's" head.

I wanted to go, but the "Tiger's" next move riveted me to the spot, all attention. He was doing something which I felt would prove of interest. With the thumb and forefinger of his left hand he was mechanically wiggling a loose tooth in the front of his mouth and I stood there speculating how much longer he would continue the grim operation, ere he would jerk it out.

In another moment the "Tiger's" Hell hole had faded.

I was back in my own cell. The "Pirate," the Doctor, and "Give-a-damn" had returned to my dungeon. It was the fourth day after my double jacketing. A Senate investigation committee had come to the prison, and fearing that the truth might leak out if I should die, the "Pirate" ordered "Give-a-damn" to cut the ropes quickly. Before he did it, the prison "croaker" gave me a hasty examination.

With a leer on his face he straightened up and coolly remarked to the "Pirate," "Well, Warden, you fixed him all right this time! He's as dead as a door nail."

I recall the whole thing so vividly. It seemed that I was standing over to one side of the cell looking down upon my poor scarred body which lay in a lifeless heap before me. I had not journeyed far during this experience in "the little death."

I wondered if I would ever again occupy the miserable shell. It had always seemed to me that if I remained away after they took my body from the strait-jacket I should never be able to inhabit it again, and this time above all others, I was loathe to give them the satisfaction of saying they had killed me.

"Give-a-damn" cut the ropes and rolled me out. I was resting on my back. There was a struggle. My eyelids fluttered, opened, and in an instant I was smiling up into the "Pirate's" face, to his great relief.

"There! There," he shouted at the top of his voice to the "croaker." "Damn him, I knew he was only faking!"

"No wonder he can smile!" said "Give-a-damn" laconically. "He's paralyzed!"

"Paralyzed!" the "Pirate" jeered with a dry laugh. "Get him on his feet and he'll stand all right!"

Obeying orders, 'Give-a-damn'' dragged me up, then let go! Of course after such a lacing the life could not return to my body all at once.

I reeled, bent at the knees and pitched sideways, gashing my forehead against the wall, to the great amusement of those who had endeavored to kill me.

"He's a fine actor! He's got nerve enough to do anything!"

I replied in a husky whisper, "You're right! Of course I did that on purpose, and if you will continue lifting me up I will keep repeating the performance as many times as you like, just to amuse you! I am only sorry I couldn't have died long ago in the jacket to put you out of the misery of having to bother torturing me!"

"But," I cautioned, "since you didn't succeed in killing me and since I smiled, I have won a little wager which will cost you just five cents. Don't forget the 'Tiger's' sack of tobacco!"

At this the "Pirate" raised his hands to his hair as if to tear it out by the roots. Then, realizing that it was dangerous for him to remain, since he had done his worst and could do nothing now but trample upon me with his feet, he moved to the cell door.

My husky voice stopped him. He turned to hear what I had to say.

"Just one moment, 'Pirate,' I have a little prophecy to make," and I smiled again while the blood from the gash in my forehead trickled warmly down my face.

"This is the last time I will ever be tortured in the jacket! One year from today I will go out of this dungeon never to return to it; and better still, four years from the day I leave the dungeon I will walk from the prison a free man with a pardon in my hand. More, the Governor of the State will bring that pardon in person to San Quentin!"

The "Pirate" laughed. "Stark mad! He's gone stark mad," he said and quickly left the solitary without another word, "Give-a-damn" and the prison "croaker" following closely at his heels.

I was alone! Until evening I lay on the floor in a half conscious state. By that time I could feebly crawl about, and painfully worked my way toward the bucket. There was only a little water in it, but I cleansed the gash on my forehead and rubbed some over my bruised and burning body, dropping again on the bed, exhausted.

It was days before I could bring myself to eat a bite of food. But I did manage to rap some stories to the "Tiger" through the medium of the knuckle voice, telling of my latest adventures in the strait-jacket. "Give-a-damn," being unable to stop me, was so furious that he called the Warden.

The Warden came to the dungeon, threatening to cut off my food if I did not cease rapping.

"As you please, 'Pirate'," I replied. "I have not eaten for a long time and the thought of starting it again is annoying."

"Well then, I'll put you back in the jacket."

"Remember the prophecy I just made to you," I answered. "But even at that I wouldn't be averse to another bout in it, for I am the 'Jacket Kid.' I thrive upon it," and exposing my wasted arm I added, "See how stout it makes me!" And even as he stood looking at me helplessly I turned and continued knuckle talking to the "Tiger."

Glaring in rage for a moment, the "Pirate" cursed and stamped his feet, then dashed from the dungeon like a mad man. His last words were, "Diablo! Diablo!" His superstitions got the better of him. He thought I was the Devil. I never again saw the "Pirate" from that day.

He who had seen so many men weaken and collapse after just a few hours in that instrument of torture had given me up as one who could not be killed. How well I recalled it all in the peace of the last dungeon days.

Solitary had changed as if by magic. "Give-a-damn" no longer stalked through the corridor like a demon, watching for the first chance to entrap the "Tiger" or me into some overt act, in order that he might keep the jacket working.

Even his night guards were becoming lazy, and instead of watching the two Ishmaelites of the dungeon, they spent their time up in the guard's quarters, playing cards and drinking.

"Give-a-damn" next left the prison on a vacation. He had been gone for a couple of weeks. On his return, contrary to his usual condition from such visits, he was sober. And the marvel of all, he came to my cell, and in the most kindly way, tho shamefacedly, asked how I felt.

It was the first decent thing that he had ever done. I was amazed, and being only human my quick temper nearly got the better of me. A hot retort was choked in my mouth as I listened to the warning voice of my guardian angel.

For a moment I became weak. My knees trembled as if with the ague, when I thought how nearly I had toppled down my castles of good resolutions. It appalled me to realize how weak I was before the first blast of temptation. I, the new man, who would henceforth govern my life by the law of love, stood on the brink of the precipice ready to jump back into perdition and the folly of wrong thinking.

The very essence of the law of love is to return good for evil. I had stood adamant against the temptation of returning like for like. I had remained passive and smiling under the most brutal taunts, but now that the first kindly word had been spoken, it was so unusual, so unexpected, I was unprepared to meet it.

The incident was trivial, and I doubt if "Give-a-damn" in his crude mind divined the extent of the suffering his kindly words had caused. I felt immeasurably relieved when he left me.

He had gone to the "Tiger's" cell, and I could hear the sound of his voice. It was the augury of a change in solitary.

The "Tiger" was now knuckle tapping, this time loud, and I wondered why he had cast aside all caution. "Ed.," he called, " 'the moon is made of green cheese,' and this world of ours is topsy-turvy. Either that or 'Give-a-damn' has softening of the brain. Listen to this as a piece of news. He has just been to my cell, and has offered 'the olive branch of peace.' More, he shook hands with me, and before he left he told me that we could knuckle talk all we wanted and as loud as we wanted, that he was not going to be the catspaw any longer for the 'Pirate,' that he was a brute and he knew it and wondered how he could ever square himself with Morrell and that he was sorry for the whole rotten mess."

Solitary was indeed changing. The very atmosphere smelled different, and I wondered more about my prophecy. They never again put me in the jacket, and my wanderings were at an end.

Many times during the peaceful months that followed I tried persistently to project myself out of the dungeon, beyond the walls of the great prison of San Quentin. There was one place that drew me with the force of a magnet. It was a quiet, restful town of fruit and flowers in the interior of California.

I had often been there during the periods of my most terrible torture in the strait-jacket. On my first visit I found myself entering a large school. I recall that I did not want to go inside. The thought of disturbing the pupils in their study annoyed me. But again the force that irrevocably led me here and there in my pilgrimages would not be denied.

In those early experiments with the power of projection I was dreadfully obsessed with the belief that I was Ed.

Morrell, my real physical self, and not a spectre, a mere phantom, a shadow that had left the jacket and the dungeon. I reasoned, "I can walk, I can see, I can hear, I can smell, I can feel! More, I can talk!" But I could not explain to my mind why people never answered when I addressed them. Their indifference nonplussed me, because I believed they heard.

There were many discrepancies, incongruous, incompatible with logic and reason. For instance, I could look through people as if I were an X-ray. Opacity meant nothing to me. I could flit through doors without opening them. Solid walls were as tissue paper, intangible, non-existent, when I wished to pass beyond. A moving train going at the highest speed was just an ordinary escalator for me to step off and on at will. And yet all this never appeared to be other than real.

In the subconscious or rather supernatural states everything was actual, the genuine, and the commonplace, and it was not until my return to conscious life in the dungeon that these things would cloud and become shadowy, creating a doubt in my mind as to whether they had really happened or not.

I had no chance to check up my experiences away from the dungeon, and it was not until I had finally left solitary that the means presented and I verified many of them, such as the occurrence of the wreck of the big steamship outside of the Golden Gate, and my persistent dogging of the footsteps of a man in Alameda County, whom I in some way irresistably associated with my release from the dungeon.

And thus it happened that I ventured into the school where fate seemed to have decreed that I should meet one whom I would know in later years and learn to love. I walked up the center aisle of the room until I reached the teacher's desk. I paused there long enough to utter some apology for my intrusion, but the young woman with jet black hair, the teacher who was reading to her class, did not heed my presence.

I turned to look about through the sea of young faces. Suddenly my eyes rested on one. A weird impulse attracted me toward her. She was sitting to the right near an open window, her head bent low over a book.

I walked slowly down the aisle and stopped near her desk. She raised her head as if to look at me. She was a little Miss of twelve or thirteen.

When I entered the class room I noticed that just a few of the young faces were cloudy, almost in shadow. But the little girl, my little girl whom I picked out from among all of them was fairly radiant with light. Her blue eyes were frank, open, and trusting, and she had a sweet smile that encouraged confidence.

In a vague instinctive way, I knew we were not strangers. Still she was startled at my sudden appearance. I feared that she might lose her poise and hurried to say a few reassuring words. She moved over in her seat. It seemed to be an invitation to sit down.

The afternon session closed and the pupils filed out. My little girl carefully put her books away and was about the last to leave. I went with her. Outside another little Miss joined her. After a few words they parted and we two so strangely brought together walked toward her home. She stood at the gate for a moment, pensive, and as I thought looking into my eyes, then turned and skipped across the yard and entered the house.

That had been the first of many visits which held my soul enthralled and later served to lighten the burden of my misery in San Quentin's dungeon. But now I could go there no more. My power to project myself beyond the walls of San Quentin ended with my strait-jacket prophecy. So all that remained to solace me during the intervening months, pending liberation according to the definite time of the prophecy, was the vision of that little girl's face. It brightened the narrow enclosure and softened my memory of the years I had spent in that den of brutality.

Now I was free to think, to mull over in my mind the marvels which had been revealed to me during my spells in the "little death," and most important of all — the great revelations that came with my dungeon awakening. Feverishly I worked on that new system of Penology, which had been born in my mind from the depths of anguish.

This was the dawn of the Twentieth Century, and the world was waiting for the message, and I, the "Dungeon Man of San Quentin," now had within my grasp the solution of our appalling criminal problem. My martyrdom had not been in vain, and I counted the days still remaining, before I should step from the place that had been both my Hell and my salvation.

The poor "Tiger" remained skeptic to the last. He often tapped to gibe me pleasantly about that prophecy. "You know, Ed.," he would say, "I must admit you have done wonderful things here in the dungeon. You have defied death in the jacket, and even told me of that loose tooth of mine. I confess that was a 'knockout'."

"Yes, your prophecy about the strait-jacket seems to have something in it. The 'Pirate' has left us alone, and 'Give-a-damn' has tamed down so much I think he must have gotten religion. But," he went on, "don't forget that jails are real. They are made of steel and stone. You have no friends left. You are dead and forgotten, a life convict in a dungeon at San Quentin. With the exception of myself, you are regarded by the prison officials as the most desperate man ever confined in the history of the State."

I tapped back a few very encouraging words, then closed my knuckle talk with the "Tiger" forever, when I said "Jake, bide the time. Tomorrow the year will be up. After that you will believe!"

CHAPTER XXIX

RELEASE FROM THE DUNGEON, THE PROPHECY UNFOLDING.

The murky light which forced its way through the drab painted windows of the solitary room announced another day. From my cell I had watched the darkness fade and from then on I counted the hours.

"Now, it must be eight o'clock," I thought and mentally adding on a few minutes for good measure waited for the next hour to go by. "Nine o'clock! Yes, surely it must be nine because I have counted it by seconds, and unless my count is wrong it must be nine and well beyond."

Then I grew afraid to count any more. Nevertheless, I found myself speculating, even trying to guess whether or not it was ten. I had never before tolled off time by hours, and the horror of it appalled me. What a boon, what a mercy had been mine, that I was not allowed to know anything about the hours of the day. During my long years of isolation and silence, time had meant nothing. It was registered by only two conditions, absolute darkness and a few hours of dull gray light.

I often heard it said in prison that this was one of the things the jail system reckoned on as a punishment for the solitary convict. If that be true, then God in his infinite mercy must have intervened, because it was a blessing in the guise of a punishment. Of all the miseries that can be inflicted upon a poor unfortunate shut away from human companionship, none equal that of being forced to know each hour of the twenty-four, day in and day out. I can well imagine it would soon mean madness for even the strongest mind, and I thank the kindly fate that saved me from such an added weight to my overburdened soul.

Something happened, now! The gong in solitary sounded! It was just an ordinary bell operated from a push button outside of the big door, but it struck my ear drums like the belch and boom of heavy artillery.

I heard "Give-a-damn's" rough voice and clumsy attempt at a greeting, "Welcome, to my department! This is a pleasure, Major, this is a pleasure! Come on inside and I'll show you the place. I was beginning to think, Major, you had forgotten all about solitary. I certainly welcome this chance to meet our new Warden. Come on in, come on in!"

"Give-a-damn" and the stranger were now walking down the big solitary room, and as the two came into line with my vision, I instantly recognized the man whom "Give-a-damn" called the Major. He was the new Warden, none other than my Alameda County man, the very one whom I had followed and watched so persistently during my repeated wanderings in the "little death" from the strait-jacket.

Overcome by emotion I staggered, fairly reeled back from the barred door. Now there could be no more doubt. Yes, my experiences in the strait-jacket were true. He was the man I had so persistently visited in those mental travels. The proof was conclusive. I had never seen this man in the flesh prior to those strange events.

For a moment I lost thought of the new Warden and the things that were happening about me. My mind flashed out to the town of fruit and flowers. In an instant I was looking upon the face of the little girl in the same school room where I had last seen her poring over her books. I wondered if I would sometime meet her too.

I heard my name. It was the Major asking "Give-a-damn" to show him my cell. He stood for a moment trying to peer in. It was dark. He could not see me and he ordered "Give-a-damn," the boss of solitary, to open the door. Then he requested to be left alone.

Entering my cell, he stood looking at me for a long time without saying a word, evidently lost in the horror of the gruesome object before him. His eyes were moist as the tears welled up in them. He finally broke the silence and I heard his voice.

"Morrell, I am the new Warden!" he said when he finally broke the silence. Plainly agitated he continued, "Three weeks ago I took charge of San Quentin. From the very first day that I came I have been busy investigating your case."

"You were accused of smuggling firearms in here, for the purpose of leading a mutiny and taking the prison by assault. You were tried on that charge by the Board of Prison Commissioners acting as a court of five judges in the case. You were convicted on the evidence presented and sentenced to solitary confinement for the balance of your life."

"That was five years ago. Since then nothing has happened to alter the condition and show whether or not you were really guilty as accused. My investigation of your case has proved that you were not guilty as charged, but rather that you are the victim of a prison plot by a scoundrel who tried to profit by your misfortune."

"When the Board of Prison Commissioners held their meeting yesterday I presented the facts and demanded that your sentence to this place be revoked. Now I have come to release you. You have been most unjustly treated. I shall do all in my power to right that wrong while I am Warden at San Quentin," he concluded.

He then prepared to lead me from the living tomb where I had endured so many weary years. My voice had weakened down to a mere whisper, but before leaving the horror chamber of silence I managed to make an appeal to the new Warden that he permit me to see the poor "Tiger" and bid him farewell.

If I live through the years of eternity I shall never forget the few tense moments spent looking through the gratings of his cell door, trying to make out the gaunt features of my poor companion of the knuckle voice. I slipped the shrunken fingers of my hand through the bars. The "Tiger" held them with a firm grip. His feeble voice vibrated with joy.

"God, man, this is a miracle! Let us hope the rest of your prophecy will come true, and that you will get a pardon in four years."

The Warden drew me away, and then very prudently tied a bandage over my eyes lest the sunlight outside should blind me. In another minute the big door to solitary closed behind me. The Warden and the escort guard carried me almost bodily down the long stairway and then across the prison yard to the clothing room where the bandage was taken off.

I was dizzy, nearly stricken with agoraphobia, having come from solitary and silence to the moving world of the prison after five years of solitary confinement. Everything seemed so unreal.

Kindly hands led me to the bathroom, and as the old dirt encrusted clothes fell to the floor I stood outlined against the glaring light, a terrible and most pitiful object indeed. This was the first time I had clearly seen my body in all its shrunken horribleness.

The parched yellow skin drawn tightly over the well defined ribs, and the joints standing out like huge knots made me appear to be a very old man. The long straggling, matted beard and hair streaked with gray completed the picture of a famine stricken wretch. I wondered if I would ever be well again.

I weighed only ninety-six pounds. I was the wreck of what had been once a man. Freemen and office convicts kept coming and going while I was being washed. Everybody was trying to get a look at the "Dungeon Man." I was an object of curiosity.

THE TWENTY-FIFTH MAN

At the barber shop old Frank, the head barber, who had been in charge of the place for twenty years greeted me warmly. He too was a lifer and had known me in time gone by.

"I sure want to shave you and cut that hair, Ed.," he remarked as he tucked the towel around my neck. "How does it feel anyway to be down out of Mars?"

The transparent skin, the eyes deepset from suffering, the long hair and beard must have made it possible for old Frank to see something unusual. After viewing me intently for a moment he stepped back as if puzzled. He then called the other men to come and look at me.

"Who does he remind you of?" he asked excitedly.

There was no response. They were all silent, curious to look me over. At last old Frank blurted out, "With all respect, Ed., you're the finest living picture of Christ I have ever seen, so help me God!"

The little group of barbers stood in awe, and then came a welcome relief from the tension. "Well, I thought old Frank was ironclad! He's got it at last! The religious bug has found its way into his skypiece and I thought he was immune!" It was the voice of the ever present jester.

Several months had passed, and my return to health was almost phenomenal. Everyone marvelled at it, and I most of all felt happy because henceforth my life would have a new meaning to me. There was much to be done, and I must be ready for it.

The Warden had announced his intention of appointing me "Head Trusty" of the prison. It was the most responsible position a convict could hold at that time and carried with it almost as much power as the Warden himself had, and in some instances more, if the "Head Trusty" cared to use it for the weal or woe of his fellow prisoners.

This news dumbfounded the subordinate officials. They loudly protested their opposition, almost to a man. Even the Board of Prison Commissioners sharply counseled the Warden to be careful.

Then one day, the Captain of the Yard came over to me with the message that the Warden wanted to see me immediately.

"I have sent for you for a special purpose," said the Warden. "The position of 'Head Trusty' is vacant for the fourth time in twenty-eight years. There are over five hundred written applications." He pointed to a pile of letters on the table.

"I have read everyone of them," he continued, "and my choice for the job rests between two men. I made up my mind to set even these two aside for the present, until I took up the matter with you. I know that you can fill the duties of 'Head Trusty,' and all I will ask is that you give me your word of honor as a man not to betray my trust in you."

"There are many privileges of favor that go with this position. You will be allowed a wide range in liberty of action. The extent to which you exercise it, and how wisely will determine your fitness for the place. Your indomitable will power has stood the test. I know it from the records. That, combined with your patience will surely make it possible to overcome such obstacles as you will encounter from day to day."

We shook hands, we two who were so differently situated, and apparently so far apart,—he, the Warden of a great prison, one of the largest in America, a former military man of high rank, a good citizen of unquestioned standing, a man, gray haired and white bearded,—and I, a life convict in stripes, the former incorrigible, the "Dungeon Man" who had been regarded as the most terrible character ever confined in the history of the State. And here in the Warden's office we two strangely separated beings were this moment cementing a friendship to last until death.

In strictest confidence he then told me how he had come to accept the Wardenship of San Quentin. At first he refused it, having retired from active life. The new Governor of the State had called upon him a second time, and while the two conversed over the 'phone, this man, sitting in his study pencil in hand unconsciously tapped upon a scratch pad. He finally promised the Governor that he would think the matter over before giving his decision.

He hung up the receiver, and glancing at the paper, noticed that something had been written upon it while he was talking. Seizing the pad he read the name, "Ed. Morrell." He looked at it questioningly wondering over the strange incident. It bothered him, and unable to solve the enigma he called up a friend who was a State official. Through him he learned that the name was that of the notorious "Dungeon Man of San Quentin."

The next day he told the Governor that he had decided to accept his offer. "That's how I happen to be here!" he announced.

"I have never given much thought to the supernatural, nor have I been very strong on metaphysical subjects, but I certainly would like to have you explain the riddle of how your name came to be written upon that scratch pad!"

I smiled as I said, "Some day, Warden, about four years hence I will make it all plain to you. In the mean time you have cut out a big job for me, and my only concern now is that I shall make good and prove to you that you did the right thing when you accepted the Wardenship of San Quentin."

When my appointment for the position of "Head Trusty" was finally announced from the Captain of the Yard's Office, the stir and buzz of gossip fairly shook the big prison. Convicts old in prison politics sagely wagged their heads and passed sinister remarks to the effect that Morrell had at last fallen for favor. But the convicts in general were firm in their belief in me. They insisted that prisoners would receive better treatment than ever before in the history of San Quentin.

For many months I went about my work quietly, attracting very little attention from anybody,— just studying conditions within the walls. One thing troubled me greatly. There were many convicts, some of whom had suffered long years in prison, a great number of them life timers, friendless and forgotten, laboring continuously in the Jute Mill.

I often watched them dragging their weary limbs to and from their endless task. I had carefully selected a list of names from among their number and presented it to the Warden on the occasion of a timely conversation. He scanned it without a comment and fearing that he might misunderstand I hurriedly went on to explain that the greater number of prisoners on the list were far beyond the age where they should be required to perform a hard task of continuous labor.

"Splendid," said the Warden, "but what are we going to do with those men? Force them to idleness? Why, some of them will die if denied the opportunity to do useful work!"

"That's easy, Warden," I remarked. "I think I can solve the problem. The flower gardens within the prison are attended to by big husky men who hold these jobs merely through favor. Why not let the old men, overworked and worn come out to the flowers and put these burly fellows in their places?"

The weeding process commenced shortly afterward. The prison was jarred; but the voice of the jail approved.

The evil of espionage, or the "stool pigeon" plague, like a fungus growth waxes fat on our American Jail System. It is the curse of every Penal Institution, and no matter how honest and sincere the intentions may be of the most high minded Warden to stamp it out, like the upas tree it will spread its poison and pollute the life of the institution before his very eyes. It is a cankerous growth, however, which must be viewed in the light of a welcome agency that will aid materially in helping to destroy to the very foundations our rotten, topheavy, inhuman, unthinkably stupid American Jail System.

When I assumed the duties of "Head Trusty" at San Quentin, that big jail was a seething maelstrom of prison politics and "stool pigeon" intriguery. My first efforts to grapple with it proved to be but a feeble attempt. I might as well have tried to stop the rushing waters of Niagara with my hand. Still, I did accomplish a little.

The "stool pigeon" news of San Quentin gravitated to the Captain of the Yard through the nightwatch. These notes were collected and left on his desk in a pile ready for inspection each morning. This was his first mail of the day, and always received his most solemn attention. No other duty, no matter how important, could hold his interest, and why not? These notes were the medium through which the commander inside of San Quentin's walls managed to keep his finger on the pulse of the life of the big jail.

As trusty of San Quentin I was the custodian of the keys to the cells of nineteen hundred convicts. When the prison was locked up at night I took the key box to the safe located between the gates at the main entrance. In the morning I was the first man out to prepare everything for the unlock. I had enough time to spare to go to the Captain's office and examine the nightly "stool pigeon" mail. Most of it was bits of information regarding the doings of fellow convicts, complaints which might result in favor to the authors of them.

Occasionally I would come upon some serious items, possibly pending attempts to escape. I would remove these notes from the pile and keep the matter closely to myself until I had time to investigate the whole affair. They were often from jail provocateurs who treacherously betrayed the effort to escape of some confiding fellow convict. after aiding and abetting it. Their notes would describe minutely the nature of the break, even to the hiding place of the tools.

I usually bided my time until a favorable opportunity presented in which to examine the prisoner's cell. If the work of damage had not progressed too far, I would leave everything intact, but would remove the tools; then keep my counsel for days.

During that time the poor unfortunate suffered all of the torments of impending doom, worry and remorse. The effect of thinking about what might occur was worse than the infliction of the most condign punishment.

When I saw the proper mental condition had been produced I would start action by having one of the convict assistant trusties bring the harassed man to the office. He was left sitting upon "the mourners' bench" where he would be stared at by all who passed and occasionally quizzed by some of the officers about "his trouble." After nearly an hour of this new form of third degreeing he would then be taken back to his work without a word of information to relieve his tightened nerves.

I remember this was done in one very serious case for a week before the man was brought into the place we called "the old leather room." There behind closed doors, I took him to task about his plans, pointing out that a thousand convicts walked through the front gate to liberty with heads erect, for every one who made his escape over the wall. I showed him that even if he should make his "getaway" from the narrow prison enclosure he would still be a convict confined in the larger jail of the world, and that such an experience would soon prove that the outside was far more terrible than the iron bars, guns and guards of San Quentin.

There was not a single instance where such a method with my fellow convicts failed. Further efforts at escape would stop without their being exposed to the awful dangers of the jail's punishment which I never knew to cure anyone, including myself. Redemption was achieved always in this new way; and in the privacy of that "old leather room" at San Quentin destiny often used me as the instrument to fashion a new set of tools whereby another misguided soul was saved for a life of usefulness and future rehabilitation.

My work as "Head Trusty" of San Quentin became easier as time went on. Even those who had doubted my intentions in the beginning changed visibly and commenced to hold a keen respect for the "Dungeon Man."

When I first assumed the duties I had the privilege of selecting my own convict assistants. Instead of the old gang who had formerly strutted about in that capacity, dressed in finely tailored suits of convict cloth, with subdued hue of stripe visible only on close scrutiny, men cold, arrogant and unfeeling, without the least pity for their unfortunate fellows, I substituted convicts old and prison-wise who had never been given a chance, principally because they would not carry or barter tales for favor. The others were ingloriously marched to the Jute Mill stripped of their togs and finery.

The Captain of the Yard at San Quentin was a new man who had come there with the Warden who took me from the dungeon. He knew little about the operation of the inside of the big prison, but nevertheless he was shrewd and far-seeing, and above all conscientiously just. He wanted to learn everything. His greatest desire was to see that each convict should be treated fairly and impartially. He abhored the prison pet system, and it soon became bruited about that he was responsible for the changes taking place. I was just as pleased that this was so. It made my work easier and relieved me of assuming too much responsibility.

The next in command in line of authority to the Captain of the Yard, was the Turnkey of the Prison. He was the only officer who retained his position from the old Administration; but that was not unusual in his case, because he had weathered many political upheavals and prison cleanings. He was the oldest prison official in point of years of service in the history of the State, and is still in the same position at San Quentin. He was the Turnkey who fearlessly accompanied us to the Jute Mill during the mutiny.

The Turnkey was known as a stern disciplinarian, but an honest, kindly, and just man nevertheless, and the best proof of this is that during his long stewardship in that man-killing jail, he never forfeited the love and respect of those confined of San Quentin. The convicts called him just "Captain Dan." In his case that name had a meaning. It was a term of endearment.

"Captain Dan" knew me from the day I entered the prison, and during the new Warden's investigation of my case, while I was still in the dungeon, he was the only officer who had expressed a doubt of my guilt. His stand in my case greatly strengthened the belief in the new Warden's mind that I was innocent. In fact it was commonly known about the prison that it was through his silent investigation that the Warden learned of all the circumstances of the jail intriguery which had robbed me of life itself.

He was the first freeman to shake hands with me on the day of my release from the dungeon, and the first to congratulate me when I was appointed to the position of "Head Trusty." Our duties brought us together a great deal and through him I learned much of the old prison plot. Most of it proved a revelation to me.

And now I was to hear something about the old Captain of the Yard, the man whom Sir Harry had made his tool. This man continued to hold his position under "the One Eyed Pirate," and often during the years guardedly broached a growing suspicion and doubt of my guilt to the Turnkey. It bothered him greatly.

When he finally left, forced out through the arrogant authority of the "Pirate," his last official act was to make an abject appeal that my case be reopened. His conscience troubled him. He feared I was innocent, the victim of a miscarriage of justice. The "Pirate" only taunted him contemptuously by replying, "If you thought Morrell was innocent, why in Hell didn't you declare yourself years ago? Why make me the goat in your mess which happened long before I came here?"

The poor Captain of the Yard left the place in deep humiliation, a broken old man, but he was destined to have his day of revenge. My man of Alameda County, the new Warden, remained only a short year in charge of the big prison and the former Captain of the Yard was immediately appointed in his place.

On the first day of his return he called on the 'phone from his executive office outside to have "Ed. Morrell" sent to him at once. When I entered the Warden's private office, he stood up and looked at me a long time. I was not the shadow he had expected to see.

Evidently relieved his face lit up. In the next minute he had put his arms affectionately around my neck. It was the only way that he could express the depth of his feelings. We were soon sitting together behind closed doors, talking about future plans.

Impulsively he went on, "Ed. Morrell, I am the happiest man in the world to think that you have done all of these things for yourself, and without a friend. It must be a miracle, my boy, it must be a miracle!"

"But you have only made half the journey yet," he went on. "Your pardon must be the next consideration. But at that, even now you have more influence in the State than I have myself. Why, Ed., the President of the Board of Prison Commissioners, Senator Felton, thinks more of you right now than of any living man; and there is the Lieutenant Governor, also on the Board, who swears by you.

Then again, I have been told only this morning that every Sheriff in the State who brings a prisoner here, knows you and all about your work. They will be with you to a man."

"Tell me how you have done these things. Where did you get the power? Still I can see it all. I have only to look in your eyes to realize that you are one man in a million. God, if we had only known better! How much misery and suffering we could have saved you!"

I stopped him right there. "You are wrong, Warden! I would not exchange my experiences in the dungeon for anything in this world," I said. "No, not even if I knew before that I must suffer twice as much as I did, because it was there in the darkness of the dungeon that a merciful God came to my rescue."

I left him much concerned over my words. He was growing very old and such reference to the supernatural affected him deeply. During the rest of his administration, we had many conferences, and he often deferred to my judgment in the most weighty things concerning the affairs of the prison. There was a perfect understanding between us.

As Captain of the Yard for years, he had been regarded as one who was very harsh, but everybody conceded that he was scrupulously honest and absolutely free from the taint of prison graft. From the day that he returned to the institution as Warden until his death he never lost an opportunity to sing my praise to everyone who visited San Quentin. He worked heroically to wipe out the past and I am sure that his conscience was clear regarding the part he played in my condemnation to a living death, when he passed from this world. In his death I lost a wonderful friend.

The fourth fated year since my release from the dungeon was now here. When I left that dungeon I had only the one friend who fought for my release, the man from Alameda, the new Warden, Major John W. Tompkins. Much water had passed under the bridge since then, and I could count my friends by the legion; but the most cherished thought of all, I had won the love of my fellow convicts to a man, and every freeman on Point San Quentin respected me.

CHAPTER XXX

THE PROPHECY FULFILLED, A PARDON.

Much has been written regarding the unfortunate who passes through our criminal machine, and a great deal of speculation has been ventured on what constitutes the severest part of his ordeal. True, his arrest, trial, and conviction for crime represent a terrific upheaval, and it has been often shrewdly suggested that if the whole affair could end with that, the shock to the nervous system would in itself be sufficient to reclaim many.

This period is indeed a grave crisis, but I have studied the question closely and believe there are just two great high-lights in the convicted one's disgrace, the day of his incarceration and that of his release. The first is marked by confusion and humiliation combined with a strong feeling of horror and dread as he attempts to adjust his stunned nerves and mind to the drab surroundings of a prison cell, while the approach of his time of release produces a confused mental excitement over the thought of freedom.

He tries vainly to grapple with the demon of worry which obsesses his mind, and at last is overpowered with the thought that all is lost and naught remains but the empty shell of shattered hopes. Home ties broken, and loved ones gone from his life forever, he fears the world will greet him with a cold rebuff, that there is nothing to live for, and when the hour arrives he is cowering and utterly wretched.

During my four years as "Head Trusty" of San Quentin I never lost an opportunity to help lighten the burden of an outgoing convict. I have seen strong men break down and cry like children over their impending freedom.

When Lieutenant Governor, Warren R. Porter, my staunch friend, who was then acting Governor of the State of California presented me with my pardon on the night before my release, marking the fulfillment of my prophecy, he stood in front of the Captain's Office with a party of friends, ladies and gentlemen. They gathered around close, perhaps inspired with a desire to see what effect the news would have upon a convict serving a life sentence when suddenly informed that he was a free man.

They must have felt sure I would break down and cry, because many were well acquainted with my strange history. However, none knew my philosophy of life.

The scene was ordinary until the Governor spoke. They did not know that a great bond of friendship existed between us, and his words were a surprise.

With his hand resting upon my shoulder he said solemnly, "Ed. Morrell, here is your pardon! God in his mercy knows you have earned it! In giving you your pardon I do not know of anything in the world that could make me happier."

"Tomorrow, when you step through that gate to liberty, with all your rights as a citizen restored, I know you will make good. Your sterling character and ironbound determination must spell success for you. There is a great work ahead and the world is waiting!"

I grasped his hand firmly. There was much I wanted to say, but as in all big moments, the words were commonplace. "Governor, let the pressure of my hand bespeak all that is in my heart! It is getting late, and I want you to come over to the hospital with me," I added.

Arm in arm we crossed the yard. I was taking him to see an old soldier, a convict, to plead that he be pardoned so that he could be taken to the Soldiers' Home to die. I went over his wonderful war record hurriedly, told how, when but a mere boy, he had used his own belt to strap Admiral Farragut to the rattlings of the Flagship, when the fleet was running the blockade of the batteries at Mobile.

The dying man was made happy by the Governor's promise that he would be pardoned on the following day.

We again went out into the yard. The Prison Band burst forth in peals of music. They had planned a farewell concert for me in the big room, but since the Governor had come inside of the Prison, the Warden ordered them released, and in the yard they played in honor of the Governor and his friends, and "the pardon of Ed. Morrell."

I had barely five hours sleep, then jumped up and put together my treasured keepsakes, including my notes and writings. I left the cell without stopping a moment to analyze my feelings. There was too much to be done at the office. Hundreds of prisoners were waiting to shake my hand and wish me "good-bye and Godspeed."

I realized then what it meant to possess fully the love of one's fellow men. My hand ached.

The first moment that I could liken to shock occurred when I stood dressed in my new citizens clothes before the full sized mirror in the clothing room. My emotions were tremendous.

Long years before when I was transferred from Folsom to San Quentin I had looked in that same glass. It had not changed a particle. I had! I was then just in the prime of young manhood. And in a moment before that glass, spectre-like the tangled threads of my life passed by.

Once more I was a little boy with my mother in a mining village of Pennsylvania. She called me her "little man," because I had started to work at the tender age of nine, a slate picker in the coal breakers. In another year I went down into the depths of the coal mine to work twelve hours a day with just enough oil to keep a tiny lamp lighted while I opened an air trap-door and allowed a train of cars to pass through.

Even at that early age, in my loneliness I visualized strange scenes and distant lands. One day an explosion occurred in the mine. Why I should have survived was ever a mystery to those who found me, and I knew not why until I experienced my dungeon travels!

Next, I had run away from home and was in the New York Bowery. In a little while I crossed to the Jersey side of the New York Bay. It seemed as if a directing hand were guiding me for I did not then know why I stowed away on a cattle boat bound for Europe, nor why, at this time, I knew so much about the sea that even the Captain marvelled at me. I had put in my appearance the second day out.

At Liverpool I eluded the vigilant watch on the boat. Soon, I was wandering through the big city. But tiring of it in a few days I made my way up into Scotland. From there I landed in a coastwise vessel at the Harbor of Cork in Ireland.

I spent a wonderful month tramping through Ireland. I left the Emerald Isle at Dublin for London going straight to the one place of all, Whitechapel. But I did not remain there long. The filth and hunger, and the dirty doss houses disgusted me. My young untrammeled mind craved for the free open air or the wild dashing of the ocean, and now I achieved my great adventure.

I was stowed away on a P & O Boat bound for Australia, but deserted my floating palace at Naples, Italy. I would have a whole month before the next boat to wander about the big Italian City. The rough, but kindly natives made my stay one long holiday. There was food in plenty for the mere asking and it required a great effort to drag myself from the place, but my steamer was ready to sail and I must go.

My wanderings through Australia are now merely a memory. Just one big thing stands out. I was stowed away on the Steamship Zealanda outbound for San Francisco, California, the land of gold, the place of my earliest dreams since childhood. I shall never forget my first sight of the Golden Gate as the big ship slowly plowed into the harbor.

The hand of Destiny then directed me down into the San Joaquin Valley, where the feud between the California Outlaws and the "Octopus," the railroad, was at its height. Through the whirligig of fate I joined the band. Then came the final crowning act of all, the County Jail holdup, and the long chases through the mountains, the quick trial and my condemnation for life!

I was next standing in the Warden's Office, waiting for that great Mogul to turn around. Then the ten ton bowlder loomed up to view before my eyes, followed by plottings and counter plottings to escape and the racking tortures on the Derrick and the Chloride of Lime Cell.

Again, I was manacled to the bullchain with twenty-four other transfers, Incorrigibles, dragging our bodies through the man-gate, twenty-five Ishmaelites leaving Folsom Prison, transferred to San Quentin. Next I saw myself the leader of a mob in a mutiny in the Jute Mill, felt myself being dragged naked to the water chamber in Kid's Alley, saw the short bull chain of the dungeon, lived through the long weary days and nights in torture, ravaged by hunger and cold, felt the sensations of beings plotted against by Sir Harry, the "stool pigeon," went through the trial before five unrelenting judges, who sentenced me to that tomb of the living dead for life on a charge of having imaginary guns smuggled into the prison.

The picture of the strait-jacket flashed before me, the long years of excruciating torture without human companionship, and the knuckle talk with the "Tiger." I saw again the "Pirate's" face as I made the prophecy which had now been fulfiilled to the last detail; went through my release from solitary, and felt the long hair and straggling beard, five year's growth, and my shriveled body, sore infested, burnt, and skeleton-like.

That release from solitary had occurred only four years before, and yet ages had intervened. In but a few moments all of this went hurtling through my mind. I was still before that glass in the clothing room.

I was indeed a new being! Aged, most certainly, with eyes a little hardened perhaps, but clear and steady as an answer to my thoughts.

Did I fear the future?

No!

In a few more minutes I had left San Quentin forever, a free man!

On the boat going over to San Francisco, I picked out a quiet spot on the upper deck, where I could enjoy to the fullest, the great expanse of water, sky and land, my first glimpse of the big world from which I had been so suddenly cast down and out.

As I stepped from the Ferry Boat in San Francisco, someone called my name before a gaping mob. I was amazed! I had forgotten what people were like.

Several newspaper men were snapping cameras in my face. Then, a gaudily dressed man approached.

"Mr. Morrell, come with me! I'm the manager of a show house on Filmore Street. I will give you one hundred dollars a day and sign a contract for four weeks just to step out on the stage and make a little talk to my audience."

Several friends burst through the crowd and forcibly rescued me, shoving me into a waiting cab. In a little while I was within the protecting shelter of a room in one of the big hotels in San Francisco.

Alone, I sat down and tried to think. My nerves were at the breaking point. I was now suffering from an attack of agoraphobia, as on the occasion of my release from the dungeon, only this was worse. There were so many fast moving objects in a city.

Everything passed me with the speed of a bullet. I was in utter confusion, my rate of motion being hopelessly lost.

Then, something strange occurred! I who had lived a thousand lives, suffered a thousand deaths, who had never been known to give forth a sob even under the most terrifying conditions, was crying. Through that channel, the pent up feelings of years of suppression flowed, and I felt relieved.

During the last remaining year of the five I spent in the dungeon waiting, with the faith of a martyr, the fulfillment of the prophecy given to me at a time when my cruel jailers were trying to throttle the last breath of life from my body in the strait-jacket, and when there did not seem one chance in a million that I should survive the siege, I cast aside every atom of my former puny fallible judgment. I had vowed that henceforth I would rely with the simple faith of a child in God's protection that surrounded me, and which had been made manifest when my jackets were stretched asunder and I was saved from death.

After that everything was clear, I no longer doubted or questioned, and as the months went by my faith increased apace, until at last the door had opened and I walked out of the dungeon. During the four probationary years waiting for my pardon I had ample evidence that my life was saved for a great purpose. But strange to relate, I viewed my experiences as something peculiarly sacred, yes, even holy and not to be bruited about for scoffing minds to ridicule. There, in the privacy of that hotel room I prayed as never before, in thanks that I had been spared the living nightmare of life imprisonment, and in gratitude that the Christ Spirit had found its way into my soul through the darkness of a dungeon and would aid me in the great work for humanity which my experiences had privileged me to undertake.

My tightened nerves relaxed. In another few minutes I fell asleep. It was dark when I awoke, a new man,— Ed. Morrell, the man he is today!

CHAPTER XXXI

YEARS IN RETROSPECT.

Two glorious months had passed. I stepped off of the Ferry Boat in San Francisco with my skin tanned to a brown, light of foot and with plenty of red blood coursing through my veins. I weighed nearly one hundred and fifty pounds, and my leg muscles were hard as iron from walking.

I had just returned from a lone pilgrimage in the Sierra Nevada Mountains. I had been in the far reaches of the Kern River Canyons, one of the wonder spots of the world. Two long months communing with nature, man's greatest healer, had completely restored me to health. I was now ready for the work which was cut out for me to do.

My first public announcement was given in a long article to the Sunday Press of San Francisco. It was a statement setting forth the principles of the Honor System. It created a great deal of attention. At that time it was extremely revolutionary, and brought down upon me varied comments favorable and unfavorable. One eminent editorial authority dissected my theory and cast its fragments to the public winds, concluding with the charitable remark that I should not be taken seriously, that a great deal of allowance should be made for a man who had suffered such shocking brutalities and long years of prison confinement.

But the seed had been sown on fruitful soil all over the Far West, and needed only time to garner the harvest.

In another month after my return, everybody in California was talking. I had just finished a series of big mass meetings in various sections of the State. My revelations about the world behind prison walls startled and stunned the public. It was the first time in this country that a voice had ever penetrated to the outside from the darksome shadows of a prison to tell the ghastly story of the things that are done to American men in American Jails, and that voice had come out to the world to demand if such things must be.

The backwash from this public agitation fairly deluged the lagging press, and spurred it on to action Now they were clamoring insistently that something must be done to sweep clean the whole unmentionable mess. Prison Reform was in the air, the entire State of California was aroused as never before and rankled sorely under the public disgrace, shocked beyond measure that such things could be tolerated in this Christian nation and in the Twentieth Century.

Hundreds of invitations to speak kept pouring in on me from all sections. People everywhere wanted to hear my message, and letters of encouragement and offers of advice and financial assistance if need be were received daily. The sleeping soul of the Golden State was aroused.

The Legislature of 1909 was about to convene, and I appeared before that session with a program. The very same Capital, where I had been paraded in the dirty Folsom stripes, while the rabble howled with delight and threw peanut shells into my unprotected face, was now to hear the sound of my voice in defence of the State's condemned and degraded unfortunates.

Thru my efforts, the immediate result was a parole law, which included benefits for life convicts. When the measure was dissected after it became a law shrewd politicians marvelled that such extreme legislation could have been even contemplated.

The wisdom of this law has since been amply demonstrated, for statistics show that life convicts stand well at the head of the list of paroled men who have made good.

The next two years were devoted to the lecture platform, arousing public opinion to the highest pitch, and finally when the Legislature had convened again, I presented another measure for the abolition of all forms of corporal punishment in that State, which included Insane Hospitals and Juvenile Reformatories as well as State Prisons, County Jails, and in fact every institution of detention!

Speaking before a joint session of the Legislature, I exhibited to view, the bloody strait-jacket, even allowing some of the law makers to sample its torture, and the measure was passed with hardly a dissenting voice, at last ending the long chapter of horrors which had caused the fair name of California to become a disgrace and a stench in the nostrils of the civilized world.

The victory in the last session of the Legislature created a profound sensation. My power on the public platform arrested the attention of even the most callous skeptics, men who believed utterly in the theory of the rod of iron for all law breakers, began now to see the folly of our whole criminal system.

It seemed nothing short of miraculous that so much could be accomplished in so little time and now temptation was wafted into my face. Luring offers were made to have me spectacularize my life. Playwrights, show men, and agents from motion picture companies dogged my footsteps in San Francisco, using every argument imaginable to have me turn from my chosen work and reap a harvest of golden coins from the dramatic elements of my strange life.

One worthy imitator of the celebrated P. T. Barnum put it this way, "I say, Morrell, fortune smiles but for a day. Your sun is shining bright. Beware of the fickle-minded public. You will be dead and forgotten in a year. Make a clean up, man, make a clean up! Don't be a damned fool! Sign this contract with me as your manager and I will make a cool million in cash for you before another year is out!"

I respectfully declined the offer, and I wondered what would be my chances with that man on a jury trying me for my sanity. He left thinking I was mad.

Jack London and I were very dear friends, and we had often talked about my experiences in the dungeon, particularly those phases pertaining to the "little death" in the strait-jacket. He was fired to a frenzy of enthusiasm to incorporate the remarkable elements of that part of my life between the covers of a book.

"God, Ed., do you know what this means to me?" he often said. "It has been the ambition of my life to put across a staggering punch against the whole damnable, rotten American Jail System. I want it to be my masterpiece."

We were in the Saddle Rock Restaurant in Oakland the day I finally consented, but it was only with the understanding that the story should be a direct appeal to save the life of the poor "Tiger," my silent mate of the knuckle voice in the dungeon.

The restaurant was full of guests who were startled from their quiet dining, when the great Jack London jumped up from the table and rushed across to my side and fairly hugged me around the place, like a little boy just released from school, but Jack London was always a boy. Even his work was play to him. He loved action, life, and the outside world, but most of all he loved humanity and I had promised to give him a new weapon to use in the defence of his fellow man.

The recollections of the couple of months spent on and off at the London Ranch in the "Valley of the Moon" while the material was being compiled for the "Star Rover" are memories of Jack London which will be treasured all my life. A strange bond of love, which he often mentioned to our mutual friends, existed between us until his death.

Jack London's masterpiece, the crowning achievement of his life, will live imperishable in American Literature, as one of the greatest pen pictures ever created by an American artist. More, in depicting the horrors of my torture in the strait-jacket in the dungeon at San Quentin, Jack London hurled the most damning indictment ever recorded against our whole iniquitous American Jail System. May his memory rest enshrined with love, in the hearts of the American Public, through all the ages until time shall end!

And now the secret is out! I have been married quite a few years and my wife is,— should I stop and let you guess? No, that would be unfair, because it all seems so wonderfully strange. She is none other than just "the little girl" whom I used to visit at school in that interior town of fruit and flowers, from my jacket Hell in San Quentin's dungeon.

From the very first when I had gone into the classroom and picked out the little girl sitting near the open window, I never lost faith but some day we would meet and that she herself, now grown to womanhood, would play an important part with me in my life work.

The whole affair troubled me. It was the one big link in my chain of experiences which I had not been able to piece together. I had made a trip to the little town and had gone to the school without even asking directions from anyone. I located the desk near the open window, and from that point back trailed to her home to find that the place was occupied by strangers. She had moved away and was now living somewhere in San Francisco. There the trail ended.

But I was not discouraged. I knew I must wait for fate to untangle the threads that mysteriously drew me to her. And like all good things in my life it came about when least expected and at a moment when my thoughts were furthest from the quest.

Quite by chance I had met a friend in San Francisco. Before we parted I promised to call at a certain address for another meeting. It was nearly nine o'clock at night when I found time to keep the engagement.

I had rung the bell and stood waiting. A young woman of about eighteen opened the door. From the bright hall light I could plainly see her face. My first moment was one of startled amazement. I recognized her instantly. "Good God," I thought, "she is my little girl!"

My first impulse was to ask if she did not recall me. Then, common sense came to my rescue, and I almost laughed over the incongruous situation.

Still, I could see that she gazed fixedly at me, just as she did years before when I stood near her desk in the classroom, and again when she stopped at the gate to her home and looked pensively into my eyes. Yes, there was something in her back memory and now, wonder of all, she was smiling.

In an effort to hide my confusion and avoid an awkward situation, I politely asked for the friend whom I had called to see. In the sweetest voice imaginable she told me my friend was out, and was not expected until late, then invited me to come in and wait.

I offered some apology and declined, but promised to call again. The door closed and I walked down the street like one floating in thin air. That meeting was one of the happiest moments of my life.

After our formal introduction, and she learned who I was, she confided to me that her most interesting study in the University was Sociology, and that she had always had a dream that some day she would center her life work on the great problem of prison reform. Then she asked if I would help her in her studies.

From this time on we were almost inseparable, but it was a long while before I confided to her the secret of our strange association. I was overjoyed when she confessed that she believed it all. Not one iota of it was unreal to her. She had seen me in her day dreams as a little girl.

We were sitting on the highest rock overlooking the ocean, near the Cliff House. Her hand was resting loosely in mine. We had been talking about the coincidence of our meeting. She turned suddenly and with the frank expression which had so impressed me in her childhood looked straight into my eyes.

I have known you always," she said. "The moment I opened that door I recognized you as the man in stripes who had come to me in a vision in the school room. It is surprising but I have felt your influence guiding me from that day to this."

I was happy beyond measure, but a thousand times happier still when she promised to be my wife after her school days had ended. Thus was completed the chain of my prophecies. The last, the best one of all.

Fifteen years have passed since my return to the world and a life of action, and as I reflect upon them, I feel that it was a great privilege for me to have gone to prison, to have suffered all the horrors it is possible for a fiendish system to conceive, to have known through experience the nerve racking darkness of a dungeon, that I might bring to the world the story of the jail from the inside, and with soul ablaze, offer a solution for the ills, which reflect upon humanity and insult the intelligence of this great American Nation in the form of a tremendous tax burden, not to mention our prison made criminals, periodically released a thousand times more hardened and ready to take up crime than they were on the day of their first apprehension.

Since my initial victories, my voice has sounded from Coast to Coast, always pleading with a lethargic public to arouse itself and recognize the danger of our ever increasing criminal problem.

Colorado, Oregon, Arizona, and later Washington have all fallen in line with the trend of the new spirit of the Twentieth Century and have broken away from the cruel, man-handling blood terrors of the past. Oregon, under the influence of one of its noblest sons, Governor Oswald West, put the Honor System in full operation in that State, and Arizona under its first Constitutional Governor, Hon. George W. P. Hunt operates its State Prison strictly upon Honor principles, thereby testifying mutely to the wisdom of an enlightened public conscience.

Even Canada, whose Immigration Officials tried to bar my entry into that country now appreciates the value of the work I did there, particularly in British Columbia where I exposed the Westminster Jail and the blood horrors of the Stony Mountain Penitentiary. In fact all Western Canada has reason to remember my work.

In 1917 I appeared before the Legislature at Harrisburg in the State of Pennsylvania, where I spoke at a joint session in behalf of a measure which I had presented for the creation of six Prison Farms, for the purpose of cleaning out the horrible County Jails in that State. I was the first ex-convict in the long history of this commonwealth who had ever been accorded the unique honor and privilege of addressing that State body of law makers.

I spoke for nearly two hours, and the members to a man listened to my message in rapt attention. One representative from a rural County stood up and spoke when I had finished. He "allowed" that he had been coming to the Capital at Harrisburg as a representative of his district for "nigh onto twenty-eight years" and he never thought that he would "live to see the day when a former outlaw, and an ex-life convict to boot, would be permitted to stand up there on that rostrum and hurl defiance into the faces of us law makers."

"And now I want to say he has opened my eyes," he said, "and I am with him heart and soul."

I was given a rising vote of thanks. Since then Pennsylvania knows my work intimately.

During the war I was called to Washington. There before the law makers of the Nation I offered a convict legion of twenty-five thousand men between the ages of eighteen and thirty-six, who stood ready to volunteer and leave the jails of this country to go and fight in the front line trenches of France.

In those intervening years up to the present, millions have heard my voice, and marvelled over my power. Governors, Judges, Statesmen, noted newspaper men, great American Authors and Poets, many foreign men of letters, world renowned psychologists and psychiatrists know me and my work, and call me friend.

And now the twenty-fourth year of the century is here. My work for the last fifteen years has been only one of preparation, just plowing and breaking up the soil and clods of public ignorance, stupidity and prejudice, to allow the air and life giving sunshine of love to beat down upon our cesspools and plague spots dotted all over this nation in the shape of loathesome jails and penitentiaries. The end in view is that a public conscience will be at last aroused and they will be leveled to their very foundation stone, so that in their place we may erect the structure of the New Era Penology, the real message which I brought from the dungeon and have kept waiting these fifteen years until the world should be ready to receive it.

Always, that power which saved me in the dungeon, that voice which kept me from madness, leading me onward and upward to higher things, stands revealed in all my work. I am satisfied that I have lived and suffered for a purpose.

THE END

THE AMERICAN CRUSADERS

(INCORPORATED)

FOR THE ADVANCEMENT OF

THE NEW ERA PENOLOGY

BY

ED. MORRELL

WITH A SPECIAL FOREWORD BY

DR. THOMAS TRAVIS

AUTHOR OF "THE YOUNG MALEFACTOR"

BULLETIN NO. 1

NATIONAL HEADQUARTERS:
MONTCLAIR, NEW JERSEY

FOREWORD

After carefully reading Bulletin No. 1, the first public statement issued by the American Crusaders Incorporated for the advancement of the New Era Penology, I am so struck by the whole tremendous question of Crime, the Criminal and the Jail that I cannot refrain from calling attention to some outstanding pertinent facts.

Never before has there been such widespread interest manifested in the man behind the bars. Perhaps it is due in some measure to such abuses as the Florida Convict Camps have just brought to light. Perhaps it is also due to just such work as this for which we are now asking your interest and co-operation.

At any rate a new angle in the matter is being presented, —the mass of people are beginning to ask—What happens to these men we put in prison? Does this prison and punishment business for which we pay such tremendously high prices, do enough to justify the money we spend on it? Just what does it accomplish?

Does prison reform men? It may punish them, but does it prevent others from entering lives of crime? What do we who pay for the prison system get out of it? Does it either protect us or reform them?

What do such Crime Waves as we now have mean? If the present system is satisfactory or even fairly good why does it not decrease crime? Such questions are being asked — the whole country is asking them. We want a real solution of this crime business.

Scientific students of prisons and the prisoner see the thing from one standpoint; police agents see it from another; wardens and sheriffs see it from still another. All of them have something to contribute to this question.......
BUT HOW ABOUT THE MAN WHO HAS BEEN THROUGH IT ALL — THE MAN WHO VIEWS THE SYSTEM FROM THE STANDPOINT OF BOTH LAYMAN AND CONVICT, VIEWS IT FROM ACTUAL EXPERIENCE ON BOTH SIDES OF THE WALL?

We have in Mr. Morrell a man who has felt the knife deep in his quivering vitals. He knows how the criminal feels, he knows what the criminal thinks, and what effect all this prison system, past and present has on the prisoner, and what is more upon the public at large. Morrell is a freeman, and for the past fifteen years has devoted his time entirely in the interest of the taxpayers of the nation who are supporting a costly system which manufactures rather than reforms criminals.

If you were trying to find out what was the matter with your fine expensive automobile, would you not be very much interested to have your auto talk and tell you what was the matter?

Certainly you would.

In Bulletin No. 1, tho it is merely an outline of the "New Era Penology," Ed. Morrell does speak up, at last giving the world the benefit of his long years of research both as a prisoner and freeman. The long silences of solitary confinement speak; the soul starved for years speaks. The man who has been strait-jacketed, tortured, speaks, the man who has lived and breathed behind bars speaks, the personality, living, vital human, speaks; and last but by no means least the pardoned life convict speaks after fifteen years of effort as a free acting agent outside the prison walls, not with mere froth, but in grim, short, clear words boiled down through the years of solitary confinement, through the many experiences as a freeman dealing with the ex-convict and studying prison conditions.

Here is what Ed. Morrell sees and what he feels in his soul ought to be done. Read it, even if you do not agree with it. READ IT. READ it and think over it; and then tell us whether you think we are all right now, or whether we need a change. READ IT, a message from the inside out and from the outside in. You who are free, READ IT.

DR. THOS. TRAVIS

Montclair, N. J.

THE NEW ERA PENOLOGY
CRIME, THE CRIMINAL AND THE JAIL.

Theory of the fundamentals of criminal law must be changed before we can effectively grapple with this worldwide problem. True foundation lies in discarding of old methods and abolishing archaic fifteenth century jails.

The American Crusaders inaugurates a Nationwide campaign of public education for the advancement of the New Era Penology.

The fullness of time has come for the introduction into America of an entire change in the method of handling our criminal population and in the procedure of criminal jurisprudence.

Let it be stated emphatically, there is no more urgent or imperative duty resting on those who have the best interests of our common country at heart than the service of informing and arousing public opinion so that the citizens of this country will be led to demand these changes which are sorely needed.

CRIMES RAMIFICATIONS

Universities of crime, officially styled State Prisons, dot the various commonwealths of this nation. Also, there are upward of 3,500 County Jails, and thousands of lockups and police stations, not to mention the primer and grammar grades of crime, technically termed juvenile and correctional institutions.

In these places our fellow human beings are confined, men and women, boys and girls, yes — and even children.

Some of these jails are easily several centuries old, tyrannized over by political henchmen holding their jobs for what? Simply as a reward for their partisanship — visionless men with whom tyranny becomes an obsession. The whole American Jail System can be summed up as one of persecution and cruelty on the one hand, or on the other its reverse evil, coddling paternalism.

By this system men are either hardened or weakened and ultimately sent out totally unfitted to assume the duties of citizenship and usually to commit worse crimes than those for which they were originally punished.

The population of our jails roughly approximate over eight hundred thousand. This army of human beings fluctuates in and out of these bastilles, and there are over a million other men dependent upon this vast horde of lawbreakers for a livelihood, the latter being officers of the law; judges who conform to every classification of the criminal court from the Supreme to the Petty Bench; policemen, from the uniformed to the plain clothes man, including about 70,000 constables, nearly 4,000 sheriffs, 12,000 deputies; and Jail Wardens, Superintendents of Institutions, Warders, and Gun Guards, including therewith thousands of clerical and underling assistants, making up a grand total of about a million who support their families from this difficult occupation of trying to check and control crime.

Therefore, approximately two million people are supported year in and year out by the toilers of this nation, who live law abiding lives, at an annual cost which has increased yearly until in 1922 it reaches the staggering proportion of over eight billion dollars.

These statistics are based upon the calculations of one of America's noted authorities, William B. Joyce, President of the National Surety Company of New York, who states it is the bill we paid for the cost and loss of crime and asks, "What are we going to do about all this?"

To quote further from this eminent authority, "It is worth repeating that the great bulk of all moneys collected by means of taxation is not devoted, as popularly supposed, to the maintenance of armies and navies. The average annual expenditure in this single country devoted to the prevention of crime and the prosecution and punishment of lawbreakers would twice rebuild all the fleets of the world, and pay the current costs of any three Governments.''

CRIME PARADOXES.

We are forever manufacturing criminals when the purpose of our system is, and always has been to check crime and protect the honest citizen.

If the management of an industrial plant had from forty to seventy per cent of its product returned as unsatisfactory each year, how long would it continue business on the same old lines? Would it be for years?

No! And yet, this is the stupid uneconomic way of attending to the State's business!

But what is this system that manufactures jail hardened, habitual criminals out of common, accidental lawbreakers; and what is our jail?

Just this, a criminal court finds a man guilty of crime. The Judge turns the crank of the criminal machine and out drops a card with his sentence stamped thereon, the length of time of that sentence usually depending upon the degree of the convicted man's offence, which summarizes the history of a case in our criminal courts of today.

Our Jail System consists of just prisons,— hotbeds of crime, debauchery, and deviltry; disease infested, foul, immoral stench ridden dens, where those confined have little to do other than trade information regarding how to commit more crime; places for the encouragement of cruelty both in keeper and confined, where abnormal conditions pervert all those who come under their baneful influence, where initiative and energy are sapped until men must perforce become mere elemental beasts, to be released at the expiration of that arbitrary criminal court sentence without one effort having been made to fit these unfortunates for lives of usefulness. Henceforth they are doomed to return, thus keeping up the weary treadmill grind.

Ancient, Mediaeval, and Modern viewpoints all rub cheek by jowl in the American Jail System. Vicious coddling paternalism in some States shakes hands with the devil's limbo of the Spanish Inquisition in neighboring States of this great civilized Christian Nation.

Today, Florida's horrors are fresh in all minds. But there are many Floridas. In ten States the law permits the leasing of prisoners, peonage, a system of shocking brutalities and violence. In these ten States the jail is used as a speculative institution and convicts are its stock in trade, leased out as so many mechanical "robots" to be used for the accumulation of wealth for the temporary slave owner.

In eighteen other States we have convict contract labor, another form of peonage slavery, but operated by the State as manager in chief for the benefit of favored political henchmen parading in the guise of convict labor contractors. In these institutions the State exercises the use of the lash, the whipping post, chains, dungeons, and solitary confinement, and many other unmentionable cruelties to goad on the lagging, underfed prison slaves.

Where will the Mediaeval Jail System, which still operates in this enlightened age of the Twentieth Century, end? There is but one conclusion, namely that if the monster evil is allowed to continue poisoning the very stream of our social life, the nation will eventually drift into disintegration and chaos.

The futility of our criminal court system may be better understood by quoting one of the leading jurists of this country in passing sentence upon a group of offenders.

Judge Hammond, of Georgia, said, "I am to sentence these men about whom I know nothing, of their crimes I know very little, I am to take their words that they are guilty, but there is no recourse. This is the custom. But it should be changed. There should be a psychopathic laboratory to which these men should be taken and skillful persons should study them and their offences and recommend a rational curative treatment. Some of them would be released forthwith, others would be necessarily restrained for life."

"I am helpless, however, to do more at this moment save that action which the statutes prescribe. I am now preparing, gentlemen, to launch out upon the most barbarous, haphazard proceedings imaginable."

THE NEW ERA PENOLOGY AND ITS FUNDAMENTAL PRINCIPLES SIMPLY STATED.

How much better if Judge Hammond of Georgia could have uttered these words, based upon the law of the New Era Penology:

"Friend and brother, it has been determined by an unprejudiced tribunal that you have violated the law. As for your intentions we do not presume to judge. As for your motives, they can be known only to yourself and God. As for your act, it makes no difference what it was, except that it was dangerous to Society — with all other points the law does not concern itself. The fact which has been established shows that you are a dangerous element in the social group — you are an obstruction to its onward march — you are out of gear with its intricate machinery."

"Your relations with God we leave with God, for we neither grade your crime nor brand any man as criminal. Your relations with Society, Society has the right to regulate, and Society decrees that you remain in exile from it until you have shown by your conduct and regenerated life that you are fit for return."

"Every help will be given you, every resource of the State will aid you, every incentive will be offered you to learn your lesson. When you have learned it, be that time long or short, Society will welcome you back again, because your very return will show that you have worked out your own reformation — that from the bitterness of experience you have learned the truth you would not or could not learn without it. Friend and brother, until that time comes, farewell — and may God be with you."

HIGHLIGHTS IN THE FUNDAMENTALS OF THE NEW ERA PENOLOGY.

A complete realignment of the Criminal Code, to bring all States under jurisdictional control of a central governing body as a Department of State similar to other Departments of State of our National Government, with a Cabinet Officer under control of the President and the National Congress.

The Criminal Courts of the Nation to operate in specified zones, each working in harmony, within its zone, and with the Courts as a united whole.

The function of these Courts will be solely concerned with the innocence or guilt of the accused. That determined, the function of the Court ends. If the accused be proven innocent according to the evidence presented, the duty of the Court is to discharge him immediately. On the other hand, if the accused be found guilty according to the evidence presented against him, the Court will at once remand the convicted violator of the law to the Central Station within that specified zone for examination, treatment, and training.

This done, the function and power of the Court ends. There will be no appeal from its findings. Should a miscarriage of justice occur the damage may be easily repaired through the operation of the system in vogue at each zone training station.

Let it be granted that the accused lawbreaker is innocent of the crime committed; but the findings of the Zone Investigation Station are that, while this boy or man may happen to be innocent of violation of the law, still he needs the care of the State.

The Physical Department of the Zone Station reports him very much under par.

The Psychopathic Department of the Zone Station reports him hardly above the grade of a moron mentally.

The Educational Department of the Zone Station reports him utterly without learning, barely able to read and write. He is illiterate.

The Vocational Training Department of the Zone Station reports him a blind alley worker. Left to himself, untrained, he will never get anywhere.

Thus the complete findings of the Zone Training Station clearly show that, while the newly admitted inmate may be entirely innocent of any crime, he is nevertheless under his proven handicaps manifestly unfitted to meet the requirements necessary to become an efficient member of the Social Group, and hence the State determines to exercise the right of jurisdictional control for a sufficient length of time to help him overcome his defects.

In the usual case passing through the Zone Court, where there is no question regarding the guilt of the accused, a magistrate of the Court of Equity, operating in harmony with the Zone Court determines the amount of damage done by the lawbreaker, and accordingly passes a fine sufficient in amount to cover complete restitution, which must be paid to the injured party in the case at issue, this fine to be fully paid from the labor of the convicted man. Also, there will be added to the fine any other costs involved in the Court procedure of the case, so that no honest citizen of the social group will in future bear any costs involved in criminal actions.

In other words the concept of the new penology is: Let those of the Social Group who desire to indulge in the expensive folly of crime foot the bill. Honest citizens must and will refuse to shoulder any future taxation burdens con-commitant with crime.

This, in a nutshell, summarizes the simple fundamental principles of the Criminal Court procedure which will operate under the tenets of THE NEW ERA PENOLOGY.

The bugaboo of the whole question has been the criminal jails of the Nation and how to remedy their evils. Their further continuance, once the operation of the New Era Penology is inaugurated, is simply incompatable.

The question of doing away with the jails of the Nation is no longer a hope — a speculative theory. It is a concrete, fundamental fact that we do not need these sink holes of the dark ages to hold in isolation our anti-social brothers.

The practical operation of the honor system, clearly proves this contention. And later demonstrations in the workings of the New Era Penology as witnessed at Occoquan and several other places in these United States, amply show that we can do away with jails, walls, bolts, bars, guns and guards.

The institutions of the future, which will replace the myriad jails operating in manifold duplication all over this nation will be very simple. In fact they have already been provided for us. During the late World War our Government cleared off vast tracts of land in various sections of this country, for concentration camps to train the newly recruited boys for the duties of soldiers. These vast reservations are fully equipped to house and accommodate hundreds of thousands of human beings and can be utilized quickly for this great National purpose. They can, as by magic, be turned into vast bee-hives of industry where they can be fully equipped to take care of the human material sent through the psychopathic laboratories of each central Zone Investigating Station.

Many of these reservations will be entirely devoted to the work of handling extreme cases of deficiency, abnormal human beings, morons and criminal imbeciles.

Other reservations and their industries will be specially provided to care for the by-product of murder, meaning by this term that all unfortunates who have committed a violent homicidal deed will be there isolated, for the balance of their natural lives, where they may work out their destiny as God intended that all human beings must do. In making this provision for murderers the New Era Penology emphatically states that the murderer must and will be compelled to support the needy dependents of the tragedy. In other words we will henceforth refuse to wantonly destroy murderers, traitors, pirates, ravishers, incendiaries, and vitrol throwers, recognizing it as a stupid waste of human life, representing a total disregard of the value of latent energy and man-power to be found within the bones and muscles of all human beings.

The question may be asked, "How are we going to operate these institutions, future bee-hives of industry, and not run counter to the rights of free labor out in the open industrial world?

We emphatically state that the problem is at once solved when we answer that all those of the anti-social group who are laboring within these reservations are doing so on a basis of fair and equitable competition with all other labor in this country at large.

In other words, the wards of the State must be paid in full for the work they do. The rate of wages paid within the confines of the institution must be the same as the prevailing rate of wages paid for a like work in the industrial world at large, and why not?

If we, of the law abiding citizens, refuse to foot the bill and thereby, through the superior power of the force of numbers compel our anti-social brothers to pay in total for their criminal depredations, surely, in justice, let it be said that we must make ample provision for them to be enabled to do so.

OUTLINE OF AMERICAN CRUSADERS PROGRAM.

1 — To substitute for our present penal system a rational curative and correctional system based upon the principles of The New Era Penology.

2 — To place the entire penal system of the Nation under the jurisdiction of the President of the United States, a Cabinet Officer and Congress, by an Amendment to the Constitution.

3 — To realign our criminal code by:
- (a) Abolishing the Jury System in criminal cases and substituting a tribunal of judges.
- (b) Abolishing the office of District Attorney and substituting a Public Investigator and a Public Defender to determine the innocence or guilt of the accused.
- (c) Abolishing all arbitrary court sentences and substituting the remanding of the individual to the Central Zone Investigation Station.
- (d) Establishing a Court of Equity which shall determine the fine necessary to cover restitution to the injured party and to the State.

4 — To create physical, psychopathic, educational and vocational departments in the Zone Stations to diagnose each individual case and to outline the proper course of treatment and training.

5 — To establish Industrial Training centers modeled after the army vocational rehabilitation system for the various groups of offenders:
- (a) All law breakers who have satisfactorily passed the physical and mental tests.
- (b) Law breakers who have been classed as mentally deficient or criminally insane.
- (c) Murderers or those who have committed violent homicidal deeds. (These cases will be isolated for the balance of their natural lives and compelled to support the needy dependents of the tragedy.)

6 — To establish a scale of wages for prison labor corresponding to that paid free labor for similar work, thereby enabling prisoners to be self-supporting and to pay off their fines.

7 — To establish a chain of employment agencies to secure work for the State Trained Pupils of the future.

8 — To deport all criminal aliens, who represent about fifty percent of our criminals, and to establish an international bureau of criminal identification to co-operate with the Bureau of Immigration.

9 — To establish an international commission to suppress the indiscriminate manufacture of all narcotic drugs; each nation to have the privilege of manufacturing drugs necessary for medicinal use under Governmental control.

10—To suppress crime news and all information which might suggest crime to potential law violators.

AN APPEAL

Fellow citizens, fathers and mothers of this Nation, join hands with us in this great twentieth century crusade to promote a nationwide educational campaign for the correct understanding of "The New Era Penology" and of the imperative necessity that our penal institutions be no longer subjected to the ignorance and incompetence inseparable from their connection with partisan politics, to the end that public opinion will be aroused and that a force shall be created for the furtherance of The New Era Penology.

Aid the American Crusaders, Inc., to spread the light of reason and let the spirit of Christianity pierce our loathsome dungeons of the land — to the end that we will arouse lethargic citizenship duty in all the people of this great country.

Without this necessary revelation as to what our prisons and criminal judiciary system really are, no intelligent progress will ever be made.

We believe there can be no greater public spirited work than this, and it is our profound conviction that once the public at large realizes the immensity of the undertaking and the benefits most sure to follow, the work of the American Crusaders, Inc., for the advancement of the New Era Penology will receive nationwide support.

DR. RAYMOND S. WARD,
Secretary-Treasurer
of the National Organizing Committee.

Montclair, N. J.

THE AMERICAN CRUSADERS

For The Advancement of
The New Era Penology

Honorary Patrons Subscription Form

Prevention, not promotion of crime; Redemption, and not the damnation of men, the true purpose and intent of the new system.

"Correction instead of corruption"; justice instead of injustice; civilization instead of barbarism.

I herewith give in cash the sum of .... Dollars, or promise to pay to the American Crusaders, Inc., the sum of .... Dollars, in quarterly installments.

Name ....

Address ....

Make checks payable to
    DR. RAYMOND S. WARD
      Secretary-Treasurer, of the
         National Organizing Committee.
         Montclair N. J.

CPSIA information can be obtained
at www.ICGtesting.com
Printed in the USA
BVHW08s2242310518
517844BV00010B/57/P